The circle blazed silver.

A translucent wall of light rose up to surround me, the fire, and Dragos.

He lunged forward, shifting as he blurred across the circle. Before I could touch the handle of my knife, he knocked the legs out from under me. I hit the ground hard. He slid to a stop at the edge of the circle. Where his fur brushed the barrier, it wilted in a sizzle of holy power.

I feinted to one side but rolled the opposite direction, across the campfire. It wasn't hot enough to give me another attack of the big and uglies, but the move tricked Dragos. He shot past me, snarling and trailing ribbons of saliva from his jaws. I caught a whiff of his rancid breath as he passed. Then I was on my feet, my big knife in hand.

He feigned a leap, but I anticipated it and retreated around the circle. I left a good couple of feet between me and the barrier. Having seen what it did to a werewolf, I had no desire to test its powers on hellspawn. Even if it didn't hurt me, I wouldn't want to be outside the circle, where all the pack could have a go, according to Azra. I think the werewolves knew that, even though I hadn't translated that part of her message for them.

Dragos transformed again. One second he was a huge timber wolf. The next he was a man-wolf, six feet tall in a crouch, hands become razor-sharp claws. His arms had at least two feet of reach on my knife. I regretted never taking the boss up on his sword fighting lessons . . .

The Pathfinder Tales Library

Prince of Wolves
Dave Gross

paizo
Seattle

Paizo Publishing, LLC, the Paizo golem logo, and Pathfinder are registered trademarks of Paizo Publishing, LLC; Pathfinder Roleplaying Game, Pathfinder Campaign Setting, and Pathfinder Tales are trademarks of Paizo Publishing, LLC.

Cover art by Dan Scott.
Cover design by Sarah Robinson.

Paizo Publishing, LLC
7120 185th Ave NE, Ste 120
Redmond, WA 98052
paizo.com

ISBN 978-1-60125-287-6

Publisher's Cataloging-In-Publication Data
(Prepared by The Donohue Group, Inc.)

Gross, Dave.
  Pathfinder tales. Prince of wolves / Dave Gross.

  p. ; cm.

  Other title: Prince of wolves
  Set in the world of the role-playing game, Pathfinder.
  ISBN: 978-1-60125-287-6

  1. Imaginary places--Fiction. 2. Magicians--Fiction. 3. Fantasy
fiction. I. Title. II. Prince of wolves.

PS3607.R67 P75 2010
813/.54

First printing August 2010.

Printed in the United States of America.

For my friend Pierce Watters

Prologue

Radovan awakes in the dark. This is not a dream.

He lies on his belly, a garlicky mass filling his mouth. He gags as he pushes the nasty lump out with his tongue. He feels his arms pinned behind his back, thumbs bound tight by what feels like rough twine. He smells pine sap, and his right cheek is sticky where it presses against the floor. Deck?

Agony crackles to life all over his body, bangs on the back of his skull, thunders along his spine, pounds deep in both shoulders, and shrills in his knees and shins. A wave of nausea rolls through him, and he can't distinguish the sickness from motion. How could he be back on a boat so soon? This is not a dream.

He slides to the right, his tender shoulder pressing against a wall. He arches his back, and his head touches another barrier a few inches away. He tries to raise his knees, but his buttocks hit the same low ceiling. Is he in a crawl space? He flops to the left, and the floor moves with him. A muffled voice outside the walls that surround him shouts something like, *"The devil alive!"* Radovan isn't sure of the exact words. His Varisian is still shaky, but he realizes he is in a box.

A coffin.

"Alive!" he yells, but his tongue feels numb from the garlic that dissolved in his mouth for who-knows-how-long before he spat it out.

"Let me out!" he thinks he says.

The coffin shifts hard to one side and then wobbles before the men set him on the ground, still inverted. The voices rise in argument, and Radovan can make out only a few of the words: *"dead alive," "dead not-dead," "devil,"* and *"curse"* or something like it. He spends a second wondering why he is face down, another on why his thumbs are tied. Then he focuses his mind on what to do about it.

He raises his knees again, trying to ignore the sickening pain and push open the coffin lid. A coffin nail squeals, but it hardly budges. There isn't enough room for leverage. He rocks side to side, hoping one of his elbow spurs can dig into the soft wood on either side. The band around his thumbs prevents him from striking with any force, but his weight lifts the coffin's edges, thump, thump, thump.

"Alive here!" he shouts. *"Not dead! Not dead!"*

Footsteps retreat from the coffin, and the men outside lower their voices in conference. Radovan hopes they are fetching a crowbar, some hammers, an axe, whatever it takes to get him out of this coffin. He's crawled through smaller apertures before, sometimes sewer drains, and once even through an exceptionally foul privy to gain access to a Chelish noble's home vault, but he has never done it without the clammy fear that always accompanies him into such tight spots. It catches up to him now, settling in along his spine like a wet cat that has crawled out of a cold river.

He hears activity outside, but nothing near the coffin. Someone is stacking things nearby. Tools? Weapons? Radovan has an unpleasant thought. They are stacking wood.

His mind reaches for any useful Varisian phrases he can remember, but before he can grasp one, they evaporate and he resorts to the Varisian words he knows best. No one can mistake his meaning now. A harlot in Caliphas once told him that he curses like a true son of Ustalav.

The coffin rises again, unsteady in frightened hands. He imagines the men outside leaning away from the box, afraid to put their hearts too close to the devil inside. They rush toward where Radovan heard them stacking wood, and the coffin flies, giving Radovan half a second of weightless vertigo before it crashes onto what sounds like a pyre fit for a Linnorm king. The twigs are still snapping beneath his weight when he hears the whuffle of torches and the sound of men thrusting their brands into the wood.

Radovan thrashes and twists. The twine cuts into his thumbs and hot blood wells on his skin. He kicks straight down, but the sound of rising flames is louder than the impact of his bare foot.

The bastards took my boots, he thinks. For a mad second the thought of how much he paid the Egorian saddler for those fancy red kickers diverts the course of his anger. "Give me back my damned boots!" he screams. He doesn't notice that he has reverted to Taldane, the common tongue.

He feels the heat of the fire beneath him. A little heat doesn't bother him—he picks iron skillets off the stove without a mitt—but soon he feels his eyelashes wilting. The flames grow so bright he can see them through the fine seams of the coffin bottom. He knows what happens next, and for a second he considers whether it might have been better to let them bury him alive.

This is not a dream.

Chapter One
Princely Trappings

Forgive me for transporting our correspondence from my customary letters to this journal. In the absence of reciprocal communication, however, I shall keep this record in hopes that I may deliver it personally into your hands. This medium might elicit more informality than you have come to expect, and I hope you shall receive it in the spirit of camaraderie. Yours have been among the most welcome of the reports I compile for the Society.

Naturally I grew concerned upon the return of my undelivered missives, all the more so upon receipt of the report from Doctor Trice, whose dearth of resources leaves him without a clue as to your current whereabouts. Of course I sent inquiries to my personal contacts in Caliphas, but upon discovering that the whispering lilies twinned to the bulbs you carry had all perished in my greenhouse, my concerns became fears. I pray it is a mishap only that has eliminated our last avenue of communication. I shall proceed in the hope and belief that you are awaiting my assistance.

I must admit that my anxiety is heightened by your tantalizing hints as to the object of your expedition. My researches in both the Egorian Lodge and my personal library have uncovered scant references to this *Lacuna Codex*. It seems to have played a part in the earliest conflicts between the last Kings of Ustalav and the agents of that dread lich known as the Whispering Tyrant. And yet if so, one would expect some mention of the *Codex* among the catalogues of spoils at Lastwall, but my correspondents there report no such reference.

The only additional information I gleaned before departing Greensteeples was a reference to a similarly named tome, roughly translated from the ancient Thassilonian. If these are two references to the same book, then the knowledge contained within is far older than you might anticipate. Worse, my information suggests it has its origin in the earliest known writings of the cult of Urgathoa, the Pallid Princess. My greatest fear is that you run afoul of a contemporary cell of that awful following, for the atrocities of their necromancers are exceeded only by the depravity of their disciples. It is difficult to know what you expect, of course, since it has been over eight months since your last report.

Such a long silence after such tantalizing hints about your expedition naturally piqued my concern. You can imagine my surprise, however, when the Decemvirate itself contacted me to inquire about your latest report, an inquiry that I was unfortunately unable to satisfy due to my lack of information. Admittedly, my initial reaction was to be cross that you had sent redundant reports that, however unintentionally, offered my superiors in the Society the impression that I have been less than supportive of your endeavors. Coupled with rumors of recent misfortunes in my home city of Egorian, such communications undermined the confidence in which the Decemvirate has held my performance these past sixty years.

It is not my intention to air my concerns outside of the personal rapport we have established in the time since your reports were assigned to my attention, and I assure you that my interest is primarily to assure myself of your safety and success.

Thus have I come to Caliphas, accompanied by only a valet and bodyguard. I shall employ additional servants locally and follow your trail, as I am certain you have marked it well and subtly. When I find you, I shall place this journal in your hands, and you will weigh it as proof of the great value of your work both to the Pathfinder Society and to me, your friend and colleague, Venture-Captain Varian Jeggare.

Despite lacking experience beyond the borders of Cheliax, my new valet has demonstrated a commendable aptitude for bureaucracy, so I left the tedious affairs of foreign passage largely in his hands. Unfortunately, certain key comforts of travel were lost during an incident about which I still harbor suspicions, and the remainder of the voyage to Caliphas was less than agreeable. I shall leave it at that, for now.

My hope is that time away from our native city will provide respite from the late unpleasantness, and not for myself alone. You may recall that my longtime bodyguard, Radovan, while orphaned, is principally of Ustalav heritage. One hopes that he will find some solace among his people, even if he was born and raised in Cheliax. I wish he could see my inclusion of him on this venture as a reward, as I intended. Let us hope that he does not cause me to regret retaining him in service.

It occurs to me now that the three of us—you, me, and Radovan—share the dubious blessing of mixed parentage. Except in his legacy of the red carriage, my elven father is unknown to me. Orphaned so young, Radovan remembers little of his parents, or so he has told me, and naturally he knows nothing of that infernal ancestor who forever cursed his line as hellspawn. I use the term "cursed" deliberately, for while many might apply it carelessly to you or me, the people of Cheliax, damned as they are for serving the Prince of Lies, reserve an acute disdain for those in whose veins runs the blood of Hell. For my part, I have never felt entirely welcome in human society, even as a child. Not since the death of my mother and the rise of the devil-worshiping House of Thrune, certainly. Perhaps you and I shall discuss the matter further. I doubt the subject would be of interest to Radovan, who often strives to pass for human.

Our ship arrived in Caliphas two days ago, and my first order of business was to interview Doctor Trice at that insane asylum he employs as a Pathfinder lodge. His demeanor suggested that he might be at risk of becoming one of his own residents one day, and I sense that the locals enjoy a certain black amusement in the fact that most of his patients are former Pathfinders. Needless to say, I was greatly relieved not to find you among those in his custodianship.

Trice could only confirm that you had consulted him upon your arrival; he could not tell me where you planned to search next. I shall not reprimand you for failing to share more information with him, for despite the code of our Society, not every member will aid you as I have. I do not know enough about Trice to say whether he can be relied upon, and so I must trust in your judgment in the matter.

After leaving Trice, I considered dispatching Radovan to cull what information he could from the markets and public houses while I reintroduced myself to the nobility of Ustalav. Sadly, Radovan has never exhibited the least interest in the Pathfinder Society, and has in fact come dangerously close to insolence in his jests about what he calls our "little club." Perhaps I am still annoyed with him for the liberties he takes in fulfilling his duties. A bodyguard is not expected to protect one from oneself.

Letters had been dispatched by quick post before I invested the custodianship of Greensteeples to my cousin Leonzio, and I was fortunate enough to arrive just before a grand social occasion including representatives of most of the noble houses of Ustalav. Many were previously unknown to me, since during my past visit most of those human men and women who now rule were children. I had hoped that someone among them had heard report of your visit. Unfortunately, the current generation of Ustalav nobility was less welcoming than the former had been.

Perhaps I am unduly sensitive to the issue, but I could not help but suspect their questions about the rich holdings of Cheliax were veiled accusations directed toward my wholly inadequate gift to Prince Aduard. If not for Radovan's mischief, instead of that ghastly samovar Nicola found in the Gold Quarter, I should have presented His Highness with six cases of the finest wine the family vineyards have yet produced. Certainly no fewer than five cases.

When the evening finally became eventful, I had escaped, however briefly, the relentless pursuit of the Ambassador from Westcrown. She had summoned me to the embassy upon my arrival in Caliphas, whereupon she subjected me to a gratuitous admonishment to avoid embarrassing the throne during my stay. She was a lovely, crass, uneducated thing. She did not even offer me a drink before patronizing me, who traveled abroad in the service of the throne before her grandfather was born.

Thankfully, I saw no sign of her in the portrait gallery on the south face of the Royal Palace, where I had escaped to enjoy a glass of a tolerable local vintage. Behind me, the sharp strains of the Prince's musicians were muted as the servants closed the ballroom doors. I could still discern the melody of a common Varisian folk tune beneath the arrangement created for the occasion of the Prince's sixty-fifth anniversary. Its name varies, but I have always thought of it as "Eyes at Dusk," a song played in my native Cheliax from the long market to the gilt stage of Egorian's Grand Opera, where I last heard it braided into the overture to *The Water Nymph*.

I relished the music and wine while gazing out over the Royal Square, whose central fountain was dedicated to the nation's founder, Soividia Ustav. The retiring sun cast a halo around the onion-shaped spires of the Grand Cathedral of Pharasma, the most imposing structure in all of Caliphas. Its granite walls absorbed rather than reflected the light, and its narrow buttresses evoked the images of an ashen forest. At the foot of the edifice, a throng of black-robed worshipers lit candles and began the Procession of Unforgotten Souls. In the twilight, their candles blazed brighter than stars as they walked single file down ramps into the waters of the serpentine pool that wound its way beneath the pediment and into the foundations. For a time they seemed only to disappear, each candle winking out one after the other as their bearers entered deeper water. It was impossible to view this solemn parade and not think of the countless dead whose graves lay in the wake of my own life.

Before I could succumb to the melancholia that has ever been the principal fault of my character, the first of the worshipers emerged from the watery passage on the opposite side of the cathedral entrance. The waters had drenched the celebrants' robes, revealing the colors of their festival clothes beneath the thin fabric, and one by one the candles miraculously winked back to flame. Thus in the weeks before the Harvest Feast do the faithful of Pharasma renew their prayers to the Lady of Graves: Let our souls be harvested a different year, not this one. Not this year. Not yet.

As if in answer to their prayers, a flock of whippoorwills rose from the cornices of the Cathedral and swept south, then north, and finally south again to resume their autumnal migration. Their song rained soft upon the square, audible even at a distance and through the leaded glass. How beautiful, I thought.

"Indeed," said a sonorous voice behind me.

I turned to see Count Yarsmardin Senir followed by other prominent counts of Ustalav. A quartet of servants—all exactly the same height—I noted, trailed them bearing trays of dessert wine. It is not often that I find myself surprised, especially by a veritable procession, although in my defense I note that the carpets of Prince Aduard's palace are thick enough to muffle the advance of a Taldan legion.

I bowed, and the gentlemen returned the courtesy in their native fashion, folded hands over their hearts. The ladies of Ustalav do not curtsy, nor do the mistresses of noblemen, but at the sight of my southern manners, one covered her smile with powdered fingertips.

"I beg your pardon, Your Excellency," I said to Senir. "I did not realize I spoke aloud."

Senir waved away my apology. His short gray hair gave him a military aspect, but as a third son, he had been given over to the monks of Pharasma until the passing of his childless elder brothers required his assumption of the family obligations. "Please," he said. "We are peers, Count Jeggare."

"I meant respect to your clerical title, Bishop," I told him.

"Ah," said Senir. "I leave that mantle within the walls of the Monastery of the Veil." Senir tugged at the collar of his purple velvet coat. It looked uncomfortable. "Have you met Count Neska of Barstoi?"

Aericnein Neska and I exchanged another bow, he clicking his heels to punctuate the courtesy. Neska had aged dramatically, as humans do, since I had first met him three decades earlier. Now the sagging wattles of his throat gave him the appearance of a vulture rather than an eagle. It was an apt change, since the vicious but futile wars he had since waged with his neighbors had fattened none but the carrion. The silver lining of his presence was that it would spare me further social intercourse with the loathsome daughters of Countess Solismina Venacdahlia, whose territory had principally contributed to the acres of graves dug by Neska's ambition.

Senir indicated a portly man of forty or so years and said, "Count Haserton Lowls."

Lowls made a quick bow and reached for my hand. I did not recognize him, for he must have been a child when I was introduced to his parents. He pumped my hand twice before Neska cleared his throat, and Lowls withdrew. "I beg your pardon, Count Jeggare," he said. Flecks of spittle clung to his bushy moustache. "I never know the foreign custom, but I wish to impress upon you my excitement that a fellow enthusiast of the arts has come among us. I myself am something of a—"

"Haserton," said Senir. The Bishop's condescending use of Lowls' personal name did not pass unnoticed by the others, each of whom glanced away or hid a smile behind dainty fingers. Lowls turned from Senir to me with a bewildered expression, as though he were a child who had been admonished for choosing the wrong fork at dinner, but he still did not know the right answer. Senir ignored him and said, "May I present Count Conwrest Muralt, the new master of Ordranto?"

Muralt had been distracted, looking over his shoulder through the ballroom doors as the servants opened them to admit Radania and Opaline Venacdahlia, the latter of whom cast me a snaggle-toothed smile as she returned from her stroll along the outer gallery. The pitiable woman had exhausted her prospects of marriage among the local nobility. That she would flirt so openly with a foreign lord of mixed blood was a testament to her desperation.

"Count," I said. Muralt said a few words devoid of charm or interest.

"Forgive us for intruding on your reverie, Count Jeggare," said Neska. "What was it that you found beautiful?"

"I was admiring the ceremony before the cathedral."

"Ever studious, eh Venture-Captain?" said Lowls. His tone was eager, but the eyes of the other men fixed upon me, awaiting my answer. I suspected one of them had manipulated Lowls into this line of inquiry. When I had last visited Caliphas, I learned that the lords of Ustalav saw me less as a scholar than as a thief of secrets that they preferred remain interred with the bones of their ancestors. "Grave robber" and "plunderer" were their synonyms for "Pathfinder."

"Only curious, Count Lowls. The rituals of Pharasma are among the most poetic I have seen."

"And you must know something about that, I imagine," said Count Muralt. "I mean, as a lord of Cheliax, you must have seen some extraordinary rituals."

I did not like the way his mouth lingered over the word "extraordinary," even if his statement fell short of insult. Everyone present, even the most parochial lord, knew that the people of my homeland were sworn to Asmodeus, whom we called the Prince of Law. To revere the Prince of Lies, as he was known elsewhere, alienated virtually everyone outside of Cheliax, yet to admit one did not was certain to send dangerous gossip back home, which was, I had no doubt, the principal function of the young new Chelish ambassador.

Politics aside, it always struck me as a supreme gesture of hypocrisy to condemn one people for obeying the Lord of Damnation when one's own nation revered the Lady of Death.

"I have witnessed many extraordinary rituals," I said.

Neska smiled at my equivocation. "It is on Pathfinder business that you come to Ustalav, is it not?"

I had spent the better part of the evening avoiding that question, and I was growing tired of the chase. "Yes," I said.

The four men awaited an elaboration, but I offered none. Instead, I gestured toward the window. "There they go," I said, nodding at the whippoorwills. "Taking with them the mystery."

"Then you are sure to follow them," said Senir. "Perhaps it would be best if you did. It has long been said that the mysteries of Ustalav sleep late and wake angry. I would not wish you to endure their ire."

"The only mystery I wish to solve," I said, "is that of a missing Pathfinder."

"Indeed?" said Senir. "And this is an errand for the illustrious Count Jeggare? I should think Pathfinders go missing all the time."

"True," I said. "But this one will be found. This one was mine."

"Was?" He had noticed my unfortunate use of the past tense, which I assure you does not reflect my hope and belief. "In that case, Jeggare, why do you bother?"

"A slip of the tongue," I said.

Senir studied my face for a moment, as if looking for a sign that I knew more than I had revealed. "Perhaps you have other reasons for coming to our land," he said. "If so, consider the fate of those who have meddled among the tombs of our glorious ancestors, those who fought against the Whispering Tyrant and those who fell to his corruption. Not all who lie beneath the soil of Ustalav sleep soundly. I give you my word, sir, as a fellow gentleman: you would do well not to disturb them."

Before I could frame a politic response, a hand slipped in to curl about my arm. Without turning, I recognized the unmistakable scent of Countess Carmilla Caliphvasos beneath a light mist of rare Kyonin perfume. As much as the smell of her bare skin, I remembered the countess's passion for things elven, my younger self included. I did not have to feign the smile I turned toward her.

To say she had not aged a day in over thirty years was no poetry. The barest dusting of powder whitened her face and décolletage, which was daring even for the young women attending the ball. The mole on her cheek was a fabrication, as was the ornate white wig that supported a lord's ransom in jeweled combs, but everything else was exactly as I remembered from the hundred sultry Caliphas nights I had spent memorizing her personal topography. Carmilla was the woman who introduced me to the wider world of sophisticated love. If you read several meanings into the term "sophisticated," why then it is a testament to your keen understanding and, I trust, your discretion.

When first we met, her seduction made me late for my winter's residence at Lepidstadt University, but I learned more at her hand that summer than I had in six months' study of Ustalav's most ancient libraries. At the time she had seemed older than I, although in truth I was at least twice her age. Thanks to my father's blood, however, I appeared as a young human of middle twenties. Now, however, the mirror had begun to mock me with its rumpled roadmap of my face, while Carmilla might as well have used a thirty-year-old portrait as a looking glass.

"I see that the rumors of your bathing in the blood of virgins are not without substance," I said. It was the sort of callow joke I made often in my youth, but she rewarded me with a smile. I extracted myself from her grasp just long enough to kiss her hand.

"Coarse slanders," she said. She batted me with a carved ivory fan I recognized as the parting gift I had given her. The weather in Caliphas had been cool since my arrival, so it required no great feat of deduction to realize that she meant to flatter me by flaunting it. She let the fan dangle from her wrist as she pressed a finger against Senir's embroidered sleeve. "Still, the bishop here watches me closely each time we dine, making sure I sample every dish made with garlic."

Senir bowed curtly at her quip, smiling but clearly not amused.

"You cannot keep our visitor all to yourself, my dear Bishop," Carmilla said, blithely ignoring the rest of our company without eliciting their offense. I cannot understand how she manages that trick, though I studied it often. "There are dozens of young people who have never met our dear Count Jeggare, and we must not deny them his acquaintance."

It is fortunate that I have had nearly a century's practice keeping the mirth from appearing in my eyes, for Senir's gaze was deep and keen. I saw in his eyes that he understood I had been rescued—and that I understood it as well. We both smiled as though we harbored no such thought. The others in our company smiled in much the same way, except for the uncouth Lowls, who blurted out something about making an appointment for me to see his sketches before his savvy mistress distracted him by demanding a return to the dessert buffet.

As Carmilla guided me away, I procured a couple of glasses of sweet wine from a servant's platter. We walked a while in silence, and she held my arm so close and pressed her warm body so gently against me that I felt a resurgence of the affection we once shared. Or the affection I once felt, anyway. There was no denying that I was not only young but, as they say, impressionable, and only a fool would assume that the experienced lady had invested so much of her heart in me as I had in her. It was a dangerous feeling, and unproductive, but I relished it for a minute as we strolled past portraits of princes and counts, each a generation older than the former. I imagined them as jealous rivals envying our revived happiness. Then I released the fancy like a captive bird freed from a cage.

"I should be displeased with you," Carmilla purred. "It wounds my pride to know you have been in Caliphas so long without sending me so much as a calling card, while you spent an entire day with that loathsome Doctor Trice."

"Incomparable lady," I said, "even the greatest pleasure is sweetened by the prior dispensation of all tedious matters, and no pleasure is greater than that of seeing you again."

Carmilla tilted her head to appraise me. "A bit thick."

"Forgive me," I said. "I am out of practice."

"What a shame," she said. "I should hate to think our liaison spoiled you for the ladies of Cheliax."

I shrugged as though I could not deny it, and she smiled to accept the implied compliment.

"Despite the intolerable length of your absence, I remain too fond to punish you as you deserve, my sweet Varian. Your youthful enthusiasms have remained bright in my memory over the years. Do not say how many." She laid a finger upon my lips. "Let that remain our secret."

As we walked arm in arm, the subjects of the portraits hung along the outer gallery changed gradually in style and subject. The recent lords of Ustalav were robust, bearded, and mustachioed men or pale ladies arrayed in costumes that would not have seemed too plain in a Chelish opera house. Their forebears were another breed entirely, hard-faced men and women more often adorned in iron than in silk, their prominent noses less often diminished by the hand of obsequious painters. As we passed beyond the remembered monarchs of Ustalav, here and there were paintings obscured by dark velvet curtains. Carmilla noticed my interest.

"The cursed and the damned," she said.

"The villains of history?" I asked.

"Not always, no," she said. "But princes whose legacies are best left to the obscurity of the Academy."

After a furtive glance to either side, she reached for one of the velvet pulls.

"Wait," I said, too late to stop her.

She unveiled a portrait whose thick veneer was as cracked as the mud of a summer desert. Beneath the rugged contours of its varnish, the figure beneath was a man of undeniably fiendish character. Upon the bridge of his hooked nose was a draconic ridge, and from his brow rose a craggy expanse that expanded to either side in long white horns where a carica-turist might extend a sage's eyebrows. Tiny white protrusions of bone dotted his prominent cheekbones, and his long chin was as sharp as a trowel. If age and lacquer had dimmed the hues for hundreds of years, one might expect his skin was originally the color of molten copper. It was the face of a hell-spawn, one quite near in ancestry to his diabolic forebear.

Carmilla released the pull, returning the portrait to obscu-rity. "Don't look now," she whispered. I could not help myself from turning to see a small group of the prince's guests round-ing the promenade behind us.

"If you kiss me," Carmilla said, "they shall have some gossip."

I could not dispute her logic, so I obeyed. It had been so long, and I had forgotten how soft and how warm and how much I felt as though I were dissolving like the last of the winter ice, and soon all other thoughts were driven from my mind. When she pushed me gently away, I felt the despair of an exile. My face burned as much from regret for lost years as from the effects of the evening's wine. Carmilla made a show of fluttering her fan as I recovered my composure. The spies had retreated, but now we had some assurance of what they would report.

"I am doubly glad you have found me," I told her. "While nothing compares to the joy of our reunion, I had hoped you might assist me in . . ." I paused to frame my request in a flattering manner.

"In that more tedious matter?" she suggested.

"Indeed," I said. "One of my colleagues is missing, and I have come to find her."

"Her?" remarked Carmilla. "Perhaps this other matter is not so tedious."

"Ours is purely a collegial relationship," I said. "It is important to our Society that I find her." Carmilla did not need assurances, but she enjoyed the pretense of my embarrassment. I wished I were a better actor, for I saw the whimsy perish on her face, so I added, "It is important to me."

She gave me a long appraisal. I feared I had broken the charm of our briefly revived romance, but she smiled. "How you have grown, my dear boy," she said. She stroked an alabaster finger through my hair, and in my vanity I wondered whether she was tracing one of the silver lines that had become so prominent in recent years. "If only you could linger a while in Caliphas. Perhaps this time you could teach me a thing or two."

"I rather doubt that, my lady," I said.

This time her smile told me she was glad I understood the hierarchy. I was her elder in years only. With a snap of her fan, she attracted the attention of a servant skulking by one of the ballroom doors and indicated our empty glasses.

"As it unfolds," she said, "I have something that may be of use to you."

I felt a pang of hope before cynicism usurped its place. Never one to disappoint me, Carmilla legitimized my suspicion.

"Naturally," she said, "I have a small favor to ask in return."

Chapter Two
Dance of the Sczarni

Just give me the goddamned money."

Nicola arched his back to look down his skinny nose at me, black eyes goggling. He had no idea how much that posture made him look like a giant grasshopper. If we'd had an audience, I might have told him so just to watch him turn red. Unfortunately, even the hired driver had wandered off to enjoy his pipe out of range of the valet's complaints about the smoke, leaving us alone beside the cart laden with supplies for the expedition. The rising sun had burned away the morning mists, and it was getting hot on the cobbled street that wound up the hill from the seething markets. We'd finished our chores, and I was eager to get back down to the market for a cool draught of the local brew.

"As you of all people should know, Radovan," Nicola said, "I take my responsibilities seriously. The master entrusted me with his purse for a reason, and he made no mention of an allowance for you after engaging our additional security. That task settled, I presume you have ample personal funds to enjoy the marketplace, or wherever it is you choose to visit in Caliphas in your free time. If not, I recommend you manage your money more carefully. I would be glad to demonstrate a simple method of monthly accounting—"

"Listen." I poked him in the chest, not too hard since I didn't want to give him a bruise he could show the boss. "You wouldn't even have that purse if not for me." The young pickpocket we'd encountered earlier had been no amateur, but I'd been doing it a lot longer than his ten or twelve years.

"And for that service I will gladly commend you to His Excellency," said Nicola. "And in personal gratitude I will overlook the matter of your attracting the constabulary."

He had me on that point. The gutter rat tried to bite me when I pinched him for the purse, and we were so close to the water that I couldn't resist tossing him in. I should have realized he'd start crying "murder" as soon as he came up for air. Despite Nicola's impeccable Jeggare livery, the guard who stopped us saw not a couple of innocent visitors to his fair land but a pair of foreigners with a fat purse. My devilish good looks didn't help. Chelaxians are unwelcome enough in most places, but hellspawn are enough to start a riot.

I took a breath and gave Nicola the little smile, because threatening him wouldn't do any good. "Listen, the guard just wanted a little taste. That's what I was trying to tell you."

"You mean something like a bribe?" Nicola's cheeks colored.

Desna weeps. "I mean exactly like a bribe."

"Don't be absurd. He repeatedly stated that his only concern was the welfare of that street urchin—"

"Who scarpered off because he was a pickpocket."

"—and the maintenance of peaceful conduct on the waterfront—"

"Which was disturbed by the urchin who lifted your purse."

"If your Varisian amounted to more than a few phrases for ordering beer and engaging the services of prostitutes, you would have understood that the man was only doing his duty."

"Then why was he holding his hand out like this?" I showed him.

Nicola looked down at my hand. I wasn't exaggerating much, but there was no way to mistake the invitation. "I assumed it was just a local gesture," he said. "Besides, he went away, didn't he?"

"Yeah," I said with so much sarcasm I was afraid I'd bloodied my lips. "When exactly did he do that again?"

"Right after you shook his . . ." He stood there a few moments with a comical expression as the first drops of understanding fell upon his face. "You paid him a bribe."

"The last of my loose cash," I said, "which is why I need to dip into the acquisitions fund." Now was the time for Nicola to realize it was easier to pay me. For a wrist-sniffing sycophant, he wasn't completely stupid. Sometimes he just needed a little nudge in the direction of reason. I waved my hand and held it out the way the city watchman had done.

"You can forget it, Radovan," he said with a sour look. "I have tried to be a friend to you, despite your obvious resentment of Count Jeggare's trust in me. No doubt you have enjoyed a more informal relationship with the master in past, but his appointment of me should leave no doubt in your mind that he prefers a more traditional hierarchy among his servants."

"Actually, I'm not a servant, I'm—"

"Please show me the courtesy of not interrupting. I am trying to help you, Radovan. Many in my position would not do the same. No, I am not referring to the unfortunate circumstances of your ancestry; naturally, I defer to the master's judgment in all such matters, and as he has seen fit to employ you despite the infernal blight on your family tree, I unreservedly support his selection. Rather, it is the cloud under which your own actions have cast you, Radovan, that prevents others from seeing you in so sympathetic a perspective as I have. Did I speak a word of condemnation after the regrettable incident of the master's wine? Radovan, I did not."

If he said my name one more time, it was going to be hard not to give him the big smile, and that always ended badly. Instead, I took a deep breath through my nose and said, "You told him that I was the one who told the sailors there was wine in the hold." I didn't know that for a fact, but the way the boss had glared at me after his conference with Nicola was a pretty good clue. The boss should have been grateful. I'm the only one who ever tells him when he's been swimming too deeply in the purple seas. All I did was mention, in a casual manner and in the hearing of the crew, that there might be a few dozen bottles of good Chelish wine stored inside the cab of the red carriage they had labored so hard to stow in the upper hold. That had to have been thirsty work, I remarked, innocent like. How could I have known the teetotaling captain would order the rest of the wine thrown overboard? I couldn't have been the only one to overhear him cursing Cayden Cailean and all his drunken minions while barking orders at his hung-over crew.

Nicola arched an eyebrow in a poor imitation of the boss, and I knew I'd guessed right. He said, "The master desired me to speculate on a likely cause for the disappearance of his personal stock, and it was my duty to obey. I did not, however, venture into disparagement of your character or any expression of certitude of your guilt. As I was saying, however, if you have lost the master's trust, it is through your own failings, not because of any imagined competition from me. Furthermore, while it pleases you to disparage the term 'servant,' my family has served the lords of Egorian with grateful distinction for generations, and I am no less proud than my great grandfather Orellius, who daily shined the boots and scabbard of the great General Fedele Elliendo, to tend the needs of our esteemed lord and master, Count Varian Jeggare."

I waited a moment to see whether Nicola had lost track of his point or had just winded himself. When he looked to me as if expecting a reply, I clapped him lightly on the arm and said, "Well, Nicola, you've got me there."

"So you understand?" he said tentatively.

"Perfectly," I said, patting him again.

"Excellent," he said. "For a moment there, I feared you might lose your temper. I am glad we had this opportunity to clear the air. Now, if you will excuse me, I must acquire a few more items for the next leg of the master's journey." He tugged at the front of his jacket, watching to see whether I would put out a hand to shake. I did, giving him a good squeeze, not quite hard enough to wet his eyes.

"Thanks, Nicola. I'm glad we had this little talk." I waved and sauntered away—I practice that saunter for exactly these occasions—patting the fat purse I'd lifted off of him. Pretty soon, Nicola was going to be the one to lose his temper.

Apart from the absence of the cries of the slave sellers from atop their scaffolds, the immediate difference between the markets of Caliphas and Egorian is the smell of garlic. We Chelaxians like the stuff just fine. We just don't steep everything in it the way these Ustalavs do. Maybe I should get in the habit of saying "we Ustalavs," since that part of my blood that doesn't come straight from Hell is all Varisian, maybe all Ustalav. I'd ask my mother, but we haven't talked much since she sold me.

Garlic is one of those things, like the storied mists, that everyone down south associates with Ustalav. Since the population is mostly Varisian, you expect a certain amount of spice along with the bangles and the veil dances, but I was beginning to wonder which came first, the garlic or the vampire?

The boss is not humorless, although he comes across that way to those who know him casually, so when he told me that the people of Ustalav eat garlic at every meal to ward off vampires, I wasn't sure whether he was having one over on me. I mean, yeah, one of the crates Nicola had on his inventory was full of silvered blades and bolts for the crossbows, plus phials of holy water, bunches of wolfsbane, all that kind of thing. That didn't bother me so much, since I had a few clashes with wererats back when I ran with the Goatherds, so I knew it was more practical than superstitious.

But the garlic, really? If that stuff worked, vampires would take one whiff at the walls of Caliphas and never come back. On the other hand, maybe that's proof that the stuff works, since most of the vampire stories I've heard take place in remote villages. Maybe the vampires of Ustalav prefer a diet of shepherds and milk maids.

As for me, I'd be happy with a loaf of that seedy black bread and a ladle of mushroom stew. As I reached the grand market, where earlier I'd picked half a dozen guards for our journey inland, something distracted me from my growling stomach. I was following the song before I realized what was drawing me in.

At first I couldn't discern its melody from the half-dozen other tunes drowning in the market noise. There were a couple of small groups of buskers, one of them including a woman with an operatic voice the boss might have enjoyed if he weren't still gazing into Elfland; no doubt his local peers were keeping him well irrigated with the local stuff. I dropped a coin into the basket beside a young girl who hammered on her dulcimer with an expression better suited to swatting flies. I stopped for a minute to watch a whiskered gnome playing the shepherd's pipes and capering around a drumming bear. He was the first non-human I'd seen in Caliphas, apart from me and the boss.

The song grew louder as I approached a crooked lane bordered by striped tents. Pinned to each of them was a sign, some with Varisian words, others with images of orbs, wands, cards, and cups. I got the picture. It was an oracle's row, and through the opening of the tents I spied palm readers, crystal gazers, bone casters, and diviners of tea leaves. Most of them were old women, one or two younger and prettier. One was a frail old man wearing a purple turban and a pound of face paint in a vain attempt to resemble a Vudran mystic. He mouthed a silent word and reached a withered talon toward me, but I walked on.

The song was close enough that I could hear the lyrics and even understand some of the words. Around the last crook of the oracle's row I found a crowd of townsfolk encircling another peaked tent, clapping their hands in time to the song. I pushed through for a better look.

The singer was a young man with long black mustaches and a little patch of a beard just below his lip. He was shirtless beneath an embroidered vest, his skin tan. His clear tenor twined with the melody of a skirling fiddle played by a lean old man with gray hair and identical facial hair. They and their fellow musicians performed on a circular pile of worn carpets, while the rest of their clan mingled among the audience, encouraging everyone to join in on the chorus. The moment I saw them navigating the audience, I knew what they were: Sczarni.

All over the world, these particular clans of the wandering Varisians are thieves, vagabonds, con artists, bandits, pickpockets, murderers, smugglers, and scoundrels of every hue from middling gray to bloody red. They're my kind of people.

The Sczarni sang of running through pine forests, ranging the green hills, bathing in the mists of his country, something like that. Even without understanding half the words, I could tell it was joyful anthem. The audience liked it, too, adding their voices to the chorus and clapping in time to the three box drums. When the song ended, the city folk showered the carpet with red and silver coins. I plucked one from Nicola's purse and threw it, realizing only after it caught the light that it was gold. What the hell? It was a good song.

The color of my money caught the eye of one of the Sczarni women who gathered the coins. She was as pretty as a spring morning, with a faint blush upon her cheeks and just enough color on her eyelids to let you imagine it was nature rather than design that had put it there. Her eyes were the color of new moss, and when she bent to fetch my coin, the chime of her bangles drew my eye to her delicate wrists.

She knelt there a moment and looked up at me. The corner of her unpainted lips quirked, and for a second I couldn't tell whether her expression was a smile or a sneer. Before I could come up with one of my useful Varisian phrases, a boy called out to her.

It was the pickpocket I'd dunked in the harbor. His hair had dried, but his woolen clothes still drooped, and I saw a piece of gray seaweed clinging to his trousers. He spat out a few more words in Varisian, several of which I knew well. I shot him the tines, a nasty gesture with my outer fingers on either side of my throat. It's worse if you know how we execute criminals in Cheliax.

The boy complained to the Sczarni at large. The young man who had been singing asked him a question, and again I caught only a couple of words: "money" and "foreigner." It was then that I realized how foolish I'd been to flash my gold. While they wouldn't fall on me right there before the crowd, I could grow a long tail of cutthroats as I walked away.

The gray-haired fiddler said something that reduced the entire Sczarni camp to laughter, but by the boy's reddening face I knew it was at his expense, not mine.

"We do not take from those who give freely," said the beauty before me. Her Taldane was excellent, if heavily accented. "Dragos is right. You gave Milosh good lesson."

I showed her my little smile and pinched my nose. "And a good bath, I hope."

A few of the Sczarni laughed right away, and after the fiddler translated, so did the others. Milosh shot me a look meant to burn a hole through me.

"I am Malena," said the dancer. Her hair was darker than a new moon midnight, with jewels glittering like stars among the clouds.

"Radovan." I gave her the simplified version of one of those fancy bows the boss practices before the mirror when he thinks no one is looking.

Malena squinted at me. "You look Varisian," she said, "but your clothes are foreign." I was particularly fond of my new red boots and jacket. Both tooled of fine Chelish leather, they concealed the better portion of my working gear. Her compliment made my perpetual negotiation with the boss to avoid wearing the Jeggare livery worth every argument.

"My name is Varisian," I said. "I was born in Cheliax."

"But your parents come from Ustalav?"

"Maybe," I shrugged. There was a pretty good chance of that, but I didn't know enough about my parents to make a conversation of it, so I changed the subject.

"I like that song," I said. "What's it called?"

"It is 'The Prince of Wolves,' an old song," she said. "Vili sings it well." Without taking her eyes off me, she tilted her head toward the singer, who was giving me that territorial look I so often catch when talking to beautiful women.

"He certainly does," I said, attempting to throw him a bone. I could see from Vili's face he didn't understand a word of Taldane.

"You know Varisian dancing?" She shook her hands, ringing the bangles on her wrists and striking a pose I'd seen in cheap copies of famous paintings, many of which looked an awful lot like her.

Before I could answer, the fiddler struck up a dance tune. Before the second beat the audience was clapping, hands above their heads. This time the musicians moved back toward their tent, leaving the carpet free, and Malena whirled into the center like a queen upon her dais. There she struck another iconic pose, and the crowd shouted her name.

At first she barely seemed to move, but the bangles at her wrists and ankles chimed in time with the music. Then she spun, and the hem of her skirts floated up to unveil lean, muscular legs. It was a rare woman in Egorian who did not shave, and something about her downy calves tickled the back of my neck. It was either that or the scent of her natural musk as she twirled close enough to brush her hair against my face.

I know an invitation when I see it, so I followed her back onto the carpet, adding a slide to the tap-house three-step to match her rhythm. The crowd laughed, but Malena met me halfway with a side step that kept me in pursuit while she painted the air with a flimsy scarf she'd conjured from her sash. Soon the locals cheered as much as they laughed, especially when I slipped an arm around Malena's waist, then let her escape when she pushed me away in a big gesture. I made a show of touching my purse to make sure she hadn't come away with it, and the crowd howled approval. They liked laughing, and I'd given them a clown.

Malena spun away, challenging me with a pout. I mimicked the henpecked husband I'd seen in street burlesques, hands spread wide and low, face pleading forgiveness. I knelt and offered her an invisible bouquet.

She played coy, dancing around the circle to float her scarf upon the face of one man after another. Some of them waved her off as their wives scowled at them, while others reached after her, none quick enough to touch her as she faded back.

I took a step after her, but then I paused. The last time I'd taken a shine to a beautiful woman, it had all gone to hell fast. In the months since, I hadn't even returned the winks of the working girls, and they'd begun to resent it. Still, months later and so far away from home, maybe it was time to put the past behind me, move on, and assorted other platitudes. While I was thinking, Malena must have sensed my hesitation, because she drifted close past me. Her hair smelled of late summer fields, and I made up my mind. I snaked an arm around her waist, bent her low in my arms, and kissed her.

As kisses go, it wasn't my best work. I was too concerned about posing for the crowd, and she was too surprised to decide whether to give it her all or push me away. I lifted her back upright. Setting her back on her feet, I confirmed my guess that she was only a couple of inches taller than me. I took a step back, almost inviting a slap, but when she put her hand to my cheek it brought only a light caress. She smiled full into my face.

Something smashed the back of my skull hard enough to knock the sight out of my eyes. I turned and stepped back, raising my fists to protect my head from another blow. My vision cleared enough to reveal Vili pulling Malena away from me. She shouted at him in Varisian, too fast for me to follow. He ignored her, glowering at me.

Now there was something I wanted even more than a tumble with Malena. I tipped a wink at Vili and beckoned him toward me with the time-honored gesture. The other Sczarni moved away in unison, as if they'd known in advance what was going to happen. Of course, they did know, as did the audience who leaned in for a better view.

The Sczarni began to clap an irregular rhythm, and many in the crowd joined them. They'd seen this dance before. I let Vili take the lead, and he began to circle me sunwise, the way a serious fighter never does. He was making a show for the crowd, for his fellows, and mostly for Malena. I let him get comfortable with his performance while I sized him up. He was five or six inches taller, but I outweighed him by a good stone or two. I dashed forward.

A knife appeared in his right hand. It was a neat move, fast as magic. The crowd gasped, and I stopped in the middle of the carpet. The blade was the length of his hand and looked sharp. It was a simple weapon, well kept and often used. I reevaluated Vili's ability. He was dangerous.

I pulled my own knife from its built-in sheath along the spine of my jacket, where its inverted haft looked like the tail I do not have, no matter what any of those lying Trick Alley doxies say. It was twice the size of Vili's, with the diabolic curves favored by Chelish rakes and priests of Asmodeus. I had keened the edge that morning, and the afternoon sun set the silver filigree on fire.

Vili kept his mouth straight, but the gleam left his eyes. He reversed course, circling moonwise until he paused and made a show of laying his knife on the carpet. I shook my head in mock disappointment, but I stepped back and stabbed my knife deep into a jeweler's block beside a nearby tent. In my peripheral vision I saw the darting figure of the pickpocket. Keeping my eyes on Vili, I said in Varisian, "No." Then, hoping someone would translate, I added in Taldane, "Touch it, and I will beat your ass and throw you back in the harbor."

I meant it, too. That was an expensive knife.

Vili rushed me. I faded left and hooked his leg with my foot, shoving him as he hurtled past. He stumbled but turned fast, much more agile than I'd have guessed. He lowered his head and growled, showing his teeth. His canines were long and yellow. An animal stink rose from his skin, and the light hair on his bare shoulders grew thick.

I wished I had that silvered knife back in my hand.

The circle around us widened and grew quiet. Vili's growl grew deeper, and his face began to change. His heavy eyebrows grew together, the hair spreading down his widening nose and across his low forehead. His jaws lengthened, and those big teeth swelled even bigger. Before you could say 'werewolf,' he was on me.

I grabbed his long ears and held tight. His fists battered my ribs, but I was more worried about the teeth. While I focused on keeping his jaws away from my throat, his knee shot up into my groin. He howled as the spike in my leather cup split his kneecap. I'd need a tailor tomorrow, but he'd need a crutch.

I pulled him over my leg and threw him to the ground, still hanging onto his ears. He clutched at me, and I could feel his fingers turn to steel spikes, digging hard into my neck. I put my face close to his and gave Vili the big smile.

It's something I try not to do often because my teeth are not my best feature. I have to pay the street barbers extra when I want a scrape, and the kindest thing anyone ever said about my smile is that it reminded him of a box of good silver the butler had dropped.

Someone in the crowd screamed, and half the audience ran for home or temple. Even the Sczarni ceased their clapping.

"Don't make me bite you, boy," I said, heedless of the fact that he looked a good five years older than me. Judging from the smell, I was pretty sure he was the one I'd just scared the piss out of.

One of the other Sczarni shouted out a translation. Vili gradually relaxed his grip, his eyes never leaving mine, and lay still on his back. I stood up, watching for any sign of fight to return to him.

When I moved out of reach, I saw that most of the crowd had vanished. Soon I would be alone with the Sczarni, so it was definitely time to leave. I turned to see the kid fleeing from my knife, which was still stuck fast in the jeweler's block. I wish I'd seen him straining to remove it. I pulled it out, lifting the heavy block an inch before the blade came out.

Vili slunk back into the group of Sczarni. Without the crowd to mask their numbers, I counted fourteen. They cast sidelong glances toward the gray-haired fiddler, and I realized he was their boss—chief, headman, or whatever. I touched my chin to him before realizing the Chelish gesture might not translate, but he returned it in a way that made me think it did. That might mean things were settled and done, or it might just mean I could have a head start.

As I moved away, Malena said, "Wait. Do not be angry with us, Radovan. Let me cast the Harrowing for you. A gift."

All the best sayings about revenge come from the Sczarni, so I knew it was a bad idea to linger among them without a crowd nearby. Also, I've never liked Harrowers. They're worse than most other fortune tellers because every once in a while you find a true Harrower, one of those card-readers who can actually see something from a distance of a thousand days. More often you've just paid a few silver to a con artist, and you walk away thinking you've learned something about yourself, but it's just the usual Sczarni patter, some bullshit about love, some bullshit about wealth, some other bullshit about your generous nature tempered by your inquisitive mind. I could do it myself, if I could keep a straight face.

No matter how I looked at it, there was no good reason to stay for a card trick. Still, the idea of slinking off looking no braver than Vili in front of Malena—that rankled.

Before I had made up my mind to leave, a couple of Sczarni women brought out a little round table and two stools before retreating, leaving only Malena and me in the center of the carpets. The fiddler lingered nearby, maybe thinking of himself as a chaperone.

It was all out in the open in the middle of Caliphas, and there was still plenty of daylight. What the hell? I took a seat across from Malena.

She left out the introductory mumbo-jumbo I'd seen before and simply passed me her Harrow deck. The cards were old, but the edges were still sharp enough that I didn't immediately notice the marks of a card sharp. I turned them over and looked at the faces: The Juggler, The Peacock, The Queen Mother, The Paladin. I'd seen them all before, painted by other artists. Whoever had created this deck had a creepy sort of talent, or maybe the images just seemed more ominous in my current circumstances.

Satisfied that I'd smeared enough of my spirit or whatever all over her cards, Malena took them back. "Why you have come," she said while shuffling the cards. She riffled them like a dockside gambler and lay them face up not in the familiar box but in a crescent pattern with the horns facing me. "What you will find."

Finally, without comment, she placed a single card face-down between the horns of the crescent.

She began from the center with The Fiend. "This is where you come from," she said. "A place of strength."

"That's incredible," I said. She ignored my sarcasm. If her fingers were as keen as I imagined, it was no great trick to place the cards where she wanted, and after seeing my big smile, she couldn't help but realize I had ancestors from a warmer climate.

"Here are forces that compel you." She indicated the adjacent cards, the tyrant and the wanderer. She waxed poetical

43

about the aspects of the mind and personality, and I nodded without really listening. Her eyes were greener than I had realized earlier, and she had extra piercings on each earlobe. The tattoo of a snake ran across her neck and down one shoulder. I wanted to follow it, but there was the fiddler looming nearby. Would I start another fight by brushing a lock of hair off of that bare, tanned shoulder?

"These are forces that oppose you," she said. There were The Idiot and Betrayal, good choices. "And these may aid or mislead you." The Mute Hag and The Dance. That one seemed about half-good to me, present company considered, and I was getting nervous. I glanced around to see no one else in sight.

She had reached the horns of the crescent and described The Twin and The Empty Throne as the shadows of my destiny. Perfect, I thought. Next she'd tell me I was to inherit the riches of a long-lost brother, and then the fiddler would offer to sell me a land deed.

I stood up. She looked up at me with an enigmatic expression. Was she waiting for me to ask a question now? To offer her money? I touched my purse to make sure it was still on my hip, but then I noticed she had not touched the final card. I flipped it over.

The card depicted a man standing atop a moonlit hill, a scepter in his hand and a crown at his feet. Below him, a dozen glowing eyes peered out from the shadows as if waiting for a command from above.

"No!" shouted the fiddler. He kicked over the table, scattering the cards.

Something in the tone of his voice gave me a start. I'd backed up several steps before I realized what I'd done. Malena bent to pick up the cards, and the fiddler scolded her in Varisian. I caught only a few words, but their body language told me everything I needed to know. She had done something wrong, and he was furious.

"What's the problem?" I asked.

"Quickly," said Malena. She pressed something into my hand. "Here is your coin. Now go!"

The fiddler pointed at me with his outer fingers, sort of a reverse of the tines. "Get away from my family, devil," he said. "You are cursed!"

"Well, yeah," was the snappiest remark I could muster. Still, I knew my cue when I heard it. I backed away from oracle's row. Only after I'd turned the corner did I look at what Malena had given me.

A copper piece, and not even a shiny new one. The head of the ancient lord on its face was verdigris against the black grime of decades, maybe centuries. Maybe more than that. He was a handsome fellow, but with a sour look on his face, as if he'd just tasted something he'd expected to like but had to spit it out.

"You and me both," I told him.

Chapter Three
The Lepidstadt Scar

As I offered my hand to convey Mistress Tara into the carriage, her escort interposed himself so abruptly that I was obliged to step back to avoid receiving his shoulder in my chest. My acquaintance with Casomir Galdana was less than an hour old, but already I regretted my promise to escort him home.

From someone among her extensive network of admirers, rivals, and sycophants, Carmilla had learned of your intent to visit the estate of Count Lucinean Galdana in hopes of gaining access to his family library. At first I was dubious that a lord of Ustalav should open his private holdings to a Pathfinder, but I should not have been surprised to learn your powers of personal persuasion are equal to the eloquence of your written reports. Carmilla had also heard that you impressed Galdana sufficiently that you stayed at his estate at Willowmourn for several days this past spring. And indeed it is true that disdain for our Society need not be universally held through the nobles of Ustalav.

I have never met the present Count Galdana, but of his predecessor I recall only a jolly disposition and a propensity for country humor and boasts of recent hunting excursions. What gossip I had gleaned since arriving portrayed the present Count of Amaans as an avid huntsman so frequently afield that the nobles of Caliphas were more accustomed to receiving one of his near relations, this time his sister's son Casomir. In return for her information, Carmilla asked only that I escort Casomir and his cousin, Tara, to Willowmourn.

That Carmilla's request coincided perfectly with my own designs did not escape my notice, nor have I been deaf to the whispers of her desire to undermine the place of House Ordranto. Surely Casomir could have hired his own guards and carriage, but Carmilla insisted that sharing the luxury of my own vehicle would offer a favorable impression that could only aid me in gaining access to the Galdana family library. In other circumstances, I might have hesitated before allowing myself to be manipulated in such a manner, but weighing the likelihood that Carmilla was using my visit to cast suspicion on Count Galdana against the prospect of finding you, I judged the danger worth the cost.

Casomir Galdana was the icon of Ustalavic nobility. Lean of frame and cheek, he already displayed a shadow of dark beard after the noon hour, although by contrast his hair was pale as winter straw. I noted the rapier at his hip and, beneath his left eye, a familiar sort of scar. With no offspring of his own, his uncle the Count had adopted him, a gesture not uncommon among Ustalavic nobility, especially between uncles and a sister's son. In return for the honor, Casomir attended such duties as the count did not wish to fulfill personally, such as fetching their cousin from Caliphas.

Casomir's cousin Tara had lately arrived from Vudra, where her father served as the Ustalav ambassador until his retirement a decade ago. While the ambassador wished to enjoy his remaining days in the balmy climate of his wife's homeland, he desired their daughter, upon her majority, to experience his native culture. I suspect as well he hoped her stay in Ustalav society might provoke a fortuitous marriage.

Tara possesses the beauty peculiar to those of mixed parentage, if you will forgive so self-serving an opinion. Her complexion is the color of crushed cinnamon, and her eyes are so black that one must look carefully to realize that she has not used belladonna to enlarge her pupils. Yet upon this Vudran palette rests the aquiline nose common to the Varisians of Ustalav, and her hair more reflects the brilliance of spun copper than the earthy tones of henna.

Unfortunately, the young woman has spoken fewer than two dozen words since our acquaintance, all of them practiced courtesies. I suspect her constitution is ill suited to the autumn weather, or perhaps she has not yet adjusted to the local cuisine. Or perhaps she had sampled too broadly of the Prince's wine and endured the same aftereffects from which I was suffering. Whatever the cause, at least her delicate constitution offers no offense, unlike Casomir's excessive protection of his cousin.

Casomir should have been more appreciative of my presence, for without it he might have suffered more than a shoulder in the chest. When his second glance at Radovan assured him of my bodyguard's hell-tainted nature, Casomir's blunt inquiries as to his parentage ventured close to insult. Radovan understood more of the Varisian than I expected, but happily his response was polite, if not servile enough to satisfy Casomir's ill temper. I wish Radovan would redouble his efforts to learn the local tongue, for fewer natives of Ustalav will understand his Taldane as we travel away from Caliphas.

There was one more unfortunate incident of note before we departed the city. Nicola had earlier apologized for the

delay in procuring the supplies, but it was of no conse-
quence since I had postponed our departure by one day to
allow Casomir and Tara to dispense with their local obligations. Still Nicola flitted about, and there was no mistaking
Radovan's sly smile when he noticed my valet's agitation.
When I observed Nicola's constant touching of a new coin
purse, I realized what must have occurred.

I summoned Radovan to my side on the pretense of
inspecting the six guards he had chosen. They were a rough
lot, but judging from the amputees and drunkards I had
seen loitering beside the hiring post, Radovan had chosen
the most able. Only two showed any military demeanor, and
one wore a high collar that did not quite conceal the ugly
scar of a noose.

"How many convicts?" I asked Radovan.

He jutted his jaw in that half-smile that tells me he had predicted my first question. "Just the one," he said. "The question
is: which one?"

That he asked meant the answer was not obvious, unless
he were bluffing me. Radovan relishes in misdirection, a
quality I appreciate far more when it is employed in my
service rather than at my expense. The ploy should have
irritated me, but it is difficult to resist a puzzle, even a
simple one.

Thus, I discounted the hanged man, whom Radovan told
me was named Costin. The pair who struck me as former soldiers were Anton and Dimitru. They sat on a low wall near the
stables, not looking directly at us, but obviously aware of our
conversation and ready to move the moment they heard an
order. Luca, a lean fellow with a burn on the back of one hand,
inspected the riding horses before finally saddling a gray mare
for himself. Costin stood with one foot on the wall, leaning
toward one-eyed Emil. They shared a pipe carved to resemble
a sleeping bear, but despite their efforts at nonchalance, their

eyes continually flicked toward the curtained window of the red carriage, where they had last seen the beauteous Tara vanish. The last, a long-haired youth named Grigor, was missing the little finger of one hand. He looked down the sight of his crossbow for what must have been the third time since our arrival.

I indicated the third man.

"Yeah, Luca," said Radovan, sounding deflated. "But what was he in for?"

"Horse theft," I said. "He knows the beasts well, and the traditional Ustalavic punishment for theft is branding the back of the hand."

Radovan nodded his appreciation. It was not an especially astute deduction, but I expressed it confidently enough to impress him. Such occasions were becoming uncommon after so long an association. Still, the answer provided the segue I required.

"There is a lesson in that for you," I said. "Such a brand would inhibit your ability to mingle in certain circles."

Radovan normally exhibits few tells, but I noticed a slight tightening at the base of his jaw. He nodded but said nothing. There was a time when that would have been enough to confirm an understanding between us, but I felt the need for clarity.

I said, "I trust that Nicola will find his misplaced purse among the baggage."

Radovan looked toward the sun, which had just surpassed the horizon. "I'm surprised he hasn't already."

In happier times he might have amused me with a witty rejoinder, but my admonishment rankled him. Perhaps the fault is mine for allowing such informality over the years.

Too late for such thoughts. I could leave my guests waiting no longer, so I summoned Nicola with a snap of my fingers, and we boarded the carriage. Moments later, the hired driver cracked the reins, and we began our journey north, into the heart of Ustalav.

Road travel is never so comfortable as in the red carriage. Four generations of human and halfling servants have maintained the carriage since the day of my birth, yet it has never required repair. Nor has its lustrous color faded. Neither the springs nor, incredibly, the wheels have ever required replacement, although I have the latter re-shod in fresh steel as a matter of annual maintenance. Its interior is like a tiny drawing room, the facing seats covered in thick leather upholstery as luxurious as any armchair. They conceal ample storage compartments, which the servants had filled with my belongings to make room on the roof for my guests' baggage. The spacious windows still contain their original glass. Beside them, tiny enchanted lamps emit light at a touch. Unfortunately, neither of my fellow passengers seemed to appreciate the comforts as I do.

To ameliorate Tara's discomfort, I drew the curtains, but Casomir permitted no further ministrations. Once Tara began to doze, however, he surprised me by leaning forward to engage me in conversation.

"Forgive me, Your Excellency," he said. "I fear I have offered you offense. My concern for my cousin's health—"

"Think nothing of it," I said, as one does. "I hope the travel will not aggravate her condition."

"Condition?" he said archly. "What do you mean by—?"

"Her ill health," I said.

"Ah," he said. "I beg your pardon. Caliphas is the very cradle of slander in our country, and my cousin's arrival has given birth to the most despicable speculations among our peers."

"Indeed."

"But you do not need me to educate you in this matter," he said. "I understand that you too have endured the rasp of the tongues of Caliphas."

I nodded less to acknowledge the point than to encourage him to continue. For a long moment he did not, and I let the silence gnaw at him.

"Countess Caliphvasos looks very well," he said.

"She does," I agreed.

"If I understand correctly, you have known her for some time."

"That is so. We met when I was on my way to Lepidstadt University to conduct some research."

"Ah, then you must be acquainted with Master Nagrea, the fencing instructor."

I saw now where Casomir intended to direct the conversation. When I resided at the university, a few of my fellows encouraged me to engage in their graduation tradition. Upon completion of their fencing instruction, the students convey their rapiers and a large quantity of wine to a high cliff beside the river. There they take turns standing with their heels upon the edge of the precipice, wearing only a steel visor to protect the eyes. One by one, their comrades test their skill and courage. Challengers must withdraw once the defender inflicts a wound, usually a slight pinking of the arm, but only after the defender suffers a slash upon the face does honor permit him to step down. The victor's fellows toast him and pour wine into his fresh wounds to ensure a lasting scar. Among the noblemen of Ustalav, the Lepidstadt scar is more celebrated than a county signet.

"No," I replied. "My visit was perhaps before his tenure."

"Ah," said Casomir, studying my face. He undoubtedly saw from the start that I do not bear the famous scar, nor do I wear a sword. Was he trying to provoke me? It seemed such a clumsy ploy that I doubted such an obvious explanation, yet he said nothing more until we stopped at noon to rest.

Casomir escorted his cousin in a promenade around our roadside camp while Nicola directed the preparation of a cold luncheon. I found Radovan among the guards who had escaped Nicola's conscription. The locals were teaching him Varisian phrases while they stretched away the morning's accumulated aches. At first I was disappointed to hear that most of them were boasts and challenges in the peasant dialect, undoing the foundation of proper Varisian I had tried to instill in my servants during the passage from Cheliax. The vulgar dialect, however, would undoubtedly prove useful to Radovan in his dealings with the lower classes.

I watched as Radovan demonstrated one of his favorite tricks. He and Grigor, the long-haired archer, stood about twenty paces apart, each beside and slightly in front of a birch tree, each holding one of Radovan's boot knives at his side. Ever since I had insisted on having them silvered in preparation for our expedition, Radovan complained the balance was off and had practiced throwing at every opportunity. On the ground between them lay a few silver coins, their stakes. Standing to one side, Luca counted down, "Three . . . two . . . one!"

Simultaneously, each threw his knife toward the other's tree. Radovan's sank two inches into the birch wood, but an instant later he caught his rival's and hurled it back. It stuck and quivered an inch above the first knife.

"A little trick I learned down on Eel Street," Radovan told them in Taldane.

The guards murmured appreciatively, even Grigor, who had lost the bet.

I stepped forward to express my preference that we reach Kavapesta with the same number of fingers as when we left Caliphas, but Radovan spoke first.

"Say, boss," he said. "They're teaching me more Varisian: *I am bigger than I look. Do not make fun with me.*"

The Ustalavs laughed. "Good accent," I said. "The idiom, however, could use some refinement."

"*Bigger than I look*," he repeated to more laughter. The men liked him, but I wondered how skilled they were.

"As long as you men are taking your exercise, indulge me with a demonstration," I said.

"What do you want?" said Radovan. "Archery? Hand to hand?"

"Swords," I said.

"All right," he said. "Anton, Luca." The bald soldier and the horse thief stepped forward. "Show the boss what you've got," he said in Taldane, adding in Varisian, "*Do not kill or cut the head. For the bester.*" He held up a gold coin, knowing that I would replace it in his next pay purse.

Anton and Luca needed no further incentive. They drew their weapons and approached each other. The crossbar on Anton's sword bore the royal crest, a veteran's weapon. Luca wielded a cutlass, probably won in a game of chance on the waterfront. They crouched and clashed their blades a few times. Anton parried a stab at his arm and riposted, pinking Luca's forearm.

Radovan shook his head. "That was pitiful," he said to Luca. He tossed the gold coin to Anton, but I snatched it out of the air.

"I did not request a pantomime," I said. "I wish to see whether you can fight. Radovan, take Luca's place."

"Come on, boss," he said. "You know I'm no good with a sword."

It was true that I had never seen Radovan wield a sword he had not taken from an attacker, and in those cases he had either discarded the weapon or used its pommel to club his foe. He preferred to fight at close range.

"Very well," I said, removing my coat. "Lend me your blade, Luca."

The guard hesitated before surrendering his weapon and retreating. I felt its weight and made a few passes in the air. It was not an ideal weapon for a duel.

Anton put up a hand. "Please, my lord," he said. "I have no wish to harm you."

"If you can scratch me," I said, "ten gold coins."

"Ten!" he said with enthusiasm. He raised his weapon.

Suddenly I felt foolish. It had been many years, perhaps more than a decade, since I had practiced regularly. I have had excellent instruction, but that too was decades ago, and among the several reasons I employ Radovan is that I dislike personal combat.

But here, what was I doing? Was it so important to show Casomir that my lack of the Lepidstadt scar did not mark me as a eunuch? Letting this hireling scratch me would be all the evidence one could desire that I was no longer a swordsman.

Anton thrust at my knee, but I parried and retreated. He followed, but he cast a questioning glance at Radovan. I answered by beating his blade out of line and attacking his leading shoulder.

Anton caught my blade on his cross-guard as he retreated. I pressed the attack, binding his blade in a small circle before cutting in the opposite direction to strike at his arm. The tip of my blade nicked the leather bracer on his wrist, but I had not drawn blood.

"Perhaps this is not such a good idea," said Anton. He lowered his guard with a shrug. I dropped the tip of my blade. He said, "I fear I will cut you—"

He lunged full out toward the toe of my boot. I lifted my foot, stamped on his blade, and tapped his chin with the tip of the cutlass.

Anton looked up at me from where he'd stumbled into a kneeling position. Fear cast a shadow over his eyes for a second, but then he offered me a conciliatory smile. "I think maybe you have seen that trick before."

I tossed Anton the coin and returned the borrowed cutlass to Luca. Even a few seconds of swordplay had left my shoulder sore. As I turned to leave the men, Radovan walked beside me.

"What's on your mind?" he asked. Much as I valued his keen perception, I preferred he focus it away from me.

"One of our guests reminded me that it has been far too long since I exercised my swordsmanship," I said. "Do you think Anton lost purposefully to curry my favor?"

Radovan shrugged. He was not entirely without diplomacy. "That reminds me," he said. "How long before I can give the men their presents? Some of them are not used to a proper sword."

I had hesitated to distribute the silvered weapons earlier out of concern that one or more of the men would abscond to sell the valuable weapon rather than risk the perilous journey for relatively small pay. The financial loss was not my principal concern, but I had brought only enough for a small contingent of guards, and I wished all of them to be able to fend off the supernatural as well as the mundane dangers of the road.

"Unless you're ready to break out the old spell book and . . . ?" Radovan waggled his fingers in an approximation of a wizard's gesture. He watched me for a reply, and I knew the reason.

In the many years of our association, Radovan had seen me deduce the identity of a thief by the material components of the spell he had used to penetrate a warded safe. He had watched as I translated the runes of an ancient spell puzzle and altered them to reveal their hidden message. He had even witnessed my deflection of the cantrips of an amateur wizard in an otherwise sinister instance of blackmail. What Radovan had never seen me do, however, was cast a proper spell. It was a wonder that he had never pressed the issue before. The answer to his question was embarrassing, but considering the potential dangers of traveling Ustalav's roads, it was probably time he knew. On the other hand, there was an issue of propriety. He was my servant, not a peer.

"You may distribute the weapons now," I told him.

Radovan was more relentless than my great-niece's abominable terriers. "But you're ready to back them up with spells, right?"

"You did not tell them so, I trust."

"Of course, not, but I figured—"

"You must not depend upon my casting spells of any significance," I said.

"What about all those arcane books and things in your library?"

I sighed. "The study of the arcane was one of my earliest passions. Unfortunately, while I was adept at the theory, in practice I encountered certain difficulties."

"Yeah?" said Radovan. "What kind of difficulties?"

What most observers unfamiliar with the arcane do not realize is that a wizard actually casts the larger portion of any spell long before unleashing its power into our world. For most spellcasters, the act of releasing the magic is a simple matter of uttering the final triggering phrases, performing a concluding gesture, and perhaps expending a catalytic matter.

Unfortunately for me, it is also—to be blunt—a matter of expelling my last meal.

From the moment I first fix a spell in my mind to the moment I cast it, my body seizes up with cramps. I perspire in a most unseemly manner, and at times I have developed an intolerable stammer. The longer I retain the prepared enchantment, the worse my condition becomes. Even the relief of unleashing its power inevitably comes with a noisome regurgitation, which I assure you caused my fellow students in the Academae in Korvosa no end of amusement.

But that was none of Radovan's concern. It was high time I resumed a more formal relationship with the help. I waved him away and said, "The men are hungry. See to them."

Chapter Four
The Senir Bridge

Unlike huntsmen and girls, I don't find horses the least bit romantic. Granted, the damned things have always hated me, so I'm biased. A couple of other hellspawn have told me they have the same problem, but others can ride horseback all day long. One whiff of me, though, sends most draft animals screaming for the barn. The brave ones tend to wait until I get close and then try to trample me to death. Ten feet is the safe limit, so I don't get to ride up front in the red carriage unless the boss needs the extra speed.

So no matter how many times I hear riders complain about suffering from saddle sores, I know it has to beat standing on the footman's step. After five days of hanging onto the back of the carriage, my legs felt like columns of lead slag. I couldn't stand it anymore. My back was killing me, and the carriage blocked half my field of vision. I climbed up onto the roof.

Stacked so high, the luggage threw off the vehicle's balance, so I squatted beside a box of crossbow bolts for a look around. The last inhabited farms of Caliphas were a day behind us. In the morning we had passed a few crumbling chimneys, the tombstones of abandoned houses. Since then the road was the only human mark upon the land. It wound up into the wooded mountains to a pass where we'd cross into the tiny county of Ulcazar before entering Amaans, the domain of Count Galdana.

There were hours left before nightfall, but the shadows of the western peaks reached for us, their fingers inching closer with every turn in the road. I felt a chill and wished I'd worn something heavier under my jacket. I should have bought one of those woolen shirts I saw in the market in Vauntil, but after a long day spent on the footman's step, I was too tired to exchange even a half-hour in a proper bed for the promise of future comfort. It wasn't a question of cash—I'd used the money in Nicola's purse for stakes at Towers after leaving the Sczarni, so I was flush. You'd think Varisians would be better at Harrow card games, but Desna smiled on me. Maybe they just didn't play the way we do down south. They didn't even catch my pocketing their cards as I left. That was rubbing it in, I know, but I wanted a better look at a local deck.

The art was different from what I'd seen before, but that wasn't unusual. I'd seen half a dozen variations on the cards over the years. Even in Cheliax, market oracles use them for Harrowings, and noblewomen consider them fashionable, playing at casting their own portents over cakes and cordials. My old boss, Zandros the Fair, forbade the Goatherds from playing Towers, which he considered bad luck if not outright sacrilege. He'd been extra superstitious since he cheated a Varisian witch out of her savings and soon after began a slow transformation into what the smart money bet was a goat. I hadn't seen him in the better part of a year, but if there was any justice in the world, the scrofulous old bastard was running on all fours and eating out of garbage bins by now.

Of course, forbidding the boys from playing Towers only made the game more popular with us. In years of illicit games on Eel Street, I'd seen a lot of Harrowing decks, so I knew the fifty-four cards by heart. Still, I'd never seen that one Malena turned up. I remembered it vividly because of the surprise: a man holding a scepter, a crown at his feet, glowing eyes under a dark hill.

I wanted to ask the boss whether he knew anything about such a card, but he was occupied with his guests. Besides, he'd been exceptionally snooty recently, and considering his mood, I wasn't ready to tell him about my scrape with the Sczarni. I'd just have to ask the next Harrower I met. There was bound to be at least one in every Ustalav town.

The coin Malena gave me was another mystery. There was something familiar about the face of the man on it. I tried to remember whether I had seen it in a painting or printed in one of the books from the boss's library, but that didn't seem right. It was as if I'd once seen someone who looked like the man on the coin decades ago, but the memory was buried beneath the childhood I'd spent so much time trying to forget. Or maybe the mists of Ustalav were exciting my imagination.

Before leaving Caliphas, I'd paid the farrier at the stable to stamp a hole at the top edge of Malena's copper and string a leather thong through it. Since then I'd worn it around my neck as a talisman. I told myself it was a token to remind me of the smell of Malena's hair, but when it comes to Harrowings, I'm not so skeptical that I won't hedge my bet.

The carriage lights came on as we entered thicker woods. Even after five days, the effect still startled the carriage driver, Petru, who was accustomed to stopping at dusk to light the oil lamps on mundane vehicles. I hoped the boss was keeping an eye on him from inside, triggering the lights just at the moment it would cause the most alarm. That didn't seem likely the way the boss had been acting lately. He was becoming more and more like any other member of what he called the "peerage."

From the vantage of the carriage roof, I spotted the outriders. Anton and Costin rode a few hundred yards ahead, scouting for any trouble on the road. They carried their crossbows slung across their backs, so they must not have seen anything out of place. Dimitru and Emil flanked the carriage when possible, moving ahead of the team when the woods grew too thick beside the road. Bringing up the rear were Grigor and Luca. I exchanged a wave with the horse thief, pleased to see that he had not slipped away with our best mount. Not yet, anyway.

Crouching among the luggage was more comfortable than hanging onto the back of the carriage, but it tempted me to lie back and take a nap. That was no good, because even if I'd been willing to nod off, the higher we rose into the mountains, the more tree branches brushed against the roof. After touching the crossbow I kept beside the ammunition box, I crawled forward to pat the driver.

Petru started when I touched his shoulder, but he nodded at me. When we'd met, he hadn't batted an eye when he noticed my infernal heritage. I can pass if it's dark, or in a bar full of drunks, but it's obvious to most that I'm not entirely human. Few had taken it as calmly as Petru had, especially in Ustalav.

Petru was an oddly dapper Varisian of thirty or forty years. Despite his meager means, he wore a stovepipe hat with bright peacock feathers sprouting from the brim. His long tail coat was spotless, and I'd caught him brushing it each stop after he'd seen to the horses. He had a fantastic widow's peak and the sort of mesmerizing eyes you see on actors and magicians. Nicola had hired him, but I tried not to hold that against Petru. He slid over to give me room on the driver's seat, but I shook my head. No sense spooking the horses.

"How far until we stop?" I asked. He looked blank. I'd forgotten he had little Taldane. *"Much far?"* I tried in his language.

"Past bridge, two three hours. After dark."

Joy, I thought to myself. No sense wasting good sarcasm with my bad Varisian.

Before climbing back down, I took another look ahead. Anton had stopped and raised his fist above his head.

"Whoa," I told Petru. The meaning was the same in both our tongues. He reined it in, and the carriage slowed and halted.

The carriage door opened as I hopped down. "What is it?" asked Nicola.

"Not sure," I said. "Stay in the carriage."

He pursed his lips but demonstrated the good sense to do as I said.

Anton remained where he was as Costin rode back to us. I met him halfway, passing close enough to the horses to make them skittish.

"Heard a sound," said Costin. His boyish voice belied the ragged scar around his throat. "Tree falling."

"See anything?"

"No," he said. "But bandits sometime block road with tree."

I whistled loud enough to summon the other riders. When they arrived, I sent Grigor to join Costin and Anton.

"Stay in sight of the carriage," I said. "You see anything, come back to the carriage right away."

Anton snapped a salute. The others nodded, and all three rode ahead.

Ignoring Nicola, who hung his head out of the carriage window as if I'd report to him, I climbed onto the footman's post and opened the message door. The boss had already put his ear close to the opening so I could whisper to him. I told him what we knew and said, "We'll move ahead careful like, yeah?"

He nodded and murmured a comforting variant of my report to his guests. The woman was a doll. Before I could tip her a wink, the boss pulled the door shut. Probably for the best. Those noble ladies, they can't get enough of me, and judging from what I'd seen of her cousin, that'd make nothing but trouble.

We advanced at half our previous pace. Every ten minutes or so, Anton would turn back and wave the all clear. The fourth time, he held up his fist again. Rather than send Costin back, he beckoned me forward. This time I made a point of avoiding the carriage horses, but still they whinnied and stamped.

"Crybabies," I muttered.

I joined Anton, Costin, and Grigor beneath a signpost beside the forking road. While my spoken vocabulary was growing each day, I wasn't reading much Varisian. Anton pointed down the right path, translating for me.

"The Senir Bridge," he said. That was our destination. Once we crossed the river, it was all downhill away from Ulcazar and into Amaans. Anton pointed toward the western path, over which a massive fir tree had fallen. "Monastery of the Veil," he read aloud.

Unless the boss had planned to surprise us with a detour at this point, the barrier was not in our way. Still, the timing was suspicious. Someone might have wanted to make sure we had only one path to take.

"Cover me," I said. Anton repeated the command in Varisian for Costin's benefit. I said, "Tell Costin if he hits me by mistake, I'll beat his ass good."

Anton gave me a grim smile but did not relay the message.

I left the road and circled around to the base of the felled tree. As I'd expected, it had been hewn down, not felled by rot. And it was just the right size of tree in just the right place to dissuade a vehicle from taking the path to the monastery.

Back at the carriage, I told the boss what I'd seen. He knew he didn't need to tell me that someone was trying to ensure we would continue toward the bridge. The woods to either side were far too dense to make driving the carriage around the tree a safe option.

"How long to clear the road?" he asked. We had two axes in the carriage but no saws.

"An hour or so," I guessed. Less, I hoped, but it's a bad idea to suggest more than you can deliver. "You want to take shelter there?"

The boss turned to Casomir. "How far is the monastery?"

"Perhaps six miles," said the young noble. He shrugged and showed empty palms. "I have seen maps but have never visited."

Probably the boss was weighing whether it was better to remain here and clear the road or else try to make it to the monastery on foot. One look at the boss's expression told me he didn't like either option, not with Miss Tara in his custody.

"We continue," he said. "Highest vigilance."

He definitely didn't need to tell me that, but maybe he thought it would impress Casomir and comfort Tara.

I climbed back up top so all the men could hear, but looking around I counted only five outriders.

"Where's Emil?"

We all looked into the woods. They were a lot darker than I had expected them to be at this hour. The black boughs drank up the light that made it over the mountains.

"*Look*," called Dimitru, pointing. Emil's horse trotted out of the gloom toward the carriage, tossing its head and blowing hard. The beast's eyes were wide, its saddle empty.

Costin and Grigor called Emil's name, but Anton and Dimitru looked to me. The veterans knew as well as I did that he wasn't coming back.

"Forward," I called. I picked up my crossbow and cocked it. "Stay close. Watch the woods."

Petru slapped the reins. I set a bolt against the bow string and hunkered down a couple of feet behind him, ready to jump up beside him if we needed to give the horses extra incentive. Up ahead the trees parted to reveal the Senir Bridge, an arcing stone span barely wider than the carriage. Once across, I reckoned we could turn and present a focused defense.

It was about then that the howling began.

The sound came from both sides and behind us. A life spent navigating the alleys of west Egorian told me what that meant. They were flushing us forward. I lifted my crossbow and kept my eyes on the road ahead, looking for the first glimmer of eyes.

Grigor shouted. I looked back to see his horse shying away from Luca's, which screamed and rolled on its back. Beyond it lay a dark red smear in the road, obscured by the gloom. From the corner of my eye I saw a blur vanishing into the forest. Grigor controlled his horse and urged it toward the carriage, unwilling to remain alone in the rear guard position.

Another man and horse screamed. Ahead of us, Anton fired his crossbow at a gray wolf that had torn Costin from the saddle. It looked like a hit, but the wolf only shied away from the road, its jaws red with gore, ready for another assault. The carriage hopped as it ran over Costin's ruined body. In as little time as it took to say so, they had taken out half our guards. They were not common wolves, and I had a guilty feeling I was the reason they attacked.

"Look!" cried the driver, pointing with his whip. I glanced left to see a pair of wolves pacing the carriage. One ran on its hind legs, like a sprinting man. Instead of paws, it had human hands gripping a crossbow taken from one of the fallen guards. That unsettling detail distracted me from the other queer thing I'd just seen: the driver's pointing arm was bare. Looking back at him, I saw he was completely naked except for the tall hat. He released the reins and whip and turned to face me. I saw not Petru but the leering countenance of the Sczarni singer, Vili.

He struck the crossbow just as I squeezed the tickler. The bolt shot off into the woods. I pushed forward to shove him off the carriage and under the wheels, but he shifted form while twisting around. Rising up, he had the leverage, his body pressing down on me as his grimace stretched into slavering jaws. I fed him the crossbow, but he tore it from my grip and flung it away.

Half-wolf, his naked skin bristling with new fur, Vili crouched low—not to strike, but to take cover. Too late I realized he'd gulled me. I heard a string snap just as I turned to see the wolf with human hands aiming at me.

I swept the air with my left arm. Desna smiled, for I caught the bolt. But then the goddess laughed, too, because the missile pierced my palm to the fletching. My hand was good as dead, but at least the silvered tip stopped short of my breast.

Someone called my name, but I couldn't tell whether it was one of the guards or someone in the cab. We hit the lip of the Senir Bridge with a jolt. I would have tumbled off the roof, but Vili caught my good arm in his jaws. He bit down, hard.

The pain covered the world in blood. All I saw was red and black. I roared back into Vili's half-canine face, but he was no longer cowed by the sight of my teeth. His claws slashed in from either side, but I blocked them with my elbows. I caught his arm with one of my spurs, and he yelped. I pulled, but my arm was caught tight. His jaws may as well have been an iron vice.

"Radovan," shouted the boss. The cab door opened, but as the carriage tilted in that direction, Vili wrenched me back in the other. The carriage wheels cracked down hard, steel sparking on the stone of the bridge.

There was no time to answer the boss. I could barely protect my vitals from Vili's claws. I couldn't reach the knife at my back, not even those in my boots or sleeves. Two or three more shakes of the werewolf's head, and I'd have nothing but tattered sinews left of my right arm. My left hand was still transfixed by the crossbow bolt, and it was all I could do not to stab myself with it.

Which gave me an idea.

I could barely feel my left hand, but I squeezed it into a loose fist and punched up from my waist. We screamed together as the silvered bolt shot into Vili's lower jaw, passed through my arm between his teeth, and finally pierced the werewolf's brain.

It had to have killed him instantly, but Vili's legs pumped once more, throwing us off the carriage roof. We flew past a gargoyle mounted on one of the bridge posts, so close I could have reached out to grab him if both arms weren't pinned to my enemy. Face-down, I had a good look at the black ribbon of river below us. My leg clipped the rails as we went over. We tumbled, and time slowed as we fell away. A couple of red stars blinked beneath the bridge, and a great orange blossom opened up where the carriage had been.

The last thing I saw were the doors of the red carriage floating down after me, each ringed in a fiery halo. Then I felt the cold hand of Pharasma, slapping me like a newborn about to cry for the first time.

Chapter Five
Willowmourn

I have always remembered my dreams.

As a child I entertained my mother and the servants at breakfast by recounting my slumbering fancies, which came to me twice or thrice each week. For my seventh birthday, she gave me a journal bound in blue lizard skin that crackled with static when I drew my finger along its surface. In it she bade me chronicle my sleeping visions, which she told me were gifts from the goddess Desna. By my next birthday I had filled its three hundred pages, and she gave me another. And so we continued until her death, when I laid aside my dream journals along with the last of my childhood. Although I no longer recorded them, throughout my adult life, my dreams have always been fresh and vivid in my mind each time I woke.

As such, it was strange to find myself in a lavish bed, certain that I had awoken from a powerful but unknown dream. Mystified by the unprecedented experience, I lay staring at the silken canopy. An eternal hunt chased along its embroidered edges as men followed hounds that pursued stags whose flight attracted wolves, which, in their turn, pursued the men. I realized then that I rested within the home of Count Lucinean Galdana.

I pulled aside the covers to discover I wore my own bedclothes. Standing, I examined my body for wounds but found not so much as a scratch. Some ambiguous gap confounded my memories of arriving in this haven. We had been on the Senir Bridge, fleeing wolves. The beasts had pulled some of the guards from their horses. Radovan was on the roof, and I wanted to climb up to help him, yet I had hesitated, weighing my desire to aid him against my duty to protect Tara and Casomir. I remembered putting my hand on the door, and there was a sound, but then . . . there was nothing else in my memory.

How much time had passed, I did not know. Was it only the next morning? Improbable, considering the distance we had yet to travel when we were attacked. The morning sun shone through windows to the east and south. A banked fire hissed in the hearth.

There had been fire at the bridge. I was certain of that. There had been a great deal of fire.

I went to a mirror beside the basin stand. Except for a bruise on the side of my chin, there were no visible injuries. The injury appeared recent and was still tender to the touch. Once its anger subsided, I became aware of a gnawing void in my stomach. I felt as though I had not eaten in days.

The pitcher was full of clear water, so I filled the basin and washed the sand from my eyes. Mother had always called the residue "Desna's footprints." Why could I not stop thinking about my late mother this morning? I had lost her so long ago, and never since had I endured such a loss.

Where was Radovan? Where were the others of our company?

A search of the unfamiliar room uncovered my necessities. I noted that the cedar wardrobe contained all of my clothes, not only those in which I had traveled. At the bottom of the cabinet were the bags containing my personal items and books, including my lap desk and this journal. The good omen cheered me, if only briefly.

A timid knock upon the door interrupted my dressing.

"Come," I said.

In crept a tiny young woman dressed in Galdana's colors, cornflower blue and white. She was about fifteen years of age, with enough experience in the household to attempt concealing her fear but not enough to succeed. She performed a nervous curtsy, attempting to mimic the southern fashion, and stared at the floor near my feet.

"What is it, girl?"

"My lord, I am sent to see to your needs."

"Indeed," I said, looking her over. I remembered enough of Ustalavic hospitality to know it did not differ substantially from the Chelish in terms of gender roles. If Nicola were unavailable, it was expected that one's host would send a male servant to assist my toilet. To send a young chambermaid with such an ambiguous task was to invite indiscretion. Even were the count a man of liberal morals, it was no small slight to assume I shared his indiscretion.

"What is your name?" I said.

"Anneke," she replied with another curtsy.

"Anneke, I desire to speak with your master," I said, knowing she would be incapable of answering my questions. My stomach added an embarrassing interjection. "Also, I wish to break my fast."

She performed another curtsy, quite unnecessarily. "My lord, Master Casomir is in Kavapesta," she said. "And Mistress Tara remains in her rooms."

"What of Count Galdana?"

"He has been away these past five weeks, my lord," she said. After a moment's hesitation she added, "And two days."

"When is he expected to return?"

"I am told he should return before the snow, as is his custom."

"His custom?"

"His Excellency hunts the western vales each autumn."

I recalled having heard some rumor of this eccentricity in Caliphas. Among Galdana's peers, there was some debate whether his venturing into the least populated reaches of his county was a sign of unusual devotion to his subjects, mere eccentricity, or madness. Of course, to certain nobles of Ustalav, there was little difference among those three possibilities.

"In that case," I said, "bring the butler to the dining room."

"Yes, Excellency." She bobbed her head and ducked out the door.

"A moment," I said, pulling on my boots. "You must show me the way."

An instant of surprise blanked her features as her eyes met mine. "Of course, my lord."

She led me through the unfamiliar house. As we descended the stairs to the ground floor, I observed a man outside. He wore heavy gloves and had wound a long, damp kerchief around his face. He knelt beside a fallen whippoorwill and placed it within a burlap bag. Before he rose, the tip of his thumb sketched the spiral of Pharasma over his heart.

I paused beside the open window to watch him as he continued his circuit of the house. Twenty paces farther, he knelt to retrieve another dead bird. The sack hung heavily at his side.

Beside me, Anneke surreptitiously traced the spiral of Pharasma over her belly.

Nodding at the young man in the yard, I said, "Your husband?"

"My husband!" she said. "Oh, no, my lord. I am not married."

"Of course," I said, masking my surprise. Now my unspoken question was whether the child she carried was Count Galdana's bastard.

Tara awaited me in a sunlit dining room. Behind her, windowed doors revealed the eastern panorama. Vast white clouds drifted across the sky, their shapes mirrored in the river. Across the water, barely visible in the distance, stood the city of Kavapesta. I had not seen it from this vantage, but I recognized the onion-shaped spires of its temples from my previous visit.

"In the name of my cousin, Count Galdana, I welcome you to Willowmourn," said Tara. She curtsied in the fashion of my country, lower than I had seen since my last visit to the ballet. Knowing that her peers in Caliphas must have striven to break her of the customs she learned in Vudra, the gesture touched me. "We owe you our lives, Your Excellency."

I returned her courtesy with a formal bow. "While nothing could please me more than to know I have aided your safe arrival, I am at a loss as to the particulars."

Tara made a pretty little grimace and glanced at the top of my head, though I felt no wound there. "We feared as much, Your Excellency."

I lifted a hand. "Please," I said. "Honor me with my given name, Varian."

She made another curtsy but declined to repeat my name. Much as I admired her good breeding, my own has worn thin over the years, and I had received enough courtesies for one morning.

"Where are my servants?" I asked.

She averted her gaze, and I knew the answer before she said it. "I regret to tell you they lie now in Pharasma's acre."

"All of them?" The question caught in my throat.

"The count's men did not recover all of your hired guards," she said, blanching. "Their bodies, that is. But Casomir tells me that your servants were buried beside the village nearest the Senir Bridge."

The news brought with it a cold weight, and I regretted the impatience that compelled me to question the young woman about such an unpleasant subject. "Forgive me," I said. "I should discuss the matter with Casomir. I am told he is in the city."

"That is so, Your . . . Varian," she said. "Upon our return, we had word that Kavapesta is beset with plague. In the absence of his uncle, Casomir has crossed the river to confer with the city masters. He will return before nightfall."

"I see." No doubt the ordeal had already taxed her frail constitution, so despite my own roiling emotions, I declined to press her further. Saving me from the need to offer an innocuous tangent, the butler arrived, followed by another servant bearing covered dishes on a platter. The butler seated Tara, who said, "Thank you, Felix." He held my chair for me before taking the dishes from the other servant and placing them before us. He unveiled them simultaneously. A trio of poached eggs in cream sauce lay upon points of toast with grilled potatoes rubbed in garlic and rosemary, the dish garnished with a gleaming rivulet of pike roe. It looked splendid, but the aroma struck me as peculiar. Tara relished the scent.

"Count Galdana has the finest cook in western Ustalav," she said. She had forced a note of cheer into her voice, but her eyes were heavy with sympathy, or fatigue, or perhaps her own sorrow. I wondered whether she was as homesick as I now felt, bereft of the only two companions I had brought from Cheliax. She pierced an egg with a silver fork and tasted it, closing her eyes in appreciation.

Confirmation of my servants' deaths balked my appetite. I regretted hiring Nicola to undertake such a long journey only to die in a foreign land. I was sorry too for the men I had hired to guard us. They were mercenaries, of course, and knew the risks, but they were still human beings, decent men each, for all that I knew of them.

Like the mercenaries, Radovan had known from the moment I employed him that one day he might be called upon to give his life in defense of mine. In the earliest years of our association, I expected that moment might come at any time. Certainly we had shared a great many dangers, and always he had interposed himself between me and the threat without hesitation. In service to my safety, he had suffered beatings, stabbings, even immolations that would have incinerated a bodyguard of purely human blood. I had begun to think of him as indestructible.

Now I could not help but imagine the last moments of his life. Had the wolves taken him? What was that fire I half-remembered? Surely that had not killed him, for in past he had proven uncommonly resistant to fire, even for one of diabolic heritage. Still, resistance was not immunity, and he could be burned by sufficient heat, such as that generated by magic. I prayed that he had at least been spared great pain, but in retrospect it seemed that most of his life had been about enduring pain of one kind or another. He carried his heart lightly, and although he gave it too easily at times, he seemed happy much of the time he worked for me.

"You must tend to your hunger, Excellency," said Tara. "The dead are beyond our help." I recognized the wisdom of her advice, even though I did not feel it. It was right to live for present necessity rather than wallow in past misfortune.

Returning her courtesy with a smile I did not feel, I took a bite of breakfast from this "finest cook in western Ustalav." It dissolved upon my tongue like decayed flesh, its putrescence spilling down my throat and up into my nasal passages. I barely brought the napkin to my mouth in time to stop myself from spitting the foul stuff back onto the plate.

"Excellency!" Tara gasped. She looked more astonished than offended. I turned away to spare her the sight of my wiping the inside of my mouth with the once-fine napkin. It was not enough to scour away the taste. I drank from my goblet, but the remaining filth instantly tainted the water so thoroughly that I dared not swallow. I rushed out the windowed doors and spat out the horrid stuff. Felix followed me outside with another goblet and napkin. Drink after drink gradually cleansed my mouth until I could control my gag reflex.

Turning to phrase an apology, I saw that Tara had withdrawn to spare me further humiliation. Despite her kindness, the heat of shame joined my cold sense of loss without countering it. Felix stood discreetly nearby until I addressed him.

"I shall take some air," I said.

"Perhaps Your Excellency desires a different meal," he said. He nodded toward a moss-draped pavilion beside a nearby grove. "Perhaps in the rotunda."

"Some fruit would be pleasant," I said. "No eggs."

Felix bowed and withdrew toward the manor house. I took the opportunity to stretch my legs along the riverbank, where clusters of dark willows bent to steep their tresses in the river. The passing current created the illusion that the wooded islands in the middle of the flow were the funereal barks of Ulfen heroes.

To the south loomed the accursed mountains of Ulcazar. I should forever hate the place for taking the lives of my servants, especially Radovan. Despite his recent disgruntlement, our association had been long and, in large part, mutually beneficial, although I had never given it so much thought before this day. At the best of times, I thought of him as more than a servant, but of course the disparity in our births rendered friendship impossible. If only I had maintained a proper distance from the start, I should not so mourn his loss now.

To die so close to returning to one's ancestral home seemed an especially cruel irony. I had never visited my father's homeland in Kyonin. The elves do not welcome half-breeds into the lands they themselves abandoned so long ago, before returning to reclaim them. Perhaps his death had spared Radovan the disappointment of rejection by his own people.

Distant thunder answered my thoughts. Far to the west, a storm front fulminated over the Virlych Mountains. It had been the same last time I had gazed upon those tortured peaks. Hideous magics still ravaged that blighted terrain, the ghosts of spells that had once slain legions now stalking the spirits of their defeated foes. Even in their ultimate triumph, the armies of men and dwarves could only contain, not destroy, the Whispering Tyrant. Some in Ustalav say the storms are his dreams.

I returned my attention to my immediate surroundings. Even by Chelish standards, Willowmourn Manor was a grand and ancient structure. It was constructed primarily of hewn bluestone, and its gables of gray slate lent it a stately aspect in the otherwise pastoral environment. Unlike southern manors, its gardens flowed subtly into the surrounding vegetation, seeming at their most exquisite points nothing more than happy accidents of nature. The gatehouse, the servants' quarters, a large stable, and several secluded pavilions all enjoyed the shelter of shade trees. Stands of poplar, ash, linden, and birch had been reduced but not replanted in regimental order, as was the custom of gardeners in Egorian. I found this truce between civilization and the wilderness most agreeable, but there was one notable exception to the rule: to the southwest lay the most extraordinary hedge maze I had ever seen. Above its borders rose fantastic topiary heads. Among the nearest I noted the heads of a stag, a bear, and a grotesque ogre. Such a frivolity would have enchanted me in my youth, and to be honest I still delighted in exploring such simple puzzles whenever I discovered one I had not previously encountered. I decided to seek out a better vantage from one of the western rooms after breakfast.

My perambulation took me past a number of the outdoors servants. A pair of towheaded boys, obviously brothers, swept out the empty carriage house. They peered at me through the corners of their eyes lest they meet my gaze and be required to doff their caps and wait upon my pleasure. I noticed no signs of my carriage within the building, and I worried what had become of it. For the first time since the beginning of our association, I was impatient for Casomir's return.

Beyond the carriage house, a hard-faced groom exercised a pair of excellent stallions in a paddock. Through the open doors of the stable I saw six equally fine animals in the nearest wing of the L-shaped building. An open kennel had been built into the outside wall, its compartments guarded by three enormous dogs who eyed me as I passed. Two were fully grown Ustalav wolfhounds, thick as mastiffs in the chest but with longer legs and a dense gray coat. Both had drooping mustaches upon their square snouts, and their resemblance to certain nobles of Ustalav might have been risible had my mood been less cloudy. The third was a younger incarnation of the elders, still developing his adult coat and lacking his parents' mustaches. He would dwarf them both when he reached his full growth. The youngster's ears rose at the sound of barking from the river, where his fellows played. After a longing glance in their direction, he returned to his vigil, eyes fixed upon the stranger that walked his master's land. Like his parents, he was destined to be a guardian.

By the time I had completed my circumvolution, Felix awaited me in the northern rotunda. He bowed and held my seat.

"Mistress Tara asks me to convey her apologies for her absence," he said. "She hopes your walk has restored your appetite."

"Convey my thanks for her consideration," I said, trying not to appear too apprehensive as he uncovered the breakfast salver to reveal an assortment of sliced melon, berries, and steaming buns. Felix watched as I sampled a bite. He released an audible sigh when he saw I was content.

"Perfect," I said as he poured a cup of tea.

"Thank you, Excellency," he said. "Is there anything else I may bring you?"

"No," I said. "You can, however, answer a few questions."

"Of course, Excellency," he said. I could not help but notice a shadow of reluctance cross his face.

"When do you expect the Count to return?" I said. "And do not say, 'before the snow.'"

He nodded. "We expect the Count, as well as the first touch of winter, to arrive within the next week or so. Forgive me, Excellency. The duration of my lord Galdana's autumn hunt varies from year to year."

While unsatisfying, the answer was no worse than I deserved for presuming upon the hospitality of a lord who had not been informed of my visit. Still, there was much I could learn in his absence and that of his proxy, Casomir. "Tell me of this plague in Kavapesta."

"Master Casomir has gone to learn more, but we have heard it has stricken dozens. Several have perished, but the priests of Pharasma have saved the worthiest among the afflicted."

He did not need to explain that those saved were among the more generous donors to the church. Wherever priests bestowed their divine cures among the people, the same hierarchy existed.

"This morning I saw a man collecting the carcasses of dead birds," I said.

"Odav, Your Excellency," said the butler. "He is my lord Galdana's gardener."

"Yes, yes," I said. "But I was inquiring as to the reason the birds have died."

"Of course. Forgive me, Excellency, but I do not know the reason. It is a recent phenomenon."

"But it is thought to be related to the plague?"

He raised his empty palms. "Perhaps Master Casomir will return with the answer to that question, Your Excellency. Until then, we must take every wise precaution."

"I see," I said. "Apart from collecting the dead birds, have you taken no other steps to prevent the spread of this plague?'

"Your Excellency, ferry travel is forbidden except by permission of the mayor or, in the absence of Count Galdana, Master Casomir. The staff are confined to Willowmourn, which has thus far been spared affliction."

"Very well," I said. "When did our party arrive?"

"Yesterday morning, Excellency," he said. "Although I am given to understand that you were another day conveyed from the Senir Bridge."

"That reminds me," I said. "Where is my carriage?"

The butler's face paled. He hesitated to answer, but at my insistent look, he said, "I regret to inform Your Excellency that the vehicle was destroyed."

His words struck the breath from me. The red carriage was my sole material legacy from the father I had never met, and, except for my home at Greensteeples, the only surviving connection I had with my late mother. It was far more than a property. For nearly a century, it had been a key feature of my household. It had been with me longer than any friend, relative, or rival. It had been a part of me, and I felt its absence like a wound in my heart.

"If Your Excellency desires privacy," said the butler, his body leaning back as if yearning to escape.

"No," I snapped. "What of the wreckage? Where are its remains?"

It seemed impossible for the man's face to become even whiter, but he faded like a ghost before answering in a near whisper, "Your Excellency, I do not know. Perhaps it was burned along with the bodies of your servants."

"Burned?"

"Yes, Excellency."

"Are you quite certain the bodies were burned?"

"Yes, Excellency," he said. "Burned and the ashes cast upon the river."

And thus I knew for certain that someone at Willowmourn was lying to me. The question was why.

Chapter Six
The Ugly Little Girl

You know what focuses the mind? I'll tell you what works for me: waking up face down inside a coffin crackling on a heap of pitch-soaked timber.

My claustrophobic twitches melted away like fat on a spit. My back felt as though someone had sewn hot stones under the skin. I couldn't feel my legs at all. The spurs on my elbows dug into the coffin walls, but the twine binding my thumbs wouldn't break. If I kept struggling, I'd soon sever my thumbs, which dripped a pool of hot blood onto the small of my back. The fire's glow penetrated the seams of the coffin, and I could see the wood blackening.

A little fire doesn't usually bother me, but this time I was in the oven. The flames prickled my face, and the smoke stung my eyes and nostrils. If this had been a hypothetical situation, I might wonder whether the flames would grow hot enough to kill me before the smoke suffocated me.

I can live without both thumbs, I decided. I jerked my elbows outward harder than ever, hoping to pierce the coffin sides. The scream came from my thumbs and rushed up to leap into to my brain and escape through my mouth. The only other sound I could hear was the hiss and pop of the pyre. After the second jerk, I couldn't even feel whether my arms were moving. I smelled the stench of my melting hair and felt a brand above either eye where my eyebrows had been.

My body lurched to the side, and cool air washed over my left arm. An instant later, I felt the freezing pain of flame rushing up it. The orange flames were inside the coffin. The sleeves of my jacket were on fire, and at last I felt my skin shrinking beneath the disintegrating fabric. I tried to blink, but my left eye was sealed shut.

I lurched again, and the coffin rolled with me. I heard a woman's scream. A distant part of my brain hoped it was not the sound of my own voice. The coffin slid fast, turned over once, and hit the ground with a splintering crash. I couldn't tell whether it was the wood or my bones that cracked, but I kept thrashing, kicking, howling.

My hands flew apart—with or without thumbs I couldn't tell. My left arm passed through a ragged hole in the side of the coffin. I shoved my hand through the splinters, smashing at the lid. For an instant I was astonished as it flew up, breaking into charred pieces as it disintegrated against the backdrop of a cloudy sky. I rolled out onto the cool grass, tearing off my burning jacket and the shirt beneath. All around, people screamed and shouted, running away. I pushed myself up to my knees and squinted through the bars formed by my fused eyelashes.

I was at a crossroads. Dead center in the intersection was a rectangular hole about six feet deep. My grave.

The gravediggers stood gaping beside an open cart attached to a lowing ox that shied from the sight of me. The fabric of their clothes was homespun wool in the grays and browns of peasant farmers. Several of the men grabbed tools from the cart: picks, a few spades, and a pitchfork. Why had they brought a pitchfork? The sight of it drew a growl from the well in my chest. It was not a sound I'd made before. The ox bolted away.

I shot the tines at the man with the fork, and a warm splash of blood wet my chin. I glanced at my bloody hand. It looked as if it had been through a meat grinder, but it was all there, more or less. More, actually. My fingers had grown half again their normal length, and the tiny bone nubs on my knuckles had grown into coarse spurs like the ones on my elbows.

The shock of the first blow refocused my mind if not my vision. A long dark shaft trembled before me. It rose out of my right leg where the tines of the pitchfork pierced my thigh, but what really upset me was seeing the long bony spike that had emerged from my kneecap. Only shreds remained of my expensive trousers, and beneath them my skin had turned the color of molten copper. There was no time to appreciate the rage building inside me before a terrific howl burst out of me.

No, it's not my usual thing, but under the circumstances it felt exactly right.

Four of the village men approached, weapons held high. Cowering lower with each step, they looked as tiny as slips, although they were all human, not halflings. I ripped the pitchfork from my thigh, gripped it just above the tines, and swung hard. The butt of the handle cracked one man on the head, knocking him cold before sweeping past to smash the cheek of the one standing beside him. A pick swung down at my uninjured thigh, but to me it was as slowly as through water. I caught it by the haft and forced it back, smashing the villager's face with its butt. The man dropped the weapon and clutched his bloody mouth.

The fourth stepped back, gaping at the spade humming in his hands like a tuning fork. Only then did I realize that son of a bitch had hit me in the head. I almost felt sorry for him as I threw him the big smile. All blood drained from the man's face. He turned his head as if to flee, but instead he only cocked his arms in a comical manner and fainted dead away.

I laughed. The sound boomed across the hill to echo in nearby dells. I never laugh like that. Nobody laughs like that.

The rest of the villagers fled like a herd of startled lambs, most of them heading toward a cluster of thatched buildings just down a gentle hill from the crossroads. Their Varisian cries were still mostly babble to my ears, but I made out the words "*devil*" and "*monster*," and those names suited me just fine. There was also an unfamiliar word they kept repeating: Azra. Whether that was some local demigoddess or their name for Pharasma or Desna, I didn't care. I felt so big and strong, they'd need a goddess by the time I came to town. They'd need a whole other village of gravediggers before I was done.

I shouted threats and curses after them. My voice was hoarse beyond recognition, and the words that emerged were strange. The language sounded familiar, but I didn't recognize my own words, even though somehow I understood them. It wasn't Varisian, and it sure as hell wasn't Taldane. Then I realized I was speaking infernal, the language of devils.

Unlike the boss, I don't speak more than a couple dozen words in any foreign language. Maybe I had more than a hundred words in Varisian by now, after help from the guards—poor bastards. I couldn't actually speak anything fluently other than Taldane, the common tongue of the Empire and many lands it had once conquered and lost. Still, you pick up the sound of lots of languages in a cosmopolitan town like Egorian, so I could tell the difference between the elf and dwarf tongues, for instance. And considering the nature of the Chelish underground, it had been useful to learn the difference between infernal and abyssal when the trail of our latest job led to cultists of either camp.

That must have been one hell of a bang on the head, I thought. Then I became keenly aware of the burning pain all over my body, especially on my face and chest. I rubbed my eyes, and the lashes came away in gummy lumps. I blinked hard, but only my right eye opened. I tried pulling on my left eyelid, but it was swollen shut. I gave up, distracted by how long my fingers and nails had grown. My vision was still cloudy, but that was not enough to account for the transformation of my body.

The villagers were out of sight now, no doubt hiding in their root cellars. Up ahead, black and red chickens darted through the muddy avenues between their homes, agitated by the commotion. Pigs snuffled and nosed the mud of their pens, which I noted were built between the houses. Filthy peasants.

Beyond the village lay a wide, lazy river. On the far side, wooded hills rose gradually to the right, which I guessed to be the south judging from the position of the veiled sun. That put me on the west, probably not where I wanted to be. The boss—or the boss's remains, I realized with a sickening feeling in my belly—had to be farther up in the mountains and on the other side of the river. From this dirty little village I could see no bridges, and no mountains either.

An itching sensation on my right buttock alerted me that my remaining clothes were still smoldering. I slapped at the fabric and tore away most of it when I saw how much smoke and flame still licked at me. Those ignorant pig farmers had ruined my new clothes! The jacket alone cost more than one of these mucking peasants earned in a year.

I'd have that out of their hides. I strode into the village with blood on my mind.

The cottage doors and windows were shut tight. I noticed that all the doors were painted red, probably to ward off evil spirits, though I doubted they'd stop me. Beneath the shuttered windows were flower boxes containing the year's last drooping blossoms. I smashed a few as I came. Maybe that would get their attention.

Immediately I felt foolish, like some drunken vandal. The moment I paused to think, I wasn't sure what to do any more. I'd never been so angry, and that was a curious thing. I'd suffered more than my share of outrages, but I learned to wait for my revenge by the time I was four years old. Since then I'd always met insult with a cool head. If it wouldn't kill me today, I could sneak up on it tomorrow. If only these peasants spoke Taldane, then I could at least beat an explanation out of one of them. Maybe I had enough Varisian to make it work. The trick was to get my hands on one without killing him.

That was good enough for a plan, and the idea of action calmed my beating heart. The nearest house would do. I reached for the door handle, and then I saw the ugly little girl.

She sat bareback upon a mottled white donkey at the other end of what passed for a main street. Under a film of road dust, her clothes were more colorful than those the villagers wore. Her vaguely brown hair formed a tangled hood that revealed only the freckled tip of her nose and the half-hidden glimmer of light blue or gray eyes. She stared at me with a calm expression that I found damned irritating.

"What are you looking at?" I said, but something else still had my voice and my words. I wanted to look around for the ventriloquist who was having one over on me.

The girl frowned when she heard me. She kicked the donkey's flanks, but the beast lowered its long, black-tipped ears and refused to budge. Its eyes were ringed in white at the sight of me. With a sigh, the girl dismounted and ran toward me, just like that. She didn't hesitate. She was barefoot, the soles of her feet black and tough. She carried no weapon, but as she came within ten yards of me, she dipped a hand into a pouch at her waist—there were at least a dozen little bags hanging from the wide leather kirtle—and spread a line of fine white ash on the ground. She stepped back, beckoning me to come toward her, to cross the line.

Right, I thought. How stupid do you think I am? I walked around the line and smiled a little when I saw the consternation on her face. Not a girl, I realized, but a woman. Her tiny stature and general lack of grooming gave her the look of a street orphan.

"*Azra,*" cried a woman from the shelter of her cottage. "*Beware the devil!*"

At last, a whole sentence of Varisian I could understand. I snarled my thanks at the hidden speaker before turning back toward this Azra. What was she? The village witch? The local madwoman? She didn't know what she was in for.

I stepped forward, just to give her a little scare, but she was too quick. She whirled away in a gesture that briefly reminded me of Malena's dance in the Caliphas market. These Varisian women sure know how to dance. So do I.

As I reached for her arm, I followed so close that I didn't see she had spread an arc of dust around her as she moved away. I'd not only crossed the line but planted my foot right on the ashen barrier. I winced, expecting a wall of magical energy to freeze me solid or make me do the lightning dance, but nothing happened except that Azra danced away and stood with one fist on her hip. She frowned at me like a gardener discovering a gopher hole among the cabbages.

Behind me, I heard the slow creak of a hinge. I turned to see the nose of a crossbow emerging from a window.

"Shoot that thing at me," I said, "and I will shove it so far . . ." There was no use threatening anyone, I figured. No one understood a word I was saying.

I debated a second between charging the window and simply running out of its field of vision, but then Azra shouted a series of short hoots that were definitely not Varisian, maybe not any language. I spared her a glance to see her shoo the man back inside and shake her head "no." The archer lowered the crossbow and pulled the shutters back, leaving just enough space to peer out at the confrontation.

Now what? I watched as Azra dipped a knuckle into a tiny jar she took from another belt pouch. She rubbed the stuff into her eyes, blinked, and stared at me.

I did not like that stare. It made me feel as though my jewels were hanging out. It occurred to me that such might actually be the case, but I checked and saw enough of my pants remained intact that I still had a little modesty left. Still, something about the way this ragged hedge witch looked at me made me feel she saw something inside, maybe something I couldn't see. It was beyond annoying—it was downright infuriating.

I bent down to put my face close to hers and opened my mouth to speak, but before I could utter a syllable, she reached up and smacked me on the forehead with the palm of her hand.

The blow was much harder than I expected, but the surprise, not the impact, made me step back. Her hand came away with a lump of green-gray goop on the palm. I felt something pasty stuck to my brow and reached up to touch it. There was something like a scrap of parchment there, but my fingers couldn't grip it. They felt thick and numb, and in a second the feeling had spread up my arms.

I took another step away and wobbled like a drunk. Overcompensating, I stumbled forward. I was going down. I could feel it, and I needed to get away from this woman—this Azra—before I was at her mercy.

I ran past her, covering yards with every step, faster than I'd ever been before. At the other end of the muddy lane I saw a small covered wagon, its side panels carved and painted with images of deer running beneath a starry sky, the moon smiling down at them as wolves crept from the shadows of the trees. I had to laugh. Not for the first time, I sympathized with the deer.

Behind me, the villagers shouted out of their windows, and Azra answered them with hoots and grunts. If I could just make it to the woods, the worst that would happen is that I'd die and be eaten by wolves. That had to be the lesser evil.

I ran around the wagon, mindful that the archer might not obey Azra's command to hold his fire. There I ran straight into the white donkey, which screamed and brayed. It bucked, turning itself completely around in two awkward hops that would have looked hilarious from a distance. I tried to leap aside, but the donkey was quicker. Its hind hooves came up and smashed me.

For the second time in recent memory, the blow felt as hard as the end of the world.

Chapter Seven
The Secret Hand

Before locating the clues you left to guide me, I uncovered two entirely unanticipated mysteries. The first delighted me so much that I briefly forgot my recent misfortune. The second deepened my suspicion that someone at Willowmourn was deceiving me, or possibly even manipulating my actions.

A few hours after my second breakfast, Tara found me as I gazed down at Count Galdana's topiary maze from his second-floor trophy room. My only companions before her arrival were the heads of prey ranging from stags to firepelt cougars to an enormous bugbear, all of which stared from the walls in mute testimony to the skill of the men who had slain them.

The added height of the second floor allowed me to see more of the topiary figures, which seemed to consist of equal numbers of game animals and monsters, but not the complete maze, which might have given me a few moments' solace as I unraveled the puzzle of its passages.

Earlier I had hoped to observe the maze from the vantage of the fourth floor, but a footman stationed at the stairway informed me apologetically but firmly that the upper chambers were unavailable to guests. Despite my obligations to the hospitality of an absent lord, this unexpected barrier only increased my desire to explore those forbidden passages, as did the pungent odor of wine vinegar that I detected from them. I wondered what mishap had caused the servants to use such a noisome cleaning agent, but chances were the answer was both distasteful and uninteresting.

Coincidentally or not, Tara's reason for approaching me was quite the opposite of restriction. She found me upon my return to the trophy room, where I had noticed a weapon frame above the hearth was absent its swords.

"Does Count Galdana carry his entire armory while on the hunt?" I asked.

"Perhaps he does," she said with a smile. "We are acquainted only by correspondence. I have scarcely more knowledge of him than you must have."

"And I have none at all," I said, discounting the gossip of Caliphas. "I hope he shall not mind my presumption of his hospitality while he is away."

"Surely he will be grateful that you conducted me safely home," she said.

I wanted to ask her more about the events at the bridge, but I knew Casomir would take exception to my questioning Tara rather than asking him directly. Much as I disliked him, there was a protocol to observe. Before I could frame an indirect query, Tara continued.

"Casomir left instructions that you are to have full access to his uncle's library," she said. When I did not immediately respond, she added, "That is why you came, is it not?"

"Indeed," I said. "I am grateful for the favor."

"I shall tell the servants you are not to be disturbed until supper," she said. She touched a bell pull beside the mounted head of an enormous stag and indicated the butler, who stood almost invisibly behind her. "If you require anything, feel free to summon Felix."

"Thank you." I noticed shadows beneath her eyes. "Are you well, my lady?"

She smiled a wan apology. "Our recent misfortunes have troubled my sleep," she said.

"No doubt that is it," I said. "But to be certain of your health, perhaps we should summon a cleric from the city."

"Thank you for your concern, Excellency," she said.

"Varian, please."

"Varian," she said. "I feel only weary and unsettled, not ill. I promise that the moment I suspect otherwise, I will ask Casomir to summon aid. Until then, it is best that we leave the priests to minister to those most in need."

"You are generous, lady."

"And you grow more courtly as you recover from our ordeal," she curtsied. "If you will excuse me, I shall retire until Casomir returns."

In her absence, and unable to examine the topiary maze from a better height, I followed Felix to the library. He unlocked the door with a key on a ribbon about his neck. I noted that he kept a ring of keys in the pocket of his coat, suggesting that the library was a chamber of especial privacy. Indeed, he did not follow me inside but begged leave after indicating the location of the bell pull.

Unlike the absent count's trophy room, which offered the uncomfortable sensation of being surrounded by predators, Galdana's library felt instantly comfortable, almost familiar. While it was but a fraction of the size of my holdings at Greensteeples, the room was practically constructed of bookshelves. The walls above the shelves were lined with the crests of various noble houses of Amaans, as well as the occasional bronze statue or marble bust my mother called "dust-catchers." And yet the library surrendered no horizontal space to anything but bookshelves, and those were crammed with books, scrolls, maps, and folios. Four banks of freestanding shelves stood among the leather chairs and divan, as did a large map table and three podiums. There was barely room left for a modest fireplace before which stood a pair of comfortable-looking chairs, a table laden with books between them. Galdana even had a credible globe, although it appeared to have been constructed generations earlier, and I immediately spied several obvious errors.

But you know all this already, for the next thing I spied was your ingenious mark. It might have taken me longer to spot it, but the late morning sun slanted directly onto the shelves you had rearranged. Recognizing the "discovery" sigil formed by the spines of green bindings moved from their former organization was a joyous moment that briefly shook the sorrow from my brow.

From that point, it was a simple matter to select only those volumes whose top edges lacked the thicker layer of dust on the remainder of Galdana's collection. Here I am tempted to admonish you for trusting that the housekeeping staff did not include a more conscientious chambermaid, but perhaps you had ample opportunity to observe the staff and weigh their deficiencies against the likelihood that one might obliterate your trail.

A brief inventory of the more recently disturbed tomes provided me with four categories and one anomaly. No doubt the histories of the region were your principal object, and it was no surprise to find religious texts similarly disturbed. Also expected was the discovery that you had removed a number of blank, bound manuscripts. I trust that you received Count Galdana's permission to use these materials in expanding your Pathfinder journal, or, failing that, that your liberation of them went unnoticed. Discretion is a great shield in the pursuit of knowledge.

As for the fourth category, I was naturally troubled not only by the presence of several treatises on the cults of Norgorber and Urgathoa but also by evidence that they had been among the most frequently perused volumes. The discovery of such books by his peers would raise difficult questions for Count Galdana, who at best would be labeled a degenerate, at worst condemned as a worshiper of those forbidden deities.

Apart from the historical, religious, blank, and occult volumes, I also noticed a cheap romance among the recently handled books. Its principal contents were of no obvious importance, but I noted with some bemusement the addition of extremely risqué caricatures drawn upon the margins.

I had seen such diversions before, hidden in plain sight among the libraries of the lords of Cheliax. Upon retiring from dinner, the ladies would gather in their parlors while the men withdrew to the library. There, after a few brandies and the distribution of those ghastly Taldan cigars, the host would pretend to show his fellows the latest composition from some wretched "author" of adventure stories. No one of breeding reads such drivel, but the true object was to display the picture drama on the margins. One holds the pages between thumb and finger and riffles the pages. The resulting motion causes the illusion of motion as the drawings—each of the same subjects but in slightly different positions—appear to come to life.

It would be a fine amusement for children, except for the pornographic nature of the illustrations, which include such quotidian dramas as the lord and the courtesan, the lord and the milkmaid, the milk maid and the courtesan, and so on. Needless to say, it never ceases to amuse visitors, or at least those who find such diversions distasteful are politic enough to feign delight. I count myself among the latter.

Enough of that. You need no description of something you have already examined. Or have you? I wonder whether you have been the only visitor to Galdana's library this year, for I have not yet deduced what interest this book could have been to you.

I would have set aside the romance with its vulgar illustration except that, upon riffling the page, I heard the most unspeakable sounds of the very activities depicted in the illustrations. Even in the event that you have not seen them, I shall spare you the embarrassment of describing either the actions or the sounds. I saw that on the back of each illustration was inscribed a rune, or rather a fragment of one.

To be certain of what I suspected, I riffled the pages again. Again the bawdy sound emanated from the book. There could be no mistaking the source. I fanned the pages as a gambler might fan cards, arranging the symbols side by side until their relationship became clear. Each was a fragment of an arcane character, three or four together combining to form the letters that compose the words of wizardry. In an enchanted scroll, such characters would have been written whole as parts of the syllables of magic. Moreover, the ink that formed the words would have been invested with the materials required for a wizard to prepare that spell in his mind, like a trap set to await only a catalyst to unleash its power.

It was a fascinating discovery, but unless I could be certain that it was you who lately investigated this book, it was not a lead worth pursuing. Perhaps one of the servants, or Casomir in his uncle's absence, had amused himself with this tawdry diversion. Lacking more compelling evidence that it had been among the volumes you had studied, I set it aside for later examination of its magical effect.

I first put aside the religious volumes because I have long been familiar with the worship of both Desna and Pharasma. My mother introduced me to the splendors of the Song of the Spheres in my earliest days, and together we worshiped her until the rise of the House of Thrune and the national obligation to venerate Asmodeus, the Prince of Law. While I have never been a devotee of the Lady of Graves, all who live must one day face her judgment, and so it behooves us all to learn what to expect when Pharasma lifts the material veil from our faces. Unlike those who find her prominent standing in Ustalav a grim obsession, I see it as a sign of strength in the national character that the people of this land embrace the ultimate moment of their lives rather than subjugate themselves to the fear of it.

Despite my dedication to knowledge of all subjects, I was loath to open those books concerning the cults of Norgorber and Urgathoa. As a Pathfinder, I have always despised the Reaper of Reputation and his various cults. To those who esteem learning, there can be no more senseless following than that which employs intrigue and murder to suppress knowledge. The most terrible tyranny is the tyranny of ignorance. As for Urgathoa, the Pallid Princess, I knew of course that she had her followers among Varisians who rejected the notion that their lives were subject to the judgment of Pharasma and, like their awful goddess, desired to extend their mortal lives beyond their natural terms. I can think of nothing more hideous than the transformation of one's self into an abomination of life.

Thus, I devoted the rest of the afternoon to studying the histories of Amaans and Virlych, the pages of which displayed the most handling. You must have been anxious to continue pursuit of your goal, for I am certain at leisure you would have shown more care.

While I have a good grounding in the history of Ustalav and the surrounding territories, I am no expert in the minutia. Perhaps that is the wrong term, for even the tiniest detail can be of great importance under the right circumstances. I followed those points you deemed most relevant by looking for the imprint of your thumbnail in the margin. In the beginning, it proved little more than a refresher of commonly known history, but gradually an untold story began to take shape.

The history of Ustalav is in many ways one of the footnotes of the history of Tar-Baphon. It was over a thousand years after the death of the wizard-king's mortal incarnation that Soividia Ustav unified the Varisian clans and gave a name to the resulting country. Even during this golden age, the fractious Varisians would not be ruled by a lone monarch. To avoid disintegration of the country, one of Soividia's descendents elected to share his power, dividing responsibility for its government among sixteen counties and thus calming the most ambitious powerful clan leaders.

For five centuries afterward, Ustalav flourished among the other nations encircling Lake Encarthan, each of its long succession of monarchs believing that Tar-Baphon had met his fate at the hands of the now-dead god Aroden on the Isle of Terror. None realized that the immortal warlord merely slept, awaiting the completion of the rituals he had set in motion centuries earlier. When he rose as the lich known as the Whispering Tyrant, Ustalav was the first human land he held in thrall.

He culled those who would not serve, raising their lifeless bodies to form his first legions. By the time he combined these with forces from the orc nation of Belkzen, the neighboring lands were unprepared for his assault. It took over five hundred years for the nations of Avistan to mount a unified defense. They might never have done so except for the rallying cry of the Taldan empire's Shining Crusade combined with the dwarves of Kraggodan and the Knights of Ozem. Armies of dwarves and men struggled against the seemingly inexhaustible might of the Whispering Tyrant for more than seventy years before the Taldan general Arnisant broke the Shield of Aroden upon the staff of the Whispering Tyrant, sacrificing his own life in the act. That fraction of the god's power contained within the artifact washed over Tar-Baphon, weakening him sufficiently for the abjurers and priests of Taldor to imprison him beneath the roots of his own seat of power, the dread Gallowspire.

Ustalav rose from its ashes not as a phoenix but as a frail shadow of its former self. The counties once known as Virholt and Grolych had been reduced to a blasted range of desolate mountains pocked with the ruins of the Tyrant's monuments. The lords of Ustalav have been content to leave that land to the restless dead, and they call it Virlych. The Shining Crusade claimed another portion of Ustalav as a bastion against the awakening of Tar-Baphon, and today that is the nation of Lastwall. Even among the central counties of Ustalav, three have overthrown their feudal lords to declare themselves the Palatinates, and the Prince has neither the will nor the power to defy them. Rather, he must concern himself with the ambitions of rivals for his seat, now in Caliphas, far from Soividia Ustav's home of Ardis.

So much of the country's history I might have recited from memory, but a comparison of the minor chronicles you consulted beside them leads me to some intriguing additions. I had not known, for instance, of this rebel lord of Virholt who surrendered his county and offered his service to the Whispering Tyrant. It is tempting to embrace the scholar's proposition that he did so to spare his people the horror of undead existence among the Tyrant's legions. Such romantic notions are seldom historically accurate, especially those forwarded by servants of the prevailing force.

Did you note the references to Virholt's conjurations and compacts? The implications are troubling in their lack of detail. Answering the question of whether this Lord Virholt bargained with infernal powers before or after entering the service of Tar-Baphon could radically alter our understanding of the fall of Ustalav.

More imminently, if you are in search of some remnant of Virholt, I hope you are prepared to face the darkest magics. It does not take an immortal like Tar-Baphon to leave deadly traps behind. Too many of our colleagues have discovered this truth in the moment of their last living error.

After this first light review of the materials you assembled, I was anxious to learn more, but I found myself weary and desirous of a celebratory tonic. I rose to summon Felix, but as I placed my hand upon the bell pull, I noticed something out of place. Behind the nearest shelf I detected an unusual shadow thrown by the late afternoon night. Something rested behind the books on the top shelf. I rolled the ladder quietly over and stepped up to peer down behind the obscuring books

Behind them were several sheaves of fine vellum. Each had been cut horizontally to form sixteen miniature books, secured on one side by a strip of brass bent over to form a crude binding. They rested atop three unbound folios, a small velvet pouch, and an inkpot.

Some preternatural warning tingled at the base of my skull. I descended the ladder as quietly as possible and crept toward the door. Listening, I heard no sign of a presence. I turned the doorknob and was surprised to find it locked from the other side. Peering through the keyhole, I saw no one in the corridor.

Now all my skin crawled with anticipation and suspicion. I strolled with feigned casualness past the windows. Apart from the young hound I had seen earlier, who gazed up through the window as if keeping watch on me, I detected no spies peering in. Compelled by that numinous feeling, I completed a circuit of the room as if exercising muscles grown stiff with inactivity. I saw no peep holes and suspected none of the various knickknacks of serving as a scrying device. Assured that I was unseen, at least by means obvious or mundane, I returned to the high shelf and removed the hidden papers.

Beneath them I discovered a further treasure: a long sword sheathed in a scabbard of white leather and gold frame, held against the wall by the weight of the bookshelf. I left it there as I descended to examine the strange little books.

They were not proper books but strips of bound pages devoted entirely to the flipbook characters I had previously encountered. The contents were spells with which I was once intimately familiar, spells I had studied in hopes that they would serve to protect me from the dangers of a Pathfinder expedition, before I regretfully abandoned them in the face of my peculiar frailty to holding magic within my mind. Yet there was something far more familiar about these "riffle scrolls," as it immediately occurred to me to call them. The realization settled upon me like a mantle of ice at the same time as I heard the sound of Casomir's carriage returning from the ferry crossing.

The writing on the strange scrolls was indisputably my own.

Chapter Eight
The Black Bird

For months after my initiation to the Goatherds, I had nightmares about that day, and how I beat a merchant's son to within an inch of his life as the rest of the gang looked on as witnesses. After a while, even when I was asleep in the pen beside the other boys, I realized the recurring visions were only dreams. Still, they held me tight until I woke myself kicking to sit up sweating in the cold dark, knowing even as a child that on the day I died there'd be another stone weighing down Pharasma's scales on the side of Hell.

This dream was a lot like those.

The boss had told me stories of the gigantic birds called rocs, bigger than caravels. He said they nested in the mountains of Qadira, blotting out the sky as they swooped down on caravans to pluck up camels two at a time, their riders still in their saddles.

I'd never seen one, of course, but in my dream—it had to be a dream—one of those rocs chased me across a broken desert. Because it was a dream, I knew what my pursuer was, even though the only way I could see it was by looking for the black void where the stars had been, or when one of its monstrous wings passed before the fat lozenge of the moon. The beats of its wings were thunder, and each one threw down an earthquake. I ran from cover to cover, squatting beside a withered tree or lying flat in a shallow ditch as it swooped past. The ground was so hot that I couldn't stand still for more than a few seconds, but each time I peered over the edge of a ragged gully looking for the next shelter, the wind frosted my cheeks.

I heard a shriek behind me. Before I could roll away, talons raked my neck and a beak pecked hard into my cheek. Bright pain blossomed over my neck and shoulder, and I flailed my arms to drive it away, falling to the side and lolling like a stunned beast.

Miraculously, I escaped, if only for a moment. I smelled the musty scent of feathers and heard the great roc scratching furrows into the cracked mud. I wanted to run, but I couldn't stand up. I rolled helplessly from side to side, caught in a dry ditch barely wider than my shoulders. I kicked out, and though my foot did not move far, it struck a sharp edge.

My shout half-woke me from the nightmare, but I felt a weight on my chest, and the feather smell filled my nose. I was lying on a carpet upon a wooden floor, not the ground, and I was moving up or backward. The space was not so small, but I couldn't shake the feeling I was back in a coffin. I tried to open my eyes, but only the right lids parted.

Through a gauzy veil the light stabbed my brain. The instant I shut my eye tight, something stabbed my chin. I reached for it, but my arms were bound tight around my body. Rocking to the side, I struck another hard edge, a box or a piece of furniture. Behind me, above my head, I heard the nickering of a beast and a popping sound, like someone smacking his lips. The jolting motion slowed and stopped.

A sudden lurch startled my stomach and shoved me upward, my skull cracking against a barrier above my head. Tiny yellow stars danced in my brain, and hot bile rushed into my mouth. I tried to spit, but something covered my face, and my own sick ran over my chin and back up into my nose.

Choking, I struggled to raise my hands to my face. Too weak to tear the fabric that held my arms down, all I achieved was the bastard whelp of a sob and a gag. I tried to sit up, but I could barely lift my feet a few inches. Even that much effort made my guts ache. If I were on the way to Hell today, this is not the way I'd have chosen to travel there.

An opening door creaked somewhere past my feet, followed by the jabber of a startled chicken whose feet I felt scratch through the fabric over my legs. Someone hissed and shooed away the creature. Its wings stirred a cloud of dust and dander. A hand touched my knee. I felt the pressure of splints on both of my legs.

The hand traveled upward, joined by another as they caught my struggling wrists. I sputtered through the vomit, unable to speak. At last the hands came to my mouth and tore open the fabric. I turned to spit, and one of the hands lifted my head to let the vomit drain out of my nose. I could breathe freely again.

"Thanks," I said in a voice frailer than a whisper. On the bright side, it was my voice, and I recognized my words as Taldane.

"Oh," said a female voice. Those hands pushed me down as I tried to sit up again. She said something unintelligible.

"Come again?"

More sounds, mostly vowels, were the only reply as the woman moved away. It wasn't Varisian, and it damned sure wasn't Taldane.

"I can't move," I said. "I want to get up." Even pushing those few words out exhausted me. I lay still, trying to gather strength but finding none.

The woman returned, this time with water that I could hear sloshing in a jug. I was thirstier than I'd ever been, but she wet a cloth and wiped my chin before giving me any to drink. She took it away before I was done. When I lifted my head in protest, she pushed me back firmly. Her hand was warm and calloused.

Next she tore open the fabric on my face and pressed her wet cloth onto my eyes. The water was blessedly cool. She wiped away thick particles, the last remnants of my burned lashes, I imagined, without much hope that I was going to see a pretty face in the next mirror. She wet the cloth again and wrung it over my brow before wiping away more of the detritus. My closed eye was tender, as was most of the left side of my face. Tiny fingers pressed against the lids and carefully pulled them open.

"Ah!" I cried. I saw a smear of blood as my left eye opened, but I could see. The vision in my right eye was normal, and after a few more moments of her ministrations, I saw where I was.

Kneeling beside me was Azra, the witch who'd knocked me out in the village. She was not as small as I'd previously thought, but it was hard to tell while lying on the floor of her covered wagon. Maybe she just seemed bigger up close.

She shifted the hinge of the table on which I'd cracked my skull and secured it to the wagon wall. She helped me sit up and left me propped against the front wall while she unfolded panels on either side of the wagon to let in the fresh air.

From the concave ceiling hung bags, stained-glass globes, bundles of dried meat, and bunches of flowers and roots. As Azra opened windows, the scent of autumn leaves blew in to mingle with the pungent aroma of the herbs. On the floor of the wagon, formed approximately in an outline of my body, lay baskets, chests, sacks of grain, clay jugs, bags of potatoes, an open box of tinker's tools, a tiny iron stove, a coil of rope, and a hundred smaller things tucked in between. Above my head was a box fastened to the wagon's front wall, and its looming there made me feel claustrophobic. I slid down, but even that slight motion triggered a new bout of vertigo.

Outside, the chicken that had tormented me chanted *balk balk balk* while marching the perimeter. Beside the rear door I saw an iron loop with a piece of twine that moved back and forth in time with the sound of the bird.

Looking down, I saw I was covered in some patchwork garment of thin gray cotton. It had been stitched together from five or six smaller pieces to form a sort of bag around me. Because of the fatigue or sickness or just plain stupidity, it took me a long time to realize what it was.

"Son of a bitch!" I tried to shout, but it came out more like a sneeze. I struggled as hard as I could—which was still weaker than a newborn kitten—to rip the thing off. One of my spurs tore through the side. I raised my arm to widen the tear, and that gave me room enough to push my hands through. My thumbs were swaddled in thick stained cloth, bloody little mummies.

Azra returned, her hands raised to calm me. I wasn't interested in calm just then.

"What the hell is wrong with you people?" I said. "You worship Pharasma, I got it, but that gives you no right to box me, bury me, or sew me into a goddamned shroud!"

She stepped back, cleared a spot on a box, and sat down to watch as I raged. As tantrums go, it was pretty feeble. I listed only a few curses in either of our languages, all of which she seemed to understand, but none of which seemed to bother her. I gave up, disappointed I hadn't shocked or at least annoyed her.

She pointed at me and placed her hands together beside her check, then turned her head to mime sleeping.

"I'm not tired," I said. That was a lie, but I wasn't ready to start agreeing with anyone at that point.

She cradled her arms and rocked them as though she held a baby.

"I am not acting like a child."

She laughed, but it came out a strange *huh-huh-huh* sound. Something was wrong inside her mouth, but I couldn't see what it was. She shook her head and frowned, thinking for a second. She repeated the baby gesture and touched the fabric of the shroud.

"These are shrouds of children?"

She nodded.

"Desna weeps." I shuddered. Wearing the shrouds of dead children had to come with some nasty big curse, the wickedest evil eye a witch could give you.

Azra was looking at my chest, where I had unconsciously drawn the wings of Desna over my heart. It's a gesture gamblers and fugitives learn to hide in Cheliax. While the worship of Lady Luck is not strictly illegal, it's enough excuse for the Hellknights to rough you up. When the witch saw my expression, she raised a curious eyebrow, but then she shook her head. She mimed a few gestures I couldn't guess, but then she flexed her arms. She had surprisingly good biceps, round and bigger than my fists.

"This is supposed to make me stronger?"

She shrugged and nodded. At her side, her hands moved absentmindedly, and I recognized a familiar pattern: the Pathfinder hand-sign for "mending."

"It's a way of healing me," I said. "You're a Pathfinder?"

No, she signed emphatically.

"Then how do you—?"

She waved the question away and signed, *You Pathfinder?*

"My boss," I said. While I'd never joined his precious little club, he'd taught me a bunch of their secrets, probably hoping one day I'd come around and ask to be initiated. That's probably why he'd taken me on this mad trip, too. Give old Radovan a taste of adventure, and he'll be begging us to learn the secret handshake and wear the funny hat, or whatever it is they do at their meetings.

All the chaos since I fell from the bridge had one good side effect: I hadn't had to think much about the boss's death. I wished I could believe otherwise, but there was no way he could have survived the explosion I'd seen as I fell from the bridge. It was a miracle I'd lived through my ordeal, and I was a lot tougher than he ever was. Now I was alone, hundreds of miles, maybe more than a thousand miles away from a home I never loved anyway. Everyone here thought I was some kind of monster, a devil, and they weren't all wrong. I wasn't going to find many friendly welcomes here. Only the boss could call on a lord of Ustalav for hospitality. I could barely speak the language.

What was I going to do?

Sleep, signed Azra. She gave me another drink of water.

"I'm not sleepy," I said.

She cupped her hand over my eyes. It was warm if not soft. I don't remember her taking it away.

I must have woken a few times during the journey, because I recall images of dust drifting on narrow beams of sunlight through the cracks between the wagon panels. I remember the feet of that accursed chicken clutching at my legs, but Azra must have shortened its leash, because it didn't roam far past my knees. I'm not sure whether that was for my protection or the chicken's, because she had removed the shroud and lay a thick woolen blanket over me. My arms were free, but they still felt like two sticks of swollen driftwood. I could barely lift one high enough to scratch my chin, and that much effort was enough to pull me back down into dreamless sleep.

A few times I heard voices outside the cart. I smelled fresh manure or pies baking, but usually nothing but the bare earth

and moldering leaves. When the chicken pecked at me, sometimes I had the strength to kick it away. Sometimes I just got
pecked. I drank water from Azra's cupped hand when she
held it to my mouth. I licked pasty gruel off a wooden spoon. I
couldn't count how many times, but it was enough that I began
to hate the stuff, which tasted almost as bad going down as
coming up. When I wasn't sweating, I was freezing cold, and
every time I felt I could drift off to sleep, that damned bird
pecked at my feet. How long I lay in the arms of the fever, I
couldn't guess.

The next thing I knew, I was sliding across the ground and
staring up at a starry sky. Azra was dragging me across the
grass on a carpet. I raised my head to see the wagon aglow
in the light of a nearby campfire. The dappled donkey grazed
nearby while the black chicken strutted around the campfire,
practicing its tortures by pecking at the ground. I wanted to
shoot it the tines, but it was easier to leave my arms by my
sides and silently promise, *You'll get yours, you little pecker.*

"Where?" I asked before realizing Azra couldn't answer
until she had her hands free. I tried to sit up, but she voiced a
decidedly negative "Uh!" I lay back and tried to enjoy the ride,
but every bump in the ground managed to find a bruise or an
open wound. I grew a little nostalgic for the earlier numbness,
because now my legs felt like a couple of burlap sacks of broken glass. Every little jolt brought a pang, sometimes a shock
of agony sharp enough to make me hiss.

Mercifully, the journey was short. Azra left me at the center of a circle of flattened grass. I guessed she'd trod the area
down earlier, but it was so uniform that I fancied a god had
laid down a giant cup before lifting it for another sip.

As if reading my thoughts, Azra knelt beside me and put
a jar to my lips. I drank what tasted like unfermented mead,
but a few seconds later I reconsidered. It tasted nothing like
honey wine, but it kicked as hard as Azra's donkey. Soon I

could perceive the movement of the stars as they slid across the globe of the night sky. It wasn't black, as I had always thought, but filled with millions of stars I had never before seen. What little space lay between them was the color of deep, clear water.

Azra walked away from me. Tiny bells chimed at her ankles and wrists, and I heard a metallic shing as she produced a pair of starknives seemingly from the air. I'd seen those before, usually for sale by Sczarni or other wandering Varisians in open markets. They were rings of steel surrounding a central handgrip. Four triangular blades radiated outward to form an awkward but potentially deadly weapon. Most who bought them in Cheliax treated them as ornaments to hang on the wall in a lame effort to appear interested in Varisian culture. Certain true Varisians, especially their clerics of Desna, learned to wield the blades to deadly effect.

My head turned slowly as I tried to keep her in sight. Like the stars, I felt as though I were submerged in deep water. The autumn breeze was a slow current. If I pushed my fingers against the carpet, I knew I would rise up to float toward the moon.

Azra bent down to light a simple clay lamp. She moved on, lighting more lamps as she chimed a circle around me. A falling star distracted me once, but I think I counted twelve of those lamps. What were they for? There are twelve caverns of the moon. Or was it thirteen? That was an unlucky number in Ustalav, too, I was pretty sure. It was hard to remember all the little lessons the boss had given us about Varisian customs on the voyage from Cheliax.

Moving my head to keep Azra in sight made me dizzy as the tails of stars whirled above us. Rather than risk another fit of nausea, I lay still and concentrated on my breathing. That was boring, so I listened for the sound of insects, but they had all died or gone to sleep. Instead I heard the faint susurrus of distant trees. The smell of their decaying leaves was faint as well, but the grass beneath me still smelled of summer.

There she was, skipping past on the left, moving moon-wise around me. Not skipping, I realized, but dancing like a farm girl propelled more by optimism than by practice. Even though her gestures looked inelegant compared with, say, the sinuous dance Malena had performed for me, the rhythm of the bells at her hands and feet was hypnotic. She raised her hands toward the sky, and when she leaped, her arms formed a crescent around the fattening moon. It winked at me as her arms passed before it, and I felt more than heard laughter as big and encompassing as the rain.

Azra charged at me, her knives flashing over my chest. Wrists crossed, she formed the wings of a butterfly over my heart with her starknives. An instant later, she danced away toward one of the lamps flickering at the edge of the circle. She passed her hand over the flame to put it out. I heard her humming deep in her chest. If it was a tune, I couldn't make it out. It wasn't melodic, but there was a natural music in it, like the rhythm of waves or the wind before a storm.

She rushed back at me again, once more crossing blades over my heart. This time I felt a tiny prickling on my chest, as if someone had touched me with a needle, although I didn't think she'd cut me with the starknives. From the point of impact, a faint blissful sensation spread throughout my body, withdrawing as she danced backward. It was gone by the time she extinguished the next lamp.

Each time she returned, she made the same gesture, and I felt a little more prickling on my skin. It wasn't painful, exactly, and that same ebbing pleasure followed. Each time the feeling faded, I felt a throb of vague despair. I began to dread what would happen to me when she returned from the last flame. Time slowed, and the sky retreated.

It occurred to me that Azra might not be healing me. Maybe she had promised the villagers that she would rid them of the monster in a prescribed ritual. Even if I had the strength to resist, I decided, I wouldn't bother. With the boss dead and no friends worth counting, I might as well be buried in the soil of my forebears. Part of my mind was startled at such gloomy thoughts. That wasn't like me. I wondered whether I was drunker than I realized.

The moon withdrew behind the clouds. In the smallest corner of my eye I saw Azra bending over the last flame, and then it died. The world went silent, even the autumn air holding its fingers still in the trees. I heard only Azra's footsteps running closer. She leaped atop me, her hands slamming my chest. Enervating radiance consumed the last of my strength, and all the lush dark night dissolved into death-white light.

I awoke naked but for a blanket she'd laid upon me. By the position of the moon, I reckoned I had been unconscious only an hour or so. The carpet was still beneath me, but Azra and all her lamps were gone.

My stomach growled as I sat up. Apart from hunger, I felt better. Actually, I felt great. The splints were gone from my legs, so I stood up. Not even a wobble. I wrapped the blanket around my waist like a bathhouse towel and walked back to the campfire.

The donkey shied away at my approach, leaving me room to warm myself. Azra had banked the fire, but she had left a small stack of firewood nearby. I added a couple of logs and poked the fire with an iron rod I found nearby. Azra seemed to carry everything she needed in this wagon. I wondered whether she had a home. More likely she was a traveling healer, although one with a lot more power than the hedge witches you could sometimes find in the Long Market. Whatever spell she'd cast on me, it had worked wonders.

I dropped the blanket to inventory my bits and parts in the light of the campfire. The pitchfork wound was barely visible on my thigh, and there was only a pale mark on my hand where the crossbow bolt had pierced my palm. My thumbs felt as good as new, although I now had a ring of scar tissue on each one. It was hard to complain about that. I'd rarely received magical healing, and never for free.

Or maybe Azra expected something in return for her ministrations. That was a question I'd have to ask soon.

My empty stomach complained again, this time loud enough to disturb the donkey. There had to be oats and dried fruit in the wagon. With some water and a pot, I could make something better than that nasty paste Azra had been feeding me. I thought all country women learned how to cook, but she was obviously an exception. I went to search the wagon and realized I had not seen my nemesis, the black chicken. Suspecting an ambush, I checked the roof of the wagon. Nothing there. Then I found the leash trailing the wagon's door toward the other side of the wagon.

"Hiding, eh?" I pulled the string and heard a squawk.

I was feeling strong enough for a bit of revenge, and to hell with gruel for supper.

Realizing Azra might be annoyed that I'd roasted her only chicken, I didn't eat it all. That was harder than you'd think, because I was famished. Fortunately, there was a sack of potatoes in the wagon. I rubbed four them in a little olive oil and salt I found among Azra's stores. I had just finished burying them under the embers and had adjusted my makeshift skirt when I heard a startled cry.

Azra stood at the edge of the light holding a basket full of clothes. The garments she wore were damp, and her previously unruly hair was clean and combed back to reveal her features. Apart from the look of stupefaction, she was prettier than I'd originally thought. Something about her freckles attracted the moonlight. I know how stupid that sounds, but that's how it looked.

Idiot! she signed, gazing around at the mess of black feathers I'd left while plucking my throttled foe.

What? I signed back without thinking. I added, "I saved you half." There was no need for me to use the finger-speech, but the boss and I always used it to remain silent, usually when we were hiding or spying on someone. It felt strange to answer my half of the conversation aloud.

She sighed and dropped the basket, shaking her head in disbelief.

You know nothing, she signed.

"Tell me," I said.

Chicken eats demon, she signed.

"I'm not a demon," I said.

Demon inside you.

I almost corrected her, but then I realized I myself had no reason to believe it was a devil and not a demon that had spliced itself into my family tree. In Cheliax, where summoned devils serve and advise the ruling family, everyone assumed my heritage was infernal, not abyssal. I had never questioned that assumption before.

"Listen," I said. "I appreciate your help, but there's a difference between real healing—for which I'm very grateful—and superstition about demon-eating chickens."

Listen, she signed with an emphatic hoot. Standing across the fire from her, I finally saw what was wrong with her mouth. Her tongue had been cut out, leaving only a ragged pink lump at the back of her throat.

"I'm sorry," I said, thinking more about the circumstances of her mutilation than the issue at hand. Why had someone cut out her tongue? Because she was a witch, I reckoned. And then worse possibilities came to mind, the sort of thing that can happen to any woman who doesn't do what the wrong man wants. I felt a sudden wave of sympathy.

It took some time for her to explain. Sign-talk is not exactly a proper language, so she often had to resort to mime for words for which she knew no sign. And she was still plenty angry, so it was hard to catch it all, especially when she had to sign out words letter by letter. Her Taldane spelling needed work, although I knew better than to tell her so. At last I understood most of what had happened to me since the fall from the bridge.

I had wondered why Azra had not simply killed me back at the village when the villagers so obviously wanted to do just that. It turns out they had not initially meant to kill me but just to bury me. They'd thought I was already dead when a couple of the local boys fished me out of the river. When they saw my spurs and the other signs of my fiendish heritage, they decided I was a witch or a demon. Burying me face down, thumbs tied behind my back, with a garlic poultice in my mouth, was their way of making sure I would not come back to haunt them as the "dead undead," the worst kind of evil spirit they had around here. Once they felt me move inside the coffin, they realized I was the "live undead," the kind of monster with whom they'd usually negotiate. In their panic, they decided the distinction wasn't important since they'd already offended me by putting me in the coffin. Thus, the pyre.

Azra had just arrived in the village, which she visited a couple of times every year. As I'd guessed, she was a sort of itinerant healer, wise woman, and apparently a tinker, judging from the tools in her wagon. When she saw me, she had tried to catch me inside a magic circle. When that didn't work, she began to doubt I was a demon after all. She cast a spell to take a good look inside me, if I understood her signs correctly. She didn't explain exactly what she saw there, but whatever it was, she decided to heal me instead of kill me.

The chicken was a gift from the villagers. He was meant to peck out my evil while I slept. I was pretty sure we were having some translation difficulty at this point. "Do you mean my sickness?"

No, she signed. *Your demon.*

"All right," I conceded. "But I'm not possessed. My mother was hellspawn. I have a little devil in me."

She raised her eyes toward the sky in exasperation. She was definitely prettier now, whether because of her bath or some effect of that dance she had used to heal me. The way she focused her attention on me while we argued made me keenly aware that I was hungry for more than roast chicken. I remembered a stupid line that had worked for me before.

"Maybe you'd like a little devil in you?" I dropped the blanket and held out a hand.

Her angry expression collapsed for a second as she gaped at me. Sometimes I get that. I like to keep fit. Perhaps there was a way for me to repay her after all.

She made a flicking gesture with one hand, and a silver glint shot off of one of her rings and stung me on the chin.

"Ow!" I said. I'd gotten no for an answer before, and I knew how to take it. "Sorry, that was a clumsy—Ow!"

She stung me again, this time much lower than my chin.

"All right, all right!" I grabbed the blanket and covered my most tender targets. "It was only a suggestion."

She chased me around the fire, stinging me in between angry gestures of *dirty*, *damned*, *demon* until a lump of embers exploded from the campfire with a terrific report. The wagon rocked slightly, and the donkey shied away from it. Azra and I both stopped cold, staring at the fire and the pulpy half of an over-baked potato sliding slowly down the side of the wagon.

"Hungry?" I asked.

Chapter Nine
Lacunae

It is my sincerest hope that you were spared the acquaintance of Count Galdana's nephew during your visit to Willowmourn. His behavior since my awakening has been, if anything, even more offensive than during our ill-fated journey from Caliphas.

Upon his return from Kavapesta an hour before sunset, Casomir made no inquiry whatever about my condition. At first this indifference seemed a blessing, for it gave me ample time to return the mysterious riffle scrolls to their place beside the hidden sword. When curiosity caused me to take it upon myself to request a conference, Felix returned with his master's refusal unadorned with excuse. After preparing a fire in the hearth and lighting the library lamps, the butler left with a promise to bring me supper an hour later.

The possible explanations for Casomir's indifference were easy to weigh. That he did not treasure my company was obvious. That the affairs of the manor and Kavapesta occupied his thoughts was possible. That he wished to avoid the many questions that churned in my mind, however, seemed the most probable explanation.

I choose to receive his discourtesy as an opportunity to continue my examination of the sword and scrolls. Drawing the curtains, I returned to the bookshelf and removed them from their cache. I lay them upon the map table, in which I could conceal them given a moment's warning by a footstep in the hall or the turning of the door latch.

The ornamentation on the sword's scabbard included the stylized cornflower I had seen in the borders of the Galdana family crest throughout the manor. The blade itself was of an alloy so pale that it momentarily appeared to be made of bone. Upon its blade were inscribed the spirals of Pharasma. They formed a long, tapering trail from the hilt of the blade to a point halfway to its tip. Closer inspection revealed more tiny spirals etched faintly around the originals, each surrounded by its own smaller satellites, and so on to seeming infinitesimal iterations. What charm they invested in the blade I could not know without further study, but my preliminary theory was that it was baneful against the restless dead or, if it were truly powerful, an enchantment assuring the spiritual destruction of the lives it ended. I sheathed the blade and replaced it behind the shelf.

Inside the velvet pouch I found various substances used in the preparation of arcane spells, each wrapped in a bit of fabric. Among them were a few spiral cones of incense, a bit of horsehair, a pinch of sand, a fragment of crystal, a small mirror, and a tacky substance I am almost ashamed to admit I recognized immediately as bat guano, the material component of the last spell I learned before abandoning my pursuit of wizardry in favor of a life of gastrointestinal comfort.

The scrolls themselves were the most intriguing enigma. That they were inscribed in my own handwriting was obvious, but I had no recollection of having created them. Furthermore, they appeared recently composed, which suggested either that someone had forged my writing or that I myself had made them after arriving at Willowmourn but had since lost my memory of the event. They were all spells I was theoretically able to cast, if the act of imbuing my mind with them was not so disabling. There were spells of slumber, fascination, and the conjuration of a phantom steed, all of which I had once found simple. One was unfamiliar, and I could not tell by reading its segmented runes exactly what it was meant to do, although those arcane syllables I recognized suggested a mirroring effect. There was even a scroll for the mighty fireball invocation that I once strove to learn before admitting I was not destined to be a wizard. Seeing the spidery characters of its runes inscribed on the vellum reminded me of my fleeting image of fire on the Senir Bridge. I wondered whether it was possible that I had caused the explosion. If so, that would explain in part Tara's thanks for her safe arrival at Willowmourn. Still, that theory was difficult to accept, since I did not remember preparing such a spell before the incident, but I had no way of knowing what other gaps riddled my memory.

It occurred to me that I had not yet tested one of the scrolls. I selected one containing a common cantrip and held it as I would the haft of a sword, but with my thumb upon the upper edge. I bent the stack of vellum and let the strips flutter out. As each snapped away, the characters I—or some imitator—had written sparkled and vanished. The ghostly twin of my hand briefly appeared over my real appendage before disappearing. This I had seen before, although never without a tight nausea uncoiling in my stomach. I felt the connection between my own hand and an invisible point of force. It moved where I pointed, and I could feel its location as perfectly as if it were my own finger moving about the room. Mentally directing it across the room, I plucked a book from the shelf and pulled the volume back to my real hand.

"Ha!" The exaltation leaped from my mouth before I could stifle it. I listened for any sign that my outburst had been overheard. Hearing none, I returned the book to the shelf just as I had taken it.

What a wondrous discovery! My sudden joy sank as I realized I did not know how to duplicate the effect. It could not be as simple as inscribing scrolls in the traditional manner. During my training, I had naturally explored that craft as an alternative to holding the unreleased magic in memory, as adept wizards do so easily. Unfortunately, even consigning magic to a scroll caused me illness. I had to learn how this mechanism differed.

If it were I who had crafted the scrolls, then it seemed likely that I had found the secret somewhere within this library. And assuming you had not discovered the trick before me, there was no reason to think I would find the secret among the shelves on which you had placed your research. After concealing the riffle scrolls and Galdana's sword under the map table, I brought a lamp close to browse the other shelves.

Soon after I began, Felix interrupted me with a knock at the door. Murmuring an apology about the absence of my hosts, he laid my supper on a desk. I was so absorbed in my search that I did not notice his departure. For over an hour I combed the shelves in the library before discovering what I sought in the first place I should have examined: among Galdana's collection of romances. Its cover disguised it as one of the same sort of adventure stories, but I spied a scrap of paper rising from the top pages. That was exactly the sort of makeshift bookmark I used during research.

I laid the book beside my cold meal of sliced lamb with wine sauce. Little white crescents of congealing fat swam in the dark pool in which drowned the dejected vegetables. After a cautious sniff, I elected not to sample the latest offering from Galdana's kitchen, for I detected a familiar odor of decay. It was just as well, for at the moment I had a greater appetite for knowledge than for food.

Bound within the covers of the romance, bisecting the two halves of the fiction, I found a slim passage of arcane theory. In merely sixteen pages, it outlined an alternative process for producing scrolls of arcane spells whose powers would be released by the riffle process I had uncovered. In answering the question of creating the riffle scrolls, however, the hidden document raised several others. By what dire enchantment had I forgotten finding this secret in the first place? Who wanted me to forget it? Or was it the discovery of riffle magic that I was meant to forget? Probably not, I decided, since if that was the purpose of the thief who had stolen my memory, why leave me free to roam the library where I had first discovered the secret?

Casomir was obviously antagonistic to me, but I had to consider Tara and every member of the household staff as suspects. It was, after all, Tara who had encouraged me to continue my research into your whereabouts, which in turn led me to the rediscovery of these scrolls I had apparently created.

Another question came to mind. How much time had I lost? I opened a window, but I could not view the moon from that vantage, and the young wolfhound had remained on guard. His low growl persuaded me not to climb out for a better look. On a whim, I fetched my uneaten supper and flung a slice of lamb onto the sward. Whatever discipline the beast had learned dissolved at the scent. He ran and gobbled it in three quick bites, returning too quickly for me to use the diversion for an escape. No matter the origin of the foul scent I detected on the meat, it proved no deterrent to the canine appetite. An experiment occurred to me then, but I could not conduct it inside the manor. Wrapping one morsel in a scrap of paper and tucking it into my pocket, I threw the remaining meat to the hound. He caught each slice before it hit the ground and wolfed it down.

Selecting what seemed the more potentially useful of the riffle scrolls, I concealed them on my person. They were small, but not so tiny that I could carry them all without conspicuous lumps beneath my clothes. The rest I returned to the cache where I had found them, beside Galdana's enchanted blade. Felix arrived moments after I pulled the bell.

"I trust your studies were fruitful, Your Excellency." His tone was servile but not unctuous. If I were to allow my imagination to run away, I might have thought it too perfect.

"It is a start," I said, thinking it more than possible he would report my words to whoever was manipulating me.

"Your room has been prepared," said Felix. "Shall I conduct you there now?"

"I would rather speak with your master."

"I regret to inform you he is indisposed, Your Excellency."

"And Mistress Tara?"

"She, too, has retired for the evening."

"Then I must follow their good examples," I said. "But I find that I am not yet drowsy. Perhaps you could bring me a brandy."

"As you wish," he bowed.

As I followed Felix back to my room, I noticed in several places the absence of swords in wall plaques where one would expect to see them. So it was not only those blades from the trophy room that were missing. Unless Count Galdana brought a small company along on his autumn hunt, it was absurd to think he had taken them. Weighing the value of catching the butler in a lie against the advantage of keeping my observations from my adversaries, I decided to remain silent on the matter.

In my room, the chambermaid who had awoken me that morning slid a brass bed warmer between the bedclothes.

Even through her sleepy expression, I detected a glimmer of apprehension as she saw us enter. If I was not mistaken, the object of her fear was not me but Felix, who greeted her curtly. "That will be all, Anneke."

"Stay a moment," I said, knowing that the butler could not graciously contradict the wishes of a guest. "I would like you to bank the fire while Felix fetches my nightcap."

The servants exchanged a look, and this time it seemed it was I who caused Anneke's look of trepidation.

"Very good, Excellency," said Felix. "I shall return at once."

"No need to hurry," I said in hopes of reinforcing the assumption he must have made about my motives. "Take your time."

Felix left the door ajar. I shut it behind him, and Anneke retreated to the fire. She cringed as I approached, but I came only so close as to communicate in a low voice.

"How long have I been here?" I said. "Do not lie to me. We haven't time for such charades."

"Your Excellency—"

"We've no time for stammering or courtesies, either. Spit it out, girl."

"Whatever Master Casomir has told you is the truth—"

I grasped her arm firmly, but not brutally. "How long?"

"I don't know!" she cried. "I was summoned only yesterday."

Interesting that her arrival coincided with the gap in my memory.

"Why? What happened to the other maid?"

"I don't know," she said. "Perhaps it was her time."

"What do you mean?"

"She was to have a baby," said Anneke. "The child must have come sooner than she thought." Her unfocused gaze told me she was searching for a plausible explanation, not a fact she already knew. I released her arm, only distantly regretful of my crude behavior.

"Where is she now?"

"I don't know," said Anneke. "The village. Maybe the city. Nobody knows."

"How can that be?"

"I don't know," she protested. "She was gone when I arrived."

I considered the further coincidence that both Anneke and the woman she had replaced were with child.

"Who is the father of your child?"

The question struck her like a dagger in the heart. She stared at me, eyes pleading with me to withdraw the question.

"Tell me," I insisted. If Felix were fleet, he could be back at any instant.

She shook her head and looked away, but I heard her whimper, "I was sent away the day he left."

"Who? Count Galdana?"

She hugged herself and shook her head, refusing to answer. I heard footsteps upon the stair. I tousled her hair and whispered, "Unfasten your blouse. Just the top buttons—quickly!"

The moment I predicted Felix would open the door, I stepped away from Anneke and said, "Willful wretch! Away with you."

Whether she was clever enough to follow my cue or simply welcomed the opportunity to escape me, Anneke bolted from the room. I felt the reproachful heat of Felix's eyes on my neck until I turned to face him, and he lowered his gaze to the salver he carried. Upon it rested a crystal snifter and a small decanter of amber liquid.

I lifted my chin in an imitation of an especially imperious nemesis back in Egorian. "Well? Set it down and leave me."

I listened for the sound of his retreat. When I heard his foot on the top stair, I went to the door and tried the latch. The discovery that it was unlocked did not make me feel better about being trapped in the library during the day, but it was a relief all the same. For a moment I considered following Felix down the stairs, but first I opened the windows and gazed at the southeastern sky. The moon had risen well above the misty horizon, its bright figure veiled in clouds. Recalling its shape the night of our ambush on the Senir Bridge, and comparing that with its waxing gibbous shape, I estimated I had lost seven or eight days to the gap in my memory.

A week or more, and no memories for it.

The principal question vexing my thoughts was what exactly had happened in that period. If I had simply lain unconscious, there would be no reason to tell me otherwise. Besides, I had the evidence of the riffle scrolls to tell me I had been awake and active. I felt certain of it now: I had created those scrolls.

I raised the brandy to my nose and sniffed. As I had feared, there was a cloying, meaty odor beneath the sweet scent one would expect. Recalling the occult material I had found in the library, I recalled that one of the omens of Urgathoa's displeasure is the corruption of food. I leaned out the window to hurl the offensive liquor out of the glass.

Out of the corner of my eye I glimpsed a shadow on the moon, but when I turned to face it I saw nothing there. It could have been a cloud, but a moment later I smelled the unmistakable odor of vinegar and heard a bump upon the roof. It was too solid an impact to have been caused by a bat or a bird, if any remained alive nearby. I looked out once more. Seeing nothing but the usual tenants of the night sky, I shuddered in the chill and closed the windows.

The longer I remained in Willowmourn, the more I embraced the clichés of the mysteries of Ustalav. It was a strange land even to its natives, and at this rate I would soon be searching for monsters under the bed.

It was time I became more aggressive in my investigations not only of Count Galdana's library but also of the puzzles of

Willowmourn. I had a mind to slip out of my room and explore the upper floors, but discovery would jeopardize my ability to finish the research left for me. Besides, I had not one but two experiments to perform before I would be confident in my ability to elude the house guards and unravel the local mysteries before setting off to follow your path. One more night's sleep, I decided, and then I would act.

Felix woke me and attended my toilet before leading me to the pavilion for breakfast. As we walked across the sward, I spied two of the grounds staff talking beside the paddock. The groom listened as the gardener, Odav, spoke urgently. When the groom saw me, he placed a hand on Odav's shoulder. I saw by the faintest turn of Odav's head that the groom had warned him not to look in my direction. Felix also noticed the exchange and attempted to distract me with a banality about the mild autumn morning. I pretended his ploy had succeeded and devised a ploy to speak with one or both of the servants as soon as I could arrange to do so unseen by the butler.

Casomir rose and bowed as I arrived. "Count Jeggare," he said. "I am glad to see you are recovering from our ordeal."

"Master Casomir," I said, bowing to him and to Tara. I observed two faint but fresh lines upon Casomir's face, one of them virtually invisible against his older Lepidstadt scar. "I am sorry to see you are injured."

"What?" he feigned ignorance, but his hand rose involuntarily to his cheek. "Trifling scratches from the crash," he said after a brief hesitation. He was surprised that I could see the wounds, which I gathered had been recently healed by magic. Perhaps his human eyes did not perceive them in the mirror, but my father's blood gives me keener sight.

"Speaking of the accident," I said, "perhaps you can help me remember the particulars. I seem to have suffered a blow to the head and a resulting confusion of memory." In truth, the only blow to the head for which I had present evidence was a bruise on my jaw, which was unlikely to have caused trauma to my brain.

"Ah," he said. "That is to be expected, or so the priest tells me. I had hoped to bring him back here, but the plague demands the attention of all of Kavapesta's healers."

I nodded as if I believed him. "Perhaps if you describe the events after we reached the bridge, you might help me remember."

Casomir glanced at Tara, who nodded and said, "Do not worry that you will upset me, cousin. I may seem fragile, but I grow stronger in the care you have shown me since our homecoming."

"Very well," said Casomir. "Unfortunately, my own memories of those moments before our crash are a jumble. Your men cried out that we were pursued by wolves, but we could not see them from inside the carriage. There was certainly something chasing us. The horses were terrified."

"I remember the wolves," I said. "I saw one drag one of the guards from his horse."

Casomir nodded. "If we had time to find a defensible location, perhaps things would have gone differently. Before I could act, you had opened the carriage door and cast your spell. There wasn't enough room, unfortunately, and the blast carried us over the rail and into the rocks on the far side of the bridge."

"You saw me cast a spell?" I asked.

"Well . . ." Casomir frowned. "I do not understand magic. My great-great-aunt was a wizard of some renown, but none of the Galdanas since have shared the gift."

I opened my mouth, intending to correct his understanding. Wizardry is not a gift, it is a discipline earned by long study and the exercise of intellect. It is sorcery that is a gift—or a curse, depending on one's perspective. Realizing that my interjection was not only pedantic but pointless, I closed my mouth and nodded to encourage him to continue.

"There was a great explosion," he said. Beside him, Tara nodded agreement. "Naturally, we assumed you had hurled a fireball at our attackers, scattering them."

It was a logical assumption, except for the fact that I had not prepared a spell of any sort in more than fifty years. The only reason one would assume I was even capable of casting a spell was that he had seen the spellbooks in my luggage. I was certain that I had not revealed the books to Casomir or Tara, so either one of them had surreptitiously examined my luggage or, perhaps, they had learned from Carmilla that I once studied magic. After all, it was Carmilla who had arranged our traveling together.

And yet I had a clear image of fire in my mind, so I believed that something had exploded on that bridge. I knew only that I had not been the cause of the conflagration. The trick was in confirming whether Casomir was lying or simply misinterpreting his own observations. Without looking directly at her, I observed Tara's reaction. Both she and her cousin appeared utterly sincere in their recollections of the misfortune at the Senir Bridge.

"What happened afterward?" I asked.

"The crash rendered you unconscious," said Casomir. "All the servants were dead or missing, and the wolves fled."

"So you did see the wolves."

"Yes," said Casomir. "But only as they fled the explosion. Several ran into the woods, their fur alight. It is a wonder they did not set the entire forest afire."

"And what of our rescue?"

"The peasants of the nearest village saw the flames and sent help," said Casomir. "They brought us down the mountain in a hay cart, sending word to Willowmourn of our misadventure.

The next morning, my uncle Lucinean's carriage arrived to convey us home."

I nodded. It was a cogent story, simple enough that it could be absolutely true, apart from the omission of seven or eight days' additional events. Did Casomir not realize how simple it was for me to notice the difference in the moon? Granted, even an otherwise reasonable mind can overlook an obvious detail, but I could not help taking offense at his low estimation of my intellect. Still, it was better not to reveal how much I realized of the truth until after I learned much more about the reason for the subterfuge.

"Thank you," I said. "I recall some of what you have told me. I still cannot understand, however, why the wolves attacked in such force. Do you have any idea?"

For the first time, Casomir looked as though he were thinking about what I had said rather than repeating a prepared story. "No," he said. "I have no idea."

And for the first time since he had spoken that morning, I believed him.

Chapter Ten
The Fiddler's Revenge

Before I had a chance to smooth over our misunderstanding, Azra retreated inside the wagon and shut the door, leaving me to sleep outside. At least I didn't have to worry about sudden attacks from my demon-eating chicken. Still, after what Azra had told me, I couldn't bring myself to eat the rest. I buried the remains in the dirt beside the fire and sat down, wondering whether there was any truth to what she'd said about the demon inside me. Devil. Whatever.

Hedge witches blend the divine and arcane with hokum and old wives' tales. Even for a city boy it's sometimes hard to decide whether you're getting a magical potion or just snake oil. In general, if I can see it or feel it, I figure it's the real thing. If I can't, then I'm not buying.

Not that Azra had asked me for anything yet. If she did, I didn't have much to offer, apart from my unwelcome proposition. The last of my own clothes were probably ashes back in that village beside the river, and everything else of value had probably been traded for a kettle or a new pitchfork. All I had now were the secondhand rags of a pig farmer. At least they kept me warm and covered my tender bits, which still stung from whatever charm Azra had zapped me with. She was wicked in a temper!

I had a lot of time to think about her reaction while I huddled beside the fire. Eventually I began to appreciate how Azra must have seen me before retreating to her wagon. Even after I'd figured what her missing tongue might mean, I hadn't the good sense to realize the last thing she wanted was a naked man making crude advances. I wracked my brain for an apology that matched the offense, but I couldn't think of one big enough.

When she finally emerged from the wagon, Azra wouldn't look at me, much less sign to me.

"Good morning" got me nothing in return. She ignored "How about some breakfast?" and simply secured the last of the camp supplies back in the wagon. I skipped humor and compliments to avoid another quarrel. "You look exhausted," I tried. "Want me to drive for a while?"

That got her attention. I could see she was considering the idea. "Just point the way," I said. "And maybe harness that donkey to the cart. I'm not so good with animals."

She pulled a sarcastic face but didn't bother signing her retort. Instead, she spelled out L-U-M-I-N-I-T-A.

"The donkey?"

She nodded and went to the beast. She stroked Luminita's nose and fed her half an apple from her skirt pocket. I kept a healthy distance. Azra beckoned me closer.

"Not a good idea," I said. "You saw what she did to me last time."

She shook her head and waved me over.

"Seriously," I said. "Animals hate me."

Azra sent me a glare that invited no argument.

"All right," I said, slowly approaching. Luminita brayed and tossed her head. Azra kept stroking her nose and cooed in her ear. She traced the wings of Desna on Luminita's cheek. The path of her finger left a brief, glittering afterglow on the donkey's fur.

Come, Azra signed to me.

I took another few steps. Luminita's eyes widened. She stepped anxiously in place, edging slightly away until Azra gently tugged her back and waved me closer.

When I was about three feet away, Azra held up her hand to stop me. Luminita nickered softly but held her ground. There was no question that what I'd just seen was real magic.

Azra mimed the action of slapping reins and pointed west. She went into the back of the wagon, and I took the driver's seat. When I shook the reins, Luminita obliged by pulling away at a slow but steady pace.

The road was little more than a footpath, but it wound between the hills and crossed streams at their shallowest. Luminita knew the way, and I held the reins loosely in my lap as I admired the scenery. To the west and south, mountains rose up beyond brown fields and the black rectangles of distant farms. There were still traces of green on the north side of hills and beneath stands of trees, but the rest had surrendered to tawny autumn colors. I counted four more ragged Vs of geese flying for warmer climates. Their destination reminded me that I ought to find the boss's body and return him to Egorian. I wasn't well acquainted with his relatives, but the staff at Greensteeples would know who to inform.

On the other hand, I was in no hurry to return for my own sake. Without the boss there, Egorian held more bad memories than good. Before we'd met, I'd been little more than a common criminal, not that my condition had bothered me at the time. I just didn't know there was a better place for me. Since becoming the boss's lookout, spy, and finally bodyguard, I'd learned more each year with him than in a decade among the Goatherds. Zandros never would have taught me to read anything other than an account ledger, and I never got to keep more than a fraction of what I stole for him.

The fact was I could never repay the boss for all he'd done for me. I wished I'd told him so before it was too late.

The wagon panels slapped open behind me. Azra leaned out and directed me to stop. I pulled on the reins as I'd seen drovers do, and Luminita slowed to a stop. I couldn't help grinning. Because it was something I'd never been able to do before, driving a cart was one hell of a lot of fun.

Azra handed me a pair of buckets and pointed to a nearby stream. By the time I returned with water, she'd unhitched Luminita and was brushing her flanks. I set the larger bucket a few feet from the donkey's head, and she stepped forward to drink.

"How long's that charm last?" I asked Azra. She ignored the question and instead fetched a wicker box from the wagon. She set it before me. *From village*, she signed before returning to the wagon, where she shook out the carpet on which I'd lain during her healing ritual.

In the basket I found the scorched remains of my once-fine leather jacket and pants, along with the best pair of kickers I ever owned, almost completely undamaged. Where the fabric had burned away, someone had patched the clothes with scraps of leather. The stitches were coarse thread, but they were tight and regular, sewn by a practiced hand. It looked a mess, but it would suit me better than this pig farmer's garb. Better yet, all of my tools remained inside the sleeve pockets, along with my remaining throwing knives in their hidden sheaths. Beneath the clothes lay my purse, amazingly still full of the coins I had left after returning what I'd lifted from Nicola.

I felt a queer pang of loss remembering Nicola's death. It was one thing to miss the boss, but I did not expect to mourn his obsequious valet. I'd never liked Nicola much, but I should have been able to keep him out of trouble. Instead, it was my fault the wolves had come for us. In drawing them to the boss, I had become the opposite of a bodyguard.

Azra touched my arm and offered me a look of concern.

You are ill? she signed.

I wiped the moisture from my eyes and gave her the little smile. "Road dust is all."

She wasn't buying that, but she let it go. She made me watch as she checked the wheels for damage. Afterward she showed me how to inspect Luminita's hooves for stones. The donkey was shod like a draft horse, and up close I realized how small she was compared to one. She had to be stronger than she looked to draw that wagon for days at a time. Azra sent me to refill the buckets while she replaced Luminata's harness and hitched her to the wagon once more. When I returned, she climbed into the driver's seat and slid over. She looked down, inviting me to join her there. I climbed aboard.

As we rode, I asked her why the villagers had returned my things. She pointed at me and signed, *Live undead, dead undead*. She waggled her hand palm-down and grimaced. *Difficult to know.*

"That doesn't make any sense."

Dead alive, maybe you forgive, she signed. *Dead not-dead, maybe you haunt.*

"They could have listened a little closer for my heartbeat."

She signed, *Look demon.*

"So I'm hellspawn," I said. "It's not my fault. Some ancestor I never met had a dirty little secret. That's no reason to turn me upside down, tie my thumbs, and set me on fire."

Maybe you curse them.

"I'm not a witch," I said.

They bury me, I curse them, she signed. *I curse them big.*

I was beginning to wonder whether I'd have been safer back in the village, but Azra had done me no harm since knocking me out, and I was willing to let that go after she healed me. Later I told her why I'd come to Ustalav, including the boss's idea that I'd enjoy a visit to my parents' homeland. I was pretty sure both my father and mother had been born here before they traveled to Cheliax. Azra asked me more about them. She frowned when I explained I didn't know much more. I left out the sordid details, but I think she understood my parents hadn't raised me.

Azra seemed more interested in my encounter with the Sczarni, especially the Harrowing Malena had cast for me.

What fortune? she signed.

I had to admit I wasn't paying much attention to the cards. I tried to remember them to humor her: The Tyrant, The Empty Throne, The Dance . . . I couldn't recall the rest. While I didn't mention it to Azra, I had been a lot more interested in the contours of Malena's shoulders than in the results of her Harrowing.

"There was one odd card," I said. "It was a man on a hill. There was a crown at his feet, and in the shadows there were lots of eyes. I never saw that one before."

Azra turned her whole body to look at me. She spelled out S-C-Z-A-R-N-I and made the sign for *dangerous*.

"You don't need to tell me, sister."

She signed some more, but I couldn't follow it all. It was something about this particular group of Sczarni, that they were wolves. I explained I had already learned that the hard way, but I realized she knew much more of the Pathfinder finger-speech than I'd learned, or else there were different dialects.

"You must know a Pathfinder," I told her. *Pathfinder,* I signed for emphasis.

She nodded but did not elaborate. I knew enough to change the subject.

"This looks like a tinker's wagon," I said.

She nodded. I took the reins from her, and she let me have them. After a few moments, she added, *Uncle. Tinker.*

That jibed with what I'd seen inside the wagon. "You too?" I asked.

No, she signed. Then she nodded. *A little. I mend people.*

"Thanks again for that," I said, grateful for the opening. "Say, I was a little giddy when I saw how much you'd healed me last night. If I came across as an ass—"

She waved that off and set her eyes on the horizon. All right, I thought. On to another topic.

"Pretty soon I should go back to the bridge where I fell," I said. "My boss—his body, anyway—I should take it back home."

She looked at me and signed, *You can't.*

"What do you mean?"

Too late.

Oh, no, I thought. I should have realized by the size of the moon last night. Assuming those villagers fished me out of the river the morning after I fell, it should still have been a waxing crescent. "How long?" I asked.

She made the sign for villages and held up three fingers.

"How many days?" I asked.

She spread the fingers of one hand and with her other hand added another finger.

"Desna weeps," I muttered. She wasn't kidding it was too late. If no one else had found the boss by now, he was food for wolves.

"Why didn't you heal me sooner?" I tried not to sound angry but failed.

Moon too small, she signed. *Hurt too big.* As if that explained anything.

"Great," I grumbled, but I knew it wasn't her fault. If not for her, I'd be dead of my injuries.

That wasn't right. If not for her, I might have gone on a murderous rampage in that village. Part of me wasn't grateful for that, but most of me was. I don't often lose my temper. Of course, I'm not usually buried alive, set on fire, and stabbed with a pitchfork.

We drove a while in silence while I felt sorry for myself and she left me to it. Eventually I asked, "Where are we headed?"

Village, she signed, adding a curious gesture I didn't recognize.

"What village?" I asked.

She repeated the gesture but saw I didn't know it. She tried different signs.

Broken village, she signed. *Sad village. Cursed village.*

We stopped beside a pond that night. Azra told me not to take water from it, but even a city boy knows not to drink still water. Fortunately, between the buckets we'd filled earlier and her big jug of fresh water, we had plenty for Luminita and ourselves. Azra handed me an iron rack and spit from the wagon and pointed at a ring of black stones that had obviously been used by hundreds of previous travelers. Beyond it were a pair of crude tables, but my hope of dining at them vanished when I saw the signs of Desna and Pharasma carved onto their surface. Roadside shrines.

While I prepared the fire, Azra gathered vegetables from a sack hanging in the wagon and began to prepare them on the tinker's table on which I'd nearly brained myself earlier. When I saw how she was chopping them in quarters, I offered to trade chores with her. She gave me a skeptical frown but turned them over along with a chopping knife and a packet of waxed burlap. Inside I found a good-sized chunk of peppered mutton, no more than a couple of days old. It must have been a gift from the last village she visited before reviving me. I smelled the hanging herbs and pinched off a few leaves from the ones I wanted, along with a couple of cloves of garlic from a bulb she'd previously plundered. The knife she'd given me was about as sharp as a candle, but her uncle had attached a good sharpening wheel to the worktable.

I could work with that.

An hour later I presented Azra with the nearest approximation possible, considering local resources, of Malla's grilled lamb with garlic and vegetables. It smelled delicious, a damned sight better than that gruel she'd been feeding me during my convalescence. Better even than the black chicken, although the little pecker had tasted delicious before Azra's scolding.

Azra's dubious expression had melted when she got her first whiff of supper, and she nodded her approval as she ate. I told her about plump, cheerful Malla and how I would sneak into the kitchen to steal a taste before she served the boss's supper. I almost lost my appetite when I considered that I would probably never see her again.

Azra raised a hand and turned her head as if to listen. I strained to hear, but there was nothing louder than the hiss of our cooking fire. Beside the wagon, Luminita raised her head high and lifted her ears. Azra stood up and walked away from the fire, still listening. I followed her lead and moved in the opposite direction, keeping her in sight but listening intently for anything that might have alarmed her.

There was nothing.

I looked back at her and signed, *What?*

She waved it away, frowning. She gave up a moment later and signed, *Nothing,* but I couldn't believe she would bolt up like that for no reason. We returned to the campfire, but she ignored her unfinished meal and went to the wagon. From various compartments above the tinker's table, she added charms and roots and little phials to the pouches on her kirtle.

"What did you hear?" I asked.

Wind, she signed with a self-effacing shrug.

"Tell me."

She met my gaze and sighed resignation. *Wolves,* she signed.

I uttered a Varisian vulgarity. Azra gave me an inquisitive look, and I asked, "Do you think they could have tracked me all this way?"

She nodded without hesitation.

"We should move on."

She shook her head and pointed at the wagon.

Closer to fire, she signed. She went to bring Luminita closer, and I fetched the wagon. It was not as heavy as I'd expected, and I pulled it to the side of the fire opposite the altars. Once wagon and donkey were nearby, Azra studied the area while weighing a fat pouch in her hand. I couldn't tell what she was looking for, but she saw me staring and signed, *Wood. Plenty of wood,* before pointing to a spot beside the fire.

I fetched all the firewood from inside the wagon and went back for the bundle tied to the side. I was about to jog over to a small stand of trees a couple of hundred yards away when Azra stopped me with a hoot and shook her head. She beckoned me back to the fire where she poured out a line of gray ash in a circle maybe twelve feet in diameter. She stopped just short of completing the circle, leaving an opening of about two or three feet. There she set up one of the stools from the wagon and sat outside the circle, directing me to sit beside the fire, inside the circle.

"Now what?" I asked.

Wait, she signed.

"For what?"

Dark.

They came shortly after moonrise, from all sides. The hell of it was, I knew they came for me. I'd put the woman who'd healed me in danger.

Luminita was the first to sense their approach. She stamped and brayed, but she did not flee. Maybe she knew she could not escape, or maybe Azra's charm continued to make her docile around beasts like the wolves and me.

By the time I saw the glimmer of their eyes outside our fire's light, Azra rose from her seat and stood in the gap of her ashen circle.

I talk, she signed, pointing at me. *You talk,* she signed, sweeping her finger to indicate the intruders.

I watched her hands and translated in my biggest voice. "Do the Sczarni respect their promises?"

"You know them?" I whispered to Azra. She ignored the question.

One of the wolves came closer, padding just inside the firelight. He was a big silverback, with eyes so pale they reflected the color of the flames. He stretched the way wolves do when they rise from sleep, head and forepaws low, hindquarters high back. Then he sat back, his canine body transforming into a long human figure that rose from a squat to stand over six feet tall. Big as life and naked as the second he was born, Dragos stood glaring at me. He was slightly less hairy as a man, a trifle more gray. He looked like a white, grizzled version of Vili.

"You know why I have come, hellspawn," he said. "Azra knows I respect her territory. Now you tell her what you have done to earn the vengeance of the Sczarni."

"I told her already," I said. "Vili attacked me and my . . . party." I had almost said "friend" and choked on the word. He and those with him killed all the others. If you want blood for blood, you've had more than your share already."

"Devil bastard, you killed my son. My son! I will rend you to pieces and feed them to my family."

I had a dozen good Varisian words to say to that, but Azra interrupted with a howl. *One and one,* she signed to me. *Inside circle.*

"Seriously?" I said to her. "You want to make me fight him?"

You have teeth, she signed, glancing at my boots. She must have seen me replace my silvered knives there. She pointed to herself and the wolf pack. *Agreement.*

"I get it," I said. She couldn't break whatever territorial arrangement she had made with the Sczarni werewolves. To do so would put the villages under her protection at risk. Even I had to admit that my life wasn't worth risking hers.

She signed again, and I nodded as I understood her message. "You and me, old man, in the circle," I told Dragos. "But if any other wolf tries to enter, she'll kill you both."

Dragos glanced at Azra, one bushy eyebrow raised. His expression seemed less offended than impressed. He bowed toward her, somehow making the gesture graceful despite his nudity.

Azra signed some more. I translated with some embellishment.

"Two more conditions, she says." I avoided Azra's indignant gaze when she heard my altered version of her message. "I can't leave the circle either. And if—when—I put the old wolf down, the rest of you must swear to forgo further vengeance."

"She did not say that," said Dragos, calling my bluff. "Blood calls for blood, and Azra knows it. If a thunderbolt should fall upon me before I kill you, if the earth should open up and remove my teeth from your throat, my people will let you run until the next moon. That is the law of vengeance."

Azra gave me a look that told me I was out of time. The pack crept up for a closer view. For a second I wondered which one was Malena, but then Dragos walked through the gap in Azra's magic circle. She closed it behind him, dropped her pouch of ash, and wove a sinuous pattern with both hands. The circle blazed silver. A translucent wall of light rose up to surround me, the fire, and Dragos.

He lunged forward, shifting as he blurred across the circle. Before I could touch the handle of my knife, he knocked the legs out from under me. I hit the ground hard. He slid to a stop at the edge of the circle. Where his fur brushed the barrier, it wilted in a sizzle of holy power.

I feinted to one side but rolled the opposite direction, across the campfire. It wasn't hot enough to give me another attack of the big and uglies, but the move tricked Dragos. He shot past me, snarling and trailing ribbons of saliva from his jaws. I caught a whiff of his rancid breath as he passed. Then I was on my feet, my big knife in hand.

He feigned a leap, but I anticipated it and retreated around the circle. I left a good couple of feet between me and the barrier. Having seen what it did to a werewolf, I had no desire to test its powers on hellspawn. Even if it didn't hurt me, I wouldn't want to be outside the circle, where all the pack could have a go, according to Azra. I think the werewolves knew that, even though I hadn't translated that part of her message for them.

Dragos transformed again. One second he was a huge timber wolf. The next he was a man-wolf, six feet tall in a crouch, hands become razor-sharp claws. His arms had at least two feet of reach on my knife. I regretted never taking the boss up on his sword fighting lessons.

The werewolf's muscles tensed for a leap, but I knew he wasn't as reckless as Vili had been. I kept low to receive his charge. He came across the circle like a reaper with two scythes, the first claw sweeping toward my legs. Instead of tumbling over it, I leaped forward, stabbing at his other arm. His long claws raked my shoulder, but I shoved the blade deep into the nook of his elbow. I got a good twist in before he wrenched his arm away. He meant to take my blade with him, but those wavy edges aren't just for show. They cut a pretty red blossom out of his flesh on the way out, exposing a raw white iris of sinew beneath.

Dragos roared his fury. I had a feeling that was bad for him, so I made it worse. I blew him a kiss and tipped him a wink. He rushed me like a bull, and this time I rolled back, kicking up at his belly as he flew over. It was a bad angle, but there was enough force behind the blow to send him sliding partway through Azra's barrier.

Divine energy seared through the pelt on his leg and hip. The blast left angry red flesh that bubbled and withered in a flash. He scrambled back inside, yelping like a kicked dog. I was there first, waiting with a kick to the face.

That was stupid. Shifting instantly back into wolf form, he caught my right ankle in his jaws and savaged it back and forth. For an insane instant I thought, *I just had that fixed!* Dragos's transformation soothed his own wounds. Still hairless, the flesh of his burned leg looked weeks healed.

I kicked his head with my free foot. The second shot caught him in the eye. He flinched enough for me to drag my wounded leg out of reach of those teeth. His canines were longer than my fingers.

Scrambling up, I favored my injured leg but could still stand. My defensive crouch was lopsided, so I left it that way. I passed my knife to my right hand, hoping draw his attack to that side. He'd shown himself to be a canny fighter, but I was betting on his anger overwhelming his sense.

When he hesitated and retreated a few steps, I hedged my bet. Maybe he wasn't as furious as he was letting me think. I passed my knife from hand to hand—a stupid thing to do usually. At the same time, I shuffled side to side, feigning a flinch when I stepped right. I saw in his eyes that he'd caught it, so the next time I made a move, he rushed forward.

As his jaws opened to envelop my right hand, where he expected me to catch my big knife, I kept it where it was and instead pulled one of my backups from my sleeve. His jaws clamped hard on my forearm, but I had thrust deep into his maw, my throwing knife slicing the vulnerable interior of his throat. The instant his jaws snapped open, I shoved deeper inside, twisting as hard as I could. He bit again, his teeth rasping against the bone of my forearm and killing the sinews of my wrist. My hand was dead inside him, but I kept pushing it in from my shoulder. It was agony for us both, but only I could howl.

His body convulsed. I wrapped my legs around his chest and squeezed tight. His claws raked my back, but my patched jacket blunted the attack. His left paw was as dead as my right hand, and I dropped my knife and bent his good leg back. He could eat my arm, but he had nothing left to strike me with.

A big grin creased my face. I let my jaw crack out of line and welcomed the pain as I saw the wolf's eyes widen. I opened my jaws and pressed them hard against his throat. He struggled, and I increased the pressure, but I did not bite through. It would have been so easy. I wanted him to know I could do it.

I held him for long seconds, sinking my teeth a little deeper each time he moved. Gradually he relaxed his limbs. Finally, still gagging, he opened his mouth wide. I took my mouth from his throat and sat back, still straddling his chest. Tenderly, I removed the limp ruin of my arm from his mouth and looked down at him.

He averted his eyes and coughed. His bloody throat spasmed, and his body transformed again, this time more slowly than before. From wolf to hybrid to man, he lay there on his back, head turned away to avoid my eyes.

"I killed you," I said in that hoarse voice that stays for an hour after I open wide. "I can kill you again, any time."

Dragos said nothing.

"Abandon your revenge."

A grimace twisted his face. Tears he could not shed for his own injuries now diluted the blood that smeared his face.

I bent close to his face and screamed, "Swear it now!"

"I will," he whispered, his voice rougher than my own.

"Tell them all!" I yelled.

"I forswear the life of my son!" he cried. "There will be no more acts of vengeance." The last word stretched into a painful whimper as his body dissolved once more into wolf form. Whatever healing the transformation granted him must have been spent, for his wounds remained raw and moist.

I looked up to see all the wolves around the circle bowing low, their heads upon their forepaws.

"The rest of you," I shouted. "Swear it!"

A few of them whimpered, but one raised its head and howled. It was a black-pelted, green-eyed female, and I had a feeling I'd seen her before in other clothes. A couple of others followed her lead, and then as one the pack raised their snouts and sang to the moon.

I looked at Azra. She remained standing calmly at the gate she had closed in her magic circle. She nodded at me. I took that as confirmation of the wolves' oath, but she had a queer look on her face as she looked at me. Was it fear or surprise? It could have been something else entirely. I wasn't sure how much I liked it. Whatever it was, she made another sinuous gesture with both arms and waved the magical barrier away. The glowing walls vanished, but the silver border still glimmered in the moonlight.

I stood up, hoping I didn't look too shaky. My limp hand passed over Dragos's muzzle as I rose, my own blood dripping into his bleeding mouth. He lifted his snout and licked my knuckles.

A dog licks the hand it cannot bite, the boss once told me. At the time he was describing the rebellion in Sargava, but the words had stuck with me.

The black female padded inside the circle. I stepped away from Dragos, thinking she was going to him, but she came to me and licked my hand as he had done. One by one the others followed, each tonguing my hand before moving back to lie down, eyes away from me.

Only the female met my gaze. She shifted into human form, and there stood Malena, as I had guessed. Her naked body was leaner than I'd imagined. I could see her ribs and sharp hip bones through her pale skin. She knelt and kissed my uninjured hand. Behind her, Dragos whined in protest, but he hadn't the strength to resume his human form. His voice would not be heard again tonight.

"It is as the Harrowing foretold," said Malena. "You are the Prince of Wolves."

Chapter Eleven
The Hedge Maze

Upon leaving breakfast, ostensibly to return to the library, I strolled once more around Willowmourn Manor. Once out of sight of Casomir, Tara, and Felix, I performed the first of my planned experiments for the day. Removing the bit of meat I had saved from last night's supper, I sniffed it, detected no objectionable scent, and took a bite. It was perfectly savory lamb meat.

Some force tainted the food and drink inside the manor, but not outside. And inside, the effect seemed to apply only to me, not to Tara nor, presumably, to the house servants. If the putrescence was an omen of Urgathoa's displeasure, then I was the only one who displeased her. There was no one else I could trust, not inside the manor.

Before returning to the library, I followed approximately the same course I had taken on my walk the previous morning, only this time with a slight detour to the far side of the stables. From the nearby paddock, the groom called out commands to a horse he was leading through its paces. I approached and leaned upon the paddock fence as though to observe his work, but when he looked at me I glanced toward the nearby stable to emphasize that we were out of sight of those within the manor. He was a clever fellow and took my hint, coming near me as he continued to call out to the horse.

"You are Anneke's father, are you not?" This close to the man, there was no mistaking the familial resemblance. He had undoubtedly heard gossip about my ruse with the chambermaid last night, and I would have to smooth it over to make him cooperative.

"It is dangerous for you here," he said, ignoring my question. He sketched the spiral of Pharasma over his heart. "It is dangerous for all of us, but you still have time to escape. Take Anneke with you. She is a good girl. She will serve you the way you like."

"You don't understand," I said, wincing at the implied offer to prostitute his daughter. "The incident with Anneke was all a charade. I promise upon my honor that I did not interfere with her. Now tell me, what is this danger?"

He shook his head and made the common Varisian warding against the evil eye. He would not put a name to the source of his fear. "It comes at night. You must go before then. I beg you, take Anneke with you."

"How can I believe you if you won't explain the nature—?" He glanced over my shoulder, and I turned to see a sour-faced Felix approach. I turned back to the groom and pointed to the hedge maze, asking him banal questions about its age and how many gardeners were required for its maintenance. He caught on at once, but he did not have the knack for obfuscation. I hoped that Felix would fail to note the apprehension on his face.

"Your Excellency," said the butler. "I hope Bogdan is not troubling you."

"On the contrary," I said. "It was I who interrupted his work. Thank you, Bogdan."

The groom knew a dismissal when he heard it, and he returned his attention to the horse with an expression of obvious relief.

"Perhaps Your Excellency desires admission to the library," said Felix. "I wish to ensure that you are not kept waiting while I attend my other duties."

"Most thoughtful of you, Felix," I said. "I shall fetch a few things from my room and meet you at the library in ten minutes."

"Very good, sir." He bowed and departed, passing near enough to Bogdan to whisper a reprimand. As the butler turned away, the groom's gaze implored me to do as he begged. I turned away and followed Felix into the manor.

If I have learned nothing else from my time as an active Pathfinder, it is that when a common fellow warns you of danger, it is wise to heed his advice.

Of course, I did not overlook the terms of his warning. If I had until nightfall to escape this unnamed peril, there was still time to perform my second experiment, conclude my investigation into your likely next stop, prepare my travel bag for a hasty departure, and perhaps even confirm my suspicions about the nature of the curse on Willowmourn. If by remaining I could overcome said curse, I would be glad to do so, but if the theory taking shape in my imagination was correct, the source of the evil was not something that I wished to face without the assistance of several men at arms, a proper mage or sorcerer, and at least one senior cleric of Pharasma.

In my room, I donned the most durable of my garments and folded my heavy woolen coat into my travel bag, which already contained my necessaries. I covered them all with this journal and my book of spells. When Felix saw that I meant to carry the bag into the library, I addressed his suspicious countenance by remarking that I wished to copy certain passages from Galdana's books into my own notes. I might have gone so far as to invite him to count my books before and after my visit, but there is a limit to how far I will accommodate an inquisitive servant.

When Felix locked the library door behind me, I consulted that forbidden tome of Urgathoa, *Serving Your Hunger.* At first I could not imagine why I had found it among your other materials, and I still wonder whether it was you or my forgotten self who placed it there. In light of new evidence, the book's title alone was almost sufficient evidence to confirm my suspicions that Casomir or Tara, or both of them, and perhaps some of the staff, were worshipers of Urgathoa.

The tome's vile contents assured me that tainted food and drink was long understood to be an omen of the Pallid Princess's displeasure, which somehow I had invoked, surely by whatever actions I took during my missing days. A review of its other contents in comparison with the scattered history of the traitor lord of Virholt was sufficient to clarify its relevance to the object of your journey. Spells and other unholy knowledge held by the apostles of Urgathoa were among the secrets Virholt had been commanded to steal for the Whispering Tyrant.

Before I could turn to my next task, Felix surprised me with an early luncheon, or so I assumed it to be. I clumsily concealed *Serving Your Hunger* in a thick volume of the Galdana family chronicle, feeling all the while like a schoolboy discovered with his fingers in the pages of a volume of Qadiran erotica. It occurred to me that Felix must have been unaware of the tainted food phenomenon or else he would not provoke my displeasure by bringing me food he knew I could not stomach.

For the first time I questioned the butler's complicity in the mystery of my missing time. He and Tara were both present during my reaction to the revolting breakfast yesterday.

Casomir, however, was not, and his cousin's courtesy and the butler's discretion may well have kept that information from him. Was it possible that a follower of Urgathoa could be ignorant of her omens and their effect on outsiders? Certainly not if that outsider had already once run afoul of the apostle's schemes.

I bade Felix leave the meal on the desk, as he had done the previous evening. When he lingered to await further instructions, I assured him I was engrossed in my pursuit of clues to your whereabouts and desired no further interruption until I rang for him. He departed somewhat reluctantly, I thought. If not an adherent of the Pallid Princess, he was at the least a spy for his master.

During a closer study of the chronicles of Amaans and its neighboring counties, I saw why you sought this *Lacuna Codex* and what horrors it must contain. The Lord of Virholt was a double traitor, cursed by his people for betraying them to Tar-Baphon, yet his true rebellion was against his wicked master. Already a practitioner of diabolism and necromancy, Lord Virholt only pretended to use his art in the service of Tar-Baphon, all the while gathering power in the form of rare spells and rituals that he kept hidden from the Tyrant. Whether he did so to liberate his people or to usurp Tar-Baphon's powers for himself, one cannot know from these histories. What is certain, however, is that he fell in battle after Tar-Baphon learned of his treachery. What you have been seeking all this time, I now believe, is the location of the dark spells Virholt stole before his death.

Having exhausted the fragmented chronicle of Lord Virholt, I turned to Galdana's maps. Only after an hour's frustration did I resort to dusting the maps of Vyrlich with blotting sand to reveal the invisible path of your stylus as you traced the regions that interested you into your Pathfinder journal. At last I saw your trail clearly.

I wrote a succinct letter addressed to the Bishop of the Cathedral of Pharasma in Kavapesta. I hesitated before mentioning the name of Countess Caliphvaso, unaware of the local Bishop's political affiliations and thus uncertain what influence Carmilla's name would carry in Amaans. Ultimately I relied upon citing the name of my absent host and included a brief description of the occult materials I had found within the house. What action to take, I did not presume to suggest to His Excellency. I could venture a guess, however, that it would involve a great deal of divine fire.

Concealing the letter in my sleeve, I turned to my next project, the second experiment that I had longed to conduct. The presence of riffle scrolls in my own handwriting suggested or even proved that I was capable of creating them, but the process described in the pages hidden within the romance seemed far too simplistic, as if the author assumed certain foundational knowledge of the reader. There had to be something else that my forgotten self had discovered. All the same, before I risked setting out on my own, I had to arm myself with magic.

My misgivings were well founded, for my first attempt to re-inscribe the mage hand cantrip I had expended the night before was an utter failure. Considering the un-triggered riffle scrolls I still possessed, I decided I preferred to keep all of them on hand in case I need to use them before unraveling the conundrum of their creation. There was, however, the one strange spell among them.

Examining it in riffle-scroll form was a puzzle within a puzzle, as each character one would inscribe upon an ordinary scroll was inscribed in two or three successive fragments. That was not strictly true, I realized, as I examined them further. Some strips were composed of the end of one character and the beginning of another, or in some cases a whole character with a fragment of the next attached. I could perceive no logic to the pattern of these gaps. If only I had the original spell to compare it with.

Then I realized the spell must exist somewhere within the library. I stood and turned, feeling my heart sink at the sight of so many hundreds of volumes to search for a single reference. The prospect was all the more daunting since I had uncovered two instances of hidden knowledge already—the bawdy illustrations and the instructions for constructing these riffle scrolls. Peering outside, I saw my canine sentinel lying on the grass beneath the library windows. My imagination wanted to detect some unnatural sign about the dog, but his fixation on me was perfectly explicable. He licked his chops when I opened the window.

The sun had already begun its western decline, and I realized the hour was much later than I'd assumed. I had little time to finish my preparations before departing, and there was still the issue of Galdana's hidden sword to consider. I wished to take it with me, but it was impossible to conceal it on my person. Even the larger of my satchels was insufficient to engulf it, and I had brought only the smaller. Perhaps the solution was under my nose.

I carved several thick portions of foul-smelling ham from my luncheon plate and fetched the sword from its hiding place. At the window, I showed the hound the meat. Immediately he sat down, head erect and alert. I threw the meat past him, and as he leaped after it, I dropped Galdana's sword to the flowerbed on the ground below. It was not fully concealed, but I calculated that one would not notice it on casual observation. The hound returned to his original place, tail thumping in anticipation.

"Lie down," I commanded, and he obeyed. I rewarded him with another treat. We repeated the ritual until the meat was gone, whereupon I closed the windows and returned to the final problem. It was not urgent that I test the unknown spell, but if I had inscribed it as a riffle scroll, I must have had a reason. If necessary, I could copy it into my spell book later.

Perhaps I already had.

I retrieved my long-unused spell book from the satchel and opened it where I had left the ribbon marking the last page I had consulted. It was not, as I had remembered, the fireball invocation. Rather, after that reminder of my failed study of wizardry was a new spell composed in my own hand but inscribed with fresher ink. It bore the intriguing name of "steal book."

My eyes hungrily devoured its instructions, which described a singularly elegant means for transferring the contents of a book to another blank volume, leaving the first one empty. Thus, it was not intended to duplicate knowledge but to abscond with it. I found the idea at once dangerous and exciting, and the moment my mind began to consider applications for the spell, my subconscious latched onto the clue I had been failing to understand: I knew how the riffle scrolls worked.

Rereading the book thief spell and comparing it with the riffle-scroll version, I saw that the gaps in the characters were analogous to the spell's somatic components, those gestures a wizard must perform in order to bring about the magical effect. But it was not a direct correlation, and it required a great deal more focus and comparison before I realized the locations of the breaks were also influenced by the verbal components. Yet there is a third point to the great triangle of arcane magic, and that is the material component. The pattern among the characters did not seem to account for the sand and guano and crystals a wizard must carry with him, and then I understood completely. The ink upon the riffle scrolls was completely ordinary; unlike one who reads a traditional magic scroll to unleash its spell, the user of a riffle scroll had to carry with him the material components. That explained the presence of the velvet pouch I had found with the scrolls.

Why had I made the book thief spell into a riffle scroll? What volume had I intended to steal? And why would I use the spell rather than simply take the book itself? The answer to the latter question was immediately obvious: to make the owners think the book still remained among the library, while I walked off with its copied contents. But where had I found the original? Were there other spells hidden somewhere in Galdana's library.

I silently chided myself for a fool and turned the page to see whether I had copied any other spells. On the page after the book thief, I saw not a new spell but a note in my own handwriting. Reading it, I felt cold fingers upon my spine: "The Daughters of Ugathoa devour the mothers of men."

I realized then that Bogdan was not behaving as a panderer earlier, offering me his daughter for my dishonorable use.

He was begging me to save her.

The sound of the scroll riffling across my finger attracted the footman's attention, but his head lolled back and his eyes closed before he saw me. I reached him barely in time to ease his slumbering body onto the third-floor landing. After laying him against the wall, I placed the expired riffle scroll in my pocket. The rest remained tucked inside the waist of my trousers, where they made me appear as if I'd spent the past weeks overeating instead of starving. That thought reminded me of the thrill I had experienced while burglarizing the kitchen before ascending the stairs. There was a time when I would never have stooped to petty theft. Radovan had always done such things for me.

I had tarried too long over the puzzle of the riffle scrolls before finally pulling the bell to summon Felix. By the time he arrived to open the library door, the sun was half-hidden behind the Hungry Mountains. I thought I had over an hour, but it now appeared I had only minutes before full dark.

"Where is Anneke?" I asked, too impatient to pose the question indirectly.

"Your Excellency," Felix began in apologetic tone.

"Where is she?" I demanded, straightening my back to emphasize my height, if not any legitimate authority over the butler.

"At this hour she should be preparing the upper bedchambers," he said. "If there is a problem—"

"No," I said. "I shall retire to my room for an hour, and then I wish to have supper in the dining room."

"Very good, Excellency." He bowed and moved to lead me there, but I said, "I will conduct myself. Your attentions are more urgently required in the kitchen, judging from recent mishaps."

His face colored, but he bowed again and retreated. I found my way first to the entrance, where I left my bag beside the preserved foot of a mammoth, now serving as a repository for walking sticks. Alert to any observation by the other house staff, I crept up to the third floor and incapacitated the sentry with a sleep enchantment before proceeding as quietly as the carpeted halls allowed. I moved as silently as a burglar.

I listened for sounds of housekeeping, but at first all I noticed was the overwhelming odor of vinegar. If anything it seemed stronger than it had before, and I no longer imagined it was the residue of recent cleaning. As I followed my nose to its source, I heard a human voice. A man's voice uttered rhythmic grunts, as though struggling to open a stubborn portal. The sound emanated from the same room as the acidic odor. I crept forward and knelt at the door, peering through its generous keyhole. Through it I had a narrow view of a candlelit room. To one side I saw a large enameled bath, apparently unoccupied. To the other I saw the corner of a bed swathed in red velvet and the soles of a man's naked feet.

Propriety demanded I withdraw, but the thought that Casomir or one of his servants might be raping Anneke incited me to the risk of testing the door handle. It was, of course, locked tight. Trusting that the man inside would not hear it over the sound of his own exertions, I removed the appropriate scroll and discharged its magic. I felt a tingle of the spell's power rush away from my fingers, but except for the slapping of its leaves and the faint clicking of the lock, it produced no other audible effect. The man inside did not pause in his endeavors, so I dared to turn the knob and open the door a few inches for a better view.

The naked man was indeed Casomir, although I could see only a sliver of his averted face. I could not immediately identify the woman whose body lay beneath his, for its singular feature was the absence of a head.

Behind me, a woman gasped. Anneke stood behind me, gaping at the dreadful tableau. She dropped the sheets she had been carrying, but they barely made a sound as they struck the floor. Before I could raise my finger to my lips, she unleashed an ear-splitting scream. I closed the door and pulled her toward the stairs.

"Run," I commanded, pushing her before me.

Halfway down the stairs I wondered whether I had truly seen a red cover on the bed or simply white sheets steeped in blood. What lay beneath the surface of the vinegar bath? My curiosity perished within the grip of my panic and the need to convey Anneke to safety. I thrust my satchel into her arms. When I grasped the handle of the entrance door, I found it was locked solid.

"Felix!" shouted Casomir from two floors above. I pushed Anneke against the wall and pressed my body beside hers. We watched with suspended breath as the butler ran through the foyer and up the stairs without turning toward us. When he was out of sight, we ran to dining room and tried the windowed doors. Also locked. Abandoning my last attempts at stealth, I hurled a chair through the glass windows and cleared the sharp remains with a nearby candlestick before ushering Anneke onto the darkening lawn.

"To the stables," I said. "Hurry!"

I circled toward the west, pausing only to fetch Galdana's sword from the flowerbed. Desna smiled on me, for not only was it still there, but there was no sign of the guardian hound. I ran toward the stables, intending to enact the first part of my escape plan. Anneke screamed again. I saw her standing on the open lawn between the manor and the stables. She turned away from something she had seen in the sky above her and ran as if Hell itself were at her heels.

I looked where she had looked but saw only clouds against the moon and stars. But there, something moved among them, a rogue cloud, or some ragged cloth caught in a violent wind that had risen only as I turned my eyes skyward. Whatever dreadful thing floated up there, its presence chilled my blood and turned my feet to stones.

While I had promised nothing to her or to her father, I felt a pathetic obligation. I had not placed the wretched girl in harm's way, but I had manipulated her in my efforts to misdirect Felix and Casomir, deepening her involvement. Even if she were not carrying the bag containing my valuable books, I should be a villain not to follow her.

There was no time to ponder the moral question. I ran toward her, but she turned toward the hedge maze. I altered my course to follow her, but Bogdan intercepted me, bursting out from the stables.

"Save her, my lord," he cried. "I beg you, find her and flee this place!"

"What chases her?" I asked.

"The black cloud," he wailed. "The corruption of the house, the sins of our masters—"

I would have slapped the babbling out of him, but the hand I raised still held the sheathed sword. I should have found a belt for the scabbard, but such a trifling detail had slipped my mind during the day's astonishing discoveries. "I will find your daughter, but you must do something for me."

"Anything," he pleaded. I had to grasp his arm to keep him from kneeling and clutching my knees.

"Take a horse and ride to the ferry," I said. I thrust my purse and my letter to the bishop into his hands. "Bribe the ferryman, kill him if you must, but take this letter to the cathedral."

He nodded dumbly, trying to understand. "But how will you—"

I shook him hard to keep him from thinking. "Just do as I say, or they will catch your daughter."

We ran side by side until he entered the stable and I veered off into the hedge maze, following the sound of another scream.

The moon would not rise for an hour or more. The dull glow of sunset reflected off the clouds to reveal only the uppermost fronds of the high hedges. I listened for another sound of Anneke's location as I felt my way along the path. My recollection of the maze from the limited perspective of the trophy room gave me some idea of the right course, but I did not know whether Anneke knew her way through. I called out her name.

"I am here to help you," I shouted. "Your father sent me."

I heard a sibilant sound emanating somewhere above the hedgerows. It sounded like the hiss of a mountain cat, but I could not envision one light enough to climb the foliage and stalk us upon the maze walls. This was something else, something with no need to perch upon a ledge. A shadow passed before the moon, but it had moved behind the hedge wall by the time I looked up. I smelled vinegar in the air. This was something from the house.

"Anneke!" I called again, this time in a stage whisper. I heard rustling from a few passages away. I summoned the image of the maze I had consigned to memory and turned to seek the shorter route to its source. "Stay where you are, girl. I will come to you."

Someone—or some thing—rushed along the passage adjacent to mine. The foliage shook, and another miasma of the vinegar smell washed over me and clung to my skin. The scabbard trembled in my hand. I drew the weapon. The blade buzzed with hatred, the thousand spirals on its blade blazing like miniscule galaxies. The resulting illumination cast my surroundings in stark lines of black and silver, banishing all color.

Deeper in the maze, Anneke shouted, "Please don't!" Her screams mingled with a sound like hail falling through deciduous trees. A cloud of leaves and stem fragments filled the air, along with another sour stench.

I hacked at the hedge with the enchanted sword, but whatever its powers, it was no more effective against the thick vegetation than any common blade. I rushed through the circuitous path until the light of the sword revealed a wet black bench beneath an enormous topiary figure of what might once have been a giant boar. The beast's head was missing, and long gouges ran along its nearest flank. I slipped on the wet path, and for a mad instant I imagined I had trod in the blood of the enormous vegetable sculpture. It was indeed blood steaming in the chill autumn air, splashed all over the path and the nearest hedge walls. Among the pools, I spied fragments of bone and ruined scraps of flesh. A hank of pale hair clung to the base of the bench, and nearby lay a tangle of narrow cloth strips that had been the chambermaid's dress. Nearby lay my satchel, glistening with gore.

Hot and sticky fluid dripped upon my face. I raised the sword to fend off whatever hovered above me. The thing screamed in fury and levitated farther away. Past the blinding light of the sword, I perceived only a vague impression of a tangle of dangling gourds and vines, all slick with black blood.

More than the sight or the horrid smell, some invisible aura of the thing filled me with absolute abhorrence. Every nerve in my body was poised to flee, but an ineffable indignation fired my heart to deny the impulse. Before I could think of what I was doing, I snatched a scroll from my waist and riffled it upward.

The spell was born as a spark but soon grew to the size of a man's fist before striking the monstrosity above me. There it blossomed into a blinding cloud of flame, throwing me to the ground and blasting the hedge walls away in every direction. Where the blaze touched the foliage, a hundred tiny fires raised their infant cries.

I scrabbled away, retrieved my satchel, and ran by the light of the sword to the maze's exit. There I sheathed the weapon to conceal its light. I expended another riffle scroll to conjure a phantom steed, and then a translucent horse fearlessly stood beside the fire, allowing me to mount before bolting away from the conflagration. We ran south toward the ferry until I could no longer hear the baying of the pursuing hounds, whereupon I turned the steed westward, toward the mountains of Virlych and the object of my quest.

Chapter Twelve
Children of the Damned

When I snapped his arm, the boy's scream cut deep into me. I felt the eyes of the old women on the back of my neck as he thrashed and wailed. Azra cooed and stroked his protruding forehead. Tudor moaned and looked up at her. Standing above his head, Azra signed to me, and I did my best to translate it into Varisian for him.

"Good, she says," I told him. "You did good. Only a little more."

I pulled hard on his arm, and he screamed to burst my ears.

The Sczarni werewolves had followed us to the accursed village, trailing Azra's wagon in human form like a line of immigrants. I don't know where they kept their clothes, but the morning after my fight with Dragos they were all dressed and waiting at their own camp about forty yards from ours. They had just disassembled a tent. I recognized the fabric as that of the one I had first seen in Oracle Alley back in the market of Caliphas. When I looked up from dousing our campfire, it was nowhere to be seen. None of them carried anything larger than the leather satchel borne by the big barrel-chested man I'd heard Malena call Cezar, and they had no pack animals, not even a pull cart. Another mystery of the Sczarni.

Uncertain how they would treat me this morning, I hesitated before approaching them. When finally I walked toward them, Azra emerged from the wagon and snapped her fingers for my attention and directed me to finish breaking camp. When she saw the Sczarni waiting nearby, she scowled. Within minutes, she harnessed Luminita and hitched her to the wagon. When she slapped the reins, I had to run catch the wagon and climb up beside her. Looking back, I saw the Sczarni following us on foot.

"You invite them along?" I asked.

She looked at me as though I'd again said something stupid.

"Why are they following us?

She snorted her derision. *Prince of Wolves*, she signed.

"It wasn't my idea," I told her. "I only hope it's not one of those situations where you're king for a month and then they eat you." She didn't smile, but it was only mostly a joke. The boss had told me wild stories about Mwangi tribes who proclaimed visiting explorers their new king. Most of these unlucky travelers figured Desna had smiled upon them until they noticed the ceremonial bath was getting awfully hot.

"Say," I said. A bad thought had occurred to me. "This is the second time I've had a tussle with a werewolf. I got chewed up pretty bad both times. I'm not going to . . . you know." I made claws of my hands. "Grr."

She laughed, and I counted it a triumph.

You ate chicken, she signed.

"Yeah, so?"

Full of demon. She pointed at me. *No room for wolf.*

"I don't know what that means," I said, but maybe I did. Maybe the werewolf curse only worked on proper men, not hellspawn.

"I'll tell Dragos he's still the head man," I suggested. "Send them on their way."

She gave me another exasperated look. *Not prince, Dragos,* she signed.

"Then who?" I asked. "Was it Vili?"

No more prince, she signed.

"Why not?"

Ask wolves, she signed impatiently. *But do not trust. Show weakness, they eat you.*

"I'll stretch my legs," I said. I was still stiff after she healed me again after the fight. I'd been surprised that she also healed Dragos. I wondered just how far this agreement between them went. Were they allies? I didn't think so, judging from the looks she gave them, but then I didn't expect a cleric of Desna to be on such agreeable terms with a pack of Sczarni werewolves, either.

I walked beside the wagon. The Sczarni kept up what looked an easy pace for them. Now that I knew what they were, it was no surprise that they were all lean and long-legged. I should have seen the clues even before Vili showed me his teeth back in Caliphas. Dragos had the same thick, converging eyebrows as his son, and I noticed several of the others, including Milosh the pickpocket, had slightly pointed ears with tufts of hair at the tips. There was no looking at them now without noticing how wide their mouths were, and how prominent their canine teeth.

Malena hastened to walk beside me. She offered me a burlap parcel.

I took the package. Inside were a couple of hares, skinned and gutted.

"For you," she said in Taldane.

I nodded thanks. "Listen," I said. "This might sound ridiculous, but your people don't, say, eat your prince on the full moon or something?"

"Not so ridiculous," she said with a breathy laugh. Her Varisian accent was every bit as sensual as I'd remembered, but at the same time it made pins of the hair on the nape of my neck. "But no, we are not cannibals. Should Dragos kill you in later challenge, you will not be eaten."

"That's comforting." I thought about what she had said as we walked beside the wagon. And I thought about what she hadn't said. "When you say you aren't cannibals . . . ?"

"That means we do not eat our people."

"Right," I said. "So Azra, she is one of your people?"

"Of course not. She is a powerful healer. We respect her territory. She respects our ways. Sometimes we trade."

Beside us, Azra slapped the reins. Luminita picked up her pace, and we had to step quickly to keep up. It was little effort for long-legged Malena, but I was on the verge of running.

"How do you know which ones are her people?"

"They mark their villages," she said, drawing in the air. I recognized the wings of Desna, but then she added a coil.

"Desna and Pharasma?"

Malena nodded. "Birth, dreams, death," she said. "All of life. She is very powerful witch."

Although worship of some other gods is tolerated back home, all are subordinate to Asmodeus, the Prince of Law. Outside of Cheliax, he's more commonly known as the Prince of Lies. Either way, the people of my country are used to worshiping more than one god, even if one is the one you worship in public, the other only behind closed doors.

"Tonight, come to our camp. I have a tent," said Malena. She threw a brief glance toward Azra's wagon and then looked full into my eyes and added. "I would never make you sleep outside."

Behind us, Dragos scowled at her. I resisted the urge to taunt him with a smile. Beside him were another man and young Milosh, imitating his elder's expression. The other Sczarni—two women, two men, and another teenager whose sex I couldn't guess—walked with their gazes on the horizon. I got the sense there were mixed feelings among the Sczarni about this whole Prince of Wolves thing, and it wasn't hard to see who was on which side.

Azra slapped the reins again, and I got the message.

"I'll think about it," I said to Malena, thinking of hot baths. "Let's talk more at the village."

"No," said Malena. "We do not enter that place."

"Why?" I asked. She made that evil eye gesture and said no more. The wagon continued to pick up speed, so I dashed for the driver's seat and climbed aboard. Flushed from the run, I smiled at Azra and showed her the hares.

She turned her head, lifted her chin, and ignored me for the rest of the journey.

Long before we reached the village, I knew we were entering cursed territory. We passed the burned ruins of a farmhouse, and from a nearby tree hung the corpses of an entire flock of sheep. Azra made the sign of Pharasma over her heart and encouraged Luminita to move faster. All I could think of was the time it must have taken for someone to tie all those nooses and pull them up into those branches. Then I thought of what would motivate a man to do that, and I felt queasy.

Our destination lay at the eastern foot of the Virlych arm of the Hungry Mountains, a craggy range of gray stone and black forests. Its tallest peaks vanished into the clouds. Low-lying mists pooled among the trees and through the precipitous valleys, their movements contrary to the prevailing wind. Strange colors lurked within those vapors, the sickening hues of gangrenous wounds.

The first signs of habitation were the lonely effigies mounted in the harvested fields. They differed from southern scarecrows in two respects: the sacks that formed their heads blazed with garish embroidery suggesting leering faces, and between their wicker legs jutted enormous carved phalluses. I'd seen enough fertility fetishes in the boss's library to catch the gist, but it still made me chuckle. Azra looked at me, puzzled. I guessed she didn't think it was so funny. We followed the road over a round hill and descended into a small valley blighted by the ugliest village I have ever seen.

To call the buildings hovels would be to give the term a bad name. About twenty ramshackle structures of weathered gray wood squatted within an irregular border formed by a fence painted with what must have been tar. Stuck all along the fence were glittering bits of broken glass, colored beads, feathers, chips of pottery, and all manner of colorful garbage. The nearby fields had all been gleaned down to the soil, which here was not the rich black I'd seen elsewhere in Ustalav but a ruddy brown mix of soil and clay. Sheep and chickens roamed the avenues between the shabby little houses. Pigs wallowed in a large pen, mercifully on the other side of the village, and up on the nearby hills I spied a flock of sheep. Among them was a figure I took at first for a giant. Upon seeing our wagon, he whooped and hollered a word over and over while running down toward us. He repeated it six or seven times before I realized it was Azra's name mangled by a cleft palate.

As we drove near the fence, more villagers rushed out to open the gate. My first good look at them nearly turned my stomach. They looked like freak show rejects.

Many of them had the tiny pin heads I'd seen only in the sketches of bizarre Mwangi tribesmen in the boss's library. The only difference was that these people were clearly Varisian, but with short, conical skulls and weirdly uniform facial features.

Others had malformed limbs, including one legless fellow who waddled toward us on a pair of arms that resembled plucked goose wings. One was a walking skeleton, nearly seven feet tall but not a stone heavier than I am. His clothes draped over him like the canvas concealing a new statue.

They clamored for Azra, and their jumbled voices sounded like a dozen different languages. I had to concentrate to recognize the language as Varisian. Those who didn't have obvious speech impediments seemed to have adopted those of their neighbors, but there was no consensus among them. The babble added a headache to the vertigo their distorted faces gave me.

For a second it appeared they would swarm Azra and pull her from the wagon, but she passed me the reins and went willingly into their arms. Each of them wanted to touch her hair or the cloth of her garments, and she didn't so much as flinch at their hideous appearance. Women with faces like rotten squashes pressed root-like infants into her arms, and she kissed their cheeks as the crowd escorted her into the village. All the while they jabbered at her, but she seemed to understand it all, nodding and signing back or miming her replies.

I looked behind us. There was no sign of the Sczarni, as Malena had warned me. For a fleeting moment, despite the danger, I wished I had stayed with them instead of entering this accursed village. At least I had the donkey to tend to, a good excuse to stay well back from the freaks.

"Just you and me, sweetheart," I said to Luminita, slapping her reins lightly. One of the larger buildings was a stable with several empty stalls. I drove there and jumped off, approaching Luminita in a wide circle. I hadn't noticed Azra's casting her calming charm on the beast this morning, and I wasn't ready to take it on faith that the donkey wouldn't stomp me into the mud when I reached for her harness.

"I hope you were watching closely when I beat the hell out of that werewolf last night," I told her. "Not that I'm threatening you, Luminita, but you and I have a certain history of kicking."

She remained motionless, turning her head to keep an eye on me. I reached carefully for her bridle, but she tossed her head out of reach.

"Damn it!"

An inarticulate voice called out. I turned to see that giant running up to me, one finger digging around in his nose. It was almost but not quite impossible to understand him. He'd said something like, *"Let me get that."*

I waved a hand toward Luminita. "Be my guest."

A string of drool dangled from the corner of his mouth as he came forward to remove Luminita's harness. I stepped back to avoid getting any on me. Somewhat closer to seven than six feet tall, he looked like a husky teenage boy except for his jutting cliff of a forehead, a hare lip, and ears that could have been a couple of heads of shriveled cauliflower. His eyes were far too close together. He favored his left arm, which had an extra crook in it. At the time, I assumed it was just another of the hundred birth defects I'd seen among his neighbors. It did not seem to impair him as he unhitched the wagon and led Luminita into the stable.

"Huh!" said the giant, slapping himself on the chest with a sound deeper than a bass drum. His finger immediately returned to mining his nose. "Tudor!"

I tapped my chest. "Radovan," I said in my best Varisian inflection. I still had trouble with anything more than simple sentences, but common phrases came to mind more quickly. *"Thanks for help."*

He stuck out his sticky hand. While I'm not the squeamish type, I stepped back.

"Must go," I said. *"Azra . . . waits."*

"Huh huh!" he said, bobbing his head and grinning.

Azra was nowhere in sight, but I guessed her location from the crowd of villagers beside one of the shacks. They peered through the window and relayed reports to those who could not see inside.

Most of them were women, I noticed, and despite my initial impression, not all of them suffered from obvious defects. That said, you couldn't hold a beauty contest in this village. Even the least homely of the villagers would have sent a legless pirate fleeing. Their faces appeared to have been slightly crushed from all sides. Something was grinding down on them.

I felt a chill from above and looked up at the mountains. There was no thunder, but queer lights pulsed in the shadows beneath the cloud line.

I strolled the lanes between the hovels to stretch my legs, and soon the local gang was following me. The eldest couldn't have been much older than ten, but her face looked like a crone's. Even the youngest had deep lines etched around her eyes. A fingerless boy clutched my hand between paddle and thumb, looking up expectantly. His irises were lozenge-shaped and the color of egg yolk. Tiny islands of the same color floated in the whites of his eyes. It took an effort not to withdraw my hand.

"*Hello,*" he said, tugging at me. He led me into the village as the other freakish children followed.

They showed me a puddle that smelled like equal parts rainwater and goat piss. Their intention wasn't clear until I saw movement in the water. The children screamed and scrambled after the three-legged frog trying to escape their clutches. Sweet Desna, I thought. In this village, even the vermin are cursed.

Before the little herd could trample the thing, I reached in and snatched up the frog. It puffed its throat and blinked.

I offered it to the flipper-handed boy, but he recoiled. The eldest girl took it from me. Her smile was that of any little girl, and I had to wonder whether she would die of old age before she turned fifteen.

Before I could make my escape, the children dragged me to another of their favorite sites. We crept up beneath a windowsill on which a pair of berry pies cooled. The children raised their noses to sniff the sweet aroma and took turns daring each other to stick a finger in. When I reached up to steal one for them, they squealed in protest. They spoke so fast I caught only *"Tudor" something-something "hungry,"* so I left it alone.

We made a circuit of the village, pausing to skip stones across the sheep pond or pat some friendly mongrels. We paused at a barn long enough for the eldest girl, Rusa, to recite the tale of the day a boy had gone missing until he was found trapped inside, "treed" by an aggressive goat but unable to call out for help because he was mute. She spoke slowly and clearly enough that I understood almost every word. Her tale renewed my appreciation for Azra, who not only communicated well without a tongue but somehow also still channeled the magic of her goddess. Or goddesses. I still did not fully understand what she did, and I'd never understand how she did it.

The adults we encountered saw that the children had commandeered me and nodded, as if that were the custom when strange hellspawn entered the village. All of them smiled or waved a greeting. Despite their frightening appearances, not a one of them tried to bury me alive or set me on fire. That made them my favorite villagers in all of Ustalav, so far.

Shortly before the children had exhausted me, one of the village men came to summon me. He bade the children return to their homes, and they reluctantly obeyed. Then he took me to the barn, where I saw six of the strongest men of the village had managed to pin Tudor to a table.

The big shepherd looked at me with terror in his eyes. *"Nuh, nuh!"*

Azra signed to me. *Help.*

It took me a moment to work up the nerve to break Tudor's crooked arm, but I knew it would be worse if I failed to break it on the first strike. Every second I hesitated would only increase his terror, so I didn't have a choice.

After it was all done but for the screaming, I held his arm out straight, Azra adjusted my grip, made me hold it there, and affixed a splint to Tudor's arm. He had fractured it months ago, shortly after her last visit, but he had been far from home with his flock. Without help to splint it, he had let it heal crooked. Azra could repair it with magic, but only after it had been re-broken and set straight. No one else in the village would dare to break the giant's arm. The big idiot was more than twice my size, and I wouldn't be sticking around to risk his revenge. The way he blubbered like a baby, however, I had a feeling he'd forget about it before his next meal.

As Azra finished tying a sling around Tudor's neck, she signed to an old woman who translated. She spoke as to a slow child, so both Tudor and I could understand. *"Do not move that arm,"* she said. *"Do not take it out of the sling. Do not disturb the splint, or Azra will hex you with blisters."*

Azra stepped away to wash her hands in a tin basin.

I gave Tudor a light punch on his good shoulder. "She'll do it, too, kid," I said to Tudor in Chelish. In Varisian I added, *"Listen to her."* Tudor gave me a rueful look. His unbound hand absently returned to pick his nose.

The old woman who had translated for Tudor pointed him home with a promise of supper. *"Yes, and pie,"* she said. That incentive made him break into a gallop.

As Azra dried her hands, I reached for the basin, but the village woman grabbed my hand and stepped close enough to set my eyes watering with the garlic reek of her breath.

"My lord," she said in the same simple cadence she had used to lecture Tudor. *"We are poor. Other villages do not trade with us. We have no money to buy things we cannot grow."*

The way she gripped my hand, I expected her to beg, but she stood tall, staring up into my face with one good and one cataract-blanked eye.

"Listen," I said, but she grasped the coin I wore around my neck and kissed it.

I looked to Azra for advice, but she had walked away. Gently, I removed the woman's hands and tugged open my purse. Maybe a few coins would help. Or maybe half of my money, and I could make up the rest when I got back to Caliphas and the Towers games. Still, I had been living off Azra's charity for days. What the hell, I figured. I cinched the purse shut and put it into her hands.

The old woman went down on her hands and knees. I barely stepped back in time to avoid her kissing my feet.

"You are good lord," she said, clutching my trousers. *"Long time you have been gone. Now you help your people again. Pharasma spare you. Desna smile upon you."*

"Come on, now," I said, reaching down to lift her back to her feet. I tried a little Varisian, remembering that the locals call all old women "grandmother" as a sign of respect. *"Please stand, Baba."*

"Prince Virholt," she said. She pointed up the side of the mountain, which had grown dark purple in the twilight. *"Tomorrow, Tudor will take you to your village. There, your ancestors will bless you."*

She scurried off, clutching the purse. I washed up, chuckling to myself. If these Ustalavs kept putting me in charge of their families and villages, I'd be running the country by spring.

As I emerged from the barn, Azra waited for me beside a lantern on a fencepost. She crossed her arms across her breasts, and I saw a world of disapproval on her face.

"How do you like that?" I asked. "First I'm Prince of Wolves, now I'm Lord of the Freaks." Still smiling, I walked right into her slap. The blow stung worse than her spells.

"What was that for?"

They are people, not freaks.

"It's just a joke. I've been called worse plenty of times."

She lifted the coin from my neck and took a closer look. She snorted and flung it back to strike my chest. *Prince of fools.* She flicked four fingers off her thumb at me. I didn't know it as a Pathfinder sign, but the meaning was unmistakable. She scowled and turned as if to leave. Instead, she turned back and signed slowly at me to make sure I understood every word. *Rich men,* she signed, *they praise. Give money, call lord.*

"Well, of course," I said. "You didn't think I took that seriously, did you?"

The truth was I had sort of hoped there was something to what the old woman had said. All my life I'd worked for someone else, first a small-time crime lord, later a bored and overeducated aristocrat. It would have been something, just for once, to be my own boss. All it took was a little hand-licking and foot-kissing to give me delusions of grandeur. The realization made me see myself in a humiliating new light.

Azra spun on her heel and walked into one of the larger huts. I stood there alone, feeling like an imbecile.

"Desna wept," I complained to no one in particular.

Chapter Thirteen
The Haunted Vales

After the terror of my last hour at Willowmourn subsided, I surrendered to the thrill of riding my phantom steed across the farmland of northern Amaans. Where we encountered fences, the horse leaped effortlessly to gallop across the stubble of harvested fields. When I leaned forward, the beast's smoky mane floated up to touch my face, soft and fine as silken threads. The steed's silent gait left no mark upon the ground, and it uttered no sound of exertion, although I felt its cool chest expand and fall with respiration. I sat so easily in its conjured saddle that I felt as though I were flying rather than riding. During my studies in the arcane so many years ago, I had never enjoyed this exhilaration without the accompanying misery of the nausea.

I spied fewer farmsteads as I traveled farther from Kavapesta. Against the starry horizon, the silhouette of the Hungry Mountains loomed ever higher to the southwest. To the south were the infamous Hundred Haunted Vales of Amaans, home to the most wretched of the county's denizens. Travelers were warned, rightly or not, that those who dwelt in the shadow of the mountains in Virlych were slowly driven mad, even their bodies corrupted over generations of stubborn but doomed settlement. I could only speculate whether Count Galdana's annual progression through shunned territory was a sign of his own madness or an obligation to his subjects.

More importantly, I wondered whether he was a party to the events occurring at his home. If the late Anneke's child was Galdana's bastard, his absence could be his alibi during her murder. Immediately I discarded that theory. It was foolish to assume anyone, even an eccentric like Galdana, would go to such lengths for a murder that could have been handled with far less ritual and more discretion. Whatever had been happening in Willowmourn, I did not think its purpose included the death of Anneke. Far more likely, her death was an indulgence of one or more cultists of Urgathoa.

The question of why Casomir had turned on Tara remained. Once I'd seen Anneke alive, the warm, golden skin tone of the corpse had been unmistakable. It was hideous to imagine lust alone had caused Casomir to murder and rape his cousin, but no less horrible are the degenerate rituals of Urgathoa. I preferred to speculate on what he could hope to gain by such an act. Perhaps it was a sacrifice intended to elicit a gift of power from Urgathoa. It was possible he craved infernal power to overthrow his uncle's seat. The monster he sent after Anneke was evidence that he already commanded considerable strength.

Whatever the answer was, with my note I had passed the problem into the hands of the divine authorities in Kavapesta. Perhaps it appeared cowardly to flee rather than join forces with them, but my priority remained to find you. I am still not satisfied that the cult manuscript I found in Galdana's library is unrelated to your search. If there is a connection, then I feel ever more keenly the need to find you sooner rather than later.

My imagination whirled until my phantom steed slowed its pace, a sign that it was soon to vanish. I estimated by the course of the constellations that the time was well after midnight but still hours before dawn, long after I had expected the spell to elapse. I mused upon the possibility that my arcane ability had increased over the years, despite my focus on theory rather than application. It was a logical conjecture, but one I could not properly test without access to spells I had not yet inscribed in my own book.

Before the steed vanished, I directed it toward a low dell and dismounted. There the horse walked a short distance away and turned to gaze back at me as its semi-substantial body gradually faded from this material world. As it vanished, I raised a hand to bid it farewell. A cool autumn breeze lifted my hair, and the cold hand of loneliness fell upon my shoulder.

I gathered what deadfall I could find as the ground mist gathered for the morning fog. Without a flint and steel—the necessities in my travel bag included no camping gear—I weighed expedience against the hope that I could duplicate the riffle scrolls. Ultimately I expended another cantrip to start a campfire. Huddling in my coat, I lay beside the fire a long while, struggling to escape the tangled net of questions gripping my imagination until finally slipping under the surface of sleep to sink down toward dreams.

The mists were thick enough to extinguish my fire before I awoke. For the first time since awaking at Willowmourn, I remembered my dreams. Only this morning I wished otherwise.

I shuddered to recall images of Tara's decapitated body rising from its bloody bed to point an accusing finger at me. Even if I could not protect her, once I assumed Count Galdana's hospitality in his absence, I had a duty to avenge her. I should have had the courage to remain and face Casomir and his familiar, or whatever abomination it was that had slain Anneke.

Without so much as the campfire, the enveloping mists smothered the daylight too much for reading. Unsheathing Galdana's sword, I saw that it no longer emitted radiance as it had the previous night. That effect must have been a reaction to the monster I had faced. The question was what quality of the creature evoked the sword's power. I supposed for now that the horror was of undead or infernal origin, but proof would require further study.

The more urgent matter at hand was determining whether I could reproduce the effect of the riffle scrolls. Despite the morning gloom, I made a crude podium of my bag and arrayed the necessary materials upon my lap desk. Hunger pangs distracted me, but if what I suspected were true, I would be better served by waiting before eating.

My caution proved wise. After drawing only a few of the broken runes upon the riffle pages, my stomach gurgled. As I continued, my discomfort grew more and more noxious, rising from my gorge to tickle at the base of my throat. Briefly I considered pausing to force myself to expunge the contents of my stomach, but I pushed on, hoping that I could complete such an elementary spell before the act became involuntary. I held my handkerchief ready as I inscribed the final rune.

My nausea vanished like a burst soap bubble. It did not merely subside; rather, I felt as hale as though the infirmity had never touched me.

At last I could wield the powers I had once toiled miserably to master. Of course, the need to inscribe the spells on these unorthodox scrolls entailed some disadvantages—unlike other wizards, I could be more effectively disarmed—but there were obvious advantages as well: triggering a scroll was quicker than casting many spells, and all of its verbal and somatic components were performed in advance. Like an orthodox wizard, however, I still needed to carry the appropriate material components and spell foci on my person. I felt a certain measure of pride in my earlier, forgotten deduction of this process. Moreover, I felt pride in my rediscovery. What I had accomplished before, I could do again.

By the time I had re-inscribed the cantrip as a riffle-scroll, the mists had almost completely evaporated. I blinked as I rose from a cramped writing posture—an unfortunate habit developed in my academically oriented youth—and surveyed my surroundings. The dell at day was utterly different from the location I had seen at night. From the bottom of a shallow depression, I gazed up at a sparse ring of trees standing sentinel around me. The spot where I had lit my fire in the dark could not have been better shielded from the eyes of any who might have pursued me from Willowmourn. Unfortunately, it also offered me no vantage from which to calculate my location relative to the mountains. A limbering stroll would be my third order of business after testing my first new riffle scroll and breaking my fast.

I squeezed the last of the deadfall in my coat to dry it and lay the wood atop the dead fire. Resentful of the waste of writing material, I tore a page from one of the blank folios, crushed it into a ball, and set it under the branches as tinder. I held my breath as I riffled the cantrip. As the last of the strips snapped out from beneath my thumb, the paper alit with orange flames. When I had recovered from a spontaneous cheer, I foolishly looked about to ensure no one had observed me behaving like a child one-tenth my age. The confirmation of my solitude dampened my spirits, even as the fire took hold of the wood.

The warmth was a comfort, although the fire offered little illumination in the mist. I re-inscribed the scrolls I had cast earlier, pausing to consider whether I should replace any with different spells. Unable to anticipate the nature of the threats I might face on the rest of my journey, I trusted to the selection my unremembered self had made. Some intuition suggested he might have known more than I had rediscovered since my second awakening.

The unexpectedly long duration of my phantom steed encouraged me to attempt to create an addition to my existing repertoire. Using another blank sheaf, I copied the steal book spell from the existing riffle scroll. Once satisfied that it was as accurate as I could make it under present conditions, I directed the scroll to this journal and let the strips flip off my thumb. I felt the tingling sensation of magic on my fingers, but I detected no visible effect on the open pages. However, upon the riffle scroll itself, the characters glimmered as though the ink had been mixed with diamond dust. That was interesting, for theoretically the characters should have vanished with the discharge of the magic they contained, but seeing that they did not gave me an insight into the operation of the spell.

I removed another of the blank folios from my satchel and opened its pages. Before riffling the scroll again, a sudden misgiving made me stay my hand. I counted the pages and was assured there were more in the blank volume than I had covered with my writing in the journal. Holding my breath, I directed the scroll at the folio and let it slip. As the leaves riffled free, the glimmering characters flashed and vanished. Instantly, the very same passages I had written in my journal appeared on the fresh book, leaving the original blank.

This time I celebrated my triumph in a more seemly fashion, by eating sparingly of the food I had stolen from Galdana's kitchen. I had taken only a few pounds of cured meat and a bag of shelled nuts, knowing I could forage or even capture game with magic, but it was prudent to ration from the start rather than to find myself wanting later. I expected to find few if any inhabitants nearby. Judging from the rumors I'd heard of the Hungry Mountains within Virlych, it was even possible the area was devoid of edible flora and fauna.

When I finished eating, I gathered my belongings and smothered the fire. There was no convenient way to secure Galdana's sword at my hip, so I wedged it in the mouth of my satchel, where it resembled the walking stick of some business clerk. My vanity frowned at the image I must have presented, but I countered by reminding myself that there was no one to observe me.

I walked up the nearest rise and surveyed my surroundings. The mists had retreated to the southeast, gathering their force at the foot of the mountains. It was neither fear nor curiosity alone, but both together, that reignited the thrill of discovery. With the new riffle scroll, I summoned my phantom steed and rode into the Hungry Mountains.

By noon I debated whether to stop for a rest. Terror and confusion had compelled me to remain all night on horseback, with the added benefit of using the full duration of my conjuration to escape the horrors at Willowmourn. Today, however, I faced a choice between tending to my health and gaining a few extra miles toward my goal. Both options were attractive, but at last my hunger, coupled with my inability to eat while riding, persuaded me to stop.

I chose a sunny hill that commanded the surrounding land for miles around. The Hungry Mountains encircled me now, although in the far south I knew they parted at the southernmost point of the Gorcha Pass. The mists had all but vanished, crawling back into the narrow valleys of Virlych, where purple and green lightning flashed within the gloom. Somewhere in that obscure territory lay the tomb of the man who hid his wicked knowledge from the Whispering Tyrant and perished for the offense.

As I took a portion of my stolen provender from the satchel, I spotted movement half a mile to the east. There was an animal running in my direction. Incredibly, it appeared to be the same hound that had stood vigil beneath the library window as I studied at Willowmourn. My eyes sought the fields behind him for any sign of additional pursuit, but he appeared to be as solitary as I.

It was incredible that an ordinary dog could have tracked me so far across the county of Amaans. My phantom steed left no prints, and upon its back I should have left virtually no scent trail. The speed at which I'd ridden the night before was sufficient to outdistance any mundane pursuers, and even with its huge stride, the hound could never match the pace of my steed. It would have had to run all the time my steed galloped, continuing as I slept and inscribed spells. All questions of finding me aside, the animal's fortitude must have been supernal for it to have come so far.

The lack of other pursuers was puzzling. Surely if this animal had come so far, its elders and masters could do the same. I could not imagine what reason Casomir would have for releasing the hounds but not following, unless something had distracted him from his pursuit. Perhaps the Bishop of Kavapesta had reacted swiftly to the note Bogdan carried, forcing Casomir to flight. That possibility had some merit.

The hound barked at the sight of me. His tongue lolled as he marched forward, obviously exhausted. Whatever motivated his pursuit, he continued by sheer force of spirit. If he meant me harm, I did not doubt he posed a threat. More likely, however, he was sent to find me and alert others to my location, even if I could not yet see them. In either case, the wisest course was to kill him and continue my flight with greater vigilance.

The hound increased his pace as he came within scent distance. I drew Galdana's sword, which produced neither sound nor light, and fetched a riffle scroll into my other hand. The spell would incapacitate the dog, but afterward I would still face the need to execute him.

Raising the sword as the dog came close enough to attack, I saw him lick his chops. And yet he did not attack. He came within three paces and sat, panting at me with an expression of weary expectation, heedless of the weapon I had poised to strike at him. I lowered the sword, and the dog scooted closer, still sitting.

It was his begging posture. The hound had come all this way merely to be fed.

There are times when the natural impulses of man and beast amaze me more than any magic spell. It seemed preposterous that a dog should follow me, hardly more than a stranger, all of a night and half a day to beg for food. It had to be a trick of Casomir's, the dog under some geas to find me and alert other followers to my presence. Killing it was the only reasonable choice. It was the intelligent choice. The responsible one.

It was, alas, not the choice I made.

Tucking the riffle scroll into my belt, I fetched the dried meat from my satchel. The dog inched forward, and I showed him my palm and said, "Sit." The hound obeyed, licking the spittle from his jowls and bobbing his big rectangular head.

I gave him the meat a morsel at a time, none larger than the pad of my thumb. Each time he rose or crowded me, I corrected him with a sign or a word, and he amended his behavior. It reminded me in some ways of the first days of a new servant's employment, when my hours are filled with the constant intrusion of errors and misapprehension. Unlike most of the drivers, valets, cooks, and gardeners I had instructed over the decades, the hound was a quick study, obeying not only the simple commands to sit, come, and lie down, but also to stay, turn, and heel.

It occurred to me then that I might have known the hound longer than I remembered. Just as I had previously learned and forgotten the riddle of the riffle scrolls, perhaps I had also befriended and trained this animal before my memory was stolen. Unfortunately, I became so engrossed in my conjecture and our current training scenario that I realized too late that I had fed the voracious creature more than a day's ration of the meat. I replaced the remainder in the satchel, wary of a rebellious growl. Instead, the hound lay down, head upon his paws, and slept at my feet.

I prepared my belongings to resume the journey, hoping that the sated beast would wake to find no one near and return home. Yet imagining his reaction to finding himself abandoned caused me to waver in my resolve. Cursing the unwelcome sympathy, I prayed I would not regret it later. I sat beside the hound, placed my hand upon his shoulder, and waited for him to awake.

Chapter Fourteen
The Old Village

Tudor climbed like a mountain goat. His huge stride took him easily over rocks I had to climb. I tried not to think about his baba's boast that he knew the mountains better than anyone else because he had so often gotten lost in them, coming home half-starved days or weeks after the last time anyone had noticed him tending the flocks. Azra followed close behind me. In the beginning she had tried to persuade me not to go to the old village. The discussion turned into another quarrel until I said I'd go without her and she stomped away. Now I was glad she had come, because I was starting to worry about what we might find.

It was her fault I even wanted to see the place. The night before she had kept berating me throughout supper, throwing signs so fast she looked like a street fighter trying to intimidate an opponent. Not for the first time, I suspected she had a larger vocabulary of signs or had created many of her own. Unfortunately, she had also taught her full vocabulary to the local women, who felt the need to translate after I decided to ignore Azra.

At one point, everyone around the table stopped eating and stared at me. A few tittered or clutched their hands over their mouths.

"*We made a bed for you upstairs,*" said a motherly woman whose only visible deformity was one floppy ear. "*But you would prefer to sleep in the barn?*"

"*No,*" I said. "*Why?*"

"*Azra says it is your custom to sleep with animals.*"

"*It is a mistake,*" I said to the woman, whose name I thought I remembered as Gabi. "*I confuse Azra with her donkey.*"

Azra shot back a gesture that needed no translation. A few of the villagers laughed, but more looked on perplexed. You'd think they'd never seen a quarrel before.

Gabi tugged on my sleeve. "*Who taught you finger-talk?*"

I almost said, "my boss," but I was on my own now, so I said, "*A Pathfinder.*" Despite the regret I felt thinking about him, I had to smile. In Varisian, the term "Pathfinder" also meant "trouble-maker" or "grave-robber." Many folks back in Egorian saw the boss that way.

"*A Pathfinder visited us last spring,*" said Gabi.

That got my attention. If there was any chance this was the boss's missing Pathfinder, then I owed it to him to figure out what had become of her. "*Where did the Pathfinder go?*"

She pointed out the window, into the black void where the Virlych Mountains blotted out the stars. "*The old village,*" she said, making the sign of the evil eye.

I asked more about the Pathfinder, but mention of the old village had killed the atmosphere. All the locals would tell me before retiring to their own homes was that a strong woman had appeared in the spring, asking the way to the old village. When I asked what she was looking for, the only answer was shrugs and more signs of the evil eye. If I wanted the answer, I'd have to look for myself.

In the morning, I sought out Tudor and asked him about the old village. Understanding him through his speech impediment was still a struggle, but I learned another couple of dozen words in Varisian by trial and error as he told me what he could.

Long ago, the villagers here had lived farther up the mountain. They had once been rich, he said, mining iron from the base of the nearest mountains. Their lord became a hero in the earliest days of the struggle against the Whispering Tyrant, and when he fell, as heroes do, the village was destroyed. That had to have been centuries ago, maybe longer, but history is the boss's hobby, not mine. When I asked Tudor how long it had been, he stretched his arms as wide as he could.

Both of Tudor's arms were now straight as arrows, after Azra performed her healing dance under last night's pregnant moon. The whole village had turned out to watch, and I welcomed the chance to see the ritual from a different perspective. Turns out it wasn't just the delirium of my injuries that made Azra look beautiful as she healed me. Something changed in her when she drew down the power of her goddesses. Her features didn't transform, exactly. She didn't get taller, her hair didn't suddenly become thick and smooth. Her nose was still a stubby little button. But there was something about the way the light moved on her, as if drawing your eye to tiny, common details of any woman that you suddenly realized couldn't get any better than they already were. It was like the moonlight was coming from inside of her.

Yeah, I know. I should sell that line to a minstrel. Maybe I can get a copper.

Whatever her reason, once she got wind of our side trip, Azra demanded to come with us. Tudor loved the idea, so there was no persuading him to slip away with me while Azra doled out balm for warts and tea for menstrual cramps. I thought of a joke about selling love potions in the world's ugliest village, but my sense of self-preservation kicked in before I could utter it. Azra finished her ministrations before noon, and the three of us set off to climb the eastern slope of the Virlych arm of the Hungry Mountains.

The hike took longer than I'd expected. Tudor said it would be only a couple of hours, and maybe it would have been had he traveled alone. There was nothing like a proper foot path, only occasional goat trails that crisscrossed the rough slope. By the time I was ready to abandon my curiosity, we'd committed so much effort to the trek that I kept it to myself until the sun was within a hand's span of the western peaks. I would have turned back then, but Tudor whooped and ran toward a grassy crest.

Over the edge was a plateau that spread a mile north and south, and at least half a mile west toward the base of the next rise. There it ended in a box canyon with walls of red rock. At our feet, smothered in wild grass and wilting flowers, the shattered fragments of a road ran south to north. To the south, the husk of a covered bridge spanned a trickling mountain stream, while on the other side a barren red ridge provided shelter from the north wind. I counted three mine entrances along the base of the cliff, each with a few remaining boards hanging from their open mouths. The village founders had built it within good natural defenses, but none of them had saved it from destruction.

Where the village had stood was now a stony garden of overgrown foundations and the bases of tumbled walls. In the village center slumped a tiered fountain smothered in multi-colored lichen and rippling shelves of bruise-colored fungus that seemed to throb in the afternoon light. When Tudor saw me staring, he clapped and honked with laughter. *"Scared, huh?"*

"How long until dark?" I asked.

He frowned at the sky and held his hands about a foot apart.

Whether that was a couple of hours or a couple of minutes, I decided we had better make it a brief visit. The sky was still bright, but the shadow of the mountain was moving toward us. "What was it this Pathfinder was looking for?"

Tudor beckoned us follow and galumphed off toward the west. Azra tugged at my sleeve and glanced behind us. There, standing at the edge of the road, stood a lone wolf. It looked like one of the Sczarni pack, and judging from its size, I guessed it was Milosh. I greeted him with a smile and a quick shot of the tines.

"They're keeping an eye on us," I said.

Azra signed her objection.

"I don't trust them either," I said. "But maybe they're just looking out for their prince."

She furrowed her brow at the sound of what I'd hoped was my self-deprecating sarcasm, but she said nothing else. When I looked back at the road, there was no sign of the wolf. We ran to catch up with Tudor.

In the shadow of the mountain lay the town's cemetery. The grass was thinner here, much of it hardened into red and yellow swatches. The wind had blown weird shapes into the calcified fronds. In them I saw twisted mouths, bent arms, twined fingers, a tumorous ear, and a dozen other vague fragments of human pain. The wind had plucked up the dead vegetation and balled it up to roll across the ground, rattling like empty birdcages. Here and there were the wounded stumps of ancient trees, their skins long since turned to stone.

The wind brought with it a stench of sulfur. Very funny, I thought. Before I was five years old, I'd had my fill of brimstone jokes, and I sure didn't appreciate receiving another one from an abandoned village. "What the hell is that smell?" I said.

Azra shook her head and waved away the stink. She looked cute as a ladybug, frowning with her freckled nose wrinkled.

"Rock farts!" Tudor cried. He leaped and pointed to the ground by the northern wall, not far from the nearest mine entrance. From one of the many regular scars upon the cliff face, a puff of red dust was visible for a second before it dissolved into the wind. A moment later, another dusty eruption belched forth, followed by the same stench.

"All right," I said. "Let's make this snappy. What was it that the Pathfinder wanted to see here?"

Tudor pointed to the other side of the cemetery where a lone mausoleum stood against the cliff wall.

I walked past the ruins of the cemetery gates. The stone columns had once been carved, but wind had scoured the images to indecipherable lumps and pits. On either side, red stains showed where an iron gate had once hung between them. Similar columns appeared to either side, forming a lonely picket line all the way to the canyon walls.

Tudor did not follow. Instead he pointed to a pile of stones that lay upon a stone column. He took another stone from his pocket and added it to the pile. "I go this far."

Azra and I walked past the gates. She drew the wings of Desna over her heart, and I copied her gesture. Tudor murmured a prayer to Pharasma and clung to the edge of the column, refusing to budge another step.

"You wait here," I told him. "Watch our backs."

He grimaced and bobbed his big head, equal parts ashamed and grateful that I'd let him off the hook.

Only a few of the headstones remained standing. Most leaned toward the east or lay on their faces, half-buried in the earth. I sympathized.

Past the headstones lay weathered tombs, their legends long since erased by wind and rain. Beyond the tombs, built directly into the mountain wall, was a granite mausoleum.

Sheltered by the cliff, the mausoleum had suffered less than the other monuments. I could still make out the harvest images on either side: sheaves of wheat, scythes to harvest them, and scales on which to weigh them. If the boss were there, he might have bored us with a lecture on fertility symbolism of the Ustalav branch of Pharasmin worship. If it meant he were still alive, I would have liked to hear it.

Their shattered wings reduced to rubble beneath them, a pair of angels clung to pillars beside the mausoleum's stone door. Each raised a hand to support the headstone, a hexagonal lozenge bearing a familiar graven face. I showed Azra the coin Malena had given me.

She looked at it with the same dubious expression she had shown before. She compared it to the face on the keystone and looked back at me. The skepticism melted away as she looked back at the coin, then at me again.

"Who is he?"

She shrugged and signed, *Very old coin.*

"Is he a count? A prince? He's on a coin, so he must be a big deal."

Copper, she signed with a dismissive shrug.

"Yeah," I agreed. He must not have been that important to end up on the least valuable coin.

The mausoleum looked like the sort of monument Chelish nobles kept so their descendents could visit and weep over their sarcophagi on the anniversary of their deaths. It was a grim enough custom that I wouldn't be surprised if we'd taken it from the Ustalavs.

What are you doing? signed Azra.

"Looking for a way in."

No, she signed. *Do not disturb dead.*

"Come on," I said. "I'm sure he'll appreciate a little sweeping up, a few prayers from a couple of maybe distant relatives."

No, she repeated. *Sealed. You cannot open.*

She might be right about that, I thought to myself. There were no obvious mechanisms around the door, and even though I had all of my traveling gear, that was more the sort of stuff you use to break into a warehouse office, not a thousand-year-old tomb. Besides, I told myself, I came here to find out about the boss's Pathfinder. If she had come here to investigate this tomb, she must have found a way inside.

Because I'm smarter than I look, I observed before I touched, but there were no indications of a counterweight trigger or even a handhold. I made a circuit of the little building and climbed onto its roof, but except for a trio of narrow window slits shielded by the eaves on either side, I found no portals.

The angel statues were just what they appeared to be, immobile to my prods and pulls. I spotted no signs of rust dripping out from concealed cogs or levers. Eventually I had to admit that nothing short of a wrecking crew wielding picks and hammers was likely to break through the stone door. I tried shoving with my shoulder, pressing hard in every direction against the door. For good measure, I gave the door a kick and immediately regretted it. It was solid as the mountain.

I sighed and leaned against the door, thinking of a way to give up while making it sound like my own idea rather than capitulation. At the first pressure of my hand, I felt a prickling on my palm and the stone door sank into the floor with a dry rasp.

I turned the long way around to face Azra, giving me time to don a confident mask. "You see, sister," I said. "There's nothing I can't open."

She stared into the tomb, eyes wide. I shaded my eyes from the remaining daylight and looked in too. Dust whirled up from every surface, and the floor was unmarked by any print. The interior looked like a little chapel with statues of saints and heroes lining the side walls, all turned to gaze at a stone casket in the altar's position. Weak gray light angled down from hidden slits to fall upon the top of the upright sarcophagus, which was carved in the image of a man holding a golden scepter. The carving of a crown lay at his feet. I didn't realize I was gaping until Azra tugged my arm.

What? she signed.

"Prince of Wolves," I muttered, unsure for a moment whether I was talking to myself or greeting the dead man.

She slapped my arm. I ignored her, thinking she was only going to mock me again, but she kept slapping me until I turned. She pointed behind us, into the graveyard.

Tudor's "rock farts" were appearing at an increasing rate, only now the red dust did not dissipate into the wind. Instead, it accumulated into little clouds that moved about the yard as if seeking something lost. Some disappeared into the ground, while others slipped inside tumbleweeds and wore them like armor. Within moments, more gaseous eruptions had burst from the earth around the tombstones, and the first white fingers of bones poked up out of the earth and kept emerging.

Azra hissed and pulled my arm. A starknife appeared in her hand, and she held it up like a warding totem. Before we had moved more than a few steps into the graveyard, we were surrounded.

None of the restless dead were complete skeletons, and they weren't made solely of bone. Within the red clouds, tiny metal coffin handles, blackened by age, hung suspended beside runny lumps of ground slime eked up from the deep damp. Half a skull hovered in the space a heart might hang in a human body. A tangle of centipedes wriggled in place of a head, one of the insects ringed by a tarnished silver wedding band. The spirits shambled toward us on rattling legs formed of ribs and collarbones.

I whipped a boot dagger at one of the nearest. The blade passed through without so much as changing course. I threw another that nicked a pelvis before spinning away. The spirit did not seem to notice.

"Hurry," cried Tudor, dancing in terror at the edge of the gate. Behind him, I saw the Sczarni wolves creeping toward the cemetery wall.

"Get over here!" I shouted. A dark wolf, possibly Malena, moved toward me. Two others began to follow, but a growl from silverback Dragos stopped them. He sat to watch what would unfold, and the others obeyed his example.

"Should have killed the son of a bitch," I muttered. Azra paid me no attention. She spread a ring of silver ash around us. Her hands moved like charmed cobras, and the ring flared to life, but only for an instant. Before the divine wall could form around us, the red wind whipped through and scattered the sparkling dust.

"What now?" I said.

Azra jerked her head toward the tomb while drawing another spell. She twisted her hands and snapped her palms outward. A ray of silver light shot through the nearest spirit, which sagged like a speared jellyfish and collapsed.

"Tell me you can do that all day long," I said.

Azra shook her head and continued backing into the mausoleum. I drew the big knife and covered her as best I could without getting in the way. She slapped me on the shoulder, and when I turned to look she signed, *Hold door.* She spun into a dance, her feet rising off the ground as she climbed airy steps to the top of the sarcophagus. There she continued her ritual.

"Right," I said, turning back to face the gathering mob. Each of the spirits was a different jumble of dust and mold and bone fragments, and it was hard to see where one ended and another began. Some overlapped as they shuffled forward, and that's the one thing they all had in common: they were coming for us.

I thrust my knife at the nearest spirit. The blade hissed like a hot knife in butter, and the undead thing recoiled for an instant, but then it came on again.

"Whatever you're doing," I called to Azra, "Make it quick."

Golden light filled the interior of the tomb. At the threshold, the spirits hesitated. One oozed out a ruddy tendril that steamed and exuded a strong sulfuric stink as it bathed in the divine radiance. Despite the pain or annoyance or whatever sensation a spirit felt, the thing urged itself forward, slowly at first, but then with more confidence.

"Not enough," I said. "What else you got?"

Azra shot me a look of disgust. With a flourish she gestured at my knife and set it ablaze with silver light. *Help*, she signed.

"Glad to," I growled, slashing at the spirits who pushed in through the open vault. Now my blade sizzled as it cut through their airy bodies. When I hit a bone it snapped, and chunks of greasy matter sloughed off their wounds and bubbled on the tomb floor. I slashed and stabbed like a mad butcher, but still they pressed forward. For every one I put down, they pushed me back a step.

Azra hooted for my attention. She pointed at the peaked ceiling, where more spirits oozed their way in through the window slits. One gassy figure let slip its bones and sod to thump wetly on the floor, then plopped down on top to resume control of its fragments. Azra burned it with another holy ray, but her expression was turning desperate. I didn't think she could do that again, and from the look of it, she didn't know what else she had to fight with.

The undead pressed me back, and I reached over to touch Azra's arm. I gave her a look, but she shook her head.

Then she danced.

The room filled with what looked like fireflies, and wherever they lit, the translucent substance of the spirits crackled and spat.

If we'd had three more like Azra with us, we might have won. But then the fireflies faded.

"I'm sorry," I said. "I shouldn't have—"

For a second I thought it was Azra who had screamed, but the sound came from the tomb entrance, where a blade of blinding light swept like a scythe across the undead. Where the sword touched their rotten remains, it did not just cut but destroyed. The spirits evaporated at its touch, suspended bones blackening and shattering, the muck of graves exploding into puffs of dust.

In seconds the assault was over, and there in the doorway, inexplicably accompanied by a huge dog, stood Varian Jeggare, Count of Cheliax, Venture-Captain of the Pathfinders, and my boss. He choked at the sight of me, and his eyes welled up with tears.

I felt a big mushy sentiment rising up out of my churning stomach, but I swallowed it back down and tried to think of a smart remark. Nothing came to mind.

Chapter Fifteen
Graves

Radovan was naturally dumbfounded by my sudden appearance, but, among its many other benefits, my gentle upbringing has prepared me to face the most unexpected turns of event with grace and aplomb.

Unfortunately, Arnisant, as I had named the hound, did not share my composure, leaping up and barking in excitement. I had to turn my full attention to making him sit, and then I plucked my handkerchief from my sleeve to wipe the ancient grave dust from my eyes before speaking.

"Nice dog," said Radovan. He displayed one of those lopsided grins that had become so rare in the past year or so. It fell short of the full effect of his menacing smile, but it caused Arnisant to lie down by my feet with a whimper.

"I trust you are unharmed," I replied, marveling not only that he lived but that he displayed no obvious signs of injury. The fall from the Senir Bridge alone should have been fatal. Then I noticed the starknife in the hand of the woman beside him. At first glance, she appeared to be a peasant girl, yet she held herself with the confidence one expects from a village elder. Considering the glow of recent consecration that filled the room, I supposed she was a cleric and bowed to her in the Varisian style. "May Desna smile upon you, sister."

She returned my courtesy with a nod. In other circumstances, I might have taken offense at her presumption of the higher status. Perhaps she had little experience with a higher class of people, for she left her introduction to Radovan. "She's Azra," he said. "And the big fellow . . ." His mouth fell open as if to trap a thought that had surreptitiously escaped. ". . . is Tudor."

Radovan rushed from the mausoleum, Azra on his heels. Arnisant and I followed, pausing only to retrieve the satchel I had dropped outside the mausoleum. Nearby, my phantom steed gazed emotionlessly at me. It would not last much longer, so I dismissed it with a thought, and it faded away into the nether.

The light of Galdana's sword had dimmed after it destroyed the last of the restless dead, but as a result of their residue or the lingering spirit of the place itself, the sword still produced enough light to show our way through the broken cemetery.

Just beyond its walls, a group of men and women were donning clothes they pulled from a large, worn satchel. Earlier I had seen only a pack of wolves, drawn there by the holy light and a familiar voice shouting from within. The animals had scattered at my arrival, probably cowed by the sight of Galdana's drawn blade, although Arnisant no doubt prided himself on routing them with his ferocious barking as he ran beside my phantom steed.

Judging from their clothes and the way they displayed their tattoos, I deduced they were Sczarni, the Varisians' particular breed of scum. Worse, adding the clue of their nudity to what I had seen earlier, I realized that we stood among werewolves. I gripped the sword tightly and touched a scroll tucked into my belt. Radovan and Azra approached the Sczarni as if they were familiar with them.

Beside the crumbling gateposts, a pair of naked men menaced an enormous man-child, presumably Tudor. The bullying Sczarni laughed as Tudor cringed, but their demeanor changed when Radovan strode toward them. The elder, a lean man with a fantastic white mane and long moustaches, crossed his arms in a gesture meant to convey nonchalance, but his posture revealed he was anything but confident.

"We caught this peasant spying on you, my prince," said the other man, a thick and hairy fellow with muttonchop whiskers. Despite his insolent tone, Radovan ignored that one and went straight for the old man. He feinted a grab at the throat, but when the Sczarni raised his arms to protect his face, Radovan swept his legs and knocked him to the ground. He followed the man down, striking him full in the chest with his elbow spur. I knew from past experience that Radovan's spurs were not long enough to pierce the heart, but I could not help but wince as the crack of the Sczarni's breastbone echoed throughout the canyon.

Radovan rolled up to his feet and turned his back on the injured man, who lay there wheezing, too stunned to lift his arms to the wound. Beside me, Arnisant lowered his body and growled at the strangers, while Azra hissed in sympathetic pain.

"On the ground, you disloyal curs!" roared Radovan. The other men and women fell to their hands and knees, some remaining half-dressed. While he usually maintained a cool head, I had seen Radovan angry before, fighting for his life and mine, but this time the fury was on him like a halo. "You want to follow me, you damned well come when I call!" he shouted in surprisingly credible Varisian. The rest was a string of such toxic curses as I had not heard since observing my sergeant berate the men during my first campaign in defense of the Empire.

When he had finished, a few among the Sczarni begged forgiveness, while the rest finished dressing or turned away their sullen faces. The old man glowered with barely concealed hatred as Radovan conferred in low tones with a strikingly handsome woman. She appeared to be placating Radovan, whose resistance was obviously crumbling as she maneuvered closer. He has ever been vulnerable to feminine charm.

"What was that about?" I asked Azra.

Long story, she signed, ignoring me in favor of squinting at Radovan's conference with the beautiful Sczarni woman.

"You are a Pathfinder!" I cried.

She released a weary sigh and turned her eyes to the heavens. *No,* she signed emphatically. She pointed into her open mouth, where I saw the ragged stump of her tongue.

"I am terribly sorry," I said, not knowing how else to respond to such a blunt gesture. "I am Count Varian Jeggare."

She nodded. *The dead boss.*

"Fortunately, not yet dead." The equanimity of her reply caused me to wonder how my seeming demise had affected Radovan. Judging from the motley entourage he had accumulated, any mourning he had experienced had not diminished his industry.

Tudor approached Azra, warily avoiding me and the sword I held high like a torch. His protruding forehead was only one of several signs of gigantism, and his childish expression suggested the disorder was accompanied by some degree of idiocy. I lowered the weapon to show I meant no harm, and he stood near Azra, cowering like a bullied child taking refuge behind his mother's skirts. My fleeting empathy vanished when I saw him thrust a finger into his nose. I made a mental note not to let him touch me with those befouled digits.

Radovan returned from his conference with the dark-haired Sczarni woman. "Malena tells me the Sczarni are setting camp by the old village," he said, indicating the area by the ridge with a jerk of his thumb. Near the broken road, they had already built a fire and begun removing a surprising quantity of gear and furnishings from their bag.

They are not afraid? signed Azra.

"They seem more concerned about the cemetery," said Radovan. "Besides, I told them you would curse them all if they left us alone tonight."

You do not command me, she signed.

"It was either that or beat on a few of them," he said. "I figured you could use the rest instead of dancing them back to health all night."

They will turn on you, she warned.

"You're the one who said they'll turn on me only if I show weakness," he said. "While I am strong, they'll treat me like their prince."

Azra set her jaw and lifted her fingers to sign a rebuttal, but instead she sighed and waved away his argument in a gesture of disengagement, not concession. I sensed that she and Radovan had established a history of argument. She turned her back on Radovan and examined Tudor for wounds. I noticed the boy wiping his sticky hand on the chest of his tunic.

I turned away and asked Radovan, "Prince of the Sczarni?"

"Just the werewolf ones, I think," he said.

At least he was fully aware of their true nature, but his willingness to associate with lycanthropes of any sort surprised me. He had nearly died at the hands of a wererat gang during his tenure with the despicable Goatherds.

"Are they the same creatures who attacked us at the Senir Bridge?"

"Same clan," he said. "But the one who led the attack is dead."

"Then why do they follow you now? Surely you must realize they will want revenge."

"Boss, I don't even know where to begin." Before he could continue, Arnisant began to bark somewhere in the graveyard. It began as an alert, but the sounds accelerated and transformed into a howl.

We ran toward the sound, which came from a spot just inside the cemetery walls. Tudor paused at the gate, debating whether to enter the accursed place or remain outside with the Sczarni. By the time we reached Arnisant, Tudor came puffing up behind us, afraid to be left alone among the werewolves. He was not a complete idiot.

Galdana's sword did not brighten, but by its feeble light we saw the hound was reacting to a grave. Despite the weeds and dead wildflowers upon the mound, it was instantly apparent that the grave was months old, not centuries.

"Boss, why did you come here?" asked Radovan.

I indicated the mausoleum. "If I have followed her research correctly, my Pathfinder sought that tomb."

"I hate to say it," he said, and then fell silent because he knew I had observed the same fact that he had upon entering the tomb. Before he and Azra disturbed it, no one had been inside the mausoleum for centuries.

While Arnisant stood sentry outside the vault door, Radovan and I searched the mausoleum. Working side by side with him evoked happy memories of our concerted efforts to unravel the mysteries and intrigues of my peers in Egorian. Besides, focusing on the object at hand distracted me from my dreadful suspicion of what we would find in the cemetery.

Dragos and Cezar grudgingly unearthed the recent grave as penance for failing to come to Radovan's aid earlier. I took advantage of our relative privacy to familiarize Radovan with my experiences at Willowmourn, including my suspicion that Casomir Galdana was a disciple of Urgathoa, the Pallid Princess. In the time since my escape, I had begun to formulate a theory to explain why he had allowed me access to his uncle's library. It was important to him that I continued my research, even after a first attempt presumably went awry, requiring him to have my memory blotted. Somehow he had given his scheme away the first time, before he had gained what he desired from me. It could only be that he too wished to find my missing Pathfinder, or more probably the object of her quest. If so, his object had to be the *Lacuna Codex*, which I knew was connected to his appalling goddess.

Radovan's account of his experiences since the incident on the Senir Bridge distracted me even more than did the contents of the tomb, but the ancient coin Malena had given him was even more intriguing. I agreed with his assessment that the image appeared so similar to the lord on the sarcophagus that they were almost certainly representations of the same man. Even the convergence of those clues, however, led to more questions. If this man were in fact the lost lord of Virholt, it was difficult to reconcile his prominence in the ancient chronicle with interment in this isolated village. If he had been buried with honor, his tomb should be in a more prominent location. Alternatively, if his death at the hands of Tar-Baphon were ignominious, one would expect no memorial whatever. The latter case seemed more likely, considering the dearth of references in the accepted history of Ustalav.

"You say this fellow was lord of the whole region, a king or prince," said Radovan, passing me his talisman. "But this is only a copper."

"Just so," I said. It is my habit to give him a chance to answer his own questions, but I was struck by the image on the coin. "Do you not find this image familiar?"

Radovan frowned. "At first I worried it was just a coincidence Malena was using to scam me," he said. "And then Azra told me I was being a fool about this Prince of Wolves business. But yeah, I've seen a face like that in a few mirrors."

I could only nod agreement. The resemblance was remarkable. Certainly, native Ustalavs share certain recognizable features, but I would be surprised to learn that Radovan was not a direct descendant of the man depicted on the coin. Naturally others, especially the current nobles of Ustalav, would require significantly more evidence.

"Wouldn't a king put his face on a gold coin? Or a platinum?"

"In modern-day Cheliax, that is so. But our empire is richer than other nations, and our mints produce far more gold and platinum coins. In ages past, however, and especially in an agrarian economy like Ustalav's, few of a ruler's subjects often handled a coin richer than a silver."

Radovan said, "They put the king on a copper?"

"In the days of that kingdom, they did. Great lords stamp their images on the coins of the people. Rare coins bear the images of gods and saints, not because of their greater station but because material lords know the value of fixing their own countenances in the minds of their people. The modern counts of Ustalav and even their prince have forgotten the simple wisdom of that tradition, preferring in their vanity to see their countenances on more precious currency."

"So this guy was a big deal after all," said Radovan. "And you think it's more than a coincidence he looks like me?"

"There is a certain ethnic similarity among the noble families of Ustalav."

"You mean inbreeding," said Radovan, not quite bristling at the suggestion.

"Not as such, but of course there are many instances of close marriages to maintain a family line. Obviously, inbreeding cannot be the principal anomaly of your family history."

He raised a suspicious brow, but I showed him my palm as a peace gesture. He nodded acceptance that I had intended no disparagement, and I realized how little I had appreciated our ability to communicate in an abbreviated language of gestures and facial expressions.

"But obviously," I explained, "if there is a familial connection, there must have been an infernal cross at some point. And from what I have read of this Lord Virholt, it is possible the hellspawn branch of your family tree began with him."

Radovan considered the graven image of the ancient lord, frowning as he imagined the same distasteful scenarios that had already occurred to me. I wondered whether Virholt had summoned demonic concubines for his pleasure, or whether he had made a diabolic pact exchanging some service for the intrusion of infernal blood into his mortal lineage.

At the entrance, Arnisant growled a warning. Beyond him, Malena, the dark-haired Sczarni woman, hesitated at the entrance, a pair of goblets in one hand, a tankard in the other.

"Arnisant, down," I commanded. He obeyed, but his hackles plumped his neck.

"Careful, Malena," said Radovan as she slipped past our guardian. "I think that's a wolf hound."

If Malena found his remark humorous, she disguised it well. With one eye on the hound, she set a goblet on the floor and filled the other with dark wine. "You must be thirsty, my lord."

"Indeed," I said, raising a hand to receive a goblet. She flustered me by passing the drink to Radovan instead.

Radovan barely concealed a grin. "Sorry, boss. Princes before counts."

It would have been more amusing had it happened to one of my peers, but considering none of them were present to witness my embarrassment, I let it pass with a forced smile. It was less amusing to observe Radovan's concerned glance as I accepted the second goblet Malena filled. There was no question of my overindulgence while on a mission, and prince of wolves or elephants, he was in no position to pass judgment over a count of Cheliax.

"Whose bones are these?" asked Malena, trailing a finger through the dust on the sarcophagus's surface.

"Don't you recognize him?" said Radovan.

"It is the likeness of Prince of Wolves," she nodded. "But it cannot be."

"Why do you say that?" I asked.

"His last command to my people was carry him to secret tomb, far from any village."

"Where?"

"It was secret," She shrugged. "Those who took him did not return to our people, so the knowledge could not be stolen."

Radovan's rapt expression told me that this was news to him as well. "What else can you tell us about this Prince of Wolves?"

"They say he was born here in mountains," she said, "before the time of the lich, many generations ago. He was a son of the last king of Ustalav. His father and his father's father had hunted us, but he made peace with our people."

"With werewolves?"

"No," she said. "Our people were only human then, wanderers like other Sczarni. It was this prince who gave us the gift of night that we may better fight against the Whispering Tyrant."

"The prince was a werewolf?"

"No," said Malena. "He was a great witch, very powerful."

I was pleased to hear that the oral history supported the written chronicle I had read. "What happened to him?"

"It is not known exactly," she said. "The Whispering Tyrant discovered prince was not loyal to him. He sent warlords into mountains to find him, but not before prince had buried the secrets he had stolen from the lich."

"Why didn't you tell me all this earlier?" said Radovan.

"You spend all your time with the witch Azra," said Malena with an indignant lift of her chin. "I tell you many other things if you wish."

A faint smile crossed Radovan's face, but he brushed off Malena's overture, setting a new precedent in my observations of his interactions with attractive women. Perhaps he was finally adopting a more perspicacious approach to calculated entanglements.

"The question remains," I said, "if the prince is not in this tomb, then who or what is? Is it a lieutenant? A near relation?"

"Maybe he's not here at all," suggested Radovan. "Maybe it's just a trap for the Whispering Tyrant?"

"Ghosts," said Malena. "Better not to open."

Their conjectures were as good as mine, but I could not simply leave the tomb unexamined, not after following the trail so far.

I drank the last of the wine and returned the goblet to Malena. "Thank you for the refreshment," I said. "Now you must leave us to examine the sarcophagus."

She looked to Radovan for permission, and he nodded and returned his goblet. She bowed to him, and after a moment's uncertainty to me as well. She edged past a suspicious Arnisant as she departed.

I turned back to the coffin and saw that Radovan was grinning at me.

"What?"

"Sorry," he said. "I'm still getting used to the fact that you're here, and with some paladin's magic sword. Boss, I'm glad you're not dead."

"The feeling is mutual, I assure you," I said, uncomfortable with his maudlin display. "Now, I believe my associate thought she would find something more than a corpse inside this sarcophagus, some clue as to the arcane secrets Virholt concealed from the Whispering Tyrant." I peered along the seam of the sarcophagus, noting it had been mortared shut. I was more concerned about magical barriers.

"Maybe he hid this stuff for a good reason," suggested Radovan, kneeling for a closer look at the coffin. He had a keen eye, and occasionally he spotted something that I had overlooked.

I murmured agreement.

"Then maybe it's a bad idea to dig it up, eh?"

I could not suppress a weary sigh. We Pathfinders must forever defend our activities against those who do not understand our mission. "It is not so simple," I explained. "While those of my society pursue knowledge for a variety of motives, the majority believe that knowledge should never be lost. Knowledge is never in itself good nor evil, although of course it can be turned to either purpose. For instance, what if Lord Virholt had discovered a means of destroying the Whispering Tyrant, rather than merely containing him as the Crusaders did?"

"If that was the case, why didn't he destroy the lich himself?"

"Perhaps he lacked the resources or the power," I shrugged. "Lacking further evidence, we can only speculate. The point is that we cannot know his motives until we know what he hid. Only then can we decide whether, how, and with whom to share the knowledge. Doing so could save the world great injury on that prophesied day when the Tyrant escapes his prison."

Selecting the appropriate riffle scroll, I triggered it and saw the world as though through a frosted glass, perceiving the aura of every magic effect nearby. Galdana's sword blazed with pale blue divine radiance. The statues and the

vault walls were a wavering yellow, suggesting some min-
gling of weak abjuration and illusion magics. The base of
the sarcophagus, however, roiled with dark red and purple
currents, an active and powerful necromantic aura. The
intensity of the magic was such that the Bishop of Kavapesta
would have requested help from the paladins of Lastwall
before disturbing it.

"Upon reflection," I said, "an esteemed peer recently suggested that the secrets of Ustalav do not welcome premature
awakening." When Radovan raised his eyebrow, I explained
what my cantrip had revealed.

"What about the lid?" he asked, reaching toward the golden
scepter in the statue's hand. "I think this is a separate piece."

"Be careful," I said, shooing his hand away, but then I succumbed to my own curiosity and lay a finger up on its surface.
It was flanged like a Mendevian mace, but its ornate ridges
were far too small to serve as the edges of a proper weapon.
On a sudden impulse, I gripped the scepter and twisted. It
did not budge.

"That would be worth a fat purse to the right fence," said
Radovan.

"Even more to a legitimate collector," I added. "But its
design is curious. It looks more like a key than a weapon."

Radovan moved around the sarcophagus for a better angle
and took hold of the scepter. Even as he leaned forward for
leverage, it slipped easily out of the graven lord's hand.

He looked at me with an apology on his face. "You must
have loosened it for me, boss."

"No," I said, considering what he had told me of his earlier
entrance. "The door to the tomb also opened at your touch,
did it not?"

He nodded.

"And we have ample reason to suspect you may be
descended from the same family as the man interred here. If

so, then this key may open the secret vault, the one to which the Sczarni's ancestors bore their dead prince. Between the key and the presence of an ancestor of the prince, the vault may now be opened."

A spark of greed twinkled in Radovan's eye. "You think there's treasure in this vault?"

"Perhaps," I said. "But knowledge is the treasure we seek."

"Treasure?" said a voice behind us. Dragos appeared in the doorway, naked to the waist, dirty and sweaty. He threw a dirty spade upon the floor and said, "It is done."

Your grave was little more than a shallow ditch covered with a few feet of earth, not even enough to protect your body from the ravages of rain moisture. Only because of your uncommon physiognomy did I recognize your decayed corpse.

"It's a half-orc," said Radovan, with a premature sigh of relief. Then he saw my expression and realized the truth. "Boss, I'm sorry."

The Sczarni had set lanterns around the grave while digging, and by their light I searched for some sign that I was mistaken about your identity. One look at the ring of Cayden Cailean that you were so proud to have won from your peers in Absalom dashed the faintest hope I might have held that some other explorer had met her end here.

Judging from the appearance of your body, I realized you had been dead since before my departure from Cheliax. Knowing my journey had been futile from the start was poor consolation for learning of your death. I still felt as though I had failed you.

The wound upon your throat suggested you had been taken by surprise, and not by the restless dead. Feebly, I hoped that the end had come quickly, since wishing it had never happened was useless. At least your murderer had the decency to bury you, if not well. I stepped into the grave.

"Boss," said Radovan, "let me do that."

"No," I told him. "She was my agent."

When I lifted you in my arms, your journal fell away. I passed your body to Radovan, who laid you gently on the ground. Retrieving your notes, I climbed out, wet and cold from the grave mud, and clutched them to my chest.

"Dig it deeper," I told the surrounding Sczarni. "Six feet."

Dragos snorted. "Dig it yourself, changeling."

"Do it," said Radovan, intervening before I could turn my own ire upon the belligerent Sczarni. "I want it finished before dawn."

Dragos and Cezar stalked away muttering curses, but Malena picked up one of the spades and handed it to another Sczarni woman. Milosh ran to fetch the one Dragos had left in the tomb.

I felt unutterably weary, and Radovan grabbed my elbow to guide me back to the camp. There he helped me undress and covered me in blankets within the Sczarni tent. Arnisant entered, turned around a few times, and settled beside me.

Chapter Sixteen
The Prince of Wolves

I wheeled the phantom steed around the wagon, riding as close as I could to Luminita to see how she'd react. She only tossed her head, but Azra shook her fist at me. It was hard to tell whether she was truly angry, but I didn't care. I was having too much fun. The day was turning out much better than it had begun.

Hours earlier, when I went to the boss just before dawn, he was already awake and dressed. He sat with his back against the tent pole, a span of which glowed brightly enough for him to read. In his lap was the dead Pathfinder's journal. The boss trailed his finger beneath the lines, frowning in concentration as he considered a gap of several missing pages. I spied several such gaps throughout the book, but I let him continue until he raised his head and snapped the journal shut.

"The grave's ready," I told him.

"A moment," he said. He tucked a number of odd little books into his pockets and beneath his belt. He carried the journal and his new sword with him to the graveside.

Azra, Tudor, and about half of the Sczarni awaited us there, while Dragos, Cezar, and two older women finished breaking camp. It was becoming obvious which of the Sczarni resented the oath I'd extracted from them and which hoped that I was, or could be used as, the return of their lost prince.

Still, I didn't understand their motivation for following me, unless some were simply waiting for their chance to put me down. That didn't completely make sense, since I was pretty sure they could have killed me at any time. Malena was the only one who seemed to believe in her Harrow reading, although Milosh and the two young men, Fane and Sandu, went along with her, probably hoping to get under her skirts. Tatiana, the other younger Sczarni woman, was also with them, but I sensed she hoped to snap up Fane or Sandu, whichever didn't make it with Malena. I didn't entirely believe what they'd said about honor and waiting until the next moon to challenge me. I figured it was Azra's presence that ultimately kept them in line. That protection alone was almost worth putting up with the witch's sour disposition.

Azra had covered the body in a makeshift shroud sewn of scraps she had taken from a basket in her wagon. I was glad to see it was not the same amalgamation of children's shrouds she'd used in healing me. She inserted a few handfuls of aromatic herbs into the covering, for which we were all grateful, but the boss stopped her before she could add the final stitches. He lifted the thin fabric and placed his own Pathfinder journal in the dead woman's arms and whispered something over her. Then he nodded to Azra, who sewed it shut.

Fane and Sandu lowered the corpse into the grave with a pair of ropes. They performed the action so smoothly that I could tell they had done it many times before. That tipped the scales away from the Sczarni's eating their dead, but it did little to reassure me of their love and loyalty.

Azra blessed the grave with a series of gestures, and the boss recited a prayer to Pharasma, and then another to Cayden Cailean, the god of drunks, heroes, and happy accidents. I assumed that selection had more to do with the dead Pathfinder's preference than with the boss's propensity for excessive drink, but the thought did cross my mind. What surprised me, however, was when the short ritual concluded, the boss picked up one of the spades and began to fill the grave. After a few throws, I expected him to hand it off for someone else to finish, but he kept going. The Sczarni looked at me for direction, and then Milosh reached for a spade almost as tall as he was. I took it first and helped the boss fill in the rest of the grave. It took us nearly an hour to finish, but then we slapped our hands clean, returned the spades to the Sczarni, and led the pack down the mountain.

After a long silence, the boss and I continued comparing notes about our respective adventures while separated. In a moment when no one else was close enough to overhear, I tried to explain that it was my fault that Vili and his boys had attacked us. The boss brushed it off. I got the feeling he was still too angry to hear about it. It was hard to blame him for that, especially since my bravado had cost the lives of all our hired guards and Nicola. I had never before made such a deadly mistake, and there wasn't anything I could do that would make it any better. Still, I wanted to take my punishment sooner rather than later. The waiting was worse than anything I imagined the boss might do. Weirdly, the worst part was that I wanted to apologize to old bug-faced Nicola. But now I never could.

Seeing that the boss was in no mood to talk more about the past, I asked, "What next?"

He nodded as if he'd been waiting for the question. "I must review my Pathfinder's journal in more detail to deduce what might have been on those missing pages, but the timeline suggests she did not come here directly from Willowmourn. Rather, she traveled south, into Ulcazar."

"The Monastery of the Veil?"

"That seems her most likely destination, although the monks are famously protective of their archives," he said. "Ulcazar has been the neutral ground for most of the civil conflicts since the fall of the Whispering Tyrant. Thus, its libraries have never been sacked. The chronicles it contains could date back to the very founding of Ustalav."

"What are the chances they would let a half-orc—I mean, a Pathfinder, have a look inside?"

"Marginal to nil on either count," he said. "But even if Bishop Senir does not allow me access, perhaps he can tell us more about the nature of her search."

As we approached the village of the freaks, which is how I thought of it even if I didn't dare speak the word in Azra's hearing, the Sczarni halted, even Malena. "We wait here," she said.

"I can't believe you're still scared of the place," I told her.

"We cannot believe you are not scared of it," she said. "I tell the others it is because you are a brave prince."

"But what do they say?"

She flicked her thumb beside her ear. I caught her meaning: crazy.

The freaks greeted us with as much enthusiasm as on our first arrival. Tudor assumed the role of storyteller as he recounted the events of the night he spent in the old village, fighting ghosts with werewolves at our side. Azra gave me a warning look, but I wasn't going to correct him. The villagers had so little else going for them, they needed a bard, even if it had to be a giant, speech-impaired, nose-picking idiot. Actually, after listening for a few moments, I preferred Tudor's story to most of the bard tales I'd heard in Egorian taphouses.

What he lacked in finesse, the big fellow more than made up in enthusiasm.

We stayed only long enough to accept several baskets and jugs of provisions, enough to fill most of the wagon interior. Azra kissed a few ugly babies and gave reassuring hugs to young women who had begged her to pray to Desna that their children should be born free of the worst curses that plagued them. When I heard that, even I had to draw the wings of the goddess on my heart, but I had a feeling nothing was going to get better for these people until they moved out of the shadow of the mountains.

Before we left, Azra showed the boss her folding tinker's table and set him up with a stool inside her wagon. The air had cooled enough that she left only two of the side panels open, giving him a little light and a little shelter from the breeze as he studied his dead Pathfinder's journal. He thanked her, and almost as an afterthought, he took me aside and removed one of his little booklets from his coat pocket.

"Let us try an experiment," he said. Placing a hand on my shoulder, he thumbed the booklet as one might riffle a deck of cards. A stream of deep crimson poured out of the pages and expanded in a cloud before us. Within seconds, the gas contracted to form a large red stallion, complete with bridle and saddle composed of some weird purple material that looked more like mushroom than leather.

"Mount up," he said.

"Are you trying to get me killed, boss?" I said. "You know these things hate me."

"Perhaps not this one," he said, appraising the fantastic horse with a curious expression, as if something about his spell had not come out the way he'd expected.

"Say, you cast a spell!" I said, realizing the importance of the moment. "What about your . . . ? You know. Your little problem?"

"I found a solution in Count Galdana's library," he said, smiling proudly. "Go on." He gestured at the horse.

Luminita's kick hadn't killed me, but this beast looked even stronger than Azra's donkey. I approached it warily, but the conjured horse made no reaction, even when I raised a hand to stroke its neck. Its mane was translucent flame, but I felt no heat as my fingers ran through its silky hairs. The beast lifted its head and blew, but I heard no sound even as I felt its cool breath upon my hand.

"Do not dawdle," said the boss. "It will not remain with us all day."

I'd seen it done many times before, but getting my foot in the stirrup and throwing my leg over the horse's back was harder than it looked. I ended up climbing awkwardly up, finally managing to get myself in the saddle and take the reins. It occurred to me then that I had no idea how to command one of these things. I slapped the reins as I'd seen riders do, and the horse bolted. I hung on for my life, the boss's laughter vanishing behind me. I looked back to see Azra scolding him with a gesture, but whatever he said in reply made her join his laughter.

I had an impulse to run ahead and show the Sczarni my new steed, but instead I pulled on the reins and turned back toward the wagon. I'd endangered them both enough already, so I wanted to stick close to Azra and the boss. Besides, riding circles around the wagon was good practice in steering. As a bonus, it unnerved Luminita and annoyed the hell out of Azra.

It was going to be a very good day.

The boss hadn't warned me exactly when the phantom steed would vanish, so when it slowed and stopped beside the wagon, I first kicked its flanks to get it moving again. It turned its face to gaze at me, and then my ass hit the ground.

At least everyone else got a laugh out of it. Azra hooted along with the Sczarni, and even Luminita brayed in triumph at the fall of her tormentor. I noticed Dragos and Cezar were among the few who did not so much as crack a smile at my misfortune, and it occurred to me that it wasn't the best idea to clown around in front of the malcontents. It might give them ideas.

Despite the anti-Radovan faction, the Sczarni set up a splendid camp that afternoon. They ringed the fire pit with carpets and cushions, and at Malena's behest they broke out the box drums and tambourines. Cosmina, one of the old women, cajoled Dragos to fetch his fiddle. When that failed, the older one known only as Baba set her eye upon him, and he grudgingly fetched the instrument. He tuned the strings and played a few sorrowful fragments as the rest of his family prepared for supper, which they began cooking when Milosh, Fane, and Sandu returned naked from the hunt, each carrying three or four hares. When I finished helping Azra unhitch the wagon, we brought a basket of carrots and squash to Baba and Cosmina, who shooed us away as they prepared the food. The boss remained rapt in his examination of his late colleague's journal, making notes in a fresh book of his own in between outbursts of self-recrimination for leaving his previous journal in the grave. It was good to see he was not immune to rash decisions.

He looked like he needed a break, so I fetched the most potent weapon on hand to entice him out of the wagon. I popped the cork from one of the jugs the freaks had given us and took a deep sniff. It was mead, and not half bad.

The boss raised his head as he caught a whiff. "How is it?" he asked. I poured some into a leather jack that had been hanging from the wagon ceiling and offered it to him. He gestured that I should sip it first.

"You don't pay me to be your taster," I said, but I tried it anyway. It was thick stuff, sweet but not very strong. I shrugged and passed it to him. "It's all right."

He sampled it and made a sour face. "Ghastly," he declared.

I reached for the jack, but he pulled it back. "I'll finish it," he said, turning back to his notes. I returned to the campfire, where three rabbits were roasting over the fire as Cosmina spitted three more to replace them. I dropped onto the carpet beside Azra, but she got up the moment I opened my mouth to speak.

Fine, I figured. I had only wanted to ask her why she decided to accompany us to the Monastery of the Veil. We hadn't talked all day, so I assumed something had passed between her and the boss after we left the village of the freaks. If she wouldn't tell me, I'd have to ask him later.

Malena settled down next to me, cozy as a cat. "The witch does not like you," she said.

"I'm getting that impression."

"I like you."

What she lacked in subtlety she made up for with a swell delivery. Her low voice put a thrill at the back of my throat.

"That's a pretty good start to mending my broken heart."

"She broke your heart?" Malena said so seriously I almost laughed.

"No, sweetheart," I told her. "Don't you know hellspawn don't have hearts? That's what makes us so hard to kill."

Milosh brought me a bowl of stewed vegetables and roast rabbit fresh from the spit. I decided I could get used to having servants and sycophants, but old habits kicked in. "Take this to the boss, kid."

He looked perplexed. *"But you are boss."*

I liked being called that, but it didn't change my mind. "Not your boss, kid. My boss." I pointed at the wagon. "Fetch me one on the way back."

Still confused, he ran off to obey. Malena plucked at my open jacket and found a hole in the shirt beneath.

"I think it is the prince's blood," she said, drawing the shape of a heart over my breast. "It makes you powerful enough to gather all the wolves of our land, all the scattered clans of our people. Maybe strong enough to one day to rule all of Ustalav."

"Sorry, princess," I said. Her eyes lit up at the word, and I knew which of my fine parts most interested her. She fancied my hypothetical principality. I gently removed her hand from my chest, not that I didn't like the way it felt there. "I've already got a job."

She frowned, but it was just for show. "That is not your true calling," she said. "The Harrowing was true. Long has it been said that the heir of the Prince of Wolves would one day return to Ustalav and reunite the Sczarni families."

"Tell me more about this prince," I said. This addition of the "heir" could have been her way of elaborating her original scam to make it seem more plausible. Still, the boss had told me the fellow his Pathfinder had been seeking was some traitor who had surrendered his land to the Whispering Tyrant. That didn't sound half so romantic as the Prince of Wolves, and if they were one and the same, I wasn't so sure I wanted to be related.

I saw the boss emerge from the wagon, bowl in one hand, drinking jack in the other. I could tell by the weight that he'd refilled the leather tankard with mead. When he came to the fire to sit beside Azra, she noticed it as well. She took it from his hands and drank it half down while he stared at her, astonished. She returned it to him and wiped her mouth with the back of her hand.

The witch had her good moments.

"Our babas tell the story best," said Malena. "But you still have not enough Varisian to hear it from Baba, I think."

"I'd rather hear it from you," I said, trying to make up for rebuffing her advance.

She smiled. "It was after the fall of the Last King of Ustalav," she said. "Among those who resisted the Tyrant were the three princes whose names their father buried lest his adversary learn to conjure with them."

"So the Prince of Wolves was not the last king of Ustalav?"

"Listen to the story," said Baba, who had been eavesdropping all this time. She filled another bowl with grilled vegetables and laid half a roast rabbit on top before handing it to Milosh, who brought it to me.

"The eldest prince was a great warrior, and the queen his mother gave him a blade blessed by the goddess Pharasma," said Malena. Her voice assumed the rhythm of a tale learned by repetition. "Its slightest touch would destroy the restless dead. But when he faced the Whispering Tyrant in battle, he could not come close enough to strike his foe. The adversary cast a mighty spell that boiled the warrior's blood within him, taking the sword as his trophy."

I saw the boss lean forward, offering Malena's tale his rapt attention.

"The second prince was a bishop of Pharasma. His mother gave him a mace invested with the power of all the bishops of the land, who knelt to kiss the hem of his garments when he summoned them. He led their greatest paladins and clerics in the first crusade against the Tyrant, which men have since forgotten, to their shame. Again the adversary hurled spells from afar, shredding the flesh of the noble soldiers with fragments of their own shattered bones.

"The third prince was a witch, and the queen had no gift for him. His mother was a devil sent by the Whispering Tyrant years earlier to seduce the king, but instead she had come to love him and bore his son. The child was given to the Sczarni, whom the king had promised lands of their own in return for raising the boy to adulthood. After the death of the queen's sons, the king acknowledged his son and charged him to fight the adversary. Instead, the prince fled into the countryside.

"The king and all his folk believed the prince a coward, and yet the Prince foresaw his father's death and strove instead to wage a secret war against the Tyrant. First he bestowed the gift of fang and claw upon his foster family, although his mother's lineage prevented him from sharing it with them. In his service, they slipped through the forests of Ustalav and stole into the secret places where the Tyrant stored his greatest wealth, the artifacts of ages past, the spells of ancient wizards, and secrets the gods whisper in the vast darkness that aches between the stars."

She paused, and we waited silently for her to continue. When it became clear that she had finished, I asked, "What happened to them?"

"Someone betrayed the prince," she said. Her eyes moved toward Dragos, but she stopped short of looking directly at him. "One of his people."

"That's some story," I said, but when I looked over at the boss, I saw him squeezing the bridge of his nose as he often did when comparing disparate clues to assemble into a conclusion. I had been ready to scoff at the story, as Azra did, but if he was taking it seriously, maybe I should do the same.

"It is a lie," said Dragos. "A fairy story for children, not for men. Tell them, Baba."

Baba ignored him.

"Tell them!" he demanded. She turned her back on him and reached for my bowl. I handed it over, and she refilled it before passing it back.

"Bah!" Dragos spat. He stalked away from the fire. This time no one followed him, not even Cezar.

Chapter Seventeen
Monastery of the Veil

The Monastery of the Veil must have been conceived by an architect whose dramatic instincts rivaled those of Velasco Morova, who remained the Chelish Opera's most celebrated set designer more than eighty years since his death at the hands of a mob of House Thrune supporters.

With three tiers of turrets rising smoothly out of the highest peaks of Ulcazar, the Monastery was as much a testament to the genius of its engineers as to the daring of its creator. During both the six-hundred-year reign of the Whispering Tyrant and the centuries of civil strife that followed, the Monastery had remained inviolate, a sanctuary for devotees of Pharasma and a treaty ground for warring counties. Today, even direct rivals of Count Senir deferred to his status as Bishop of Ulcazar and Master of the Monastery.

I am loath to describe our return to the Senir Bridge, even in this new journal whose pages are for my eyes alone. There were other paths that would have led us to the Monastery, but even the best of them would have taken us much longer to traverse, and I could not be certain that any of them would accommodate Azra's decrepit wagon. It was a tinker's shop on wheels, yet she was no tinker. And although the sweet and pungent aroma of the herbs she kept within the cabin ameliorated the effect, I could still detect the pong of mold within the floorboards. For the favor of conveying me to our destination, upon returning to the Vaults of Abadar in Caliphas, I should gladly pay her to have a new cart built. Such thoughts returned my mind to the loss of my cherished carriage, memories even more unpleasant than facing the reminder of the attack on the bridge.

In daylight, the bridge looked far less sinister than it had while under pursuit. There were signs of recent repair, as fresh limestone blocks had replaced those that had presumably been dislodged by the fiery blast, whether cast by my forgotten self or, more likely, invoked by some other force. I noticed blackened stone blocks among the fresh ones, their positions suggesting that the blast might have come from beneath the bridge, not merely beneath my carriage. Judging from that evidence alone, it was all but certain that the explosion had been prepared in advance of our arrival.

As we crossed the bridge, I peered down at the river below us through the open panels of the wagon. The drop was well over one hundred feet, leaving me no conceivable hypothesis for Radovan's survival of such a fall. Granted, I had always valued his durability above his fighting prowess, although the latter was not inconsiderable, yet I had to agree with him that it was a miracle he had survived. Either Desna favored him far more than even he liked to boast, or else some other force had shielded him from destruction.

I was relieved that the Sczarni had refused to accompany us up the mountain, even before I could raise the subject of leaving them behind rather than ask the Bishop to harbor such scum. Whether the werewolves awaited us upon our descent or not, I did not care. Or rather, I could not decide which outcome I preferred. If they could be trusted, they could prove formidable allies in our search for the cache of Lord Virholt, yet it was the height of folly to trust them collectively. I had no doubt that Dragos and Cezar fomented rebellion every moment they were out of sight of Radovan, and while her attentions suggested she curried my bodyguard's favor for her own purposes, Malena's motives could range from gaining influence over their "prince" to subverting his judgment or even insinuating herself closely enough to assassinate him at a weak moment. For his part, Radovan could not always be trusted to make sound judgments in feminine matters, and Malena was beautiful in her coarse manner.

Thus we arrived at the gate to the monastery with only Azra driving the wagon and Arnisant padding loyally beside the wheels. I had weighed the impropriety of allowing Radovan to arrive mounted on the phantom steed while I sat beside Azra, but he so delighted in riding the beast that I could not deny him the pleasure. It was also fascinating to observe the difference in the animal that I summoned for myself and the monster that appeared when I conjured it for him. Variations in appearance were possible in the spell, but I had made none consciously. My earliest experiments with the spell were unfortunately limited by my peculiar handicap, but I saw now that it seemed to react not to the desires of the caster but to some unspoken requirement of the recipient.

Secretly, I also enjoyed the way Radovan had earlier charged through the Sczarni from time to time, scattering them and evoking whoops from those who felt loyalty or feigned it, and scowls from those who rankled under the yoke of his usurpation. I wonder whether he did so for the very reason of flushing out his opposition from his supporters. His mind is certainly keen enough to devise such a ploy, even though his street manners often conceal the full extent of his intellect.

I expected I would rely upon his observation and insight to supplement my own as we entered the Monastery of the Veil. The gates did not immediately open at our approach, but a sentry from each of the flanking towers eyed us silently, crossbows visible but not yet aimed at us. We heard no alarm, no cries of challenge, and I knew there would be none. Every monk in the order was sworn to an absolute vow of silence, not only forgoing speech but also treading barefoot or in soft slippers to avoid disturbing the world with the sound of a footstep. Their devotion was to the unspoken wisdom of Pharasma, Lady of Graves, the keeper of every mortal soul's last secrets until She had judged and disposed of each upon his dying day. The only member exempt from the proscription against noise was their leader, the Bishop of Ulcazar, also known as Count Senir.

The Bishop arrived in the time it took for us to dismount and stretch our legs. I had cautioned my companions to leave the talking to me, which elicited a shrug from Radovan and a dismissive snort from Azra. I barely stopped myself from apologizing for a remark that could be construed as insensitive to her mute condition. Over the past few days, she had demonstrated no courtesy deserving of special consideration from a peer of Cheliax.

When Senir emerged from the gate door, I bowed in Ustalavic fashion. "Your Excellency," I said, as quietly as possible without resorting to a whisper.

"Count Jeggare," he said, hesitating before returning the bow correctly, if not lavishly. "Your arrival is an unexpected honor."

"Forgive me for intruding upon the solitude of your monastery," I said. "I seek knowledge that may lie within your archive."

"You must already know that our library is not for common use."

"I assure you that it is for no common reason that I make my request," I said.

He smiled with just a trace of condescension. "What I mean, Count Jeggare, is that even the lords of Ustalav are prohibited from viewing our archives without great cause. And you, of course, are not of our land."

Frustrated but not yet deterred, I resorted to my backup plan. "In that case, Your Excellency, perhaps you will allow me, as a guest of Prince Aduard, to inquire about a visitor you received earlier this year."

"We have received no visitors apart from pilgrims and votaries conveying offerings from their villages."

"I believe there was one unusual visitor early this past summer," I said. "My colleague, a Pathfinder."

"You must be mistaken," said Senir. The firm line of his jaw betrayed his impatience.

"I do not think so, Excellency," I said. "You see, I recovered her journal, which notes a visit on the twelfth day of Gozran. Perhaps you were absent during her visit."

He hesitated, frowning. "I am often away attending county matters," he said. "In my absence, my brothers often experience difficulty communicating with visitors unfamiliar with our customs."

"Of course," I said. "Then would you please allow me to examine your day books, or to interview those who were present?"

"Let me be direct with you, Jeggare."

"I welcome it."

"You are a friend to Countess Caliphvasos, so I have been more lenient than I might otherwise incline, but these Pathfinder activities of yours are intrusive at best, more often provocative or even criminal. Our people revere the past as highly as we do our ancestors. We do not welcome those who wish to disturb our ghosts, which after centuries of struggle are legion. Those intruders who survive their adventures leave us Ustalavs to endure the disruptions they have caused."

"Your Excellency, I assure you my intentions—"

"Your intentions, Count Jeggare, are irrelevant. Your actions are what concern me. Were not four members of your Pathfinder Society hanged in Barstoi for graverobbing last year?"

"I was unaware—"

"And were you yourself not expelled from the capital of Katapesh for trafficking in stolen statuary?"

I was surprised that he had heard of that matter. "It was not formally an expulsion but a request from the ambassador that I—"

"And does not the house of my neighbor and friend Count Galdana stand occupied by the forces of the Bishop of Kavapesta since your recent visit?"

"I only wished—"

"And are you not the owner of a red carriage that was seen approaching the Senir Bridge shortly before a catastrophic explosion that required costly and dangerous repairs lest the road from Kavapesta to Caliphas be severed?"

"Count Senir, I offer you my word—"

"I am Bishop Senir in this place," he said evenly. "And I caution you not to offer your word as a Pathfinder."

"No, Your Excellency," I said. "I offer you my word as a gentleman that I have come to your lands as no mere treasure hunter. As for any disruptions that have occurred in the wake of my travels, I beg your pardon.".

"I would rather you beg your leave, Venture-Captain."

He could not have made his feelings more clear, and loath as I was to offer further offense to such a prominent noble of another country, I was not ready to slink away defeated. I drew the spiral of Pharasma upon my breast and said, "In the name of the Lady of Graves, I request the shelter of your roof and provisions for another day's journey."

A snarl flickered on his lips, but the expression melted into a grudging smile. "You have learned our customs well, Count."

"Yours is a great nation, Bishop. I have studied its culture and history with great admiration."

"You will have a night's shelter and provender for your servants and beasts. But at dawn you must leave us and make no further requests for another year."

I bowed again. "Understood, Your Excellency. I thank you for your hospitality."

Unfortunately, Senir's hospitality did not extend to offering me a room, so after a few hours performing certain precautions with my battery of riffle scrolls, I left the wagon to Azra and sat near a central bonfire on the flagstones of the inner courtyard. It had been hours since we broke our fast, and Radovan and I fortified ourselves with strips of venison from the previous night's werewolf-caught feast. We took turns sharing our meal with Arnisant.

Shortly after noon, one of the silent monks approached. He was shrouded from head to toe in funereal gray, and he beckoned to me and Radovan.

"Both of us?" I asked.

The monk nodded assent. Radovan rapped on the wagon wall to inform Azra of our absence, and we followed the monk into the monastery. We passed through a refectory lit so dimly that the dining brothers appeared as disembodied heads floating above their bowls. Their wooden spoons made not the slightest sound when dipping into their soup, nor did the monks utter so much as a slurp.

We climbed a spiral staircase past two defensive points through which defenders could fire upon the narrow approach to the monastery, which was as much a fortress as a sanctuary. Upstairs, past an untended scriptorium, we entered the bishop's parlor.

"Count Jeggare," Senir rose from behind a simple table on which lay an open inventory of monastic comestibles. It occurred to me only then that managing the business of a county, however small, in addition to that of a monastery, however simple, may well have contributed to the bishop's short temper.

"Your Excellency," I replied.

He drew a breath and held it a moment, as if reluctant to speak the words he had prepared for my arrival. He said, "I regret the inhospitable welcome I offered earlier."

"And I have no desire to impose upon your duties."

"I have asked my brothers about your Pathfinder. As you expected, she did visit this past spring. However, she received only a day's shelter before continuing north toward Kavapesta."

"Are you certain?" I asked.

"My brothers live by the utmost discipline," he said. "Along with their vow of silence, they are dedicated to perfection in mind and action, as well as absolute obedience."

"I thank you, Excellency," I said. Considering what I had discovered about the likely date of my Pathfinder's death in the Virlych Mountains, I knew that what he said could not be true. Moreover, even if I had not already decided that his was an exact and controlling mind, the evidence of the detailed ledgers before him weighed heavily against the prospect of a visitor arriving without his knowledge.

"As you can see, your Pathfinder has left you a circular trail," said Senir. "You cannot discount the likelihood that, upon her return to Kavapesta, she recognized that she had exhausted her local resources and returned to Caliphas, and then out of Ustalav entirely."

I sighed and lowered my head to pinch the bridge of my nose. After a pause I judged sufficient to offer the impression of reluctant resignation, I lifted my head and said, "Of course you are correct, Excellency. I have simply invested so much effort in my inquiries, you must understand how difficult it is to let go of loose ends."

"I suppose that is one of the disadvantages of the inquisitive mind, Count Jeggare."

We exchanged bows, and Radovan and I followed a novice out of the parlor and down the steps. I caught Radovan's furtive look and glanced at his feet, our sign to wait for privacy before asking questions. We walked in silence until the unmistakable sound of a whipping from the courtyard caused us both to quicken our pace. The sharp snap of leather was a startling interruption to the serenity of the monastery. Our accompanying novice did not try to stop us, and we pushed open the refectory doors to a startling scene in the courtyard.

Beside the bonfire, stripped entirely naked, a monk knelt of his own volition while one of his brothers raised a lash to strike again. Already the penitent monk's back was flayed raw, blood streaming down his legs to puddle on the courtyard stone. Across from us, Azra stood before a pair of monks who blocked her from reaching the object of the punishment. She looked to me, then to Radovan. Her eyes implored us to intervene, but I shook my head "no." Here in the seat of his authority, it was worse than futile to interfere with the bishop's commands.

"Boss," whispered Radovan. I followed his chin to the base of the bonfire, where the distinctive spine of my lost Pathfinder's journal blackened in the heat. The pages had already curled to ash. I could not help but bristle at the violation of her last written words, but I controlled my anger.

"We shall leave now," I said.

Radovan turned to Azra and signed, *Where were you?*

Puzzled, she indicated a pail of water and replied, *Well.*

"Damn it," hissed Radovan. "It was all a diversion to get us away from the journal."

"Never mind that," I said. "Hitch the donkey. There is nothing more we can gain here."

We spoke no more while we secured the wagon and drove out of the monastery gate, all three of us squeezed onto the driver's seat since Radovan had dismissed his phantom steed. Twice he began to question me, but I raised a hand for patience. An hour after we had crossed the Senir Bridge, I deemed it safe enough to pause and entertain questions. We climbed down from the wagon, and I stretched my legs with a walk around the wagon while Radovan unhitched the donkey and Azra placed the water pail before the beast.

Sorry, signed Azra as I finished my circuit of the wagon. She was clever, and I sensed she had a reasonable picture of what had happened.

"It's not your fault, sister," said Radovan.

I did not say it was my fault, she signed indignantly.

"It is no one's fault," I said before they could get started. "I realized the moment we put ourselves in his custody that Bishop Senir might take exception to my continued investigation."

"If you knew they might destroy the journal," said Radovan, "why did you risk going there?"

"Because there was much to learn while he felt we were in his power."

What? signed Azra. *What did you learn?*

"Not a damned thing," said Radovan.

"On the contrary," I said. "We learned several things."

"This is where he makes us guess," sighed Radovan.

"In other circumstances, that exercise might prove educational, but we must not tarry. There is every chance that Senir has sent agents to follow us."

Radovan glanced back along the road. "I was keeping my eyes peeled and saw nothing."

I nodded and opened the wagon door, climbing in. "If they have, as Senir boasts, devoted their lives to perfection in thought and deed, then I should be surprised if they allowed us to spot them so soon."

"All right," said Radovan. "Back to what you learned."

"First, we learned that Bishop Senir was aware of my Pathfinder's death."

"You told him she was dead, didn't you?"

"No," I said. "I told him only that I had her journal."

"Then maybe he just assumed—"

I turned a disappointed gaze upon him, and he relented.

"The Bishop is not the sort of man to assume," he said. "Observing his reaction to my mention of the journal, I noted his surprise. He had expected me to report that I had found her body."

"I don't know, boss," said Radovan. "That's a pretty big guess, unless one of your spells lets you read minds."

"Never," I said. I felt an involuntary shudder at the mention of thought-reading spells. While employing them would render many aspects of my avocation much simpler, the inherent violation was abhorrent. "The Bishop also lied about the direction she took when leaving the monastery. Despite the missing pages in her journal, it was clear that she did not return to Kavapesta. To reach the old village where we found her remains by the likely time of her death, she had to have descended westward from the monastery."

"Why lie?"

"My working theory is that he ordered her murder."

Radovan made a low whistle, appreciating the magnitude of our challenge if the Bishop were opposed to our efforts. "But why not kill her while she was in the monastery, completely under his power? It's not as if anyone there was going to talk."

I frowned at his jest but said, "Probably he wanted to see where she would go and discover who else she would question about her search."

Radovan nodded, letting the thoughts steep in his mind. He burst out, "That still doesn't make a bit of sense. You said Casomir was the one who helped you follow the Pathfinder's trail. Besides, if Senir wanted whatever she was searching for, why bury the journal?"

"Aha," I said. With a glance at Azra for permission, I unlatched the tinker's table and lowered it into place. "Now you have touched the crux of the matter. Senir did not want the journal found. The agent who threw it into the Pathfinder's grave was meant to put it beyond all mortal eyes. Thus, he was punished after Senir learned that it survived, and the journal was destroyed rather than merely hidden."

"But he had to know you would see the journal in the bonfire," said Radovan.

"I agree."

"Why do it?"

"As a courtesy between gentlemen," I said, placing one of the two remaining blank folios upon the tinker's table. "Bishop Senir offers me the opportunity to turn back before our direct conflict becomes inevitable."

"We might as well go back," said Radovan. "That journal was the last clue we had to follow. Unless you've somehow managed to memorize it."

He knew perfectly well that my memory, while excellent, is far from eidetic. I had another advantage, however, that he could not possibly know. I held up a riffle scroll with a flourish and said, "Better than that."

Azra and Radovan exchanged a puzzled glance, rewarding my dramatic presentation. Holding the scroll beside the blank pages, I thumbed it to life. Gradually, the pages filled themselves with characters, all in the flawless handwriting of my late colleague. I released the breath I had been holding, grateful and relieved that the magic retained the contents of the journal even after the original had perished in the bonfire.

"That's fantastic, boss!" said Radovan. Even Azra nodded in appreciation of the powerful spell.

I turned the folio pages to admire the exact replica of the contents of the book I had stolen. As I reached the reproduction of the pages that had been torn away, I discovered the true power of the steal book spell. Where there should have been blank sheets lay the missing contents of my late Pathfinder's journal, including sketches of the Lord of Virholt, several explicit mentions of the *Lacuna Codex*, and rough maps of the area beyond the tomb beside the old mining village.

I placed my finger upon the X she had used to designate the site of her next visit. It lay deep within the borders of forbidden, haunted Vyrlich.

Chapter Eighteen
The Starknife

The boss and I agreed not to discuss what we had learned in front of the Sczarni. He also brought Azra into his confidence, eliciting a promise to keep the events at the Monastery secret from the Sczarni only after he'd filled her in. The way he spoke to her made me feel—well, not jealous, really, but irritated. He and I had worked together for years before he trusted me enough to explain his plans, but after only a few days he was treating Azra as if she was one of his Pathfinders, despite the fact that she'd made it clear she wasn't one. Maybe he fancied her, I thought, but that thought annoyed me even more. After all his sniffing and snobbery about fashion and food and the opera and fine manners, he'd be nothing but a hypocrite to cozy up to a hedge witch.

We stopped briefly at the nearest village, but only for fresh water. The boss consulted the head man for a few minutes, asking him questions I wasn't close enough to overhear. Whatever it was, he didn't figure it was important enough to share with me. I watched to see whether he told Azra what he'd learned, but he didn't.

The Sczarni waited where we'd left them, beside a stand of trees not far from a brook west of the village. I was torn between relief that I wouldn't have to help build a camp from scratch and mild disappointment that they hadn't wandered off. I was still conflicted about the Prince of Wolves situation. The feeling that it would somehow end badly for me kept gnawing at my imagination. In the meantime, the benefits were all right. I could get used to being served first, and I didn't mind the attention Malena was showing me, even if she were nothing more than a ruthless conniver. Maybe tonight she'd dance, if Dragos could be persuaded to play a lively tune.

As it turned out, Dragos couldn't be persuaded. He sat with Cezar, in sight but out of hearing of the rest of the camp. They were having an argument that included a lot of pushing and arm waving. I'd find out what it was about and which way it had gone soon enough, I figured, but I kept an eye on them. This was the part of being prince that was going to cost me sleep.

After supper, Azra set up the boss in the wagon, and he used another of his riffle scrolls to set a flameless light above the tinker's desk to study the restored journal in detail. With his hound at his feet and Azra nearby, I decided to risk a short stroll around the camp. Dragos and Cezar had returned to the fire and had their bowls to their faces.

I hadn't finished my first circuit of the perimeter before Malena approached. She greeted me with that welcoming smile I'd first figured meant she was angling for my purse. Maybe she still wanted that, but she'd also set her sights higher. No matter what there'd been between her and Vili before, she hadn't wasted any time mourning for him. And after I held Dragos's life in my hand, there was a new leader of the pack to cozy up to. I had no illusions that she fancied me for myself, but there was only so much harm in letting her let me think otherwise. I had it all figured out.

Without a word, she slipped her arm through mine and walked beside me. She slouched to reduce our height difference, but that didn't matter to me. Ever since I was a kid, I've liked climbing the tall trees. I started looking for a place where we could enjoy some privacy without losing sight of the camp. She found one first and pulled me down onto the cool evening grass.

Her lips were soft as petals, leading me in while letting me feel I was the one choosing the path. She untied my jacket and peeled it off before I felt what she was doing. She guided my hands to the strings of her blouse and found the tongue of my belt before I'd finished untying her sash. Impatient, she pulled off her blouse and had grasped the belt of her skirt when the first blow struck my head.

"Dammit, Dragos," I growled while rising. But it was not Vili's father who'd kicked me in the head. I looked up to see Azra, and then her foot as it struck my cheek. Off balance, I fell backward with my pants around my knees.

Beside me, Malena scrambled away, heedless of her fallen blouse. I admired the view for half a second before a fine coat of fur emerged from her pale skin, her breasts shrinking as her chest stretched wide and lean. The shape of her face had barely changed, but her teeth jutted from her jaw, altering her voice as she growled. "Get away, witch, or you'll lose more than your tongue."

Azra's eyes lit up with anger. She snapped her wrists as I'd seen her do once before, and I winced as Malena flinched away from a white spark upon her cheek. I knew how much that stung.

"Take it easy," I suggested to both of them.

"What we do is none of your concern," spat Malena, raising a furred hand that had grown long claws.

Azra answered with another spark, this time stinging Malena's menacing hand.

"Knock it off, both of you," I said. But when they both turned blazing eyes on me, I shut up.

"He is our prince, not yours," said Malena. "You would not even know what to do with a man, if you could find one who could endure your ugly face."

Azra's cheeks colored as though she had just been slapped.

"And even if you had a tongue," Malena continued, "you would only use it to drive him away with your scolding."

Azra opened her mouth, screeching as she flung more sparks at Malena. One broke a few strands of her hair, while another snapped the golden loop out of the werewolf's ear. Malena shrieked this time, turning away to cover her face. A second later, she turned her furious countenance back to Azra, wolf eyes peering over a snout full of sharp teeth.

Flinging one hand above her head, Azra produced a starknife and hurled the blade at Malena's feet. It sunk deep into the earth, two blades protruding less than an inch from Malena's toes as faint white sparks coruscated along the surface of the steel.

Malena froze in place, and a moment later her wolfish features retreated. A tiny rivulet of blood ran down her cheek from one of Azra's stings, and her eyes flicked nervously between the knife and Azra. She considered her options, tensing to fight or flee. In a moment she made her decision. She snatched up her blouse and ran into the nearby trees, out of sight.

"What—?" I said, but Azra turned her back on me and walked back to camp, brushing past the boss, who had run up to investigate the commotion. When he saw the starknife in the ground nearby, his lips trembled in a war between laughter and restraint.

"What?" I demanded again, but at the sight of me with my pants down, he lost all composure and set to laughing into the crook of his elbow. It was too much to smother, and he let it go and howled to the sky. I couldn't think of a time when I'd seen him so violently amused, and knowing I was the object of his mirth made it difficult for me to share it. I put my clothes back in order while he got control of himself.

"You see," he began, but he wasn't ready yet, and his explanation dissolved into tears and laughter. I began to stomp back to camp, but he called out, "No, it's important." I waited for the explanation.

"When two Varisian women of similar social status compete over a man," he said, "there is a protocol—" The laughter took him again.

"Dammit, boss," I said. "I saw what happened. What does it mean?"

He wiped his eyes with his handkerchief before looking me in the face and saying, "Radovan, my dear fellow, you are engaged to be married."

The boss was the only one who found the situation amusing, but he lost his good humor when he saw that Azra had retreated to her wagon, shutting herself in with all of the books he'd hoped to continue studying. Watching him stand beside the door debating whether to intrude was small comfort as I sat near the campfire. Eventually he returned to the fire and stood beside me, looking down at Azra's starknife on the carpet beside me.

The way the boss explained it, if I returned the knife to Azra, I was saying I accepted her claim over me. If I gave it to Malena instead, then they would fight over me, although not usually to the death, he explained. While that thought evoked a certain naughty pleasure, I didn't want to see either of them hurt.

The third option was that I keep the starknife, and at the next full moon, I was a free man. In the meantime, unless I made a decision, I wasn't allowed to lie with any woman.

Despite the lack of available women—Tatiana wasn't half bad, but I was pretty sure she had her eye on Fane or Sandu—I found that situation downright unacceptable.

In the meantime, all the Sczarni stared at me, as if expecting me to make a decision at any moment. That wasn't going to happen, but their constant attention was making me nervous. Their tent was closed tight, and I saw everyone else outside, so I knew Malena had to be hiding in there.

"If you damned Sczarni are just going to stare at me all night," I told them, "I'm going to sleep."

"Not yet," said Dragos, standing up. Beside him, Baba turned her face away from him. On his other side, Cezar nodded grimly. Both obviously knew what Dragos was about to say.

"I challenge you for leadership," he said.

"You can't," I told him. "You have to wait for the next moon." It occurred to me that I didn't remember whether that meant the next full moon or the next new moon.

"Not you," said Dragos. He pointed at the boss. "You."

I realized then what he was after. I'd deferred to the boss so often in front of the Sczarni that it was only natural they couldn't all accept me as a leader. More importantly, Dragos had to be reckoning that if he beat the boss, I'd have to answer to him instead. Not that there was any chance of that.

"Forget it," I told him. "As your prince, I forbid it."

"You cannot forbid it," Dragos said. "It is our law."

I looked to Baba for confirmation, and she nodded at me. Somebody was going to have to show me a list of these laws before I got into any more trouble. "Doesn't matter," I said. "I'm his bodyguard, so the minute you make a run at him, I'll put you down. Again," I added for emphasis.

"If you interfere, then you are no true prince, and we shall all taste of your flesh."

I turned to consult the boss quietly. "What do you think?"

"It is a conundrum," he said.

"You aren't helping."

"It is not always easy to be the master," he said.

I shot him a dirty look. "This is serious," I told him. "I beat him, but it was a near thing. He was out of his mind with anger, and I'm not sure how it would have gone otherwise. This time he's got his wits about him. And boss, you hired me as your bodyguard for a reason. What chance do you stand?"

"You forget that I have an enchanted sword," he said.

"It lights up around the undead," I said. "Not werewolves."

He shrugged, and I saw a gleam in his eye as he walked to the wagon.

"It's a bad idea," I said, but he was banging on the door. Azra finally opened up. Ignoring the fury on her face, he mildly requested that she pass him his sword. He paused to take a length of rope from the wagon and tie Arnisant to a lead secured to the wheel. The hound looked at him with suspicion but accepted the leash obediently. Her curiosity piqued, Azra followed the boss back to the camp, where the Sczarni had already pulled away their carpets to leave an open area for the duel. Malena had not emerged from the tent, and Azra avoided my eyes and kept her distance.

The boss discarded his coat and tucked in his shirt before rolling up his sleeves. I made one last attempt to talk some sense into him.

"You know, I'll have to kill him if he wins."

"I certainly hope so," he said. Then, with less jollity he added, "I have always appreciated your loyalty, Radovan." For a moment he looked like he was going to say something heavier, but instead he said, "Return the sword and Arnisant to Count Galdana, if I cannot."

"Boss," I said, but he turned away to face Dragos.

"Wait," he said, walking around the designated area so that he was not facing the spectators. He indicated the other side for Dragos, putting the fire to his right, the werewolf's left.

Dragos scoffed at the change in position. "Where you stand will not help you," he said.

"No," agreed the boss. "But it may prove less uncomfortable for the others."

Dragos didn't understand that remark any more than I did, but he shook it out of his head as he slipped out of his clothes. I regretted letting him live when I held his life in my hand. It's a hell of a thing to kill a man, or a werewolf as the case may be, and I've done it only when it couldn't be helped. Dragos was helping me come around to a broader perspective.

The boss unsheathed his sword, which reflected the firelight but produced no radiance of its own. He lifted it in a formal salute with a dandyish flourish that might have embarrassed me if the stakes didn't include his life and—I had to admit it—if I didn't admire his courage so damned much.

Dragos made a show of rolling his shoulders and opening his mouth to show off the fangs that emerged from his widening jaws. Across from him, the boss pointed his blade at his opponent and assumed a duelist's stance completely unsuitable for this kind of fight. Just as I was about to call out to tell him so, his left hand came up and pointed at Dragos.

With a slip of his thumb, the boss riffled one of those little scrolls and sent a pea-sized ball of flame shooting toward Dragos. The flame grew as it flew forward, the size of a pumpkin halfway, larger than a man just before it reached Dragos. Caught in mid-transformation, Dragos leaped away from the danger, but he was not quick enough to escape the blast.

The sound of the explosion deafened me, and the rest of the Sczarni covered their ears and threw themselves down. Azra crouched low, and behind us Arnisant unleashed a torrent of barking. The only one who did not recoil was the boss.

He sprinted across the grass toward Dragos, who howled and rolled on the ground to extinguish his burning fur. He pressed the point of the sword against Dragos' throat and set his foot upon his chest.

"Yield," said the boss.

Still smoldering, Dragos wriggled as much as the sharp blade would allow, shifting back into his human form with much less hair to burn. He'd had recent practice at defeat, so with his next breath he cried, "You have won!"

The boss removed the point of his sword and offered his hand to his defeated foe. Dragos rolled away, hiding his face from his family, who had seen him defeated a second time since I had known him. The flames of the boss's spell had faded, but I saw a rebellious fire still burned in Dragos's eyes. I went to him.

As I passed the boss, he slapped me on the shoulder and said, "You see, there was nothing to fear." I liked the sound of his confidence, even though I could hear the echoes of the fear it masked. He'd been in mortal peril, and the fact was that once again I was the one who'd put him there. Dragos had no reason to challenge him except to regain the status that I had taken away.

I knelt beside Dragos and put my hand on his shoulder. He flinched from my touch. "I know how you feel," I said quietly enough that no one else could hear. "The people must respect their leader."

"You understand nothing of the Sczarni," he hissed.

"Not everything, it's true," I said. "But I do know that I gave you a gift last time we fought. You have proved unworthy of it, and now I must take it back."

His eyes poured hatred at me, but what he saw in mine changed that emotion to fear. He understood what I had to do.

I swept my knife from its sheath and drew its silvered blade across his throat. He gripped my arms and pulled me down, claws growing from his fingers to sink deep into my biceps. Its damage done, I dropped the blade and held him tight as his blood sprayed out over us both. The struggle was brief, but he pulled me down before his grip loosened and he surrendered to my embrace. We lay a while together, not speaking but somehow finally communicating through the last long lock of our gazes. As I watched the reflection of life vanish from his eyes, I knew at last we had reached an understanding.

Chapter Nineteen
The Last Crusaders

The mists drew a mourning cloak over our return to the west. Azra posted two pairs of lanterns at the corners of her wagon, although a passing traveler might hear the hiss of their wicks before spotting their light. Even the Sczarni carried torches to guide their steps, or perhaps they bore them to honor their departed.

Before we broke camp that morning, the Sczarni buried Dragos with no ceremony apart from the wailing of their women. Even Azra, whom I had expected to officiate in some manner, had stood apart as they lowered him into his grave. Radovan, however, had taken it upon himself to throw the last handful of earth upon his rival's grave. It was not, so far as I knew, a custom of Varisians or the Sczarni, but it had provoked no objection from the mourners. In fact, it was Radovan who ordered our journey to resume without as much as a glance toward me for approval. After summoning the phantom steed for him, I climbed aboard the driver's seat with Azra, for I was no longer in a mood to ride within the wagon, even with

Arnisant lying on my feet. It was not a day to spend apart from human company.

Despite the muffled clops of Luminita's hooves and the rattle of the wagon, the rich accents of Sczarni voices reached my ears by some queer path that wormed through the surrounding mists. I could not make out their meaning, but their tones were neither angry nor truly mournful, as I would have anticipated. Rather, they seemed to pass debate among the members of their dwindling family. I recognized Cezar's dark bass and the sweeter strains of Malena's and Tatiana's voices, but even young Milosh spoke his mind, although his voice had only begun to descend the broken hill from sharp adolescence to rich manhood. Periodically their discussion ebbed until an affirmative syllable uttered by Baba, the grandmother and acknowledged matriarch, set the tide of conversation in a new direction.

I could not overhear the content of their discussion no matter how I strained to listen. Soon after I surrendered all efforts to read by the dull light of the wagon lanterns and sat upon my magical copy of my late colleague's journal to protect it from the cold drizzle. There was nothing more to divine from its pages, and I had already exhausted comparisons with the local maps I retained after leaving the rest of my own journal in the grave. I did not regret the gesture, despite its obvious impracticality. Had I been thinking more and feeling less, perhaps I should have trapped its contents with a riffle scroll. In retrospect, I would almost certainly have retrieved it by now in a moment of frustration, and I suspect I would only have regretted cheapening my gesture. We have so few chances in this life, even one so long as mine has been, to offer sincere sacrifices to those who deserve our gratitude, and I have missed so many in past decades that those chances left to me have become all the more precious.

It was in that spirit of lost opportunities that I finally spoke to Azra.

"Where do you spend the winter?" I asked. It would not be many weeks before the roads of Amaans became impassable for a single-donkey wagon.

Here and there, she signed.

"Do you not return to your home village?"

She offered me a look intended to express annoyance, but I detected a shadow of sorrow beneath it. She tilted her head back to indicate the wagon. *This is my home.*

"Every door is open to a healer," I said. "I have not yet thanked you for healing Radovan. At present I am bereft of my usual resources, but upon my return to Caliphas, I shall have a suitable reward sent—"

She waved away my promise and shook her head.

"You could use it to help your people."

She shook her head firmly, reminding me of a very old joke about Ustalavs. When a Chelish peasant finds his cow dead, he prays that Aroden grants him another cow. When an Ustalavic peasant finds his cow dead, he prays that Pharasma kills his neighbor's cow. The national tendency toward gruff self-sufficiency can seem mean-hearted to outsiders, but I find something admirable in it.

"Why then do you help us?" I asked. "Is it because you once knew a Pathfinder?"

She signed *no* and kept her eyes on the road ahead, although we could see precious little of it in the mist.

"Is it for Radovan?" I asked.

She said nothing, but I noted the tightening of her jaw.

"Surely you must realize that by challenging Malena as you did, you offered the distinct impression—Ah!"

She punched me in the arm, a blow surprising not only for its suddenness but for its power. I had to clutch the lantern-post to prevent myself from tumbling onto the road and under the wheels. My first thought was that she had gone mad. In Cheliax or even in Kavapesta or Caliphas, a woman of her station would have been flogged for an assault on a person of my station. My second thought was the realization that she had probably never set foot inside a city or upon the grounds of a manor house. No doubt she had her own ideas of whom she could strike with impunity.

Even so, a count of Cheliax is not to be cowed by a single thump by a hedge witch. I shifted into a more defensible position on the seat and said, "What will you do if he returns the knife to you?"

I must confess that I flinched slightly when she shrugged, but she did not resume her assault upon my person. The ghost of a smile played at her lips, and I realized her secret. I had watched Radovan take the knife and fold it into a burlap sack in the wagon.

"He doesn't have the knife, does he?"

She attempted to make an enigma of her smile, but it was then that I noticed the tattoo on the inside of her right wrist. I craned my head over to see her left wrist. As I'd suspected, there was an identical tattoo.

"Show me," I asked.

She peered around to see whether anyone else was looking. No one was in sight. She flicked her wrist like a prestidigitator, but rather than a scarf or a playing card, a starknife appeared in her hand. I had been watching her wrist, so I caught the glimmer of stardust as the weapon appeared. With another snap of her wrist, the starknife vanished.

"Clever," I said. "Radovan can offer the knife neither to you nor to Malena, and so she may not impose upon his attentions until the next moon and yet you need not fear he will accept your proposal."

Azra smiled like a master criminal whose plot could not be proven, even though her adversary had guessed it.

"I wonder," I mused, "at the moment you threw that knife, which of those conditions was principal in your mind?"

She turned a wrathful face toward me, and I clung to the lantern-post.

Our progression across Amaans continued for three more days, most of that time through obscuring mist and light rain. When we paused to rest, the Sczarni drew near but did not join us, instead forming a circle around their magic bag to share the food they had stolen or hunted. Not for the first time, I prayed that Radovan could maintain control over them. They were cutthroats at best, monsters at worst, and it was impossible to anticipate their behavior without understanding more clearly why they followed him. I wanted to know much more about their legend of the Prince of Wolves, but I sensed it was too soon after Dragos's death to intrude upon their privacy.

Radovan had used the phantom steed to impress the Sczarni, even though they had to have seen me conjure it for him each day. I suppressed the urge to conjure it for myself, reestablishing my proper place in the hierarchy. If for a while Radovan were the one to whom the servants bowed, the first to receive a meal, the one exempted from the village chores, well, I could bear it. For a while.

It required more patience to practice my diplomacy on Azra, but gradually she became more responsive to my inquiries about the county, and I in turn limited my observations about her personal motivations. When I shared with her my youthful worship of Desna, she nodded approvingly, and eventually I learned more about her dual loyalties to Lady Luck and the Lady of Graves. She considered herself a cleric of both goddesses, yet her use of the starknives suggested an especial affinity to Desna. Pharasma's spheres of influence were universal: fate, prophecy, birth, and death. On the other hand, Desna was a goddess most often worshiped by individualists of all stripes, including, not coincidentally, Pathfinders. Considering those things Radovan had shared with me about her, I realized at last why the Sczarni held Azra in such esteem.

"Was it your father or mother who came from the Sczarni?"

She turned wide eyes upon me, surprised at my elementary deduction. I raised a palm for truce, but she did not strike me. Instead, she drew a deep breath and signed, *Father.*

Gradually I pressed the inquiry while we traveled, and a trifle at a time, she shared her story with me. Through a succession of signs and amendments to my questions, she signed that her father had been a Sczarni tinker, which I understood to mean he was a highwayman on the road and a confidence man in the village. Her mother was one of undoubtedly many village girls who had succumbed to his charms, yet for some reason he had returned upon the news that he had gotten her with child. His wanderer's heart did not let him linger long, however, and he had left behind the wagon as an inheritance for Azra when he abandoned her mother, an incident whose similarity to my legacy of the red carriage did not escape me.

She told me little else of her life, for when my questions touched upon the reason for her leaving her home to travel among the villages of Amaans, healing the sick and injured who in return supplied her with subsistence, a cool calm settled over her, and she would respond no more. Whatever impelled her to adopt this life, I gathered, it was not dedication to charity alone.

She signed, *Why do you go back?*

She saw that I did not understand her question.

You found the Pathfinder, she signed. *Why go back?*

That was a fair question, and I surprised myself by hesitating to respond. Perhaps I did not know the answer. Yes, the search for lost knowledge is a principal cause of our Society, and I felt an obligation to complete the search my colleague had begun. But it had become a more personal issue since someone had caused the deaths of my servants upon the Senir Bridge. The more I pondered the question, the more I believed two forces had worked against us that night, and the Sczarni werewolves had been only one of them. More galling was Casomir's attempt to manipulate me, especially his theft of my memory. What I wanted—"revenge" is such a tawdry term, but only fools believe they can have justice. Even acknowledging my own resentment, I knew it was not what I most desired.

"I want to know what has been hidden," I told Azra. "And I want to know why."

She frowned at me and shook her head, but not as if she failed to understand. Her eyes were filled with pity.

The village of freaks seemed even more miserable than it had appeared during our brief previous visit. Apart from any fear of the site's curse, the Sczarni seemed perfectly rational in refusing to enter, and even brave Arnisant sneezed at the first scent of the place. Our arrival was not met with the joyous welcome Radovan had described receiving earlier, although the pathetic beings that shambled out of their hovels to greet us smiled and bobbed their malformed heads to each of us in turn. Their clothes were the same color as the mud upon which their hovels squatted, and I would have bet one of my best farms that one could not find a lump of soap within the weird fence that ringed the village.

I was glad that Azra and Radovan had agreed that this visit would also be brief. They wished to enlist Tudor as a guide through the mountains of Virlych. Knowing the lad was both easily frightened and, to be kind, of limited intellect, I was dubious of their plan. Upon learning that none of the Sczarni had ever ventured into the mountains, nor had Azra traveled farther west than this wretched village, I saw no alternative but that we take advantage of whatever familiarity with the region Tudor might be able to share with us. Arnisant endorsed our selection by nuzzling the big lad's hands, although I suspect the reason for that had more to do with Tudor's failure to wash them regularly.

We left Azra's wagon and outfitted Luminita to carry tools and a week's provisions for four, expecting the Sczarni could supplement our stock by hunting. That seemed a viable plan until we returned to their camp outside the accursed village and found their numbers reduced by half. Cezar, Malena, Sandu, and Tatiana remained, but Fane, Milosh, Cosmina, and Baba had assumed their bestial forms and departed. One of them was still visible in the distance, a dark gray wolf loping north at an easy pace.

"What is this?" I said. "Find out, Radovan."

He joined the remaining Sczarni for a quiet conference. Beside me, Azra tugged at my sleeve.

Do not command him in front of wolves, she signed.

I opened my mouth to protest, but she was correct. No matter how much it rankled to pretend a subservient status to my own employee, demonstrating our true hierarchy would only invite further challenges.

Radovan returned. He sent Tudor to check Luminita's pack and spoke quietly enough that only Azra and I could hear him.

"Apparently," he said, "they left while I was in the village because they didn't want to go to Virlych."

"That is a good sign," I said.

"You think so?" said Radovan. "We're going for a hike in a place that scares off werewolves."

"I meant it is a good sign that the Sczarni do not wish to choose between breaking their taboos and disobeying your commands," I explained. "It means they respect you."

"Or fear me."

"There is little difference to a people as violent as the Sczarni," I said. Glancing at Azra, I added, "No offense intended."

Azra ignored my amendment and pretended not to notice Radovan's raised eyebrow. I made a mental note that the two of them were not as well acquainted as I had assumed. In the future, I would be more circumspect in references to Azra's background.

"So we're going with those who're left?" said Radovan.

I was surprised he asked. "Of course," I said. "I have not come this far to give up at the foot of the mountains."

He nodded, but I could tell he had misgivings.

"One other thing," I said. "When we are in the company of the Sczarni, I shall pretend to defer to you rather than risk further confusion among—well, let us call them 'your people.'"

"Yeah?" he said in a familiar tone of skepticism. He knew there was a second clause.

"Yet I trust that you shall not forget the true nature of our relationship."

"Of course," he said. "I got it, boss."

"Excellent," I said. "Now, then, it is time you commanded us to follow a path west by northwest, as well as Tudor's familiarity with the terrain allows."

Tudor proved such an apt guide and scout that I began to suspect he was an idiot savant. When Radovan first sent the giant boy to scale a ridge and report what he could see of the other side, I feared the lad would require rescue, thus wasting the rest of our day's efforts. Not only did he return in half the time I had estimated, he also described what he had seen with such accuracy that upon seeing the area myself, I could not recall a cartographer of twenty years' experience who could have duplicated his feat. Even aside from his uncanny aptitude for dead reckoning, Tudor had the singular virtue of tirelessly bearing a pack rivaling the weight of those Luminita bore. If not for his deplorable personal hygiene, I might have considered educating Tudor in the basic tenants of the Pathfinder Society and enlisting his service on a regular basis.

Rising to Tudor's unspoken challenge, the Sczarni adopted their lupine forms and scouted ahead in two pairs. Soon after, two of them returned suddenly, their hackles raised by the sight of one of the region's lightning phantoms. I had previously observed the phenomena only from a great distance and wished to observe them more closely, but no enticement could persuade the werewolves to return us to the site. A couple of astonished looks from both Radovan and Azra reminded me that curiosity is best served with a measure of prudence, and so I relented.

There were other wonders to behold. We passed the remains of a face carved into the mountainside ages earlier. Only a single eye bordered by a shattered cheek and brow remained, but dark shapes moved within the hollow pupil. Consulting my map, I saw that the eye was fixed on a point southeast, toward the Gardens of Lead. Behind it, to the northwest lay the lost city of Casnoriva, and farther still in that direction stood dread Gallowspire, the bastion and prison of the Whispering Tyrant.

Contrary to the rumors that no living thing resided within the borders of Virlych, we spied game trails. Cezar noted, however, that we had found no fresh spoor, only an occasional mess of bones and skin. We saw no more signs of migrating geese, but I spotted a lone scavenger wheeling over something dead or dying to the southwest. The Sczarni scouted shorter distances each time they went out, and Arnisant remained close beside me.

As night fell, the fog rose from the foot of the mountains while the heavy belly of the sky loomed above our heads. The light of our campfire cast a jaundiced ring in the narrow limbo between the vast obscurities. What little we said before sleep we spoke in whispers, and we sat our watches in silence.

Late on the second night, after I had retired from a restless watch with Cezar, Sandu shook my leg until I stirred. He lifted a finger to his lips for silence and moved along to wake Azra. Ten paces from the fire, Radovan and Malena knelt and pointed toward a dim light less than a mile distant. Taking Galdana's blade in hand, I joined them. We watched to see whether the intruding light flickered, indicating that someone had passed before it.

"There," said Malena. I followed the direction of her finger to see the partial outline of a pair of horses tethered not far from the fire. Beside them, the tiny silhouette of a man slapped his arms against the cool night air and paced to stay awake during his watch.

"Who else is mad enough to travel here?" said Radovan.

"Apart from the lingering dead?" I asked.

"You're frightening the women, boss," he said. Azra struck him in the shoulder, but it was a light, soundless blow that put a faint smile on his lips.

"Grave robbers," I said. "Cultists, necromancers, treasure seekers, the truly mad, if Desna smiles."

"You're frightening the men, now," he said. "What if Desna laughs at us?"

"Then those are paladins from Lastwall, and they have seen our fire as we have seen theirs."

Seven hundred years ago, the surviving members of the Shining Crusade founded the nation of Lastwall to maintain vigil over the ruins of Gallowspire, where the Whispering Tyrant fell, and the battle-plains of Belkzen, where his defeated orc legions had fled. Despite the final sacrifice of their great general, the crusaders were wise enough to know that the lich had merely been contained, not destroyed, and his legions had been scattered, not annihilated. Ever since, the peerless cavalry of Lastwall patrolled both the frontiers of

Belkzen and the wastes of Virlych. They had a reputation for impatience with those who trespassed these lands.

Radovan asked, "Do we run?"

"That would be pointless," I said. "Even if we turned to flee directly back into Amaans, they would overtake—"

Before I could complete the thought, a chorus of drawn swords sang out and a dozen brilliant lights blazed up around our camp. After a moment's blindness, I saw every member of our party cast in stark lines of trembling black and incandescent white. Surrounding us, just inside the ring of illumination, stood eight armed soldiers.

Arnisant barked a late alarm, but his surprise spoke volumes about the intruders' stealth. A hand sign was insufficient to calm the hound, and I had to repeat myself to make him sit and stay by my side.

"Drop your weapons," demanded one of the soldiers. He spoke Taldane with a light Varisian accent.

"Sneaky sons of bitches," grumbled Radovan. We had both been fooled by the decoy at the campfire, but Radovan took such things personally. A few years spent in noble society, where every compliment is a scheme and every courtesy a lie, and he would learn to take it in stride.

The Sczarni looked to Radovan for a cue. Wisely, he did not turn to me, but everyone saw me gently lay Count Galdana's sword at my feet. Radovan nodded, and the Sczarni threw their knives to the ground.

"I know what we agreed," whispered Radovan. "But I think you'd better take this one, boss."

An armored man on an enormous pewter-colored stallion rode through the ring of soldiers. Like his soldiers, he wore the shield of Lastwall on his tabard, but upon his shoulder I recognized the insignia of his rank. Two more mounted soldiers came up behind him.

To the captain's left was a wizard wearing one of those absurd chinstrap beards with whiskers so erect that he appeared to have been struck by lightning. He wore a ring on every finger and clutched a basilisk-hide tome adorned with a dozen little pockets on the cover, each marked with a rune indicating the material component of a spell, most of which I recognized.

On the captain's right was an armored woman with the sword of Iomedae embossed in gold upon her steel breastplate. She looked tiny beside the men, but her eyes radiated the calm assurance of an adept paladin or cleric of her goddess.

"Captain," I said, offering a military bow. "I am Count Varian Jeggare."

"Damned Chel," muttered one of his soldiers, a woman who might have been handsome but for her broken nose and prominent jaw. Her abbreviated term for a citizen of my country was a pejorative becoming more and more common among the Chelish holdings in the west. Hearing it from a defender of Lastwall saddened me, for their credo had always seemed pure in its simplicity and focus: to defend all of Avistan, regardless of political differences, from the return of the Whispering Tyrant. Even when Cheliax separated from the Empire of Taldor, they had remained neutral. Time changes all things, however, especially those that were once good.

"Captain Menas Neverion," said the captain, ignoring the discourtesy of his underling. The tracks on his face had taken at least fifty years to form, and some sage quality in his eyes made him seem even older. His Taldan name and curt demeanor dampened my hope that he would be of a lenient persuasion. "What are you doing in these haunted lands?"

There was little hope of misleading a man in the company of a paladin or priest of Iomedae, who had served as the herald of Aroden before that god's cataclysmic death. If not for the absolute power of the Thrice-Damned House of Thrune, the temples of Iomedae would likely have replaced those of

Aroden. Instead, the dark temples of Asmodeus now stood on ground once consecrated to Aroden. The obstacle before me was to tell as little of the truth as the captain was likely to accept.

"I came to Ustalav to locate a missing colleague," I said. Calculating both his next likely question and his reaction to my obvious reticence, I added, "Regrettably, I have found only her corpse. Thus, I wish to retrace her steps in hopes of returning with a complete report of her last days."

The captain did not look at his lieutenant, but I observed the worshiper of Iomedae nodding to herself. She did indeed have the means to detect a falsehood.

"And these natives?" he said, indicating the Varisians with the least turn of a finger.

"Guides and guardians," I said.

He frowned dubiously at my brevity, but without a sign from his lieutenant, he let it pass. His expression soured as his gaze fell upon Radovan. "And this . . . hellspawn?"

"My associate," I said, hoping not to diminish Radovan's authority in the eyes of the Sczarni. But I knew that answer alone would not suffice, so I added, "My bodyguard, Radovan."

The captain shook his head. "This will not do, Count," he said. "We do not welcome intruders into these lands."

"I understand your concern, captain," I told him. "But you will of course allow that these are not your lands. They remain a part of the Principality of Ustalav, and Prince Aduard himself received me in his palace upon my arrival."

A disbelieving laugh escaped his lips before the captain turned to his lieutenant, who nodded to confirm the truth of my claim before leaning close to whisper to him. He turned a scowl back to me and demanded, "And you will of course allow that these people are not simple Varisians you have employed to guide you."

I concede his point with a nod. "Young Tudor here is from a village near the mountains. He is our guide. Azra is a cleric of Desna, a healer, whose value to any venture in these regions I know you appreciate." I placed my hand over my heart and bowed to his lieutenant.

The woman beside the captain nodded toward Desna, a gesture of respect among worshipers of different but sympathetic deities. The tenants of Desna, while far fewer and less onerous, were no less virtuous than those of Iomedae.

"And these rogues?" The captain glowered down at Cezar, who glared back up. I could almost see the hairs on his arms bristling, and I sent a silent prayer to Desna that the werewolf would not lose his temper.

"A Sczarni family," I said. The captain reacted with obvious surprise that I had not dissembled, but if a thousand-mile foreigner could recognize the difference between an honest Varisian and one of their wandering thieves, it is foolish to assume he could not.

"Such company does not speak well of your character," said the captain.

Barely restraining myself from bristling at the provocation, I said, "In fact, they are in service to my bodyguard."

His lip curled. "The hellspawn."

"Listen," said Radovan, stepping forward. "I may have grown up on the streets of—"

"Silence," said the woman beside the captain. "If you wish to keep that infernal tongue in your head, you will stand back and await the verdict of your betters."

Radovan stopped himself just short of displaying his full smile, an expression that could only have resulted in outright conflict, one that I did not expect we could survive, much less win. Behind him, the Sczarni bristled, but he waved them back.

Before I could attempt another tack, Azra pushed past us both and signed angrily. The captain's horse retreated a step, and the man himself flinched at the ferocity of her approach. He recovered his composure and demanded, "What did she say?"

I could not suppress a smile at the literal meaning of her gestures, but I said, "She begs to disagree with your characterization of Radovan."

"Why does she not speak?" he asked.

Azra opened her mouth and pointed in the same vulgar manner she had shown me earlier. I sighed at the lost opportunity for a more graceful communication.

"I can translate," I said, but the captain shook his head and signaled his wizard, who took a pinch of black and white powder from a pocket on his book and began to intone the words of a spell. I tensed, and I felt the others with me bracing for an attack, but I recognized the signs he traced upon the air. I signaled Radovan that we were not under attack.

"*It's all right,*" he relayed to the Sczarni. For the first time I had noticed, his Varisian sounded perfect.

The wizard and his captain exchanged nods, and the captain looked once more at Azra. "With all due respect to the Song of the Spheres," he said, invoking Desna's formal title, "what is the nature of your association with this hellspawn?"

Not hellspawn, signed Azra, adding a rude nonverbal gesture to her response. *He is a valuable man.*

The wizard whispered the translation, but the captain scoffed. "Please, sister, I can see with my own eyes what he is."

Your eyes are blind, she said. *They see Sczarni, not Desna's children. They see demon, not son of Ustalav.*

The wizard flinched before relaying the translation, but I saw by the flint in his commander's eyes that he reported it accurately. Radovan stood behind Azra, unable to see her gestures. He stepped around for a better look, but she stepped in front of him to block his view.

This man is descended of princes, she signed. *If you try to stop him, Desna laughs at you. If you harm him, I will curse you all.*

Chapter Twenty
The Hall of Weeping Consorts

I looked up the limestone cavern walls into the towering faces of six statues. If they had ever been painted, the pigment had long since dissolved. Still, centuries of cave water oozing through various minerals had streaked their features with color. Beneath a translucent veneer, their eyes wept purple tears, and traces of white and green ran down their polished faces.

Each statue depicted a woman of the sort of ancient beauty you find only in artwork from fallen empires, and don't let anyone tell you the woman had nothing to do with the fall. Two of the faces smiled, one as though she kept a secret, the other as though she'd just revealed one. The others wore similar enigmas on their faces. Still, there were other clues as to their personalities.

One had a couple dozen rings piercing the flesh of her neck like a choker. Another statue had eyes of amber crystals bigger than my fist, although one had fallen to the floor so long ago that its cracked remains were cemented to the cavern floor by a mound of chalky runoff. The two on the far ends wielded ornate knives and turned slightly toward the center as if to menace each other or their intervening rivals. In the center were the two tallest figures, a bosomy matriarch whose lush lips spoke more of seduction than of motherhood, and a slender girl who held a basket teeming with small furry creatures against her belly.

"All right," I said to the silent statues. "Speak up now. Which one of you dirty little sluts is my Baba?"

The day after our encounter with the patrol from Lastwall, the boss still wouldn't tell me what he saw Azra signing to them. The way the corner of his mouth quirked up when I asked, I knew it had to be something humiliating. During my convalescence after the scuffle with the torches and pitchforks gang, Azra had seen me at my most pathetic. The way the soldiers hurried off after her tirade, I wouldn't be surprised if she told them I was plagued and contagious.

On the other hand, there was that business with the starknife. The boss was still being cute about that when I asked him what he thought was going on, and I was beginning to think he was the one who'd stolen the starknife from where I'd hidden it in the wagon.

Part of me wanted to think Azra just didn't like seeing anyone else have a bit of fun. Even if she'd been serious about laying a claim on me, I'd offer fat odds she'd changed her mind when she saw me put Dragos down. There was no way I could explain why that was necessary, not to a healer.

Before I could work up the courage to confront her directly, the boss stopped us a couple of hours after we set out. The break was welcome after the tense night we'd had. I hadn't slept a wink, and I think the same was true of the Sczarni. Fortunately, the mist had risen earlier than it had the past few days, and the sun winked down at us a few times. Consulting his journal and a handful of loose pages on which he'd drawn rough maps, the boss turned slowly to survey the territory.

We stood about halfway up one of the lower peaks, surrounded by endless stands of fir trees. To the southwest lay a
tiny mountain lake fed by a meager stream. Its water was a teal
I'd seen only in paintings, and the boss mentioned something
boring about its mineral content causing the color. Sheltering
us from the north was a crescent-shaped ridge of ruddy earth
and exposed granite. There was no sign of habitation, human
or otherwise. Even the vulture the boss had pointed out to me
earlier had vanished. More likely it was feasting on whatever
had been waiting to die.

"Would you be so kind as to scale that tree, Your Highness?"
said the boss. He was becoming more of an ass all the time
about the Prince of Wolves thing. I didn't understand what
had changed, but all I got when I shot him a warning look was
this stupid little smile that made him look like a schoolboy. He
was enjoying some private joke, and I had a feeling Azra was
in on it. Sure, I could have asked her. When I thought about it,
though, I knew I definitely preferred to go climb a tree.

The boss stood at the base while I shimmied up the trunk.
The tree's needles and cones were different from the pines of
Cheliax. The boss probably could have told me its name in five
or six old languages and described a dozen hedge remedies
using its bark, but I saw no point in giving him the pleasure.
I looked down at him from a height of maybe thirty feet and
thought about dropping a cone on his head. As if reading my
thoughts, Arnisant looked up and closed his panting jaws with
a snap. I took his meaning, one bodyguard to another.

Fifteen feet more and I didn't dare test the strength of the
tree trunk further. I snapped off a few branches for a better
view and had a gander. It always amazes me how different
things look from such a small change in perspective, especially a vertical change. The rock face to the northwest looked
completely different than it had from the ground. The vertical lines in the stone looked less like the effect of erosion

and more like the marks of picks and saws disguised to look natural.

The boss called for me, but I ignored the distraction. I had the strong sense that I was missing something right in front of my nose. I closed my eyes and opened them again. For half a second, I thought I detected some pattern inscribed upon the cliff, but the harder I stared the less I could see.

"Radovan!" he called again. I shouted back, trying to describe the effect of what I had seen—or rather, what I hadn't. Saying it aloud made it sound stupid, but the boss looked excited.

"Look at the sun," he cried.

Years earlier, he'd given me the opposite advice during a case involving an escaped firepelt cougar and a stolen icon of Sarenrae. "You told me never to do that!"

"Just for a second," he shouted. "Look at the sun, shut your eyes for a moment, and look back at the cliff."

My heavy sigh threatened to shake me out of the tree. I closed my eyes, looked up into the sun for an instant, and closed them again. Turning toward the cliff, I opened them again. Yellow and green spots flashed before my eyes, but as they faded I saw, or thought I saw, a convergence of lines near the base of the ridge. They were visible for only a second. When I blinked, they were gone.

"All right," I said, calling down to him. "There's something there." As I looked back at the ridge, again I glimpsed those lines that looked like a confluence of rivers, only so sharp and regular that they had to be crafted, not riven by nature.

"Find a bearing and come down," said the boss. The first part was easier said than done outside of a city full of distinctive buildings and monuments. These mountains were much less reliable, especially when the mists rolled into the valleys. I chose a couple of prominent trees and a cluster of boulders as my landmarks, imagining how they'd look from the ground.

Back on the ground, I had to hustle to catch up with the others. The boss already had them marching toward the ridge. When we reached it about an hour later, I saw nothing of the lines I'd seen before.

"Are you certain this is the spot?" said the boss.

I double-checked my landmarks. They were right where they should be, and from where I was standing, I should have been looking directly at the point where the lines on the ridge converged. "It has to be, but it looks wrong from here."

The boss put a hand on my arm. "Is it as if there were something missing?"

"That's it," I said. The sun had veiled itself with clouds, so I couldn't use that trick again soon. I closed my eyes for a few seconds, but I saw nothing but bare rock face when I opened them. The others imitated my action, even the boss, with no better luck. After a few minutes, I felt foolish and turned away.

Out of the corner of my eye I glimpsed a vault door. For an instant I saw it plain as day, a tall stone hexagon similar to the mausoleum door back at the old village. When I turned to look directly at it, there was nothing. I turned away again, and there was an even more fleeting image in my peripheral vision.

"This is going to sound weird." I explained the effect to the boss. The others listened intently, the Sczarni asking Malena to clarify with a translation now and then.

"The more you pursue it," suggested Malena, "the more elusive it becomes."

"Sounds like a woman," I said. Malena smiled at the remark, then sobered up when she saw Azra glaring at her. But Malena had an interesting idea.

"Say, boss," I said. "The way you've described spells some-times, you make them sound like living things. Like they want things, get mad, or take revenge."

He shrugged. "Practitioners of the arcane arts often describe spells that way, but it is usually more a figure of speech than a description of real sentient powers inherent in the spells. In the case of homunculi, golems, and other animated objects that take on a semi-sentience, however, it is perfectly valid to describe them as having motives, at least to execute the commands of their creators. In Thurmal's *Treatise on the Incarnations of Major Arcana*—"

He went on like that for a while, but I'm pretty sure only Arnisant was listening after he started quoting sources. I was thinking about women, and how some of them tell you the opposite of what they really mean. Sometimes it feels like a trick, maybe a test you have to pass to earn the privilege of her company. But other times, maybe most of the time, I think it's a defense mechanism. Like a door that doesn't want to be found by anyone who wants to find it too badly, or for the wrong reasons.

I turned my back to the door and thought about why I wanted to enter it. Sure, it was a big deal for the boss to find out what his Pathfinder had been seeking before she died. And yeah, I agreed it was a good idea to find whatever it was they were looking for before the bad guys did. But really, I hadn't thought much about what was in it for me. If I was actually descended of this Lord Virholt, maybe I was the one who had the most to gain—or lose—by looking inside this hidden vault.

If there was proof I was descended from this Prince of Wolves, that could get me locked into a room full of more responsibility than I ever wanted to see. I still felt a queasy shudder of guilt every time I saw the way they looked at me since I killed Dragos. It would have been better if they'd been angry or frightened, but when the pack looked at me now I saw only a longing for direction. They wanted me to tell them what to do. The more I thought about it, the less I wanted to be the one to do that.

I had to admit there was another reason I was curious about the contents of that tomb. I'd been the unwanted child of a criminal and a whore. The first part of my life was spent in slavery, and the most I'd ever managed to improve my lot was to become a servant—no matter how much I liked to use other words for it—to a lord who wasn't half as bad as his peers.

In the time I'd worked for the boss, we'd helped a few people who deserved it and hurt a few more who didn't. More often all we managed to do was perpetuate the constant struggle between people of his class for a slightly better position under the queen. In their world, I was invisible if I was lucky, and I spent a lot of my time waiting in the rain while the butler opened doors for the boss. Except for a few lonely wives who called me back to discuss a matter they'd just remembered about that last case, none of them wanted to see me again.

Even on the street, the villains I used to run with were suspicious of my new career. Some of them would still deal with me, but even those who tipped me information for some of the boss's coins still watched me close to see if I'd start putting on airs. My best friends on the street would still put a knife in my back if it meant a pay purse, and not necessarily a fat one.

What it all amounted to was that those who didn't hate me for being Hell-touched could hate me for working for this Pathfinder. And those who didn't hate me, well, they were mostly no better than I was—thieves and harlots, servants, slaves, and now Sczarni. But this Lord Virholt, this prince who fought against the Whispering Tyrant, he might have been something else. Sure, he could have been a traitor. Maybe the popular histories were right, and he sold out his people and got caught with his hand in his master's purse. But he might have been a great man. If what I'd learned about history was worth two coppers, chances were both stories were right. He was a traitor and a great man. If that were true, maybe there was hope for me, too.

I heard a scrape of stone that reminded me of the tomb opening in the forgotten village. I didn't dare turn around, but I said, "Did you hear that?"

Azra shook her head, and the Sczarni looked at me curiously. The boss turned his head to listen, but I could see from his expression he saw nothing behind me. Arnisant whined and sat at the boss's feet.

I took a step backward, and I felt cool air on my neck. I heard the sound of distant sighs and a tinkling of a spring. I smelled wet stone.

"See anything?" I whispered, still stepping back.

The others shook their heads, and when they moved to follow me, I held up a palm to stop them. "Wait."

I walked backward, careful of each step. When I felt I was closing in on the ridge wall, I shut my eyes, but I kept moving. I changed direction slightly when I felt a puff of cool, damp air lift my hair. At any moment I expected my heel to strike a wall, but instead I walked into cool shadows and stepped on a faint depression in the ground. I looked down and opened my eyes.

I stood in a stone threshold. At my feet was the lip of a stone door easily twice the size of the one at Virholt's false tomb but of the same design. Behind me was a dark cavernous space, and beyond the threshold I saw the others standing with expressions of wonder on their faces.

"Radovan!" called the boss. "Can you hear me?"

"I'm right here," I said. "Close your eyes and follow my voice."

The boss can be obtuse at times, but you don't have to tell him twice when what you say makes sense. He was the first to arrive, and I kept talking as he reached out blindly. When he was close enough, I grabbed his arm and pulled him across the threshold. One by one the others followed, except for Arnisant, who sat and whimpered in frustration at hearing his master's voice call to him from what looked like a wall of solid stone. Eventually the boss leaned out and pulled the dog in by his collar. After a brief struggle, Arnisant leaped up to greet his master, who corrected him with a curt gesture and, "Sit!"

It took another quarter-hour or so to retrieve our supplies from Luminita and guide everyone back to the cavern with a rope the Sczarni produced from the bottomless bag. We left the donkey to graze outside, lit our torches, and turned to explore the hidden cavern.

The first hour of exploration was what you might call exciting, if your idea of excitement is the constant fear that you're about to brush against a trap or step through a false floor. It was also an exercise in patience. Every time one of us made a move, the boss hissed to stop us. He kept repeating anecdotes about careless Pathfinders who had ended up impaled on a rusty spike or ground to paste by a falling boulder. The problem was that he was making the Sczarni more nervous than cautious, so I distracted him with an innocent suggestion.

"Sure would be good to have a map of the tunnels we've passed."

No sooner were the words out of my mouth than he ignited a pocket lamp and sat to sketch out the first few caverns we had explored. I beckoned to Cezar to accompany me, and together we scouted ahead with one of the torches. When we found the spot where tiles covered the cavern floor and the cavern walls gave way to buttressed passages, I had him hold the light while I crept forward to examine the floor. After twenty minutes of visual examination and a few prods here and there, I realized that my experience breaking into houses in Egorian didn't translate well into exploring centuries-old vaults. It wasn't that I got nervous, exactly, but suddenly the admonishments about cautious procedures didn't seem so prim.

The boss lost all interest in his map the moment he heard what we had found. We returned to the man-made area and lit more torches before gradually entering the inner chambers. The tiled hall led north to a wide gallery that expanded to the east and west. There we found the six statues of Prince Virholt's consorts, each of them three times my height. They were divided into two groups of three by a waterfall that splashed over a basin clogged by centuries of sediment. The fall had carved its own basin out of the nearest tiles, forming a little moat bordered by tilted and eroded tiles around the original vessel before the clear water drained into the earth below.

The rest of the gallery was tiled in icons of saints and heroes of Pharasma. I'd seen similar images for sale in the markets of Caliphas, their ornate borders distinctly Ustalavic. The boss was drawn to them like the proverbial moth. He paused only to warn us not to touch anything before he had a chance to look at it. The Sczarni needed no such warning, standing as far as possible from the walls and statues, until at last they relaxed enough to sit on the floor. Azra and Arnisant trailed the boss, while I had a good look at the ancient consorts. I had an idea who they represented, so I searched for hints of tails or hooves. Except for a few curious features, they all looked human enough. In the right light, so do I.

Eventually the boss joined me, and we worked together the way we'd done so often when examining an unfamiliar chamber. This time, he had the advantage of real spells to cast, so I waited for him to trip a scroll before getting too close.

"The entire place radiates lingering magic," he said, "but none of the statues more than the others. It's an antechamber, not the vault itself, but whatever its defenses, I suspect they are mechanical rather than magical."

I moved in for a closer look. Sure enough, I spied seams on most of the statues indicating joints that might move to strike or pin careless trespassers. I aimed to be a careful trespasser, so when I'd seen all I could, I kept my touch light as I ran my fingers over the statues.

Even under a coat of hardened sediment, I felt the indentations where the mechanisms were set into the stone. The armed consorts on the ends seemed designed to eviscerate anyone who triggered them, although I found nothing on them or on the nearby floor that would set them loose. Likewise with the others, although I had a feeling the crystal eyes were once a part of a deathtrap. With any luck, the erosion that had removed one eye had also ruined its ability to kill, petrify, or otherwise mutilate me. When I signed to ask the boss whether the statues could suddenly come to life, he shook his head, but only after a moment's hesitation.

No no? I signed. *Or maybe no?*

"Probably no," he said, since there was no sign for his favorite equivocation. I don't know why I felt the need for silent communication, except that I had a creepy feeling the consorts were listening to us.

"There's something wrong with each of them," I said. "Either they're all traps, or else one of them hides a door that looks like a trap."

"Nothing I have read provided a physical description of the king's consort," said the boss. "But I am certain if one of these statues conceals a passage, it is the one that looks like the Prince's mother."

"You sure there was only one consort?" I said. "He was the king, after all."

"A good point," he said. "But we don't actually know he was king. The Sczarni see him that way, and his sons as princes, but most references I have read refer to him vaguely as a lord, not even a count or prince. We know that the mother of the third prince was a devil, but none of these statues features any indisputably fiendish features."

"There's the one with the crystal eyes," I suggested.

He looked at me thoughtfully. "Do you have a feeling about that one in particular?"

I shook my head. "They're just statues."

"Perhaps so," he admitted. "But if the statues mask the entrance to the vault, they may be designed to offer a clue only to descendants of the Prince."

"And I'm just supposed to know which one is my ancestor?"

"My conjecture is that Virholt left some secret to be passed down to his descendents, perhaps through the Sczarni were-wolves. Over so many generations, however, the knowledge may have been lost."

Maybe Dragos had known something he did not wish to share before I'd killed him. Probably not, but I still felt a little sick when I thought of what I'd done—not that I regretted it, exactly. It had been necessary. Or maybe the ones who knew something useful were from a different family. The way the werewolves talked about their kin, I got the impression they were scattered all over Ustalav. If we couldn't figure out how to get past the ladies, maybe we'd have to search for them.

Or maybe the secret was with me after all. I thought of what had happened to me when the villagers put me on the fire. There was a lot I still didn't know about myself. That thought reminded me of the scepter we'd taken from Virholt's tomb. I'd been carrying the thing for so long that I'd gotten used to its weight in the side of my boot. It wasn't nearly as heavy as it should have been if made of solid metal, so either it was hol-low, or it was only plated in gold.

"Have you found anything that might conceal a keyhole on the statues?" said the boss.

I had no idea what to look for, so first I gave the ladies another look to decide which was the most likely to hide a door. It was not easy. Maybe I shared a resemblance with Prince Virholt, but assuming his consort was a devil, she'd come in disguise. Whatever she'd looked like, it had come down through—what?—thirty or forty generations. Maybe more, considering the short lifespan of most hellspawn in human society. Still, I gave it a try.

My first choice seemed too obvious, especially if this was meant as some sort of test. I don't know anything about the fashions of Ustalav seven hundred years ago, but those neck piercings didn't strike me as something that would catch on among the local nobility. Besides, if there were a clue, I figured it would be more subtle than that. The boss had already examined the statues up and down, so I didn't waste my time looking for a hint of a tail or a hoof-like foot. Instead I looked at the faces.

The one with the crystal eyes was interesting. One of the few things I remembered about my mother's face was her eyes. Except in the mirror, I'd never seen eyes of that same molten gold color. Still, there was something about the woman's wide jaw and round cheeks that looked completely unfamiliar. More importantly, something in my gut told me that I still had not seen the mother of a line of hellspawn.

I went to the basin and splashed cool water on my neck. Behind the waterfall, a dark shape loomed above me. I flinched, but it hadn't moved. Only my bending over the basin had made it appear so. I beckoned the boss over to take a look. We exchanged a nod and raised our hands to form a peak within the falling water. In the clear space between our arms, we looked up into the eroded face of a woman with a prominent horned brow. Beneath her pointed chin was a green bronze door set into an iron-reinforced archway. In the very center of the door was a large keyhole that looked a perfect fit for the key.

"Hello there, Baba," I said.

After opening the secret door with Virholt's scepter, I pried up a few of the loose floor tiles, and the boss helped me jam them beneath the chin of my ancestor to divert the waterfall. It was good to see him get his hands wet, if not dirty. He wasn't above physical work, but he tended to leave it to me when we weren't actively on a case. That's how it felt now: we were on the case.

We joined the Sczarni, who'd had the good sense to check for a draft before starting a fire for warmth. The werewolves peered suspiciously at the hidden consort we'd uncovered, and I could tell that none of them relished the idea of going farther into the mountain, especially not under such a face.

"Why we doing this?" said Cezar. His Taldane was improving as fast as my Varisian had these past weeks. Sounded like we'd met in the middle.

"Knowledge," said the boss. "Understanding."

Cezar gave him a blank look, so I translated for him. "Gold," I said. "Jewels. Riches beyond your imagining."

"This I like," said Cezar, repeating what I'd said in Varisian to Sandu and Tatiana, neither of whom was fluent in the common tongue.

The boss admonished me with a look, but he couldn't dispute what I'd said. "While it is true that a Pathfinder often discovers material wealth, it must never be his principal goal."

"That's all right," I told him. "You can have my share of the knowledge, and I'll take your share of the treasure."

He sighed, and I knew I'd pushed it too far. It was fun to gig him about the noble designs of the Pathfinder Society, but in his heart the boss believed in it. I think he considered our intrigues in Egorian his way of being an active Pathfinder without having to sleep out of doors. But most of the time he only read about the adventures of his active agents, who sent him reports of the things they had experienced and he could only enjoy vicariously. When I thought about it that way, he seemed sort of pitiful.

"Whether or not you choose to join the Society," he said, "you all became ersatz Pathfinders the moment you set foot inside this tomb."

"Sure," I said, hoping he'd let it go at that. But of course he didn't.

"While the Society prefers its members be introduced with a modicum of formality, the open secret of our organization is that our most prominent members were recognized as Pathfinders after the fact."

I nodded to humor him—I'd heard this before—but when Malena and Cezar whispered translations to their comrades, a hush fell over the Sczarni.

"What does this mean?" asked Cezar, relaying the question they all shared.

"It means that, like it or not, you have accepted a solemn duty to share the knowledge that we discover here, but to share it wisely. It must not be given to those who would use it for destruction, or those who would hoard it for themselves. Knowledge withers in captivity."

"You're talking about knowledge the way wizards talk about spells," I said.

"An apt metaphor," said the boss. "In the wrong hands, both knowledge and magic can cause great misery. It falls to us to ensure that whatever we discover does not do so."

Cezar frowned for a long moment, coming to a conclusion. "I agree with Prince," he said. "You take my share of knowledge. I take gold."

The Sczarni laughed, and I caught a hint of a smile before Azra turned away. The boss's face colored slightly, but he shook his head in surrender. His argument was hopeless in this company. Still, I understood what he'd been trying to do. We needed the Sczarni committed to the task in case things got dangerous. The problem was that the things that mattered to the boss didn't carry much weight with the Sczarni. I had an idea what would and I hoped I had learned enough Varisian to make it work without a translator.

"Listen," I said, raising my voice just enough to make it echo through the gallery. The Sczarni quieted, and even Azra gave me her full attention. *"The Count has his reasons to explore this place. But so do the sons and daughters of those who fought the Whispering Tyrant. Whatever it is that Prince Virholt left here, it was to be found by us, no one else. Deciding what to do with what we find is our duty to him. It is your duty to me."*

The Sczarni murmured grudging assent.

"And if there is some gold in there," I said. *"I think it is also our duty to take it."*

"Long life to the Prince of Wolves!" shouted Cezar. The others joined in with his cheer. Azra held her head in her hands, and I couldn't see her face. The boss looked at me with a curious expression. I couldn't tell whether he was irritated or confused. I'm sure he'd tell me later in words I would not misunderstand.

I realized there was one face missing.

"Where's Tudor?"

Everyone looked at everyone else, as if to say *not my fault.* We heard footsteps at the end of the gallery entrance.

"Here," said Tudor, lumbering forward. Behind him came a crowd of his fellow villagers, clubs and torches in their hands. Among them were a couple of faces I'd never expected to see again. Casomir came in right behind Tudor, his slim sword drawn. His other hand supported his cousin, who despite appearing delicate still had her pretty head on her shoulders.

"Tara," said the boss. "Of course." The color drained from his face as he stared her. His jaw locked in a determined expression I'd seen many times. He'd just realized something he had missed before. I hoped it wasn't the kind of mistake that would cost us all more than we could pay.

"Here, mistress," Tudor said, pointing at the boss. "Here they are."

Chapter Twenty-One
The Vault of Secrets

How stupid of me.

My first thought was that, should I survive to tell the tale, I would always begin with the preamble that the spell that blotted out my memory had undoubtedly also impaired my reason. There was no other excuse for my hasty assumption that the decapitated body I had seen at Willowmourn was proof of Tara's death, even if the body were indisputably hers. If my revised theory proved correct, I had seen her head that night as well.

Tara leaned heavily on Casomir's unoccupied arm. Behind them, a small army of freaks from Tudor's village shuffled into the Chamber of Consorts, as I had labeled it on my map. Most were men and boys with grotesque features but strong bodies. They must have been strong and hardy to have followed us so far into the mountains. I did not relish the thought of fighting such a mob, even with Radovan, Azra, and the werewolves beside me.

Casomir smiled. His belligerence gave me hope that I could entice him to parley. Many missing pieces fell into place once I realized Tara's true nature, and I understood at least one thing that must have occurred during my forgotten days at

Willowmourn. I brushed a finger across my unmarked cheek. "I neglected to compliment your new scars earlier," I told him. "They lend you a most becoming symmetry."

His smile vanished. "You will pay for that," he said, "a thousand times over."

Clutching his arm, Tara sighed and blinked like a sleepy lover. "He does not remember," she said. "Tell him."

"He does not deserve the satisfaction," Casomir said. Behind him, the villagers continued to pour in, shambling to either side to stand listlessly against the walls. Whatever charm enslaved them, it did not seem to rule Casomir.

"Yes, tell me, Casomir," I said. "Why have you chosen to follow this creature?"

"Tell him, Casomir," murmured Tara again. She tugged at his arm, wobbling as if drunk or ill. She appeared to be exhausted from the journey, but it was equally possible she had been weakened by too much time spent in sunlight.

"But my lady—" Casomir began.

"Why not tell me yourself, Tara?" I addressed her in her native Vudran.

"It is more satisfying to watch him writhe as I make him tell you," she said. *"Bring me the book I seek, and you may take his place."*

"What do you wish of this book?"

"What is he saying?" demanded Casomir. A glance from Tara chastened him, but he raised the point of his sword as he turned back to me. I sensed Radovan was tensing to intervene. I showed him my palm and trusted he would similarly restrain the Sczarni. Tara was obviously stalling us with this talk, but what we could learn from it could be worthwhile.

"Tell him," said Tara a third time, and this time the voice brooked no argument. "Tell him everything."

"We have come for the *Lacuna Codex*," he said. "In it are spells mightier than any known since before the first death of Tar-Baphon. They shall be returned to my mistress in the name of the Pallid Princess."

"How did you find us?" I asked.

Casomir barked a scornful laugh. "You think we let you keep my uncle's sword without good reason? It calls to my mistress. Wherever you take it, she can find you."

Considering that the blade had also saved Radovan and Azra from the restless dead at Virholt's tomb, I did not feel entirely foolish for falling into that scheme. On the contrary, judging from the sword's reaction to my last encounter with Tara, I suspected they were the fools for letting me retain it.

"What occurred on the Senir Bridge?" I said, hoping my own stalling was not so obvious that it would provoke Casomir to impatience. He had revealed so little, and yet it made perfect sense of my fragmentary understanding. Casomir and Tara, or one of them, had known of my Pathfinder's mission long before her arrival at Willowmourn. Who had tipped them off? Carmilla, Doctor Trice, or any of a hundred others who had heard their gossip could have done so. More to the point, why?

"It was as I told you, except that the last of the werewolves fled when the bridge itself exploded," he said. "That was no work of ours."

"And at Willowmourn," I said. "What happened to me there before your mistress took my memory?"

"It was much as you remember after your second awakening. She gave you the freedom of the library, and you searched for the books your Pathfinder had disturbed. You said you were close to discovering her path when you began to snoop around the house. You disturbed my mistress at dawn as she returned from her hunt."

I ignored Casomir and addressed Tara, who continued to luxuriate as if waking from a long slumber. "The pregnant maid," I said. "The one I don't remember. You chose Anneke because she too was with child."

"*A delicacy in my land,*" said Tara in her native tongue. Her head was erect now, her eyes bright and open. She had awakened. She tugged off her velvet choker, revealing an angry red line around her throat.

"*Penanggalan,*" I said. My memories were still missing, but I felt I had made this revelation before. I had only read of such abominations, undead whose heads and organs rise out of their torpid bodies at night to fly out and prey upon the living, especially newborns and pregnant women. I understood the vinegar bath now: the creatures needed to steep their organs in mildly acidic liquid to squeeze them back into their bodies at dawn. Penanggalan were prominent among some of the world's most hideous death cults, and they were known by many names. I pointed an accusing finger at Tara. "*I know you now, marsh hag. Bodiless witch. Daughter of Urgathoa.*"

"Stop speaking that savage tongue!" demanded Casomir. Behind me, the Sczarni growled, but Radovan stayed them with a word.

Tara shuddered, her arms falling limply to her side as she raised her chin. The wound around her throat opened, and a stench of vinegar and rotting flesh swept over us. I plucked the handkerchief from my sleeve and covered my mouth, gripping Galdana's sword in my other hand. The freaks began to scream, cowering at the transformation of their enslaver. Some turned away as if to flee, but their feet would not disobey the terror that pinned them to the floor.

With an ugly wet sound, Tara's head rose from her body. It dragged out its spinal cord, esophagus, and its central veins and arteries, all bearing the putrescent fruit of her internal organs. The lungs expanded after passing through the impossibly narrow passage of her neck, gasping with respiration. Her heart throbbed, dripping glistening amber ichor. Liver, spleen, kidneys, bladder, and intestines followed with a half dozen other sordid lumps I recognized from the cadavers I studied in my earliest days at the Acadamae.

"What is it?" cried Cezar.

"*Vampire,*" I said, using the Ustalav term.

Behind me, Tatiana screamed a curse that dissolved into a fearful yelp as she shifted into wolf-woman form. Radovan's expletive was both succinct and unmentionable, and I heard the familiar sound of his knife escaping its sheath. I wracked my memory for known weaknesses of the Vudran vampire, but if I had ever learned them, they were as absent as my first days at Willowmourn. I dropped my handkerchief and signed to Radovan, *Wait.*

Casomir released Tara's headless body and let it fall unceremoniously to the ground. Before it struck, he lunged at me. No doubt he expected to catch me off guard, but I parried with Galdana's sheathed sword. Casomir's blade sliced the white leather of the scabbard, but its point passed several inches from my thigh. I felt Galdana's blade humming inside.

Surprised by my defense, Casomir retreated a step. I shook the scabbard off the blade and adopted an elementary guard. The blade blazed white, and I heard Tara's disembodied head shriek at the touch of its rays. I kept my eyes on my immediate opponent. Recognizing my stance as a learner's position, Casomir sneered. "What makes you think you can defeat a Lepidstadt master?"

Even without the corroboration of the fear he tried to disguise as bravado, I knew the answer at once. I drew his attack with a feint to the knee. When it came, I caught his blade and bound it upward, snicking the point of my sword across his cheek, a hair's breadth from the scar I had given him before Tara obliterated my memory of our previous duel.

He raised his defense, expecting another attack to the face. While I confess I felt the temptation to mock him with another Lepidstadt scar, this was no student's challenge. I slashed his wrist and beat his blade out of guard. As if anticipating my vengeful desire, Galdana's sword leaped up to sever Casomir's throat. For an instant, the arterial fountain created the illusion that his head, like Tara's, would rise up above his body. Instead, it flopped back as he staggered two steps in retreat and fell to the floor, already halfway to Pharasma's acre.

A foul wind blew down on my face, and I raised the blade to block it. Miraculously, it did exactly that, dispelling the noisome exhalation of the floating face. If I had not seen it rise from Tara's body, I would never have recognized its transformed visage as belonging to the beautiful young woman I had met in Caliphas. Its skin had shrunken like a withered gourd, waxy yellow like a weeks-old corpse. The eyes engorged with blood, leaving not a sliver of white. Tara's hair, once resembling spun copper, now hung in undulating tendrils like earthworms bleeding on the edge of a farmer's hoe. Where the rays of light from Galdana's sword passed over them, the bloody locks writhed and shriveled.

I raised the sword above my head and bellowed the opening lines of an Ulfen epic in the original Skald. The face of the vampire creased in perplexity, rewarding my ludicrous gambit as she struggled to identify the strange "spell" I was casting, the somatic components of which were a Pathfinder sign to Radovan and Azra—*Run, now.*

With the vampire's eyes focused upon me, the first of my companions snatched up torches and entered the waterfall passage before I abandoned my ruse. I turned my mind to the problem of retreating without opening myself to an attack. I had never seen the creature in combat, only witnessed the awful remains of her victim.

"Come on," said Radovan, ushering Azra through the waterfall. "I'll cover you."

I lifted Galdana's sword an inch, and stood defiantly between the vampire and my company. He understood the message. I would not let him fight this foe for me.

"If she kills you," he said, "try to drop that sword where I can reach it."

Before I could tell whether he was joking, the screaming began.

The sound came from about a third of the village freaks. Above their agonized voices rose an eerie song from the mouth of the monster. Its words were in a language even I could not identify, despite its Vudran lilt. The villagers clutched their arms and shuddered, their skin rippling like the surface of a storm-blown lake. I hesitated, deciding whether to advance with the humming sword or to discharge a riffle scroll. An instant was too long.

Beads of bloody sweat formed on the villager nearest the vampire. He was a big brute with one stunted arm dotted just beyond the elbow with buds that should have been fingers. The blood oozing from his pores swelled to bullet-sized globules and rose up like a flock of startled birds to fly toward the monster, splashing onto its exposed internal organs. After a brief glistening, the organs absorbed the blood, and the villager dropped dead to the floor.

The vampire's face softened, briefly resembling the youthful beauty whose body it had ridden from Vudra. I prayed for Tara's sake that the vampire was an invader, and that the young woman whose body it inhabited was long since dead, not corrupted into the abomination that hovered before me.

A backward glance assured me that my companions had made it through the waterfall. I backed away from the monster, holding Galdana's humming sword at guard. The vampire smiled as it slowly followed me at a distance respectful of the sword rather than of me. The remaining villagers marched forward at her silent command, farmer's weapons clutched in their trembling hands, their faces etched in fear of the task before them and horror of the monster they were bound to serve.

The sword might keep the thing at bay, but I had no doubt the vampire would throw all of the remaining villagers at me. I had no desire to murder the enslaved wretches, so I backed through the opening beneath the waterfall until I felt my heels touch the slippery moss. With a quick upward stroke of the sword, I knocked aside the tiles Radovan had placed to divide the stream. For a second, I saw the vague images of the vampire and her minions through the sheet of water, and then strong hands gripped my ankles and pulled me down. I hit the slick floor hard and slid helplessly backward into the gloom. Every stair cracked my chin until I turned my head.

I barely managed to retain my grip on the sword. By its diminishing light, I saw Radovan clutching my legs and pulling me backward, letting himself fall in a painful slide before me. I crashed into him as we landed on horizontal ground, but before I could rise to complain of his rough treatment, he gripped my shoulder and held me low to the ground.

"Follow me," he said, crawling on elbows and knees. "Keep your head down, way down."

I imitated his example. By the light of the sword I saw we were traversing a narrow passage, its walls adorned with crumbling bas relief images depicting men bending down to transform into bestial figures, and then into running wolves. Above them was the ancient seal of Virholt, marking them as the Prince's wolves.

I paused and raised my head for a better view, but Radovan pulled me down. Scant inches above our heads, I felt a powerful gust of wind. It came several times in rapid succession, and I crouched lower.

"Stay down," cautioned Radovan shortly before a second series of gusts brushed the back of my head. He moved fast, and I came so closely behind him that we collided in a most undignified posture when he suddenly stopped.

The floor was slick with sticky fluid, black in the magical light. Even before detecting its coppery pong, I knew it was blood. Radovan grabbed some object from the floor and dragged it along with him. I brushed against a warm and bloody object lying beside the wall. Unlike Radovan, I did not have the stomach to lug it along with me. By the time we reached the ring of formed by the torches the others held, we were bloody hand and foot.

A horrified gasp escaped Tatiana's mouth. She gaped at the gory object Radovan had collected. It was the mutilated head and upper torso of Sandu, sliced diagonally as if he had leaned forward to run himself onto a tremendous razor, then sliced again across the face and chest as his severed body had fallen back through the blades that had killed him.

"Nasty trap," said Radovan bitterly. "Only wolves can pass."

I was grateful that Radovan had not been the one to lead the way, and that Sandu had not fully transformed before serving as a warning to the others. I considered how much of a threat the trap posed to our pursuers. I doubted it would long delay the vampire, but at least the villagers' screams would serve as a warning to their approach.

"Where are we?" I asked, raising the sword high. This far from the undead thing, its light was barely stronger than that of the torches. Radovan commanded the troops to spread out, and Azra took Tatiana by the arm to draw her away from what was left of Sandu. A minute later, we had made a ring of light around a circular vault. Above us, a brazen dome, enchanted to resist verdigris all these centuries, reflected and magnified our light.

The walls were cut like miniature bank vaults, four levels of perhaps a hundred compartments each. Many were left open, their empty interiors crusted with limestone sediment, but others were enclosed by leaden doors marked with arcane glyphs. A chiseled legend between each column warned of dire curses upon the heads of trespassers, each sealed with the ancient crest of Virholt.

The center of the room had collapsed, yet fifteen feet or so below the level of the remaining floor hung a central dais of green-veined white marble. It remained suspended above a deep chasm by a reinforcing framework whose exposed metal rods were weirdly untarnished, even where their mangled fingers clutched the walls of the sinkhole.

"Boss?"

"Yes?" I replied before realizing it was Cezar who had spoken, and not to me but to Radovan.

"What is it?" said Radovan.

"What we do now?" said Cezar. "There is no more place to run."

Radovan looked to me, but not for permission. I saw in his eyes what he saw in mine. There was no other choice.

"Now we fight," he said.

Chapter Twenty-Two
The Dead Undead

The shrieks went on for so long that I thought none of the villagers the monster had enchanted would survive the trap. Finally one emerged, crawling on knees and flipper-like hands. Cezar and Fane, both in half-wolf form, immediately grabbed him. It was Tudor, and he struggled as they pulled him through. Against a couple of men he might have broken free, but the Sczarni were monstrously strong in their man-wolf forms. I nodded my approval as they bound him with rope from their bottomless bag, as I'd ordered.

The boys resumed their positions beside the entrance while Malena gagged Tudor with one of her scarves and shoved him against the wall. She pointed at the chasm and warned him in Varisian, *"One move, and down you go."* I liked her better all the time, but I hoped it wouldn't come to that. If we could survive this fight, I hoped Tudor would as well.

The second freak saw the werewolves waiting for him. He froze, equally terrified of what lay before and behind him. He tried to crawl backward, but someone blocked his way, and they began screaming at each other. I didn't want to see them killed, but while the vampire's spell lasted, they saw us as the enemy. Besides, we had only so much rope to go around.

Fane turned to me for guidance. I said, *"Grab him."*

Fane stepped into the passage and grabbed the freak by a forearm the size of a man's thigh. Just as he pulled the man back, the monster shrieked out a string of foreign gobble-dygook. With a sound of a cart full of melons crashing to the ground, the body of someone in the corridor burst open. Fane stumbled backward in a hail of flesh and blood, slipping on the gore-streaked stone. He fell back toward the chasm, still clutching the dismembered arms of the villager he had grabbed.

I grabbed him by the scruff and whirled him against the vault wall, just in time. From the entrance, a cloud of shrapnel blew across the room. Jagged metal, shattered bone, and wads of bloody flesh smashed against the opposite wall to form a rough circle of carnage. The boss crouched at the edge of the blast, clutching a wound on the shoulder of his sword arm. On the other side, Azra held up a starknife that radiated a buckler-shaped light, shielding herself and Tatiana from the blast.

Between them, the bloody chunks of villagers slid down the vault walls to plop on the floor. There they bloomed with a sickening sound, growing at incredible speed into gory fig-ures the size of puppets. They had no skin, no eyes, no human features of any kind, only blood-slicked muscle and bone. The villagers who tried burying me would definitely have called these things the dead undead.

Azra and the boss attacked, she with divine radiance, he with the sword held awkwardly in his weakened hand. Arnisant dashed past the boss and bit into one of the bloody little horrors. The manikin's toxic flesh burned his jaws, sending the hound whining in retreat. I plucked the throw-ing knives from my boots to aid him, but then I smelled the rot and vinegar stench of the vampire emerging from the trapped passage. I backed up and watched the guts and head float out above the sunken floor. The vampire smiled, murmuring in her foreign tongue and turning slowly to observe the vault doors.

The surviving villagers, covered in the gore of their neighbors, pushed into the vault chamber. Fane and Cezar tore into them, throwing some into the pit, pushing others back into the mob. Much as I regretted the deaths of the freaks, I couldn't fault the Sczarni. It was well past time for taking prisoners.

Above us, vault doors snapped open at the monster's command. Books flew out of the compartments, pages flapping like birds caught in a gale. They swirled around the vampire, pausing one by one as its magic held them still to read their titles. The thing shrieked in triumph as it beheld a large volume bound in quilted fragments of human skin, some still retaining an ear, a lip, or a nipple.

I raised a throwing knife, but the boss was quicker. He conjured a spell with a riffle scroll. For an instant I saw a translucent duplicate of his hand appear. When it vanished, he gestured at the book before the vampire and pulled it toward him.

Tara shrieked in protest and turned toward him, but he sent the book flying to Azra and shouted, "She must not have it!"

Azra caught the book in both arms, still holding her starknife. She raised it to cast another warding spell, but she was too slow. Her body rose up as if pulled by an invisible noose. She flew toward the hovering vampire, which licked its lips with a long red tongue in anticipation of a feast.

I threw a knife at the vampire's face, but the silvered blade glanced off its scaly cheek as if it were as hard as marble. The next one I hurled lower, severing the viscera of a lung. The wet organ fell away, and the monster screamed in agony. It would take me five or six more shots like that to kill the thing, if that were even possible. I pulled out the big knife, and as the monster turned to face me, I let it fly.

The blade cut through the monster's exposed organs, cutting away several nasty lumps and a long rope of intestines, but not the heart. As the vampire shrieked ever louder and more shrilly, its severed pieces fell to the sunken floor with a sickening splash. The heart remained, and Azra still hung suspended beside the monster, clutching the invisible grip at her throat with one hand and holding onto the *Codex* with the other. Her feet kicked uselessly in the air. She couldn't last much longer.

"Come on, you scabby whore!" I screamed at the monster, opening my arms to show I was weaponless.

The vampire was too cunning to fall for such a lame taunt. Still holding Azra suspended, it hissed at me as clouds of blood seethed from its eyes. A buzzing pestilence surged out of its mouth to shoot down at me. I raised an arm to cover my eyes, but just then I saw a beam of light tumbling end over end toward the monster.

The boss had thrown his sword, the damned fool. The hell of it was, he almost hit the vampire. The blade swept inches past her cheek, severing only a few tendrils of her disgusting "hair" before arcing down into the chasm, where it would fall beyond reach of anyone who could wield it against the monster.

Damned fool that I am, I leaped after it.

I caught the sword by the grip and hurled it straight up. Desna smiled, and the blade cut straight through the vampire's heart and went on to puncture its skull. That was more good fortune than I deserved. Naturally, Desna then laughed and sent me three times as much bad luck to balance my account.

First, my back struck the ragged floor of the sunken platform, and I felt my spine crack. After the first instant of impact, I didn't feel a thing below my neck. I knew what that meant.

Next, released from the vampire's spell, Azra fell beside me. I wanted reach out to her, but my arms were dead, too. She brought her hands up to shield her head with the book, but her body hit the stone with a heartbreaking crunch.

Finally, the foul rain of the monster's steaming remains fell upon us both. I saw but couldn't feel the stuff burning my skin, and I heard the awful popping sound of her undead manikins growing all around us.

"Radovan!" yelled the boss. I saw him peering over the edge. Behind him, I heard the wailing of the villagers as their minds slipped free of the vampire's control. Their mute obedience gone, they screamed in terror of the attacking Sczarni.

"Stop killing them!" I shouted to the wolves. The boss repeated my command in Varisian, and the sounds of battle subsided. Beside me, Azra moaned and stirred.

"Azra," I said. "You've got to get up."

Azra pushed herself up and shook her head to clear it of the stars I knew were exploding in there. She punched me lightly in the arm, but I couldn't move a muscle. Understanding dawned in her eyes, and she tugged at my ruined jacket.

"I'm going nowhere," I said. "You have to climb up like you did back at Virholt's tomb."

Not without you, she signed. One of the bloody little horrors lurched toward her, and she seared it with a flash of light from her palm. It winced backward, but its gruesome body continued to grow. A half dozen more of its kin gathered behind it.

"Go," I told her. "Get that book out of here."

She hesitated, looking up at the boss, who fumbled with his riffle scrolls, then back at me. She was a smart woman. Neither of us had seen the boss cast a spell that could raise me up out of here before those things swarmed me, and we both knew I couldn't lift a hand to defend myself.

"I'm the goddamned Prince of Wolves," I screamed. "Obey me, and get out of here before it's too late."

There were tears in her eyes, and I'd put them there. She punched me hard in the chest. I couldn't feel the blow, but it hurt all the same. She kissed me then, tenderly. In its way, that hurt a thousand times more.

She pushed herself up and spun, a starknife appearing with a glimmer in her free hand. She ran as if up an invisible spiral stairway. When she was clear, the boss flipped another scroll and dissolved one of the nasty undead with a glob of acid. The shot was good for my morale, but I glimpsed the others crawling over my legs toward my face, stabbing and biting away my flesh as they came.

There was only one thing for it.

"Light me up, boss," I called.

"What?" He looked down, perplexed. I loved putting that expression on his face. Malena looked down at me, too, fear apparent even on her half-wolf muzzle.

"Give me some of what you gave Dragos," I said. "Burn these things off of me."

"No," he shouted. "The spell is far more intense than a bonfire. In that small space, it'll incinerate you, too."

"Just do it," I said. "Trust me." But suddenly I didn't trust my own instinct. Dragos had survived a blast, but he'd leaped clear of the point of explosion. I'd survived a funeral pyre, but that was a relatively slow burn, and even that had hurt like hell. Whatever change the fire brought out in me, I had a bad feeling it wouldn't be fast enough to save me from the heat of a magical fire. Even if it did save me from the manikins and didn't blast me further down the sinkhole, I'd still be paralyzed. Only I'd also be on fire. Still, it was a cleaner death than the one these undead horrors promised.

"Everyone back," the boss shouted. I bit my tongue to stop myself from telling him I'd changed my mind. Azra stood beside him, and for a second I thought she'd stop him. But she only looked me in the eyes as the boss chose his scroll and pointed it at me. I tipped them a wink and closed my eyes as the fire came down.

Chapter Twenty-Three
The Prince's Treasure

The blast from the fireball hurled us all back from the edge of the chasm, slamming me against the vault walls for the second time in as many minutes. All around me, villagers and Sczarni alike moaned in pain, the sound muffled as though I were listening to a conversation in the next room.

The lights of our torches flickered in the smoke from the blast. One of the brands flared momentarily as a pocket of flammable gas touched its flame. The world tilted and spun, and through the muted din I discerned a sound like brittle rain. Pages from the tomes pulled from the vaults drifted down like leaves, a few of them flaming from the explosion. I cringed more at the pain of the lost knowledge than at the wound in my shoulder. I smelled seared meat, and at last my mind cleared sufficiently that I focused on the immediate problem.

I scrambled to the edge of the pit. Azra was already there, howling a pitiable, tongueless approximation of Radovan's name. Her voice sounded distant beneath the pounding of my own pulse. Sulfurous flumes rose up through the gray smoke, choking us with its hellish stench. I found the proper scroll and released a gust of wind to blow it away. Much of the smoke had no avenue of escape, so it remained swirling in the sinkhole until finally it dispersed enough to reveal the figure standing on the sunken floor.

It was approximately the shape of a man, but it stood over seven feet tall. Its naked skin was the color of fresh copper, still hot from the forge, coiled muscles wrapped thick as a mile of cable around its bulging limbs. From its knees and elbows jutted sharp bones the length of my forearm, and black claws curled from its fingers and toes. Blunt, hornlike protrusions rose from its brow, and tiny spurs dotted its cheeks and chin. The only recognizable features on the devil before us were its eyes. They were identical to Radovan's.

I called his name, and he looked up at me. He was standing, and judging by the way his extraordinary musculature flexed as he moved, he appeared to be in perfect health. "Tell me you're all right."

"Never better, boss," he said.

I winced to hear him speak the language of Hell. Its harsh syllables sounded like incoherent growls and roars to those unfamiliar with the tongue. Behind me, the Sczarni backed away while making the sign against the evil eye, and the surviving villagers moaned in fear. I saw Tudor crouched among them, presumably released from his bonds by one of the Sczarni. It was plain that the villagers had been freed from Tara's charm upon her death. I addressed him in Varisian, "Calm your people, boy, and find some rope."

A thunderous impact struck the floor beside me. I turned to look up into Radovan's alien face. I felt the steam coming off his enormous body, almost two feet taller than his normal height. He looked down at me and grinned, and I could not suppress my shudder of fear at those vast and merciless jaws. Fane and Tatiana screamed along with a chorus of villagers, while Cezar cursed with such passion I expected his words to conjure another devil.

Beside me, Azra swept her hands through a hasty spell, spinning once in a pirouette of astonishing natural grace. She stopped with a starknife in one hand held before her stomach, the open palm of her other hand pointed at Radovan, or what he had become. She frowned at whatever knowledge the spell had given her. She stepped away from him.

"It's all right," said Radovan, dropping to one knee before her. *"I'm not mad."*

I translated the infernal words for Azra. Timidly she stepped toward him. He opened his arms, and after a brief moment's hesitation, she stepped into them. He held her tight. It seemed unlikely he would suddenly devour her, so I turned to give them a moment's privacy.

"Let us not linger here," I told the Sczarni and villagers in their native tongue. "Gather up all the pages you can find, and pat them out gently if they are still afire. Stack them here, here, and here. Move those torches away first. Afterward, see to the wounded."

Hours later, we finished conveying the last of the hidden tomes out of the vault and onto Sczarni carpets outside the mountain cache. I directed the villagers to place them just close enough to the campfire for light, but not so close as to risk burning more pages. The Sczarni erected their oracle's tent for Radovan, who retained his diabolic figure but could now communicate with Azra via Pathfinder signs. After ministering to the worst injured, Azra joined him in an effort to return him to his usual appearance. How she planned to do so, I could not imagine.

I tried not to dwell upon the image of Radovan in his fully infernal shape. His description of the earlier transformation did nothing to prepare me for the reality. The phenomenon was unlike any of the myriad supernatural qualities found among hellspawn, and my first thought was that he was more like the shape-changing Sczarni who followed him than any of us had realized.

At the moment of the vampire's destruction, my absent memories flooded back into my mind. I was astonished at how closely my first investigations mirrored my second. I had discovered my Pathfinder's trail, stumbled upon the secret of the riffle scrolls, and even befriended Arnisant by feeding him the meat I could not stomach. The difference was that, upon witnessing the vampire Tara's head flying out to prey upon the servants, I deduced the house was beset by a demon or undead creature. Intending to hunt for it the following night, I secreted Galdana's fabulous sword in the same place I had hidden the riffle scrolls I had just learned to create.

Unfortunately, I had not made the connection between Tara and the flying creature, and when I foolishly brought her into my confidence the next morning, she revealed her true nature. Without my scrolls or Galdana's enchanted blade at hand, I snatched another weapon from the wall. Casomir came to the defense of his mistress, only to discover that the reason I do not bear the Lepidstadt scar is that none of my fellow students were able to strike me before I wounded each in turn. Distracted by his interference, however, I fell victim to the vampire's magic. With a kiss as loathsome as the flesh of a swamp toad, she blotted my memory of my first days at Willowmourn.

After our conflict, Casomir must have ordered the remaining weapons removed from their wall mounts. I felt a surge of scorn as I imagined his fear that I might again face him blade in hand. Upon discovering the absence of Galdana's sword, he must have trembled even more, but now I understood that Tara had demanded he leave the blade wherever I had hidden it, knowing its antipathetic power would act as her compass to my location. Still desirous that I complete my investigations into the location of the *Lacuna Codex*, she allowed me to awaken again, coaching the servants to pretend that I had only recently arrived at Willowmourn.

Reliving those lost memories, I shuddered at the horrible fate that befell the servants, particularly Anneke. Her uncertainty had been my first clue to my missing days. How crudely I had abused her in trying to recover them, unaware of the peril she faced. If only I had been able to save her life, I could have felt blameless in my clumsy investigation. It should be a long time before I could forget her pitiable death.

Happily, I had more than enough present questions to occupy my attention. Cezar grumbled at his hasty bargain, for we had found no gold within the vaults of Prince Virholt. The *Lacuna Codex* was only one of almost forty volumes of arcane and historical secrets. It would take me weeks if not months to peruse them all, but for now I contented myself with a brief inspection in preparation for an inventory to catalogue them by type and importance. I began with the *Codex* itself.

If anything, Casomir's boasts had understated the potency of the spells within its pages. While little more than an adept of arcane magic, and that only because of the trick of the riffle scrolls, I had some comprehension of the ultimate magics that mortals could wield. I could not hope to cast them myself, at least not without decades more of study and practice, but I could recognize a gate spell or the dread killing word. The spells within the *Codex*, however, could annihilate whole armies or sunder the very fabric of reality. Now the tales Malena had recited of the Whispering Tyrant's triumph over Virholt's brothers seemed less like an elaborate romance and more like an unvarnished chronicle. Allowing such powers to come under the authority of a creature like Tara was unthinkable.

I set the *Codex* apart, trusting that its ghastly binding would keep curious Varisians away from it. Then I had second thoughts and mused aloud, in Varisian, that I had never seen such a potent curse laid upon any book and that I would not touch it myself if I were not such a powerful wizard. The whispers among the villagers and Sczarni alike suggested my ruse would be sufficient, at least in the short term.

As I turned to examine the other books, I felt a warm touch upon my shoulder. I recognized Malena's distinctive scent even before I turned to see her face. Between the soft hair that floated beside my cheek and those green eyes, I could see how she had proven such a danger to Radovan back in Caliphas. He was forever vulnerable to superficial beauty. There are, of course, worse failings in men, and I cannot pretend immunity to the wiles of certain women, but fortunately my standards are higher than Radovan's. Even if they were not, I was protected from any charms Malena might seek to employ by the vast disparity in our social positions.

"Can I help you with this task?" she asked. Her Taldane was not at all bad. In fact, it was rather attractive in her Ustalavic accent.

"Only if you can read Old Varisian," I said, noting with a certain satisfaction the disappointment in her eyes.

"Not I," she admitted. "Tatiana can read a little, but maybe not this Old Varisian. Is it very difficult?"

"Not once you have learned it," I told her. "It does not matter. I can finish sorting them once we return home."

"Home?" she asked. "To Caliphas?"

"Certainly not," I said. "To Cheliax, eventually."

"And the Prince, he will go with you?"

Of course he will, I almost said. But at that thought I had to pause and consider the question more carefully. I had realized in recent days that I might have underestimated Radovan's connection with the Sczarni, perhaps his connection to all the people of Ustalav. We continued to uncover evidence that he was the distant heir to the last king of the land. While it was preposterous to expect the human lords of the country to consider even for an instant that a hellspawn foreigner might sit among them, Radovan's claim was the sort of thing an ambitious man—or woman, I realized, thinking of my paramour Carmilla—could use to incite a civil dispute.

I would of course advise Radovan to conceal his identity from such people, but I could not enforce my will upon him. From the start of our association, I assured him that he was my agent, not a servant, although he understood the necessity of allowing my peers to assume otherwise and, to be honest with myself, I had often overlooked the distinction. In the past year especially, my behavior had strained our once comfortable association. He had almost left my service after an unfortunate investigation a year earlier. After all we had endured in Ustalav, I had no reason to expect he would not remain here, where there were people who treated him as the master, not the slave.

"I do not know," I told Malena. "Perhaps he will stay in this country."

She smiled at that, and I saw her gaze drift toward the tent where Azra tended Radovan. Despite Azra's trick with the starknife, which Radovan could not offer to either woman so long as Azra could summon it to her hand at will, I suspected Malena faced a more determined rival than she realized.

"Perhaps you should stay also," purred Malena.

I raised an eyebrow at her insinuation.

"Here you would be held in high esteem," she explained, "as a friend of the Prince."

"Ah," I said, oddly deflated that I had misinterpreted her overture. My value in her eyes was as a conduit to the prince. "I must return to my work, as I'm sure you understand."

She smiled hopefully, but she left me with the books. When she was out of sight, I counted them again to be sure they all remained. When I saw that they did, I wondered how much I had feared theft and how much I simply wished to think of her as a thief rather than as a woman who saw me as a stepping stone to a more powerful noble.

Apart from the *Codex*, the other volumes fell into three categories. Most contained arcane secrets stolen from Tar-Baphon and his agents, presumably via the steal book spell, to which I spied several references upon a light skimming of the text. These were the most valuable by every measure, and I intended to deliver them to my superiors in the Society, the Decemvirate in Absalom.

Another group of books concerned the secret alliance among nobles of Ustalav who, under the cloak of submission, worked to subvert the oppression of the conqueror lich. These could profoundly change modern understanding of Ustalavic history. The financial value alone, both to those who would share the knowledge contained in their pages, and to those who would suppress them, was staggering. That they should remain in Ustalav I determined at once; the problem was deciding in whose care I could entrust them.

Finally, a few books chronicled the lives, both public and personal, of the last king of Ustalav and his immediate descendants, the princes of Malena's tale. These were perhaps the most dangerous volumes of all we had discovered, not only because of their contradictions to commonly accepted history but because of the support they provided for Radovan's link to the last undisputed monarch of the country.

Wondering what mischief a lady like Carmilla could make of such materials, I chose one of the latter volumes and pored over its pages. The light was not ideal, but remembering the patrol from Lastwall, I hesitated before discharging a cantrip. If only we had been able to bring Azra's wagon into the mountains, it could have provided ample shelter for the light.

A wolf howled in the distance, and the Sczarni lifted their heads to listen.

"What is it?" I asked.

Cezar raised a hand to silence me. I did not like his presumption, but I waited until he heard another distant cry.

"Son of bitch," he said, exploring more of his newly learned Taldane. "Something coming. Something very bad."

"No," replied a sonorous voice. Just outside the glow of our campfire, a ring of masked men surrounded us. "Something is already here."

Chapter Twenty-Four
Devil's Deal

The sudden quiet warned us that something had happened outside the tent.

Wait here, I signed to Azra, knowing in the back of my mind that she'd ignore me. I threw open the tent flap and stepped outside wearing nothing but the blanket that served as my skirt. As soon as I appeared, all eyes were on me.

The Sczarni had already thrown off their clothes and half-transformed, ready for a tussle. Even the freaks clutched their clubs and rakes. I had to chuckle about that, and I couldn't explain why. Everything was particularly amusing to me since the boss hit me with the fire. Not only did I feel whole, I felt strong, invulnerable. That couldn't be true, I knew. A peasant farmer had put a pitchfork through my leg the last time I got extra spiky. But still, I felt restless, ready for a little action.

The intruders carried a variety of arms. I saw in their hands long knives, studded clubs, and wicked scythes, all of them with long hooked chains attached to their butts. Their garments were uniformly loose dark gray tunics and trousers, cinched close only at the waist, wrists, and ankles. I noticed no women among them, and they wore masks of what looked like fine pigskin but wasn't. Like whoever had bound the *Lacuna Codex*, these creeps worked in human skin. Their false faces were once real ones, patched together from a variety of sources. Their demented craftsman had left certain features in place, the hint of a nose protruding from a cheek, a tuft of beard on the brow, a fringe of eyelashes where the lips should have been. The one thing most of them lacked was an open mouth. Some wore thick stitches imitating a smile or grimace, and others had only blank space where a mouth should have been.

The exception was their leader, whose mask was featureless except for two eyeholes and a flap of skin that served as a veil over his mouth. He'd been talking to the boss, something about surrendering to the inevitable, handing over the books, and a bunch of other stuff we weren't going to do.

"Who are you mummers meant to be?" I asked, forgetting momentarily that my words came out in the infernal tongue. Still, the blank-faced man turned toward me, and I saw understanding in his eyes. Somehow, I was not surprised.

"We," said the blank masked one, hissing in the devil tongue, *"are the guardians of secrets. Surrender what you have stolen, and your deaths shall be quick."*

"That's your offer?" I said. *"I have a better one. Go now, and you can run for an hour before my wolves and I hunt, kill, and skin you."*

I couldn't see his expression, but the man locked gazes with me. The frightening thing wasn't what I'd said. It was that a big part of me meant every word and looked forward to the chase, and the flaying. A tiny corner of my heart recoiled, disgusted with me.

"Leave what you have taken from the vault," said the masked man, at last reverting to Taldane for all to hear. "Walk away and leave this land forever. I will spare your lives." His voice sounded familiar, but the pounding of my pulse distracted me. I couldn't place him.

"Never," insisted the boss, lifting the *Lacuna Codex* from the blanket and raising Galdana's sword to defend it. I noticed it did not glow as it had when he fought the undead. Whatever powers it possessed, we couldn't count on them to help us.

"Very well," hissed the intruder. He flicked his fingers, and faster than sight, a pair of his men grabbed one of the villagers and peeled back his shirt. Before the freak could cry out, they sank hooked iron claws into his chest and began to peel away his flesh. An instant later, they pulled their victim out of the fire light, and we could only hear his screams.

"Stop them!" I yelled at the nearest Sczarni, but they could not understand a word I said. Instead, they backed toward the campfire, protecting each other's flanks. *"Tell them to help him,"* I shouted to the boss.

He repeated my order, but the half-transformed werewolves hesitated, looking uncertainly between him and me. All the while, the captured villager screamed, his voice appearing first from one direction, then suddenly from another.

"It's your funeral, little man," I growled.

I reached for the leader of the masked assassins. My hand was big enough to encircle his throat, but he faded away from my grip. I growled and shot a kick at his legs, but again he evaded me with ease. He struck me just below the sternum with his fingers, reversing his hand to strike again with his palm. I barely felt the strikes after the first blow, but they pulled all my strength out.

"Give us the *Codex*," hissed the leader. "And submit yourselves for execution." Looking back where he had been, I saw nothing but shadows. Behind me, another villager howled as the intruders pulled him into the darkness.

"All right," I gasped. *"Take the books. Leave my people alone!"*

"No!" cried the boss. He drew Galdana's sword and stood protectively over his little library. "Look at their masks. They worship Norgorber, the Keeper of Secrets. They must not have them."

"Listen, boss," I began. A dart zipped out of the darkness and struck me on the cheek. I slapped it away, but I already felt the venom burning within me.

Hands slapped my bare back, and I turned to see Azra spinning close around me, whirling with both starknives in hand as she led a fading trail of blue-white light to encircle me.

"Guard the Prince," cried Malena. She and the other Sczarni rushed to surround me. For the first time in my life, I was the one with the bodyguards.

"No," I said uselessly. *"Look out for the Count. I'm going to get that slippery son of a bitch with the darts."*

Beside me, Tatiana went down hard. I didn't see what had struck her, but there was no sign of her attacker. An instant later, another villager shrieked in terror, and several of them bolted away to take their chances in the dark. One of them didn't make it out of the firelight before a chain snaked out and struck his legs, sending him to the ground screaming.

No one was obeying me. Only the boss and our enemy could understand me, and neither was inclined to do so. I felt helpless. I couldn't just stand here with Azra between me and the assassins, and I'd be damned if I did nothing and heard the villagers die, one by one. I had to do something.

My blanket fell to the ground. Modesty was the least of my concerns, but I was shrinking, and not just because of the cool night air. My fingers were no longer clawed, and my knees were spike-free.

"Wait!" I shouted as loud as I could. My voice was my own again, my words in the common Taldane. "Let's talk." I looked over at the boss. He still stood above his precious books, sword raised to defend them.

I waited what felt like minutes, but no more screams pierced the night.

"First," said that deep voice from the darkness. "Bring me the *Codex*."

I went to the boss. He shook his head at me, but he lowered his sword.

"You mustn't," he said.

"We have to do something," I said, clapping him on the arm. "These are my people. I have to protect them."

He glanced at the leader of the masked assassins, who stood once more at the edge of the firelight. He spoke quietly. "They must not win, Radovan. They are the destroyers of knowledge. They serve a god more awful than you know."

I gave him another pat on the arm, a gesture so familiar I knew it would have gotten me fired at any other time. "Trust me," I said.

After a long pause, he let out the breath he had been holding inside. His shoulders slumped, and he looked suddenly much older and infinitely weary. He put the book into my hand.

"Thanks," I told him.

When I turned back, I saw the assassins' master waiting for me. Before the fire stood Azra, flanked by the werewolves, and behind them cowered the surviving villagers. Tudor stood among them, both hands clutching a club one of his fellows had dropped. I tipped him a wink to offer him some of the confidence I didn't entirely feel. I walked toward the masked man, throwing Azra a little sign behind my back. I hoped she was looking. Who was I kidding? Of course she was looking. She couldn't get enough of me.

My nemesis looked a lot taller up close. Of course, I was a lot shorter now.

"The *Codex*," I said, holding up the book. "This is what you really want, isn't it?"

He nodded.

"Take this, and get the hell away from us. You don't get any of the other books. You don't touch so much as a hair on any of my people. This is the deal."

"Why should I accept such terms now?" he said, snatching the book from my hands.

"You're mighty powerful," I said. "No doubt about that. From what I can see, your men could kill just about everyone here."

He said nothing, so I said it for him. "Me? I'm not that powerful. But with a little help, I could definitely kill one man before I die."

Azra's got some great timing. On my last word, she crashed her starknives together like cymbals, but instead of sound ringing out a purple light flashed directly over the man, and I saw him shudder as the curse took hold. He darted to one side, but then I heard the riffle of one of the boss's scrolls and a globe of white light flared atop the man's masked head.

"We might all die," I yelled for all to hear, "but before we fall we'll fight you tooth and claw, we'll curse you and burn you and stab you in the heart."

"And by 'you,'" I said, pointing at the assassins' leader, "I mean 'you.'"

He crouched, ready to run or attack me, I couldn't tell.

"Sound good?" I called.

"Yes, my Prince," called Cezar. "To the death."

The villagers uttered a frightened murmur of assent, then repeated it in a brave chorus. "Yes!"

Finally, from my right side, Count Varian Jeggare said, "I've got your back, boss."

Our enemy stood motionless, thinking as he clutched the *Codex* to his chest. The way he tensed, I could tell he was about to bark a command and leap out of range. I prepared myself to jump after him, but then we heard the low growling from the darkness.

We looked around together, and everywhere we saw yellow eyes glimmering just beyond the firelight. I counted thirteen pairs before I gave up. There were more than a few wolves out there. More than one family. There was a whole pack of Sczarni.

The masked man stood motionless. The mountain was silent except for the low growl of the reinforcements Baba and the others must have fetched. I raised my hand, and even the growling stopped.

"You must leave Ustalav," said my foe.

"Radovan," said the boss. "Don't let him take the *Codex*."

"No," I said. "A deal's a deal. That is assuming you accept."

His eyes went wide under the mask, and I realized where I'd seen him before.

"We accept," he said. I could tell now he was trying to disguise his voice, but it was too late. "But within a month you and your master must leave Ustalav, never to return."

"Gladly," I said.

"Give him your word," said the boss.

The masked man glared at the boss but answered me. "I give you my word," he said. "I give you my word as a gentleman."

Chapter Twenty-Five
Amends

In my absence, Willowmourn had transformed into a military camp. At the closed outer gates, which I had glimpsed only in moonlight the night of my escape, six alert guards greeted our arrival. Beyond them, I saw more guards patrolling the grounds. Gardeners had cut away the burned portions of the hedge maze, revealing a bare plaza where the enormous topiary boar had perished. It would take years to restore the wonderful garden.

Two guards emerged from the gate while three remained behind its iron bars, their crossbows at the ready. The fourth mounted a horse, preparing to flee to the manor at any sign of aggression. I was grateful for the first time that the Sczarni had left us as soon as we returned to Tudor's village. Their absence during our journey across the plains of Amaans had made me keenly aware of our vulnerability to attack. I had reinscribed the riffle scrolls with my most potent combat spells, but I had lost several during our fight in the tomb and had insufficient remaining materials to replace them all.

I bade Arnisant remain with Azra and Radovan, with whom I exchanged as few words as possible since his betrayal in the mountains. I met the guards, identified myself, and informed them of the purpose of my visit. The commander gave a message to the rider and courteously requested I await the reply from the house.

Radovan and Arnisant joined me while I waited. Radovan brought me my travel satchel, Galdana's sword pinched securely in its mouth. Azra drove her wagon toward the river's edge, just beyond the walls of the estate.

"She might prefer the security of the estate," I told Radovan. "Assuming the Count extends his hospitality after I abused it in his absence."

He nodded but said, "I think she'd prefer a little privacy."

I raised an inquiring eyebrow.

"Well, we'd both prefer it," he said.

"Very good," I replied. If I had been less despondent over the loss of the *Lacuna Codex*, I might have congratulated him or, to be more honest with myself, tweaked him for the incongruity of a match between my bodyguard, a former member of the worst street gang in Cheliax, and a cleric of two deities. I still could not fathom her dual association, but further inquiry would have to wait until after I had settled my more pressing obligations.

"Listen, boss," he said. The familiar preamble indicated he was about to offer an excuse that I did not wish to hear. Detecting my impatience, he reached into one of the remaining pockets of his tattered red jacket. "I didn't want to risk your using this earlier, but now that we're here, and assuming Galdana is the sort of fellow you trust . . ." He pressed one of my missing riffle scrolls into my hands. It was the steal book scroll, which I had feared lost during the fight in the secret vault. I saw by the glimmer of its page edges that it had been activated.

"How—?" I began, but the answer was obvious. Radovan had picked my pocket before facing Count Senir in his guise as the leader of the Keepers of Secrets.

"I didn't want to flash the thing around on the open road," he said. "I'd figured there'd be plenty of time to use that thing later, preferably when we're back in Cheliax, or at least far out at sea."

"Of course," I said, admiring his quick thinking almost as much as I regretted my hasty assumption of his betrayal. Only now did I fully understand why others would follow him so readily. I could not formulate a coherent expression of my gratitude, so I said simply, "Thank you."

He nodded. "You sure you don't want me to come in with you?"

"No," I said. "Even if he cannot accept my explanation and apology, the worst the Count is likely to do is to refuse me his hospitality. If so, I will endeavor to make my approach to your camp as noisy as possible."

He ignored my jibe and said, "With all due respect, boss, I've got a feeling that none of the counts we've met in Ustalav share your idea of good manners."

So he had recognized Senir's voice also. I would have to continuously remind myself not to underestimate his cunning. I patted the pocket of my waistcoat and assured him that if there were an altercation that required his attention, I would make it conspicuous.

The messenger returned, and the guards opened the gate for me and Arnisant. I picked up my satchel and Galdana's sword. Radovan tossed off a casual salute and walked toward Azra's camp. Before I turned to enter Willowmourn, I saw him break into a run.

Count Lucinean Galdana paced beneath the recently mounted head of a dire bear. The new addition dominated the room, and as one with some knowledge of the properties of the animals whose heads he had taken as trophies, I was much impressed with his hunting prowess, especially if it were true, as I had heard from peers and servants alike, that he hunted alone.

His familial resemblance to his nephew Casomir was noticeable if not striking. They shared the same contrast between dark brows and yellow hair, but Galdana had the wide jaw and plump cheeks that I remembered from his father. Unlike his sire, however, he was rotund in no other respect. I imagined his cracking walnuts in the pit of his elbow to amuse servant girls.

He had listened with attention and patience as I recounted my experiences in the care of his nephew, Casomir, and the imposter I had known as their cousin Tara. His hard expression softened as I detailed the plight of Anneke, whose father, Galdana told me, had escaped the terrors of that night only to be found in such an unyielding state of distress that the Count had sent him to Caliphas in hopes that Doctor Trice could soothe his shattered psyche.

When I had finished my summary of events, Galdana graciously shared his perspective of the matter. That Casomir and Tara had maintained a long correspondence he knew very well. They were so close in age that their parents had hoped for a matrimonial match after years of distant friendship. Yet while Casomir had traveled to Caliphas, it was not to propose marriage but to escort Tara's coffin to the family crypts in Amaans. Galdana learned this only upon returning from his hunt, when he discovered Casomir's last letter from Vudra. It was not from Tara but from her parents, reporting the tragic news of their daughter's death from a mysterious and virulent disease.

Galdana and I pieced together what must have truly occurred. The vampire that slew Tara used the girl's seeming death to transport itself to the land where she expected to find the *Lacuna Codex*. For whatever reasons—perhaps hunger or a need to communicate with allies in Caliphas—the vampire abandoned the disguise of a corpse and adopted Tara's identity, confident that none in Ustalav except for Casomir had learned of the girl's death.

Upon arriving at Willowmourn, the vampire enthralled key servants and cowed the others into obedience. When her appetite became terrifying to the staff, she and Casomir announced the false rumor of plague in Kavapesta to keep the servants, and me, from fleeing to the city.

When Felix entered and set a decanter of wine and two crystal goblets nearby, I suspended my story. The butler hesitated upon seeing me, but after pouring the wine he bowed to his master before turning to bow deeply to me. He struggled to keep emotion from his pale face, but his eye twitched before he turned and departed the room.

"He witnessed the worst of the depravity, and he remembers it all," explained Galdana. "Fortunately, the Bishop's clerics were able to restore his sanity if not soothe his soul. He is mortified by his part in your manipulation."

"He cannot be held to blame," I said.

Galdana agreed. "I ask for your discretion in all of the unpleasant details of your stay at Willowmourn, but what you know, you know," he said. "The scandals you have learned, if repeated in Caliphas, could sully my family name for a generation."

"I give you my sincerest assurance—"

"I ask for none," he said. "Rather, I shall place my trust in your character, which I estimate to be greater than that of your Ustalavic acquaintances."

It was not my place to protest such an indirect slight against Countess Caliphvasos, but secretly I harbored my own suspicions about her complicity in the matter of delivering Tara to Willowmourn. My judgment was marred by our previous romantic association. Galdana, as a native of the land, probably had a better notion of her character than did I. I bowed my acceptance of his left-handed compliment.

"I thank Your Excellency for your understanding, and for your great courtesy to one who abused your hospitality in your absence."

"And I am grateful for your part in ridding my home of the abomination," he replied.

"Even so," I pressed, "I took your sword and these books without your permission." I nodded toward the weapon and borrowed volumes I had laid upon his desk. "I beg your forgiveness and return them to you now." I gestured to Arnisant, who stood near the window, watching the guards on the lawn go about their business. "Along with this most excellent guardian, who chased me all the way across your county to offer his protection."

Galdana nodded acceptance. "Let me offer you my advice, although you have not asked for it. Never mention these Keepers of Secrets, within or without the borders of my country. Their cult is known by another name, as perilous to utter as the name of the god they serve. It is said that even in a whisper, their master can hear it spoken anywhere on Golarion."

I almost smiled at the hyperbole, but his countenance was so grave that I could not dismiss his warning. He went to the desk and wrote a word upon a scrap of paper. He showed it to me: *Anaphexis*.

He looked into my eyes to see that I understood, and I nodded. He dropped the paper into the fire and watched it burn before returning to the seat opposite me.

I considered anew the implications of the treatises on the cult of Norgorber I had discovered among his books. Now I believed he had them not because of sordid interest or any sense of affiliation with the Keepers of Secrets. Instead, I think he was the sort of man to study his enemy. That thought led to a question about what else I had found among his books.

"Were you unaware of the tomes of magic in your own library?" I asked, thinking of the riffle scroll formulae. "Some of them were extraordinary."

"I was of course aware of them," he said, "but I have never had an interest in the arcane. Those were passed down from my great, great-aunt."

"Considering that facet of your lineage, I am surprised that you have not explored your own talents in that direction."

Galdana smiled. "You are an oddity among our class, Varian. You knew my father, and you have begun to know me. To most lords, the history of our country and the chronicle of our lineage is far more compelling than the subtleties of the arcane, although I confess a certain weakness for romances."

And pornographic drawings, I thought, but I said, "And histories, I notice."

"Yes, fortunately for us both. From what you have told me, I am glad to know my books proved useful in the pursuit of your quest."

I paused to consider my next words. Galdana had impressed me as the best sort of nobleman, and not merely because of his willingness to forgive my offenses. The library he maintained, even if he did not personally peruse its volumes, was a monument to the history of his country. And if he were, as I suspected, a foe to the followers of Norgorber, then perhaps he would be the best guardian of the histories we had recovered.

"There is a favor I would ask of you," I said. He listened with rapt attention as I described the histories of the Prince of Wolves and the war against the Whispering Tyrant. "I am loath to take them from their native land," I explained. "And as you can imagine, should they fall into the wrong hands, they could prove disruptive to an already tenuous balance among the counties."

He comprehended the magnitude of my request. "You do me great honor," he said.

"Despite the circumstances of our first acquaintance," I said, "I think it a great fortune that we have met. As my bodyguard might say, 'Desna smiles.'"

"An apt expression, although the people of our land are more inclined to beg the Lady of Graves for mercy than rely upon the whims of Lady Luck."

"And you?" I asked. "In which direction do you incline?"

"Long ago I reconciled myself to fate," he said. "Pharasma has read my life, and she will judge it on the day I die."

"May that be many years from now," I said, raising my glass. He joined me in the toast, a wan smile upon his face.

Our interview was coming to an end. I whistled for Arnisant and indicated a spot beside Galdana's feet. "Come, Arnisant."

"Arnisant?" said my host. "The legendary general. You have given the dog a good name."

"He impressed me as a heroic sort," I said. Arnisant came to sit beside me. "No," I corrected him. "Go to your master." The dog looked up at me, head cocked quizzically.

"Please," said Galdana, gesturing to me with an open palm. "I think Arnisant knows his master."

Chapter Twenty-Six
The Last Command

It was just after dawn in Oracle Alley. None of the tea-readers, seers, or phony Harrowers would arrive for hours, and a couple of ugly looks was all it took to persuade the neighboring tradesmen to go home for a proper breakfast. I couldn't say why, but I wanted a little time alone before my people arrived here, in the place where I'd first brought the wrath of the Sczarni down on my head. One way or another, my business would be done by the time the sun drank up the mists pouring through the alleys of Caliphas. If Desna smiled, I'd be done with Caliphas, Ustalav, and the Sczarni. If she laughed, then the boss would have to promote Arnisant.

Even if things turned out for the worst, I had a good last memory to take wherever I was headed. Azra and I had five nights on the trip back to Galdana's estate, where we made love for what I expected to be the last time under the riverside willows. But she surprised me. Even after she saw the caravan Count Galdana had assembled to escort the boss back to the capital with the recovered ruins of his red carriage, she followed in her wagon. I sat beside her all the way. Every now and then Luminita turned her head back to give me an accusing look as if she knew it was my fault she had to pull us across the Ulcazar Mountains. During the days, we didn't have much to say that couldn't be expressed with a touch or a kiss. The nights were a different matter, but we moved our blankets far enough that we didn't wake the boss or frighten Galdana's guards.

As we approached the walls of Caliphas, Azra slowed the wagon and let the rest of the procession go ahead. She pulled off the road and let go of the reins, as if she meant to camp there. I asked her what was wrong, and she nodded toward the city gate. A band of Varisians in colorful vests and skirts were negotiating with the guards. One of them was a dark-haired beauty with earrings big enough I could have thrown a knife through them. It wasn't Malena, but there had to be one like her in every band of Sczarni, and we both know it was no coincidence there were more of them coming into the city.

They come for you, she signed.

"Just to see me off," I said. I had my own ideas about how that might go down. It was something I hadn't discussed with her or the boss. I'd deal with it on my own.

Azra's gaze lingered on the Sczarni girl who teased her scarf around the neck of a leering guard. Even from this distance, I saw her hand dip into the poor sap's purse. When he figured it out later, I wonder whether he'd be mad or just reckon he'd gotten value for his coin. I already knew my answer. I took Azra's chin and gently turned it back toward me.

"Don't even think it," I said.

You wish you'd chosen her, she signed.

I'd learned to ignore that kind of leverage years ago, and most of the women who tumbled with me knew better than to try it. Hearing it from Azra was different. It made her seem half her age—although it occurred to me then that I didn't know what her age was. Not that I'm fool enough to ask.

"You're right," I said. "I wish I had chosen Malena instead of you."

She recoiled as if I'd slapped her. When I said it, I'd meant to be funny, but one look at her wounded expression changed my tune.

"If I had chosen her," I explained, "it wouldn't be so damned hard to leave now."

She turned away so I couldn't see the tears, but she leaned back against me, and I knew I was off the hook. The hell of it was, this one wasn't just a line. I'd meant it.

"Of course, it's not as if I really could have made a choice," I said, stroking the tattoo on her wrist. "That was some nice trick with the starknife."

She turned around to face me with a solemn expression. She flicked both wrists at once, and twin starknives appeared in her hands. She held one against her breast and offered me the other.

I hesitated. If I understood right, she was making the sort of suggestion that would have made me chuck one of my Egorian sweethearts under the chin, tip her a wink, and, soon as her back was turned, slip out the window and stay away from her street for a few months. It'd be even easier to escape here, once I set foot on a boat.

"Those assassins will be after me," I said. "It's too dangerous for me in Ustalav, at least for a while. I can't stay."

No, she signed. *But you can return.*

She pressed the starknife into my hand and closed my fingers over the haft. She kissed me hard, and her tears spilled hot onto my cheeks. Then she pushed me away. When I hopped off the wagon, she slapped the reins and drove back north.

I heard the music before I saw them. It was the same song that had lured me weeks earlier, and the fiddle sounded almost exactly the same. Then they began to emerge from the mists filling Oracle Alley.

For a moment I thought I saw the ghost of Dragos walking forward with his fiddle, but it was a younger man. There was no mistaking the family resemblance, and as he drew closer I could see it was indeed the same fiddle. This was some cousin who had inherited the instrument Dragos's son could not, since I had killed them both.

More figures emerged from the gloom. Most of them I did not recognize, but their moustaches, the embroidery of their clothes, the way the women held their heads, all were familiar. There were dozens of Varisians I had never seen before, but after my weeks running with their people, I could never mistake one of them for an ordinary Ustalav. They were not only Varisians, they were Sczarni. And they were not only Sczarni, they were the Prince's wolves.

Among the strangers I spied Milosh, his cheeks lean as though he had been running for days without rest. He looked years older than when I'd first grabbed his wrist as he lifted Nicola's purse by the docks. The way he looked at me was different, too. Instead of radiating his hatred as he had when I first shamed him before his family, he had learned to conceal his emotions. When he saw I was trying to read his face, he turned away.

Baba ambled forward, leaning on a cane I knew she didn't need when running on four legs. Cosmina walked beside her, followed by Tatiana. Fane and Malena appeared soon after. He cast a longing look at her, but she kept her distance from him. She glanced at the starknife hanging from my belt, and she looked up at my face until I returned her gaze and she looked away.

By the time they had all arrived, I counted over fifty Sczarni encircling me just as the audience had when I first danced with Malena and fought with Vili. There were no cheers this morning, not even a smile. They all looked at me, and suddenly I had no idea what to say.

Cezar stepped forward. *"Radovan Virholt,"* he said. *"You summoned us, but first I must speak."*

I nodded, trying to look confident, the way the boss did when listening to servants, but not imperious, the way he did after a few drinks.

"You took the life of my brother, head of my family," he said. *"You made us swear loyalty to you."*

There were murmurs among the strange Sczarni.

"But you did not do these things according to the proper tradition," Cezar added. He drew his knife from its sheath. As by prearranged signal, all of the others did the same. Even Baba drew the worn, narrow blade I had seen her use to chop carrots. Like her cousins and nephews and granddaughters, she pointed the tip at my heart.

Somewhere in the back of my skull, I heard the echo of Desna's laughter. I'd known it might come to this, and I came anyway. It was true, I had killed Vili and Dragos. I made no apologies for the first, since he had been trying to kill me, but the second death still gnawed at me. It had been a cold killing, an execution to save me future trouble. There had been a dozen other ways I could have dealt with him, and I'd have probably chosen one of them if I'd just taken the time to ask the boss or Azra for advice. But I'd taken the responsibility upon myself, and now I had to face the consequences. I was pretty sure they weren't going to eat me, and I'd be damned if I didn't cut a few throats on the way out. Before the thought had even formed in my mind, I felt my hand reaching for my big knife.

The Sczarni moved forward and knelt in unison. They lay their knives upon the ground, tips toward me, and bowed their heads over the blades.

"Upon our teeth," said Cezar. *"Upon our claws, upon our eyes and ears, and upon our hearts, we pledge our lives to you, Radovan Virholt, Prince of Wolves."*

I choked back the wisecrack that would have put me at ease. *"Rise,"* I told them, and then I couldn't think of two Varisian words to put together. *"Malena will repeat my words."*

She stepped forward, not quite concealing a proud smile at being singled out. I spoke in Taldane.

"As many of you have heard, I made a bargain that requires me to leave our country," I said. "If our enemy is honorable, this bargain keeps all my people safe. Including Azra and all the villages she protects."

Malena frowned at me, but she translated my words.

"You will continue to honor your territorial agreements with Azra," I said. "And if she calls to you, you will go to her. Obey her as you would me."

A man whose muscular arms writhed with snake tattoos scoffed. "How will she call to us?" he said. "Will she learn to sing to the moon?"

His laughter infected those nearby. Before it could spread around the circle, I stepped forward. "It doesn't matter," I said. "But if her wagon should fall from the road, if she should slip in the river and catch a fever, if a bolt of lightning should fall from the sky and strike her dead, then I will hold you responsible."

"What then?" said the man. He had a pair on him, which I'd have admired in other circumstances.

"Then I will break my bargain with my enemy," I said. "I will return to Ustalav. And I will find you."

The man grinned as if he were about to laugh again, but one look from Cezar's family silenced him. He shut his mouth and stepped back.

"Go now," I said. I'd thought about commanding them not to eat people, but there was no point. If I asked them for only one thing, I figured I was more likely to get it.

A few paused to get a closer look at me as they left gifts at my feet. A couple of old women kissed my hand, and one half-blind crone rubbed her garlicky fingers over my face before grunting her approval. Mostly they drifted away before the mists cleared, and I pitied the early morning drunks who hadn't made it indoors before crossing their paths.

I stopped Cezar before he left and gave him a big leather sack. He grunted with surprise at its weight. I said, "Your share."

I'd gotten a pretty price for Virholt's scepter-key, which I figured was now little more than an art object since we'd cleared out the vault. I'd kept enough to kit myself out in style, and this was the rest.

Milosh crept up to peer inside, his eyes widening as he saw how many coins the bag held, all of them of gold. He looked up at me, astonished, and I grinned back big enough to make him drop my purse, on which I'd felt his hand a moment earlier. "Nice try, kid," I said. "You need to practice."

Malena lingered after Cezar and Milosh ran to catch up with their kin. She sidled up to me and made pointed glances at Azra's starknife. If she could claim to be my consort in my absence, she'd carry as much weight as Cezar or Baba, maybe more. Azra was halfway to Ulcazar by now, and she'd never know the difference if I finished what Malena and I had started back in Amaans. I remembered the scent in the hollow of her neck, and the floral softness of her lips.

"Do you have to leave right now?" asked Malena. She slipped a finger inside my new jacket. Her finger left a warm trail on my chest.

"No," I told her. "I don't have to." She lifted my arm around her waist, but I slipped away and put my hands on her shoulders. I looked into her deep green eyes, and said, "But I will."

For the next couple of days, between visits to various merchants and the best saddler I could find, I caught myself cursing aloud. Why the hell had I turned down Malena? I hadn't made any promises, except of retribution if the Sczarni broke my lone command. By the time I realized my mistake, there was no sign of them anywhere in the market. Somewhere, Malena was complaining that I'd rejected her. If this got out, I was going to lose the reputation I'd spent so many years developing among the ladies and trollops of Egorian.

My new clothes provided meager consolation. The jacket, trousers, and boots were all soft tooled leather, just the way I liked it, but I had to settle for dark colors instead of the red I preferred. It was probably for the best, if I planned to continue working as Jeggare's bodyguard. I'd been far too conspicuous lately.

As I approached the docks, the boss descended from an ivory-paneled coach drawn by six snowy horses. Arnisant ran up behind the vehicle and sat obediently about six feet behind his master. The boss had done a much better job training that dog than he had me.

I leaned against a dock piling to light my new pipe—a gift from Baba, its bowl carved with linden leaves—while I watched the boss say farewell to the Countess. Her footmen's velvet coats were bursting with enough lace to marry off a princess and all her cousins. One of the men fetched the luggage while the boss bowed and murmured some courtesy to the occupant of the cab. All I could see of her was a slender arm nestled in dark muslin, a hand finer than porcelain emerging from the frilled cuff. The boss's eyes were fixed on the fan that hung from her wrist as he kissed her hand.

The lady's voice flowed like liquid silver, cool as the first rain of spring. "I am inexpressibly pleased that you escaped permanent injury from your ordeal."

"No less pleased than I to learn that your reputation remains unblemished by the unspeakable abuse of your trust in Miss Tara," the boss replied.

"How could I have known that she was an imposter?" she said.

"How could you?"

She hesitated, perhaps wondering whether his question was rhetorical or accusatory. I could have told her the answer. I'd heard she was plenty slippery, but so was the boss when he hadn't been tippling.

They exchanged a few more farewells the way nobles do, never using one word when they could string together a hundred. I could have had a nap before they were done.

At last the boss bowed and the carriage drove away, but his eyes didn't appear wistful. He looked like a clerk adding figures in his head. I gave him a couple of minutes to work it out, then emptied my pipe and stuck it in my pocket before joining him.

He stood beside two bags, his old travel satchel and a new leather case almost as big as Arnisant. I sent a silent prayer to Desna that he had not loaded it with new books, but I didn't like the tiered shape of its contents pressed against the leather.

Arnisant rose to greet me, pushing my hand with his big snout. The hound had filled out even in the short time I'd known him, and he wasn't done yet. I figured it was a good idea to reinforce our friendship, so I gave him the last of the sausage I'd bought for breakfast. I expected a reproving look from the boss, but he was lost in thought.

"What did you learn?" I prompted him.

"Not a thing, of course," he sighed. "My friend the Countess was naturally shocked to learn of Tara's ruse. If the creature were not already dead, she says, she would demand satisfaction."

"What?" I said. "Something like a duel?"

"Oh, no," said the boss. "Carmilla is a distinguished lady, far above the common brawls favored by the brutal sex. No doubt her retribution would be far more subtle and terrible."

"You believe her?" I asked.

He gave me that look that told me he couldn't believe I'd asked such a ridiculous question. He turned to admire the ship on which he'd secured us passage. It was a trade caravel out of Druma, *The Diamond Sea* emblazoned on its prow and bordered by what looked like enormous gems cemented into the wood. Under a canvas tarpaulin on the ship deck, I recognized the outlines of the red carriage, or what was left of it.

"Where to, boss?"

"All things considered, perhaps you should no longer address me that way."

"If you want me to say 'master' or 'my lord,' it's going to be tough." It was hard not to gag on those words. I wasn't going to last a day.

"No, those are forms I would expect from a proper servant. You will agree, I think, in light of recent events, that you are not well suited to the role."

There wasn't much I could say to that. If I'd treated any other count of Cheliax the way I'd treated the boss in front of the Sczarni, I'd be without a job and likely without my skin. And that was a trifle compared with the more serious matter of my bringing the Sczarni into the boss's expedition.

"Yeah," I said, trying not to sound too glum about it. "Agreed."

"While I can no longer retain you as a servant," he said, offering his hand, "I would be happy to think of you as my friend."

I stared at his hand, finding it hard to believe he was making the gesture to a hellspawn, to a thief, to a killer. To me.

He added, "I hope that from this point forward you will consider yourself not my servant but my partner."

"You've got to be kidding," I said. "I nearly got you killed by dragging the Sczarni into your expedition."

"True," he replied. "In fact, I expect you to accompany me when I deliver the sorrowful news of Nicola's death to his family."

"Yeah," I said. I didn't look forward to that day, but I knew I'd carry the guilt until I'd faced his widow and taken whatever she had to say to me.

"On the other hand," he said, "if not for the attack from the Sczarni, we would have arrived later at the bridge and suffered the full effects of the trap laid for us."

"Maybe," I allowed. We both reckoned it was Count Senir who had his monks plant the explosives at the bridge, hoping to stop the boss even before his investigation got underway.

"And if you had not tamed the Sczarni, as it were, would we have presented sufficient strength to negotiate with the assassins at the tomb?"

"I don't know," I said. "Probably not."

"What is important is not that you made a mistake," he said. "Rather, it is that you demonstrated your true character in how you dealt with it afterward. The way in which you dealt with Dragos—"

"I know," I said. "It was too harsh."

"No," he said. "It was wise, the justice of a prince."

It took me a moment to find my voice. "Boss," I said.

"No." He offered his hand again. "Partner. Or, if you prefer, friend."

I felt my grin slipping, and a passing stevedore let out a little shriek and shied away when he saw it.

I took Jeggare's hand. "You've got a deal, Excellency."

"Then we are agreed, Highness."

That sounded like the sort of thing that was funny once, and only in private. "I'm going to stick with 'boss,' if you don't mind."

He nodded. "Perhaps that would be best."

I reached for his luggage, but he grabbed his bags and strained to lift them. I offered to trade him the big one for mine and almost instantly regretted it. We walked toward the ship, he carrying my bag and I his.

"Tell me how things fell between you and Azra," he said. "Or did you choose Malena?"

"I don't want to talk about it," I said.

"Really? I would have expected a gambler like you to be proud of such a good luck charm as Azra."

"I don't think of her that way."

"Of course," he said. "Desna is also the goddess of dreams. Is Azra the woman of your dreams?"

"You go on like that," I said, "and I am going to puke. On you."

"Of course, Azra also serves Pharasma," he said. "Perhaps your problem is that she's the woman you'd die for?"

"If we've learned nothing else, it's that I've got more than a little devil in me," I said. "My vomit might burn your leg off. You don't know."

"I was simply speculating."

"Me, too. Ssss."

As we climbed the boarding plank, I realized I'd forgotten one important detail of our changed relationship. If being his friend meant I was going to put up with this much of his so-called humor, it could be a deal breaker, so I had to make sure.

"I still get paid, right?"

About the Author

Dave Gross has been a technical writer, a teacher, a magazine and book editor, and a novelist. He is an American expatriate currently enjoying the summers and enduring the winters of Alberta, Canada with his fabulous wife, their clever Portuguese, and two clumsy cats. His previous novels include *Black Wolf* and *Lord of Stormweather*.

Acknowledgments

Thanks to James Sutter for keen suggestions and encouragement; to Erik Mona for putting the bug in my ear in Calgary; to Don Bassingthwaite, Eileen Bell, Elaine Cunningham, Thomas M. Reid, Amber Scott, Jason Scott, Gareth-Michael Skarka, and Barb Galler-Smith for early eyes. Most of all, thanks to Lindy Smith for her relentless love and support.

Glossary

All Pathfinder Tales novels are set in the rich and vibrant world of the Pathfinder campaign setting. Below are explanations of several key terms used in this book. For more information on the world of Golarion and the strange monsters, people, and deities that make it their home, see the *Pathfinder Roleplaying Game Core Rulebook* or any of the books in the Pathfinder Campaign Setting series, or visit **paizo.com**.

Absalom: Largest city in the Inner-Sea region; current location of the Starstone, which allows mortals to ascend to godhood.

Abyss: A plane of evil and chaos ruled by demons.

Aroden: Last hero of the Azlanti and God of Humanity, who raised the Starstone from the depths of the Inner Sea and founded the city of Absalom, becoming a living god in the process. Died mysteriously a hundred years ago, causing widespread chaos, particularly in Cheliax (which viewed him as its patron deity).

Asmodeus: Devil-god of tyranny, slavery, pride, and contracts; lord of Hell and current patron deity of Cheliax.

Avistan: The northern continent bordering the Inner Sea.

Belkzen: A region populated primarily by savage orc tribes.

Caliphas: Port city located in the southernmost county (also called Caliphas) in Ustalav.

Cayden Cailean: God of freedom, ale, wine, and bravery. Ascended to godhood by passing the Test of the Starstone.

Chelaxian: A citizen of Cheliax.

Cheliax: Devil-worshiping nation in southwest Avistan.

Chelish: Of or relating to the nation of Cheliax.

Decemvirate: The mysterious and masked ruling council of the Pathfinder Society.

Desna: Good-natured goddess of dreams, stars, travelers, and luck.

Dwarves: Short, stocky humanoids who excel at physical labor, mining, and craftsmanship. Stalwart enemies of the orcs and other evil subterranean monsters.

Elf: Long-lived, beautiful humanoids who abandoned Golarion before the fall of the Starstone and have only recently returned.

Egorian: The capital of Cheliax.

Gallowspire: The unhallowed former stronghold of the Whispering Tyrant, now turned into his prison.

Garund: Southern continent of the Inner Sea region.

General Arnisant: Taldan general who sacrificed himself to imprison the Whispering Tyrant beneath his tower in Gallowspire.

Gnome: Race of fey humanoids known for their small size, quick wit, and bizarre obsessions.

Golarion: The planet containing the Inner Sea region and the primary focus of the Pathfinder campaign setting.

Half-elf: Of human and elven descent, half-elves are often regarded as having the best qualities of both races, yet still see a certain amount of prejudice, particularly from their pure elven relations.

Halfling: Race of humanoids known for their tiny stature, deft hands, and mischievous personalities.

Half-orc: Bred from a human and an orc, members of this race are known for their green-to-gray skin tone, brutish appearance, and short tempers. Highly marginalized by most civilized societies.

Hell: A plane of absolute law and evil, where evil souls go after they die to be tormented by the native devils.

Hellknights: Organization of hardened law enforcers whose tactics are often seen as harsh and intimidating, and who bind devils to their will. Based in Cheliax.

Hellspawn: A human whose family line includes a fiendish taint, often displayed by horns, hooves, or other devilish features. Rarely popular in civilized society.

House of Thrune: Current ruling house of Cheliax, which took power following Aroden's death by making compacts with the devils of Hell.

Inner Sea Region: Consisting primarily of the continents of Avistan to the north and Garund to the south, this region is the focus of the Pathfinder campaign setting.

Iomedae: Goddess of valor, rulership, justice, and honor, who in life helped lead the Shining Crusade against the Whispering Tyrant before passing the Test of the Starstone and attaining godhood.

Isle of Terror: Island on which Aroden mortally wounded the wizard-king Tar-Baphon, prompting the wizard-king's later return as the undead lich known as the Whispering Tyrant.

Kyonin: Elven forest-kingdom located in eastern Avistan.

Lastwall: Nation dedicated to keeping the Whispering Tyrant locked away beneath Gallowspire, as well as keeping the orcs of Belkzen and the monsters of Ustalav in check.

Lich: A spellcaster who manages to extend his existence by magically transforming himself into a powerful undead creature.

Linnorm King: One of the rulers of the Viking-like Lands of the Linnorm Kings.

Mwangi Expanse: The massive jungle region spanning a huge portion of Garund.

Palatinates: Three counties in Ustalav that have thrown off noble rule in favor of democratic government.

Pathfinder Society: Organization of traveling scholars and adventurers who seek to document the world's wonders. Based out of Absalom and run by a mysterious and masked group call the Decemvirate.

Pharasma: Goddess of fate, death, prophecy, and birth. Ruler of the Boneyard, where mortal souls go to be judged after death.

Prince of Lies: Asmodeus.

Orc: A bestial, warlike race of humanoids from deep underground, who now roam the surface in barbaric bands. Universally hated by more civilized races.

Qadira: Desert nation on the eastern side of the Inner Sea.

Sczarni: A subgroup of the Varisian ethnicity known for being wandering thieves and criminals, and contributing greatly to prejudice against Varisians as a whole by other cultures. Often pass themselves off as non-Sczarni Varisians while attempting to avoid detection.

Shining Crusade: The historic organization responsible for cleansing the lands of Ustalav and freeing the nation from the rule of the Whispering Tyrant a thousand years ago.

Skald: Language spoken in the Lands of the Linnorm Kings and by most Ulfen.

Slip: Slang term for a halfling.

Song of the Spheres: Another name for the goddess Desna.

Starknife: A set of four tapering blades resembling compass points extending from a metal ring with a handle; the holy weapon of Desna.

Starstone: Stone that fell from the sky ten thousand years ago, creating an enormous dust cloud that blotted out the sun and began the Age of Darkness, wiping out most pre-existing civilizations. Eventually raised up from the ocean by Aroden and housed in the Cathedral of the Starstone in Absalom, where those who can pass its mysterious and deadly tests can ascend to godhood.

Taldan Empire: Ancient realm once spanning much of Avistan, now reduced to the nation of Taldor.

Taldane (Common Tongue): Most widely spoken language in the Inner Sea region.

Taldan: A citizen of Taldor.

Taldor: Formerly glorious nation, now fallen into self-indulgence, ruled by immature aristocrats and overly complicated bureaucracy.

Tar-Baphon: The Whispering Tyrant's mortal name.

Thassilon: Ancient empire once located in northwestern Avistan and ruled by seven runelords.

Ulfen: A race of Viking-like humans from the cold nations of the north, primarily Irrisen and the Lands of the Linnorm Kings.

Urgathoa: Evil goddess of gluttony, disease, and undeath.

Ustalav: Gothic nation once ruled by the Whispering Tyrant; now ruled by humans once more but still bearing a reputation for strange beasts, ancient secrets, and moral decay.

Ustalavic: Of or related to the nation of Ustalav.

Varisia: A frontier region northwest of the Inner Sea.

Varisian: Of or relating to the region of Varisia, or a resident of Varisia. Ethnic Varisians tend to organize in clans and wander in caravans, acting as tinkers or performers.

Venture-Captain: A rank in the Pathfinder Society above that of a standard field agent but below the Decemvirate.

Virlych: Haunted portion of Ustalav never completely reclaimed from monsters and spirits after the imprisonment of the Whispering Tyrant.

Westcrown: Former capital of Cheliax, now overrun with shadow beasts and despair.

Whispering Tyrant: Incredibly powerful lich who terrorized Avistan for hundreds of years before being sealed beneath his fortress of Gallowspire a millennium ago.

EXPLORE NEW WORLDS WITH

PLANET STORIES

Strap on your jet pack and set out for unforgettable adventure with PLANET STORIES, Paizo Publishing's science fiction and fantasy imprint! Personally selected by Paizo's editorial staff, PLANET STORIES presents timeless classics from authors like Gary Gygax (Dungeons & Dragons), Robert E. Howard (Conan the Barbarian), Michael Moorcock (Elric), and Leigh Brackett (*The Empire Strikes Back*) alongside groundbreaking anthologies and fresh adventures from the best imaginations in the genre, all introduced by superstar authors such as China Miéville, George Lucas, and Ben Bova.

With new releases six times a year, PLANET STORIES promises the best two-fisted adventure this side of the galactic core! Find them at your local bookstore, or subscribe online at **paizo.com**!

"AS YOU TURN AROUND, YOU SPOT SIX DARK SHAPES MOVING UP BEHIND YOU. AS THEY ENTER THE LIGHT, YOU CAN TELL THAT THEY'RE SKELETONS, WEARING RUSTING ARMOR AND WAVING ANCIENT SWORDS."

Lem: Guys, I think we have a problem.

GM: You do indeed. Can I get everyone to roll initiative?

To determine the order of combat, each player rolls a d20 and adds his or her initiative bonus. The GM rolls once for the skeletons.

GM: Seelah, you have the highest initiative. It's your turn.

Seelah: I'm going to attempt to destroy them using the power of my goddess, Iomedae. I channel positive energy.

Seelah rolls 2d6 and gets a 7.

GM: Two of the skeletons burst into flames and crumble as the power of your deity washes over them. The other four continue their advance. Harsk, it's your turn.

Harsk: Great. I'm going to fire my crossbow!

Harsk rolls a d20 and gets a 13. He adds that to his bonus on attack rolls with his crossbow and announces a total of 22. The GM checks the skeleton's armor class, which is only a 14.

GM: That's a hit. Roll for damage.

Harsk rolls a d10 and gets an 8. The skeleton's damage reduction reduces the damage from 8 to 3, but it's still enough.

GM: The hit was hard enough to cause that skeleton's ancient bones to break apart. Ezren, it's your turn.

Ezren: I'm going to cast *magic missile* at a skeleton.

Magic missile creates glowing darts that always hit their target. Ezren rolls 1d4+1 for each missile and gets a total of 6. It automatically bypasses the skeleton's DR, dropping another one.

GM: There are only two skeletons left, and it's their turn. One of them charges up to Seelah and takes a swing at her, while the other moves up to Harsk and attacks.

The GM rolls a d20 for each attack. The attack against Seelah is only an 8, which is less than her AC of 18. The attack against Harsk is a 17, which beats his AC of 16. The GM rolls damage.

GM: The skeleton hits you, Harsk, leaving a nasty cut on your upper arm. Take 7 points of damage.

Harsk: Ouch. I have 22 hit points left.

GM: That's not all. Charging out of the fog onto the bridge is a skeleton dressed like a knight, riding the bones of a long-dead horse. Severed heads are mounted atop its deadly lance. Lem, it's your turn—what do you do?

Lem: Run!

NOW IT'S YOUR TURN...

Winter Witch

Elaine Cunningham

In a village of the frozen north, a child is born possessed by a strange and alien spirit, only to be cast out by her tribe and taken in by the mysterious winter witches of Irrisen, a land locked in permanent magical winter. Farther south, a young mapmaker with a penchant for forgery discovers that his sham treasure maps have begun striking gold.

This is the story of Ellasif, a barbarian shield maiden who will stop at nothing to recover her missing sister, and Decclan, the ne'er-do-well young spellcaster-turned-forger who wants only to prove himself to the woman he loves. Together they'll face monsters, magic, and the fury of Ellasif's own cold-hearted warriors in their quest to rescue the lost child. Yet when they finally reach the ice-walled city of Whitethrone, where trolls hold court and wolves roam the streets as men, will it be too late to save the girl from the forces of darkness?

From *New York Times* best seller Elaine Cunningham comes a fantastic new adventure of swords and sorcery, set in the award-winning world of the *Pathfinder Roleplaying Game*.

$9.99
ISBN: 978-1-60125-286-9